THE
WHITE WOLF'S
SON

Also by Michael Moorcock

The Dreamthief's Daughter
The Skrayling Tree

Gloriana

Available from Warner Aspect

MICHAEL MOORCOCK

THE WHITE WOLF'S SON

THE ALBINO UNDERGROUND

ASPECT®

NEW YORK   BOSTON

Aspect
Warner Books

Time Warner Book Group
1271 Avenue of the Americas, New York, NY 10020
Visit our Web site at www.twbookmark.com.

The Aspect name and logo are registered trademarks of Warner Books.

Printed in the United States of America

First Edition: June 2005
10 9 8 7 6 5 4 3 2 1

Library of Congress Cataloging-in-Publication Data

Moorcock, Michael, 1939–
    The white wolf's son : the albino underground / Michael Moorcock.—1st ed.
        p. cm.
    "Book 3 of the Elric saga."
    ISBN 0-446-57702-2
    1. Elric of Melniboné (Fictitious character)—Fiction.   2. Albinos and albinism—Fiction.   3. Swordsmen—Fiction.   I. Title.
    PR6063.059W47 2005
    823'.914—dc22   2005001341

In memory of
Jerico Radoc:
a generous spirit
who died too young

and for Alan Wall
and all the regulars down
at MWM, with thanks.

THE
WHITE WOLF'S
SON

PROLOGUE

*And then did Sir Elrik spye Sir Yagrin and say to him
"Fast thou, villain. Where goest thou this Daye?" Whereupon Sir
Yagrin saith: "On my Honour, I shall answer ye with arms."
Whereupon one charged the other. Ten speares did they brake until
Sir Elrik had killed Sir Yagrin and lay close to his deathe bedd with
none in all that Woode to help him.*

—THE ROMANCE OF PRINCE ELRIK
tr. from the Portuguese. Anon., London ca. 1525

THE ALBINO HUNG captive in the rigging of the great
battle barge, spread-eagled on the mainmast,
barely able to open his red, glaring eyes. He was
mumbling to himself, calling out a name, as if he felt that name
would save him. Although dreaming, he was at the same time
half-awake. He could see below him the foredeck of the ship, with
its massive catapult whose cup slaves were already filling with
flaming pitch. There, too, the White Wolf's captor strutted in his
seething rosy armor. Upon his head was the glowing scarlet helmet bearing the Merman Crest of Pan Tang, the island of the
theocrats who had long envied Melniboné her power. High-
shouldered, black-bearded, full of raging triumph, Jagreen Lern
threw up his face and laughed at his enemy. He was delighting in
his power, in the movement of his galley through the water, its
huge bulk pushed by the oars manned by five hundred slaves. He

turned to his followers, men made utterly mad by all they had witnessed, by their own demonic bloodlust, by their own cruel killing.

"Let fly!" he roared. And another shot was discharged, arcing over the water and dropping into the boiling sea just short of the fleet which had assembled to defend what was left of the world from his conquest.

"We'll get their measure with the next one," declared the theocrat, turning again to look up at Elric. He spat on the deck. There was a terrible, crooked grin on his face. He was full of his victories, swollen like a leech on blood.

"See! The white-face is nothing without that black sword of his. Is this the hero you feared? Is this all Law could summon against us—a renegade weakling?"

Jagreen Lern strutted beneath the mainmast, jeering up at the man whose crucifixion he had ordered.

"Watch, Elric. Watch! Soon you shall see all your allies destroyed. All that you love turned to heaving Chaos. Lord Arioch refuses you help. Lord Balan refuses you help. Soon Law and all its feeble creations shall be banished from our world, and I shall rule in the name of the great Lords of Entropy, with the power to make what I like of inchoate matter and destroy it again and again at a whim. Can you hear me, White Wolf? Or are you already dead? Wake him, someone! I would have him know what he loses. He must learn his lesson well before he dies. He must know that by betraying his patron Chaos lords he has betrayed himself and all he loves."

Some part of the albino heard his enemy. But Elric of Melniboné was desperately sending his mind out into the unseen worlds around him, the myriad worlds of the multiverse, where he believed he might find the one thing which could help him. He had deliberately fallen into a dream, a slumber known by his sorcerer ancestors as the Sleep of a Thousand Years, by which he had earlier learned his wizard's craft. He was now too weak to do anything else but send his failing spirit out into the astral worlds beyond his own. By this means he sought his sword, Stormbringer, calling its name as he slept, knowing that if he died on this, his last desperate dream quest, he would die here, also.

He dreamed of vast upheavals and forces as powerful as those which now captured him. He dreamed of strange lands and stranger creatures. He dreamed of heroes like himself, heroes with a destiny similar to his own. He dreamed of brutal warriors, of wonderful supernatural beings, of beautiful women, of exotic, secret places where the destiny of worlds was created. In this dream he crossed whole continents, negotiated vast oceans, fought men and monsters, gods and demons. And he dreamed of a boy who, obscurely, he felt might be his son, though he had no son in this world. He dreamed, too, of a little girl, who played unconsciously and happily around her house, knowing nothing of the enormous forces of Law and Chaos, of Good and Evil, which clashed in worlds but a shadowed step removed from her own . . .

The albino groaned. The bearded theocrat pushed back his pulsing scarlet helm, looked up at Elric and laughed again.

"He lives, right enough. Wake him, someone, so that I might relish his agony all the better."

A crewman obeyed. Knife in belt, he began his ascent of the rigging. "I'll tickle his toes with my dagger, master. That'll bring him round."

"Oh, draw a little of his thin, deficient blood. Maybe I'll drink a cup of it to celebrate his final agonies." Jagreen Lern, master of all the once-human creatures who now gibbered and slavered and anticipated their final triumph over Law, reached out his red gauntleted hand, as if to receive a goblet from one of his minions. "A libation to the Lords of Chaos!"

Elric muttered and stirred in his bonds, high above the ship's main deck. A word formed on his lips.

"Stormbringer!" he gasped. "Stormbringer, aid me now!"

But Stormbringer, that unholy black sword which had preserved his life so many times before, did not materialize.

Stormbringer was *elsewhere*, imprisoned by powerful sorcery, manipulated by men and supernatural monsters whose ambitions

were even darker, even more dangerous than those of the creatures of Chaos who sought to rule Elric's world.

Stormbringer was being used in a summoning powerful
enough to challenge the combined might of Law and Chaos and
to bring about the end of everything, of the multiverse itself.

Again the albino whispered his sword's name. But there was
no reply.

"Stormbringer . . ."

Nothing but the silence of the cold, unpopulated ether. The
silence of death.

And into that silence came laughter, cruel laughter full of the
cold joy of slaughter.

"Open his eyes for him, you scum! Watch, Elric! Watch all
that you love perish!"

The laughter blended with the crashing noise of the sea, the
terrible sounds of the war-catapults, the groaning of the slaves,
the creaking of the oars.

The pale lips parted, perhaps for the last time, barely able to
utter the word again:

"Stormbringer!"

Part One
A Much Sought-After Young Lady

Lord Elrik sate in his own red bludde
His vanquishéd foe beside him;
Saith he, "Thou kepst my Treasure near
In Castle Lorn do ye reside in."

"Take all, take all," cried his noble foe,
"Take all that I have defended
My soul's now Carrion for the bold black Crowe
But my Conscience hast thou mended."

IV

Heal'd and alone, Lord Elrik rode,
Till Castle Lorn lay behind him
"No Gold shall I need in Manor Bonné,
Where I'll finde my fair, forlorne one."

—"LORD ELRIK AND SYTHORIL," CA. 1340
    Coll. Wheldrake, *Ballads and Lays of the Britons,*
    1856

CHAPTER ONE

*Then Elric sped out of Tanelorn, seeking Mirenburg, where the next
step of his destiny must be taken. And he knew that the doom of ten
thousand years lay upon him; and that of himself he'd made bloody
sacrifice, having found the Stealer of Souls.
Now his true dream began to resume; now his destiny marched to
remorseless resolution.*

—THE CHRONICLE OF THE BLACK SWORD
Wheldrake's tr.

Y NAME IS Oonagh, granddaughter of the
Countess Oona von Bek. This is my story of Elric,
the White Wolf, and Onric, the White Wolf's son,
of a talking beast in the World Below, of the League of Temporal
Adventurers, the Knights of the Balance and those who serve the
world; of the wonders and terrors I experienced as the forces of
Law and Chaos sought the power of the Black Sword, found the
source of Hell and the San Grael. All this happened several years
ago, when I was still a child. It is only now that I feel able to tell
my story.

As usual, I was spending my summer holidays at the old family house in Ingleton, West Yorkshire. My father had been born
there before his natural parents were killed in Africa, and he had
inherited it when still a small boy. It was kept in trust by my grandparents until he was twenty-one.

Tower House was an old place. The main part dated back to the seventeenth century. There was a big late-Victorian addition, built from local granite, put on when the building was turned into a girls' boarding school in the 1890s. By the 1950s it had been split into several dwellings and sold to separate owners. My grandparents had helped my father turn the house back to its former glory. This meant that any guests generally had an entire wing to themselves. There was even a flat over the old stables, now a garage, where the permanent housekeepers, Mr. and Mrs. Hawthornthwaite, lived.

My grandparents, Count and Countess von Bek, had come to love the place and now remained there almost permanently, only going down to London for the theater season or to visit doctors and dentists. They were a hearty old couple. My grandfather was at least ninety, and my grandmother, though she did not seem it, must have been close to seventy. Everyone remarked on how youthful she looked. I was not the only family member to notice how, beneath her makeup, her face was actually younger, softer. "Good skins run in the family," said my mother. She never seemed to notice the oddness of that remark. Even Grandma's slower movements and apparent absentmindedness seemed designed to deceive you into thinking she was older. Of course, she *should* have looked older, given that she had married my granddad in the 1940s, after the Second World War. But at that time in my life I didn't really think much about it. Perhaps she aged herself to save my grandfather's pride? No one else in the family mentioned it, so I didn't think a lot about it, either.

We had been going up to Yorkshire for the summer holidays ever since I was tiny. My mum and dad had spent the summers there long before I was born. I knew every inch of Storrs Common, the brook, the old caves all around the area, the abandoned mine workings down past Beesley's farm on the path to the famous waterfalls. The falls themselves roared through a deep gorge in thick woods. The farms on the other side of the dale tried to charge tourists for walking in that beauty spot. This kept them fairly free of all but the most dedicated visitors! In Victorian times, trains had run special excursions to the Ingleton Falls, but now there was no station, let alone a railway.

All that was left of Ingleton's former glory were the reproductions of old photographs showing ladies in bustles and big hats posing beside one of the main falls. School parties came occasionally, little crocodiles of captive kids with packed lunches in their haversacks, trudging moodily along the high paths above the river. But most of the time it was still fairly remote country. I saw the occasional big red English squirrel in the oaks and hazels, and I had seen my first crayfish by the stepping-stones through that part of the river we called "the shallows." You could sometimes catch trout if you fished patiently, but the water was too fast-running to attract most anglers. During high summer and autumn there were few visitors. People were no longer allowed to park on the common across from our house, mainly because of the erosion so many walkers had created. Instead they had to park in the village, and for many the paved road up to the common was too steep.

We were used to that road. It was only half a mile, a bit less if you went the back way. Although a trip to the village took you about an hour, you could still get down to buy fish-and-chips, the occasional sweets and comics, or have a look in the souvenir shop. If it took more than an hour, it was because someone wanted to chat. We were on good terms with almost everyone there. It had taken my mum and dad a few years to be accepted, especially by our neighboring hill farmers, but now even they remembered my name most of the time.

The place nearest to us was another half an hour up the hill. Without running water, the big old farmhouse was accessible by a rough cart track which even four-wheel-drive Jeeps found hard to handle. Having no significant land attached to it, the house tended to change hands quite often. We rarely saw much of the occupants, who were almost always natural recluses. The place was known as Starr Bottom, and when we were small, my older brothers and sisters had sworn it was haunted. Shaggy free-range sheep still grazed up to the foundations of its rather neglected drystone walls.

Tower House had no gas, but it had electricity, central heating, fireplaces and a huge coke-fired stove in the big granite-flagged kitchen which had once served the whole school. It was built on the side of Ingleborough, one of the famous Three Peaks, and had a view over twenty miles of rolling hills and dales to the Atlantic at Morecombe Bay. On a clear day you could see even further from the central tower: a beautiful, rugged landscape, whose limestone glittered in the sunshine and whose hawthorns bowed close to the crags, telling of our high winds and winter snows. Our scenery was made famous in old TV series like *All Creatures Great and Small,* and preserved in its original beauty by the National Trust and the farmers who loved it.

We were a short distance from the Lake District and in easy driving distance of Leeds, so the house was convenient for almost any kind of activity. Sometimes we would drive into Leeds for the fun of it, visit one of Dad's old friends and spend an afternoon in those wonderful covered markets, the Arcades, all dark green Victorian iron girders and sparkling glass. I loved our trips to Leeds.

Only one episode spoils the memory of my early childhood in Yorkshire. I would wake in my bed with a full moon streaming into the window, showing me all the things of my daytime life: toy boxes, modeling table, audio stuff, books, various projects I had half started, but they had all taken on a mysterious and even sinister quality. As I sank back into sleep, I remember screaming a loud, terrible scream which did not wake me, but which I learned later woke the rest of the house. I don't remember much else. I always woke up very frightened.

I remember one dream which was especially terrifying and which remained in my memory (whereas the others tended to fade): *I was out on the common and had somehow wandered into a deep cave. I was lost but knew home was fairly close. I just had to find it. Below me, in semidarkness, was some sort of city with pale, slender towers like spikes of rock. And these strange creatures were coming to-*

wards me, pointing. They were not particularly unfriendly, these figures in high, conical hats, almost like elongated Ku Klux Klansmen. I couldn't make out their faces, yet I was sure they weren't fully human. I heard a shout and looked back. There was a man following me. I was more frightened of him than of the creatures approaching me. His face, too, was in shadow, beneath the broad brim of a black hat. He had a wide white collar worn over a black jerkin. A Puritan. Trying to escape them all, I darted aside and was suddenly in a deep, peaceful green-wood. For a moment I felt safe. Then I saw a man with bone-white skin and red eyes standing on a large bough over the path I was on. He was dressed in a long turban, vividly colored cloak and sashes swirling around him, his large black sword held high as he reached towards me across the treetops. "How . . . ?" he said. He was mouthing a question I couldn't hear. He could only help me if I answered him. He reminded me of my granddad, but was much younger. I knew he was trying to save me, but something was stopping him. "How . . . ? Grunewald? Mittelmarch?" Those are the only words I remembered.

Then I was running from him, too, running down towards where the men in conical hats waited for me, running straight into the tall body of yet another bizarre creature who looked down at me with kindly brown eyes. I think he was a friend of my grandfather's. A huge red fox, dressed elaborately in late-eighteenth-century finery, who smiled his pleasure at seeing me, displaying sharp, white teeth.

"Well, I suppose I'm in good hands," I said, trying to show I was grateful for his friendship.

"Paws," he said, with the literal logic of a dream, "actually. My dear mademoiselle, we must hurry . . ."

Then the Puritan was behind him, his skull-like face grinning as he lifted a huge pistol and shot the fox in the back. With a look of surprise and grief, the fox fell.

I began to run again . . .

I was screaming.

The local doctor was called, but he wasn't much help. After trying me on a few different prescriptions, he eventually admitted he was baffled. I then had a psychiatrist for a few sessions until I started to get better on my own as the dreams, or feelings, never recurred. I could still remember the people of that dream, but Mr. Handforth, the local vicar and a bit of a family friend, was the most help. He took me seriously and said I seemed to have quite a lot of "guardian angels" looking out for my safety. In his deep, cultured accents he spoke of my troubled spirit. He thought I had been a soul under attack.

"And should we worry that she believes herself under attack?" I remember my father asking him.

"Mr. Beck, she *was* under attack," the vicar insisted. "I'm convinced of it. There is no saying those forces will never be back. But meanwhile . . ." He spread his hands and sighed.

"Strange that of all of us, she should not have been spared," I was puzzled by my grandmother saying one day. I had no idea what she meant, and didn't really let it bother me much. Then, as my dreams stopped coming, I forgot all about it, though I did like the idea of the giant fox. He was like something out of *Alice in Wonderland*!

My grandparents' family estate had been in Germany, but my grandfather had given the whole place over to the nation years ago to use as a rest home for aged people suffering from dementia. Granddad was a tall, rather gaunt man, strikingly handsome as my grandma was beautiful. She was stockier, though equally striking. Remarkably, they were both pure albinos with rare red eyes, just like the man I had seen in those dreams. The two of them were clearly deeply in love. As he grew frail, she grew ever more solicitous of his health. Though my parents clearly loved the count and countess, they sometimes thought them a little old-fashioned with their decided opinions about modern pop culture! My mum and dad liked rock-and-roll, but Countess von Bek, for instance, had decided opinions about modern pop music! The only light music she was willing to accept was played by the 1930s big bands.

My grandparents' own circle of friends occasionally visited Ingleton. An odd, often bohemian collection of old people, they sometimes seemed a little remote from us but evidently took pleasure in seeing children about and almost always brought us gifts.

They would disappear off to my grandparents' wing of the house or go for long walks, talking about obscure and mysterious things. We were never particularly curious about them. Some, we gathered, had been anti-Nazis in Germany and had known our parents during the Second World War.

We spent most of the year in London, so we knew how to look after ourselves, but we enjoyed immense freedom in Yorkshire. We were allowed to range across the fells at will as long as we took our cell phones. We weren't idiots. We avoided going down into the various cave systems which ran under large parts of the hillside. These systems were the haunt of cavers, desperate to discover new and connecting routes, just as the high, shining terraces were favorite places for climbers, some of whom returned every year and were known to us. Gradually, under their expert if slightly condescending supervision, my brother and sister and I learned technical rock climbing as well as caving. Yorkshire was just the greatest place I knew in the whole world.

My adventure began on one of those slow, wonderful, dreaming, sparkling summer afternoons you get in the dales. The whole landscape takes on a magical quality. It's easy to imagine you're in fairyland. The lazy air is full of insects, the grass full of surprising little plants, such as wild orchids and fritillaria, all different kinds of mosses and the tiny creatures living in them. The hills seem endless and the days infinite. Only an idiot couldn't love it. But that day I had no company.

My dad had driven my grandparents into Lancaster to get the train to London, and my mum had gone with him, taking my brother, Alfy, and sister, Gertie, to shop for new shoes and some art supplies. They had a few other plans, so they would probably not be back until the evening. I had stayed behind because I thought one of my favorite old films was coming on the television. They had left Mrs. Hawthornthwaite, a kindly dumpling of a lady, in charge of me. Only after they'd gone did I discover that I had misread the *TV Guide*; my film, *The Thief of Bagdad*, had been on the previous week. Now I had nothing to look forward to and was doubly bored.

After lunch Mrs. H, probably irritated by my deep sighs, told me it was all right if I wanted to go down to the shallows (our end of the river where it emerged from the woods) to look for fish. It wasn't the most exciting option, but it was better than hanging around watching her load and unload the washing machine, since she wouldn't allow me to help her.

As usual, I took the cell phone. I had instructions to phone her if I needed her or got into any sort of trouble. "Mr. H can be down there in a minute or two," she assured me as she saw me off. "It doesn't matter how silly or trivial a feeling you get; just phone up. He'll know what to do. And if there's nowt to do, so much the better. He needs to be kept busy."

Mr. Hawthornthwaite, an amiable man with a shock of snow-white hair and with startling blue eyes in ruddy features, was up in the Tower mending a pipe and could be heard cursing mildly from time to time as metal clanged against metal.

I put one of Mum's old Indian bags over my shoulder. Its tassels hung down almost to the ground, but it was the best thing I had to carry my bits and pieces in, including the phone. On the way to the river I spent some while playing around in a ruined building we called the Castle. It was actually part of an old quarry, with a loading platform and rail tracks still running into it where the First World War graphite trucks used to unload, transferring the stuff to the steam train which ran along a narrow-gauge line to Ingleton Station. The remains of the graphite mill was on the other side of the village. It had blown up in 1917. Some thought it was the work of German saboteurs, but my dad said it was probably due to someone's neglect.

Rural Yorkshire has dozens of similar abandoned workings and buildings. There was still an active gravel quarry up the road from us. Occasionally we could hear them dynamiting. Their explosives were why we were never allowed to go into any local caves. A man and his two children had been trapped in White Scar Cave some years ago, hiding from a bull, and only luck had saved them. The quarrymen were not the only ones to use explosives. Even today you would hear a thump and the house would shake, usually because the least responsible cavers, the hooligans of the caving world, were dynamiting new routes into the systems below!

I had quite a decent game running in the Castle, but by about three o'clock in the afternoon I had begun to wonder about going back for tea or continuing down to the river. Then I heard a sharp crack from the direction of the woods above and assumed that the quarry was blasting, though I hadn't noticed the usual warning siren. When there were no further explosions, I swung my feet from the platform and continued on down the grassy bank from the dirt path to the river. Taking off my shoes on the bank, I waded into the clear water and was soon absorbed in seeking out whatever swam over the pebbles.

I was hoping to find freshwater crayfish, those tiny, almost transparent relatives of the lobster, but the sun on the water was too bright, and all I found were a few minnows. My cell phone was in a little holder swung across my body, and I thought I heard it start to ring. False alarm. I was on the point of giving up on the fishing trip when suddenly the phone began to make a very peculiar noise, almost as if it was warning me that my battery was low. Although I had recharged it while I was having lunch, I pulled it out and flipped it open, wondering if Mrs. Hawthornthwaite was trying to get in touch with me. She sometimes rang at teatime if there was something special, like toasted scones or crumpets, which were best eaten hot.

The phone was completely dead. I pressed the recognition button without success. There were no text messages. So I put the thing away again, thinking, a passing fluke of the hills, and returned my attention to the river until a noise from above me told me that someone was on the path. I got up in a hurry. This was all a bit spooky. There he was, a monster of a man, swinging out of the woods: a tall, bulky figure wrapped in a big leather overcoat, his head shaded by a wide-brimmed felt hat, his eyes hidden by reflecting sunglasses, with a scarf drawn up to his nose, as if it were winter and he were feeling the cold. Perhaps he was worried about inhaling dust from the quarry's latest blast.

I must admit I felt a little more vulnerable than usual as the burly man stopped on the path high above me and lifted a gloved hand in greeting. His accent was thick, deep and vaguely familiar.

"Good afternoon, young lady."

He was probably trying to sound friendly, but I gave him a cold nod in response. I hated people calling me "young lady." It seemed condescending. Perhaps a little ostentatiously I sat down and began buckling the straps of my shoes.

But the man did not walk on. "You live around here, do you?" he asked. There was an edge, an undertone to his voice, that I really didn't like.

Again I nodded. I couldn't see anything of his face at all and began to wonder if he was deliberately hiding it. He reminded me of the pictures of the Invisible Man I had seen in the Alan Moore comics my brother collected. He hardly seemed any better tempered than that character. Was that why I was so wary of him?

"Am I on the right path for the village of Ingleton?" he asked.

"You're on the back road," I told him. "Keep going and it'll take you to the middle of the square across from the butcher's. The newsagent will be down on the main road to your right."

He thanked me and began to move on. Then he hesitated. He turned, fingering the lower part of his face, still covered by the scarf. "Has anyone else come this way recently?"

I shook my head.

"I'm looking for a rather thin, pale gentleman. A foreigner. Likes to wear black. He would have arrived a day or so ago. Mr. Klosterheim? Might he be staying in these parts?"

"You could ask at the newsagent for the Bridge Hotel," I told him. "They'll put you right for where the Bridge is, on the other side of the viaduct." There were also a couple of guesthouses closer, but I didn't feel like offering him too much information. His had been a very odd question for anyone to ask in Ingleton. I wondered where he could have come from. He wore high, thick, flat-soled boots of battered leather, reaching to his knee. His trousers were tucked into the boots. He had no haversack, and he didn't look like any kind of hiker I'd ever seen. The clothes were old-fashioned without being identifiable with any historical period. Instinctively I was glad of the distance between us, and intended to keep it. Slowly I finished fastening my shoes.

He grunted, thought over what I'd said, then began moving. He was soon gone, clumping along the track like a campaigning soldier. The track was used by everyone local and curved downwards into the village. It was the shortest way and roughly paralleled the main paved road which passed our house above. For us it could often seem just as quick to go down that back road than to take the car and try to find a parking space in the village.

The encounter had unsettled me. I was getting flashes of those old, bad dreams. Nothing specific. Not even a tangible image. It was also possible I had eaten something which disagreed with me. Standing on the riverbank, I tried my phone again. It still wasn't working, although now I got a buzzing, like the sound of distant bees. I decided it was time to go home.

I wasn't used to feeling the shivers on the sunlit commons of Ingleton during a golden summer afternoon.

I scrambled up the grassy bank, reached the path, then ran up through the green hillocks over the common, past Beesley's, until I got to the back gate of our house. Mrs. Hawthornthwaite was hanging white linens up to dry on a line stretched beside part of our vegetable garden. She insisted it was the best place for laundry, since the linens especially were refreshed by the growing carrots and brussels sprouts. As a girl she had read the tip in *Woman's Weekly*, and always applied it. Her whites glittered, reflecting the bright sunshine. Starched or unstarched, they blossomed in the breeze like the sails of fairy ships.

The main walled garden was to the front of the house, still landscaped much as it had been in the seventeenth century, with junipers, cedars and poplars surrounding what was mostly smooth lawn arranged in terraces. The lawn was not good for much except looking at, since there was such a slope on it. When we wanted to play cricket or some other game, we had a flattened area out of sight behind the row of poplars and willows on the far side of the tiny stream which dropped underground long before it reached the main river. You could just see down to the back road from there.

I was half-tempted to check if the stranger was still on the path, but he would probably have reached the village by now. Something about him continued to bother me. His heavy, menacing masculinity had made its way into my head.

"You feeling hungry, dear?" Mrs. Hawthornthwaite was surprised to see me back. She looked at her watch as if wondering why I would be home so early on such a beautiful sunny day.

"A bit," I said. "Is Mum home yet?" I knew the answer.

"Not yet, dear. They were going to wait for the fresh fish to be landed in Morecombe, remember? They might have gone to the pictures, but there wasn't much on in Lancaster." She frowned. "Are you all right?"

"Yes, thanks," I said. "It's just that I saw a man on the back road. He scared me a bit."

She grew alert. "He didn't—"

"He didn't do anything except ask me the way to Ingleton and if I knew some foreign visitor," I told her. "Then he went on to Ingleton. I suggested he ask about his friend at the Bridge. It's okay. I just thought I'd come home. For some reason my phone's not working."

She accepted this. Mrs. Hawthornthwaite had a way of trusting our instincts, just as we trusted hers.

I went into the big, warm living room which looked out towards Morecombe. It got the western sun from two sets of windows. Through them you could see the roofs of the village below. I took the binoculars from the shelf and focused them on the little bit of the back road that was visible. All I saw was the vicar's wife, coasting her bike down the track. As usual, Mrs. Handforth had her big orange cat, Jerico, in the front basket. They both seemed to be enjoying the ride. Nobody else was about. I went up to my own room, planning to plug the phone in and recharge it, but when I got it out it was working perfectly. I wondered if the weather had something to do with the problem. Sunspots? I had only the vaguest idea of what sunspots were.

A bit later I had some bread and jam and a glass of milk in the kitchen. Now I was really bored. Mrs. Hawthornthwaite suggested I find a book and go outside again. I didn't have a better idea. I took one of my mum's favorite E. Nesbit books, *The House of Arden,* and went downstairs, out of the front door, through the yard, and crossed the paved road to Storrs Common.

"Watch out for that chap!" she called as I left.

Immediately opposite the house was a leveled spot, originally designed to provide parking space for visitors who planned to climb the mountain. Now, as I said, they had to park in the village. From that flat area the hill continued to rise up towards the distant peak of Ingleborough. We always said living at Tower House developed strong calf muscles if nothing else. You were either straining to go up or bracing to go down. Whenever we found ourselves on flat ground we walked so rapidly nobody else could keep up with us.

On the peak of the mountain were the remains of a Celtic hill fort. The story of the fort was that the last of the Iceni had gone there to make their stand against the Roman invaders. Armed to the teeth behind a heavy wall, they prepared for the attack. But the Romans had taken one look at them and decided to go round on their way to Lancaster and Carlisle. The Celts were nonplussed. After about fifty years of living in the wind and cold of the peak, the remains of the Iceni eventually came straggling down and got jobs on the docks at Lancaster.

I had soon found one of my favorite spots in the common, a dip in the grass where it was impossible to be seen. Here, if it was windy, you could swiftly find yourself in a complete cone of silence. The common was full of such holes, where the ground had fallen in over the cave systems which riddled the entire area. Here and there were deeper, larger holes, where the rock was exposed and which seemed like the entrances of caves but never really led anywhere.

Once below the level of the ground in the inverted cones, you couldn't hear a thing. There was no better sense of isolation, and yet anyone who knew you could easily find you *and* you could be back at home within a few minutes.

With a sense of pleasurable anticipation, I opened the covers of *The House of Arden,* a companion to another favorite, *Harding's Luck.* It was all about time paradoxes and people meeting themselves. My earlier exertions must have tired me more than I thought, because I fell asleep in the middle of the first chapter. The next thing I remember is rolling over on my back and blinking up into the late-afternoon sun. As I yawned I saw some large, round object drifting across the sky, a thin plume of smoke coming from it, a bit like the vapor trail of a plane.

Waking up rapidly, I recognized the aircraft as a hot-air balloon. A local group of enthusiasts took visitors up over the Dales during the summer, but they rarely came down this low. Nor, I realized, as the shadow of the basket fell across my hiding place, were they usually so big or so colorful. Next thing the balloon filled up my entire field of vision, and I could smell the smoke. The silk of the canopy blazed in the sun. Glittering scarlets, greens and golds dazzled me. From the rigging flew the cross of St. Andrew, the blue and white Scottish flag. I saw tongues of fire from the brazier in the basket and two very pale faces staring down at me. Then something whooshed past, and I heard a thump, a yell. As I scrambled up and out onto the common, there came the roaring sound of a powerful engine in high gear.

On turning, the first object I saw was the big antique convertible. Not the Lexus containing my parents, as I had half hoped, but a great, dark green monster with massive mudguards and a huge radiator decorated with an ornamental "B," a single blue-clad occupant, swinging off the road and onto the flat parking space. The driver's dark goggles gave him the appearance of a huge, mad lemur.

At the sound of another yell I looked back to see the balloon still dragging up the common, the silk bouncing and brilliant, the gasbag booming like a drum. The passengers had leaped from the basket. One of them had thrown out a great iron anchor and was trying to dig this into the ground, seeking to stop the balloon's progress over the grass-grown rocks. The other passenger was clinging hard to the wicker, clearly not at all happy about his situation.

This happened so swiftly, I could barely take in what was going on. None of the people seemed to need help from me, and none seemed especially menacing. It occurred to me that I ought to duck down and hide, but the driver of the car had already seen me and was waving a gauntleted hand and calling out.

"Pardon me, miss. Could you tell me if I'm at the right place? My name's Bastable. I'm looking for the residence of the Count and Countess von Bek." Pushing up his goggles, he began to climb from the car, gathering the folds of his cotton dust coat which covered what appeared to be a light blue military uniform. On his head was a peaked cap of the same color.

"Good afternoon," was all I could think of to say.

Another voice came from behind me.

"Good afternoon, my dear beautiful young woman."

Somehow I wasn't a bit offended by those rich, flattering tones, offered in the most delicious Scottish brogue I had ever heard. I turned round again. Grinning at me, the balloonist, in full Highland dress, including a brilliant kilt, was testing his anchor line now, having stopped the vessel's drift. His companion was stamping heavily on bits of flaming wood threatening to set the grass alight. Then he reached into the basket and took something out. A black, undecorated oblong box, narrow and long. Clearly an electric guitar case. He was tall and very nifty in what appeared to be European evening dress. I wouldn't have guessed he was a rock musician. When he faced me, I was surprised. I had seen him before. In my dreams! Though considerably younger, he could have been a relative of my albino grandfather or grandmother. He had the same refined, angular features, the same long, graceful body, the same slender fingers, the same white hair and subtly tapering ears, and he had the same scarlet eyes. He greeted me with an inclination of his head, then shouted across to the Scot.

"You promised us a smoother landing, St. Odhran."

The man he addressed waved a dismissive hand and removed his befeathered bonnet, revealing a shock of red hair above lively

blue eyes. With a broad, charming smile which reflected something of the swagger in his manner, he approached me. Reaching
out an elegant hand, he made a deep bow, kissing the tips of my
fingers. "You are the young Countess, I take it? I am the Chevalier
St. Odhran, forever at your service."

"I'm not a countess," I told him, still fascinated by his albino
friend. I was a bit distracted. "But I'm pleased to meet you. Would
the person you're looking for happen to be German? If so, there's
another gentleman wants to see him down in the village."

"We are all British, I fear," said the driver of the car, also pre-
senting himself in that same charming, old-fashioned way. "Even
my friend here"—he indicated the man in evening clothes—"has
sufficient residency to claim citizenship." He saluted. "At your service, Colonel Bastable of the LOTA, ma'am." His manner was
playful and won me over. He reminded me a bit of Sting and Hugh
Grant combined. "I must say, we seem to have timed our arrival
to the second. That's not always the case. I wonder if you'd mind
my asking a question. Would that house be Tower House, the residence of the von Beks?"

"I'm Oo Beck," I said. "The youngest in the whole family."

I was surprised that Mr. or Mrs. Hawthornthwaite had not yet
come out to investigate, but if they were at the back of the house,
perhaps watching the cricket, they might not have heard the visitors arrive. I had no instinctive suspicion of the three men and in
fact trusted the albino just because I remembered someone like
him in my old dreams, so I answered perhaps more freely than was
sensible. I agreed that the Count and Countess von Bek did usually live across the road but that they had gone to London. My
own parents, their son and daughter-in-law, were due back from
Lancaster fairly soon.

"Ah," said the tall albino rather sonorously. "The one thing we
had not bargained for!" Putting his long case carefully down, he
shook hands with me. His were the strongest, hardest fingers I
had ever touched before. "I apologize, Miss von Bek. My manners
have become crude." He introduced himself. "I am usually simply
known as Monsieur Zodiac."

"That's the name of a conjurer who used to appear at the Palladium," I said. "You look rather like his picture." I had seen the programs which my grandfather and grandmother had kept. "Are you a relative?"

"I had a small reputation on the halls," he admitted. "But I had not expected to be recognized by someone so young!" His smile was pleasant, melancholy, rather distant. "Your grandfather and I go back sixty years."

I explained the circumstances while the Chevalier St. Odhran, employing Colonel Bastable to help him, ran back to press the hot air from his balloon's canopy. "I'm fascinated by all those old theater things," I told him. "I mean to be an actress one day. Did you perform with the Beatles?"

He regretted that he hadn't known the group. "I was only once on the same bill. In Preston. In the early days. Now, if I might leave this in your care for a few minutes . . ." Setting his guitar case down, he excused himself and went to the assistance of the others.

I watched the three press and fold the silk and pack it into the balloon's basket. They were all tall, athletic men and plainly old friends, exchanging jokes and laughing as they worked. Yet there was a purposefulness to them which gave me a lot of comfort. I could feel myself beaming with inner contentment. Boredom was no longer threatening to spoil my holidays.

CHAPTER TWO

HERE SEEMED NOTHING for it: I must try to be a good hostess and invite the strangers in for a cup of tea. Mrs. Hawthornthwaite entered the big kitchen just as my guests and I reached the hall. She was a bit taken aback, especially when the tall men told her they already knew the von Beks and were here by arrangement.

"I'm surprised," she said a little stiffly. "Usually Mr. and Mrs. Beck let me know when visitors are expected." My parents, who under German custom could use their titles, preferred not to be known as Count and Countess.

But St. Odhran soon charmed Mrs. H, establishing his credentials with a reminiscence or two of shared early days with her employers, until the more formal apologies of his companions had her insisting to them that they should stay even when, with perfect manners, they suggested they find a tea shop in the village and return later.

"I should also warn you, Mrs. Hawthornthwaite, that up to four other members of our little band also expect to join us here," said Colonel Bastable, offering her a salute of thanks. "It would be pure imposition . . ."

She took this in her stride. I had never seen her so friendly to anyone outside the family as she was to these well-dressed yet somehow battle-scarred men, whom I think we both instinctively understood to be heroes, seasoned in unimaginable wars. "Then

I'd better get out the old tea set," she said with some satisfaction. "We've had bigger parties for the Three Peaks race, gentlemen." She wondered if she shouldn't try to contact my mum and dad on their cell phone. It was sometimes harder to find a signal for Morecombe than it was for London, in spite of what the servers always promised you. I said I'd try as soon as the big men were settled. I got them down in our comfy leather sitting room chairs, admiring our pictures and our wonderful views. Their orders for tea were hearty and manly, though Colonel Bastable generously said that while he would also find Darjeeling or something like that splendid, it really didn't matter to him if Assam was preferred by the others, so I went off to sort out what I could from our miscellaneous packets of antique teas. All we used at home was Yorkshire Gold. I decided to put that beside the big teapots Mrs. Hawthornthwaite was warming. Then I went up to our tower via the "secret" door through the upstairs bathroom, the highest point in the house, and tried to phone.

I didn't put the light on in the tower, because I wanted to enjoy the last of the evening. It was getting on for twilight now, and the mist was like a filmy blue blanket over the village below. Yellow lamps shone here and there from under twisted eaves and above rippling slate roofs touched blood red by the setting sun. Ingleton had never looked more beautiful and unworldly. In the other direction were the lights of villages all the way to Morecombe Bay: lights of homes, streetlamps, window displays, all burning the same dense yellow against the deepening blue. I could smell the fells as night came creeping up over the limestone shelves and rooks began to call out the evening roundup and turn for home.

I dialed my mum's number. It crackled and rang, crackled and rang. Then I thought someone picked up. In the hope that they could hear me, I told them we had visitors and who they were. Colonel Bastable and company had insisted they would not impose on us and had proposed taking us to supper at the Inglenook or, if we could order in time, the Hill Inn. The Hill Inn offered basic ham suppers, about the best in Yorkshire, and my vote was for the Hill. I always voted for the Hill, and I had a feeling I wouldn't be overruled tonight if all went well. Visitors, especially if from the south, always got the ham tea and the Theakston's Old Peculier. It was a sort of provincial showing off, I suppose. But it was hard to imagine a decent world which didn't have at least one of those two things in it.

Just before I opened the door to go down, I saw two figures on the main road up from the village, where it turned radically under the high limestone wall of the police station. It seemed that Sandy, our policeman, *really* wasn't in. Usually you could see the light in his back room as he watched TV and pretended he was called on a case. I recognized the heavy cloak worn by one of the figures. He was the man I had met earlier. The second man filled me with alarm because he reminded me of my old dream. He wore that same kind of wide-brimmed black hat. I told myself not to be stupid. The two strangers had managed to meet, probably at the Bridge as I had suggested. I moved away from the window in case they looked up and saw me. Seeing their shadows still unmoving, I stared into the night and wondered what they were up to.

I then went back to attend to our guests, not mentioning the strangers outside. I must admit I enjoyed playing hostess and having all those grown men responding with grave respect as I offered Eccles cakes and refilled their teacups with a brew they all agreed was the best they'd had since the various foreign parts they had all come from. I asked them if they had enjoyed their journeys.

Colonel Bastable said they had all most recently traveled from St. Odhran's place in the Highlands and before that, in his own immediate case, from Salisbury. They were surprised they had not been expected, since the message to meet had come from the count and countess, my grandparents. Just as they were tucking into a second round of Eccles cakes, homemade by Mrs. Hawthornthwaite, there came a knock at the door, and she went to answer it. Soft masculine voices in the hall. Further apologies. Then my original three visitors were standing up to shake hands with the newcomers.

These weren't the men I'd seen outside in the shadows. These were clearly all old friends and did not seem to have met for a while. They were careful to include me in their conversation, though much of it, of course, was lost on me. The newcomers were equally impressive. One had silver hair and seemed roughly the age of my grandfather, though not as frail. He was shorter and stockier than the rest, with a square face and light blue eyes, a manner of solid integrity, though a little self-mocking, with a faint accent I took to be German. Herr Lobkowitz embraced one of my tiny hands in both his massive ones. His kindly eyes were intelligent, and whereas the others had the demeanor of men of action, Herr Lobkowitz appeared to be some sort of professor. The man with him had a more pronounced accent and was clearly French. Lieutenant Fromental was a huge, gentle man with a large head, dark skin and black eyes beneath a shock of curly white hair. Although still insisting he was a legionnaire, he wore jeans, a white shirt and an enormous leather jacket, which he was reluctant to remove. As he accepted a china teacup and saucer in his hands the china seemed to turn into the dolly's tea set I still had upstairs. Herr Lobkowitz looked like a dwarf beside him.

I don't know why these men seemed familiar to me. Even their names rang a bell. While they behaved like my granddad's contempories, some were too young, but I was sure some of their names were the same as those I'd heard talked about. And, of course, it was actually my grandfather and grandmother these men had come to see. I got the impression they had once belonged to some sort of think tank at Oxford or Cambridge or maybe Westminster.

"I can't work out why my grandparents would make such an important appointment and then zip off for London," I said. "They're not like that. It's not as if they get a vast number of visitors. They'd have been talking about your turning up for weeks, normally. Yet I know for certain they won't be back for at least another day."

"They could have had a reason for calling us here early," suggested Herr Lobkowitz. "Something might have to be defended."

"You mean from those men I saw outside?" I asked.

"Which men? Are you talking about a German chap?" Colonel Bastable came to kneel beside me as I popped the last bit of Eccles cake into my mouth.

"Well, yes," I agreed, "that man and the one I just saw with his friend when I was in the tower. They were coming up the main road from the village. Not used to that hill, I bet. They had stopped to get a second wind, I'd guess."

To my surprise, the whole atmosphere changed. Immediately Colonel Bastable was on his feet while someone else doused the lights. Monsieur Zodiac peered cautiously out of the window, from where you could, if you flattened your head against the wall, just see a bit of road. It all seemed a bit melodramatic to me, and I wanted to giggle, yet there was something so serious in their manner that I soon calmed down.

"What is it?" I asked. "Are those the bad guys?"

"Never invite them across your threshold," St. Odhran said seriously. "They mean you and your family only ill."

"Grandma would certainly know what to do," I said. "But meanwhile I suppose we shall just have to be prepared."

"Prepared it is, my dear," said Colonel Bastable. "Those are beasts of prey out there this evening, and they are hungry for our blood. But even that evil pair would not come wandering into our territory so readily if they meant to start trouble at once. They are just sniffing around us, I suspect."

"Unless they possessed some enormous power which they were convinced could defeat us," said Monsieur Zodiac. He seemed the most on edge of the men. He was constantly checking the watches he wore on both wrists.

"And decided to employ it because they knew our numbers would never be weaker," murmured Lieutenant Fromental.

"You mean this is a trap that pair set for us?" Herr Lobkowitz put his head down, his hands behind his back, and began to pace. "Yet how could they have known the roads?"

"We grow too used to conspiracy, gentlemen." Monsieur Zodiac had recovered himself and leaned against the piano, lighting a cigarette and waving a dismissive hand. "They are here to spy on us. They travel in our wake." He stepped to the French windows and flung them open. The air was warm, and his action had the effect of dispelling any anxieties entertained by his companions. He flicked his ash contemptuously out into the darkness. But he moved, I thought, with wary speed, ready to contain, with instant strategies, any attack on us. I was sure I heard the mumble of conversation beyond the tall garden wall. "They trace the detritus of our passing," added the albino, addressing only the sweet-smelling garden. Then the mumbled voices stopped abruptly, and Monsieur Zodiac laughed under his breath. "If they have the power, they are saving it."

"What power? Saving for what?" I couldn't help asking.

"Power to tip us out of the world's saucer!" As Colonel Bastable glared at him, the Chevalier St. Odhran burst into raucous laughter. "Well, Colonel, she might as well know these aren't your usual child abductors. And with whatever small powers we have among us, we fight the forces of annihilation itself."

"No child should carry such burdens," murmured Monsieur Zodiac, his voice suddenly soft.

St. Odhran agreed. "But we have all known children who have borne such burdens well. True?"

It was pretty clear to me that something had gone wrong. The way they exchanged glances and lowered their voices when they didn't want me to hear was a bit of a clue. When St. Odhran began to speak rapidly in French, it was all I could do to keep up with him, though I could understand the Frenchmen when they replied to him. "They have selected their ground, then," said Lieutenant Fromental. "They must feel pretty confident."

"No doubt. We have more than enough to keep them at bay." Herr Lobkowitz sounded a bit on the grim side. "And there is much they must achieve, even after the ground has been taken and named. They were ahead of us there, I'll grant you."

"Never try to be too subtle with these people," said Monsieur Zodiac. "They are brutes. They should be disposed of like brutes."

Colonel Bastable and some of the others seemed a little

embarrassed by this, as if Monsieur Zodiac's ruthless remedies might be theirs, also.

"We shall certainly take every precaution against them." Herr Lobkowitz opened the French door and looked out into the night, sniffing the night-scented stock and jasmine. "Nothing here now."

His reassurance was enough for them. They relaxed at once. I was envious of any group of people who could trust one another so thoroughly.

Mrs. Hawthornthwaite came in. She had evidently been counting sheets and towels and so on. "I'm sure it would be no problem to put you up for a few days, gents. We've had parties of cavers and campers and even a rock-and-roll band staying before now. I'll have to wait and check with Oo's parents when they get back, of course. They shouldn't be long now. All they had to do was pick up some fish in Morecombe. Then they were on their way home. They'd have phoned if they had any other plans."

"Certainly not, dear lady." The Chevalier St. Odhran shook his head vigorously. "Ingleton has more than one hostelry, I take it?"

"Lots more," I said.

Mrs. Hawthornthwaite gave me a bit of a look. I realized then she really wanted to have the company of these men for more than just the kudos and pleasure of it. She was more anxious than she was letting on.

"Quite a lot," I said stupidly, realizing what I'd done.

"Oh, yes, gentlemen," she was forced to say gamely. "Ingleton's a famous resort, or was. Though," she added, "it's possible there won't be room for you all in the same place. And you'd want to stay together, I expect."

"We have my Bentley," Colonel Bastable pointed out. "We can easily go over to Settle or some larger town. However, if you would allow us to telephone to Count and Countess von Bek to let them know we're here . . . ?"

I hadn't thought of phoning my granddad and granny at their London flat. They'd probably be there by now. If I'd had my computer working, I would have e-mailed them hours ago. I showed

Colonel Bastable into the hall, where the telephone sat on a table covered in an old green velvet cloth. Beside it were two cutoff tree trunks—log seats. He tried to sit on one and then decided to make his call standing up. I felt a bit of an idiot for not thinking of this sooner. I gave him the London number.

"I'll be glad to pay for the call," he told me as he dialed.

I had become particularly fascinated by Colonel Bastable, who seemed to have stepped out of one of the old movies I loved to watch on the Turner channel. He even looked a bit like Ronald Colman. He certainly talked like him! He had an air of early-twentieth-century dignity about him, a way of speaking and moving which made me think of soldiers ready to die for empire, of Kipling and "the thin red line"; yet his eyes carried a knowledge, a sadness even, which denied the stereotype, as if all his experience and wisdom, perhaps even his self-knowledge, were exceptional.

St. Odhran was the most cheerful of our visitors, and Monsieur Zodiac probably the saddest. Herr Lobkowitz had considerable gravity yet seemed the most ordinary, together with Lieutenant Fromental, who appeared awkwardly embarrassed to be here, as if he felt he should be out defending his fort from Tuareg freedom fighters. For all their differences, however, the men were a glamorous and substantial group, a little reluctant, in spite of my direct questions, to go into details about why they were here. My French was not good enough for me to be a very effective eavesdropper.

When Colonel Bastable finally got through to London, it was only to leave a message on my granddad's incredible old-fashioned answering machine, which he insisted on keeping purely on the strength that it had outlasted something like twenty-six generations of upgrades.

At length, after several more telephone calls and conferences among themselves, our guests had made up their minds. To be on the safe side I phoned the Hill to tell them we'd be coming up for a ham supper.

Thanking us for our hospitality, the visitors declared that Messrs. Lobkowitz and Fromental would stay at the Bridge, where there was room. St. Odhran would stay at Oakroyd's in the village. Bastable would go on to a small hotel in Settle, some ten miles from Ingleton. I, of course, was disappointed they were not going to stay with us, though St. Odhran asked if he could leave his balloon in our unused stables. I asked if they were going to look for those men at the Bridge, and this seemed to reengage their attention. "No, but we'll keep an eye on them while we're staying there. If you don't mind, Monsieur Zodiac will take your spare bed. We determined one of us would be needed here." He paused. "If your parents agree, of course."

"Of course. Who exactly are those two men, Colonel Bastable?"

"Two wrong 'uns, dear young lady, as I said. So no invitations to come in, eh? And stay away from them when you're outdoors," insisted Bastable, glancing meaningfully at St. Odhran.

"Well, we'll be staying at the hotel tonight and will have our chance, no doubt, to get their measure." Herr Lobkowitz exchanged a glance with Lieutenant Fromental. "But you must be ready for any trick here, mademoiselle. The man you met on the road today is sometimes known as Paul von Minct, sometimes as Prince Gaynor. The man he sought and found is Herr Klosterheim. A thoroughly bad egg. Together they defy both God and Satan and plot the end of the created universe, every world in it."

"Why would they do that?" I wondered.

"Because they hate our way of life," said Colonel Bastable without any apparent irony.

After a moment's hesitation, St. Odhran and the others nodded.

"Or perhaps just because they hate any form of life," said Herr Lobkowitz.

They began to talk among themselves again, and I missed most of what they said.

Mrs. Hawthornthwaite and I were both very upset they weren't all staying. I think she felt a bit abandoned after so much talk of danger, but I quickly realized they had not half abandoned us, as it had first seemed; but rather were repositioning themselves. I had a fair idea that Colonel Bastable wouldn't be driving to Settle and, if he did, that he wouldn't be looking for a good twelve hours' sleep at some local hostelry. We were being protected very thoroughly, almost as if they wove a web around us. They created a shield against those who wished us ill. It was all that boring stuff I'd always heard from my mother. I thought I'd never really absorbed it, but now I was astonished at how quickly I was taking this knowledge for granted. I knew the danger in my bones. I had dreamed of it before. I knew how important it was to build all the defenses we were currently building. We were dealing with the threat of supernatural attack. And it wasn't the kind Mrs. Hawthornthwaite kept away by remembering which kind of lilac was best put in the bowl on the threshold and if it was better or worse luck to use your left hand to pick up a fallen fork.

I remembered something else from those early nightmares I'd had. I was experiencing the benign form of the power which had assaulted me. I recognized it now only because I had known its opposite. I knew that I couldn't be safer than with Monsieur Zodiac.

Naturally we had orders to contact people at their hotels should anything alarming happen, but I knew we were in perfect hands.

Monsieur Zodiac seemed pleased with my obvious confidence in him. I felt a strange connection between myself and those pain-filled crimson eyes.

Herr Lobkowitz patted my shoulder in a comradely fashion. "We'll go now but will be back in time to meet Mrs. and Mrs. Bek. Will you promise me you won't let the bad 'uns talk you into anything, no matter what crisis they will pretend you have initiated?"

"Of course." Again I was touched by his old-fashioned language and concern.

"And we won't let them cross the threshold of our house, no matter what arguments and sweet inducements they do offer." Mrs. Hawthornthwaite indicated her husband, nodding beside her. "We're used to witches and their ways in these parts, gentlemen."

This was news to me, but it was a kind of comfort, too. Mrs. Hawthornthwaite didn't mean cackling old ladies in big pointed hats, sailing over your head on their broomsticks. Mrs. Hawthornthwaite meant an invasion of pure evil into the dale, an invasion you could almost feel like mist curling up from the bottoms of pits and riverbeds to spread itself through every street, every room of our village. And the only forces left to fight it were the unsuspecting, unimaginative folk the likes of Colonel Bastable represented: the honest, virtuous long-term inhabitants of these valleys.

I felt absolutely safe in Ingleton. I wondered if this was, after all, the best strategy of our enemies, to attack here. Even with the deep caverns in the limestone below booming far away in the underground distance, I always felt safe at Tower House. She had no ghosts I feared.

With Monsieur Zodiac I watched the six o'clock news. I was growing impatient, wanting Mum and Dad, Alf and Gertie, to come home in the expectation that our visitor would confide more in them. I might not be allowed to stay in the sitting room, but Tower House's accoustics were so good that I'd be bound to hear the important bits of whatever was said, even if I kept out of sight on the landing which led to my room.

But Monsieur Zodiac said little more to my parents when they came in. They seemed to know who he was and were very welcoming. Dad, who was almost as thin and wiry as our guest, picked me up and hugged me as if I'd been rescued from actual danger, and Mum told me I could stay up for supper at the Hill Inn. I felt slightly guilty for having invited everyone. At that point Mum didn't actually know I'd done it. I knew she had planned on cooking haddock. She seemed genuinely grateful, however, for Monsieur Zodiac's presence and was pleased to know that his friends would be coming with us for the meal. I was rather proud of her. She was dignified and gracious, like a queen.

Messrs. Lobkowitz and Fromental came up from the Bridge after a while and waited with us for St. Odhran and Colonel Bastable. They hadn't seen the two strangers there. Mum and

Dad put out snacks and got drinks for all who wanted them. I helped Mum in the kitchen while my brother, Alfy, and my sister, Gertie, tried to persuade Monsieur Zodiac to open his case and show them his guitar. With good humor, he refused, saying he had no amplifier and refusing the offer of Alfy's. "I fear my instrument would be a little too powerful, Mr. Bek."

"Alfred," said Mum, looking up from our big Raeburn stove, "come in and help me with the nuts. Gertie and Dad can look after our guests." Alfy came in reluctantly, his big blond head bowed in disappointment, his red cheeks ruddier than usual. I think Mum had made him feel a bit of an idiot. When I tried to be friendly he snatched away and started pouring out nuts, but I knew he wouldn't stay in a bad mood for long. We heard the TV go on again. Both Mr. Zodiac and Dad seemed to be taking a keen interest in the news.

"He reminds me of the Winter brothers," said Mum. "Do you know who they are?"

"Some old pop stars of yours and Dad's?" I asked.

"I used to love them when I was in college." She pushed back her mop of brown, curly hair.

"Bloody awful R and B." Alf was being mean.

"Don't say 'bloody,' Alfy," she remonstrated mildly. "Have you finished doing those nuts."

"I love blues," I said. "Were they like Howling Wolf?"

"A bit." She grinned at me and winked. We both knew Alfy would regret his snit, as he did within five minutes, when Gert came in. She was as tall as Mum and skinny. I thought she was the most beautiful girl I'd ever known, much better looking than any of the pop stars or actresses I'd seen. She had Mum's curly hair, but it was red, and she had big hazel eyes, full lips, and a fair skin, like Alf's. She said there had been a series of earthquakes in the Middle East and another one on the American West Coast. "The worse for some time. I think that's what Mr. Z wanted to hear about. He thought we might even feel a few shock waves here. Remember the last time?"

I took some fizzy water in for Monsieur Zodiac. The others were having wine and whisky.

Monsieur Zodiac and my dad were talking about the news. "Would that be why you and your friends have come here?" Dad was asking.

"Well, sir, it has something to do with our expedition, I'll grant you."

"And what of those others at the Bridge? Assuming they are still at the Bridge."

"A wicked pair, sir. They mean your family no good. But with luck we'll see them off in a few days. We await only the arrival of the count and countess. We spoke to them on the telephone, and they are taking the early train home in the morning. They hoped you could pick them up at Lancaster Station."

"Of course. We'd better think in terms of an early night, I suppose."

"We'll be ready to be off to the Hill, I think, as soon as everyone's here. Your daughter did us the courtesy of booking supper."

Until then nobody had known I had already booked the Hill. "How thoughtful . . . ," said Dad with a bit of a grin.

I had my fingers crossed everyone would be here in good time for the ham tea I anticipated. In the end there was no problem. All the men returned in time, and Colonel Bastable ferried quite a lot of us up in his Bentley while the others had to go in the old Lexus. It was a happy, busy night at the Hill. My parents didn't know everything about *their* parents' adventures, but they knew enough to understand that all these people turning up was a bit of an honor for us. Monsieur Zodiac wasn't hungry, so I had most of his tea, too!

Soon we were back at the house, and various people were saying good night. Monsieur Zodiac stayed with us while the others went their separate ways. Again I had that sense of people posting watch. Again I felt very secure.

I drank my cocoa in front of the fire with the handsome albino. I'd heard the others speak of Monsieur Zodiac a little warily, as if he were very fierce and temperamental, but I found him very easy to get along with. I felt sort of sorry for him, I suppose. He bore his sadness, as Wheldrake says somewhere, like a steel sheath about him, so that not even the blade of his wit could strike and harm.

Before I went up to bed, the albino patted my shoulder and looked down at me through his brooding crimson eyes. He made an attempt to smile. It was kindly meant, and I saw something very much like a parent's love in his expression. I was surprised, but I smiled back.

"Look after yourself, little mademoiselle," he said.

That night I woke up several times with bad dreams. They weren't exactly nightmares, for I was always rescued before anything got close enough to me, but they left me weak and feeling unpleasant, so much so that when Dad got up early, even though the train didn't arrive for a few hours, I got up, too. He wanted to go out for a walk, and I begged him to let me go with him. I think I persuaded him while he was still sleepy; otherwise he might have remembered the warnings of the night before. But I was used to testing my safety by the limits adults set on my freedom, so, because Dad let me go with him on his walk, I thought it was perfectly okay.

It was another beautiful summer morning. As we climbed up the slopes and terraces above the house, we looked back. Tower House, all sparkling granite and glass windows, looked as magical as the limestone, with the hills rolling away behind it across to the distant, glaring sea. The West Yorkshire dales at their best.

We climbed over a stile and were soon in the fields, with a long drystone wall below us in a shallow valley and a small flock of shaggy sheep grazing above. We paused to enjoy the view again.

Dad and I had often gone on this walk. It was one of our favorites. This morning we had to cut it short, because Dad needed to get back and make the long drive to Lancaster along the twisting lanes which crossed the border from Yorkshire to Lancashire. There are still people on that border who fight those Wars of the Roses, at least verbally, and usually in the pub.

We were back safe and sound and ate breakfast before anyone else was up. Only when I had finished did I realize that Monsieur

Zodiac must have left while we were on our walk. He clearly planned to come back, said Mum, scruffy as ever in her old dressing gown, because his door was open and his bag and clothes were still in his room, although his long, black instrument case was gone. Mum, who wasn't at her best in the morning, wondered where he could be taking his guitar at this time.

"He couldn't have a gig around here. Not even a rehearsal. Could he, do you think?"

Alfy, still asleep, made a weak joke about playing in the sunrise with the hippies in Kirby Lonsdale, at which Gertie expressed her disgust. The smell of coffee filled the room, followed by the acrid smell of burning toast. Alf preferred his breakfast black.

I saw Dad off and went back out onto the common for a minute. I climbed the hill so that I would see the last of his car, waved, and began to ascend again. Which was when the earth shuddered. Then stop. Then shudder again. Then shake.

As I got to the house, the earth tossed me up and threatened to throw me into the wall before I could get through the gate.

I was winded and scared. More explosions from the cavers, was my first thought. They'd gone too far. My second thought was earthquake. I tried to remember how you were supposed to respond in such circumstances. I only knew what we'd been told to do in the hotel, on our trip to Disneyland, about getting under a secure beam and so forth.

I suddenly felt myself slipping, as if the ground had tilted beneath my feet, and I knew I was sliding towards the mouth of what we sometimes called Claffam's Cave—not a real cave at all, but a deep indent in the grass-covered limestone. I could hardly make out the grassy bottom. How had it happened that one moment I was near our quadrangle door and the next I was sliding down towards dark, slippery shale. I managed to get a strong grip on a bit of rock and hung on tight, stopping my descent.

The smell of rock dust clogged my nostrils, and I couldn't get a foothold on anything. I didn't have the breath to scream. Surely someone in the house knew what was happening and was taking the proper action.

The shale continued to clatter and hiss past me, and I was shocked to see the foreign-looking man, Paul von Minct, in the big greatcloak, shaking his dusty head out of the pit below me, his clawlike slate-colored fingers pushing back the shale as he came upwards, his long, grey face intense in its determination to keep climbing towards me. At last I started screaming. But nothing came out of my throat. This man, already described as my greatest enemy, was between me and my house. I couldn't shout, so I let go of the rock, landed on his face, knocked him over, pushed past him, and was out of the hole and back on the green of the common. I had lost my bearings. Where was the house? I heard his heavy feet running behind me, and ahead of me I saw another cave opening. I jumped in to avoid his seeing me, but I could still hear him nearby.

"Miss Oonagh. Could I have a word with you, perhaps?"

I kept my head down.

He must have known I was close enough to hear him. "You have broken the spell," he snarled. His voice was like the hard bluster of the wind. "You have shredded the net they put around you. Now you are ours!"

Then came the Puritan, Klosterheim, speaking in tones like a keening, shrieking blade on glass, behind his master. Could anyone ever forget that grating voice? Or those black and white clothes, straight out of my old nightmares? "You proved your own will, dear child. Your *own* will. You prefer to be with us . . ."

That was both so blatantly false and so nonsensical, I found some energy from laughing at it. I managed to stand, see where I was, spot the house, and start running for it.

To my relief, I saw Monsieur Zodiac beckoning to me from overhead. I had not recognized him before, since he had discarded the formal English evening dress. Now he looked just as I'd seen him in those old dreams, as if he had stepped out of one of those Hindu movies I love, with long turban ends and a flowing costume, scarfs and sashes, all of bright, beautiful colors. Why was he dressed so differently?

A growl from behind me.

"Here!"

There came a single deep note from the rock at his feet, and releasing me he reached down to pick up the black sword.

"Only this blade remains unchanged."

He gasped and reached towards me, but I was drifting past him while he shouted my name. I knew I was lost from his protection, possibly from all protection. Then I was running on solid ground in the dark, then slipping. All the others had disappeared, and I could see no opening to the cave.

As I turned while falling, the only light before me now was in the green, reflecting eye of a very large cat!

Then this light, too, blinked out.

CHAPTER THREE

WASN'T SCARED at that point, because I was confident someone would come and rescue me. I didn't think anyone had planned to trap me in the cave system. Monsieur Zodiac had, I was sure, protected me as best he could from von Minct and Klosterheim. So it was hours before I gave up and began to feel my way downwards to where I was sure I saw a faint light. It could, of course, just be the glaring eyes of the big cat I had seen in the dark, but I had no choice.

I moved carefully, trembling with cold. All I wore was a T-shirt and shorts. I was going steadily downwards, hoping to find cavers there who could get me back to the surface. Then behind me I heard a loud crack, and the ground shook faintly. Bits of stone rattled down, but nothing hit me. I had a sick feeling in my stomach, but I was trying to keep control of myself. If Klosterheim could scare me so readily, then I ought to have all my wits about me. I climbed over a ridge of rock and suddenly was looking down into a deep underground valley and the strangest city I had ever seen. It was like something out of a silent black-and-white sci-fi film. I knew it, of course. I had seen it in those old, terrifying dreams.

Crystal spires, which could almost have been natural formations, rose a thousand feet or more below me. A silvery river ran through the city center, and strange, elongated beings, scarcely different in appearance from the crystalline spikes, came and went

41

on the slopes. As in those dreams, I felt no fear of them or their city. In fact, I knew a sense of relief and wasn't really surprised by my own lack of surprise. After all, I had known the city and its strange beings all my life.

Then I realized some inhabitants had seen me and were coming towards me.

Just as in those dreams, I started to run away from them, even thought they offered me no harm. Then I saw the outlines of a gigantic fox ahead, standing on his hind legs. My thought was, I can't let him be killed by that Puritan. So I turned and ran back towards the denizens of the city. I was prepared to do almost anything to make sure the bad part of the dream didn't come true.

Two of the weird-looking creatures in pointed hoods were approaching me now. I knew they were harmless. I just *had* to change the dream, make sure the fox wasn't shot. I let them come towards me. They must have been nine or ten feet tall, with hands so elongated they reminded me of bones. The tall, pointed hoods, which could have been some kind of carapace, made them look like priests in an auto-da-fé or members of the Ku Klux Klan. Beneath these long, pointed skulls were faces at once alien and amiable, with stone-colored folds of skin, their features seemingly formed from flowing volcanic rock and suddenly frozen, utterly unhuman and beautiful. Within their strange masklike faces were eyes like ice, which clearly held nothing but goodwill towards me. When they spoke, it reminded me of the soft music of wind chimes, and though I could not understand their language, I accepted the first being's cold, long-fingered hand when he offered it. He knew I had no business being where I was. I felt confident he would soon get me home. Taking his hand, I noticed an ordinary black cat with a thin body and long ears, which had situated itself at the feet of the two alien beings. It regarded me with its almond-shaped eyes. As my hosts led me back towards their city, the cat followed. Soon several similar cats, tails high, joined us. We made a strange procession as we walked slowly down towards crystal spires.

At that point I was still convinced I would soon be reunited with my parents, or that at least Monsieur Zodiac would be contacting me. Somehow I thought they already knew about this world. I had no possible notion of the adventure on which I was about to embark.

At last we reached the city. The tall, irregular towers had an extraordinary and profound beauty. I felt an emotion similar to one I had known when visiting York Minster and Westminster Abbey, but far more intense. I had sensations of tremendous joy and was so absorbed in the experience, I did not notice the creature standing in the nearest doorway, smiling at me.

"I see the city of the Off-Moo has impressed you, young miss."

I was being addressed by that same large fox, somewhat bigger than the average man and standing a little uncertainly on his hind legs, dressed with exquisite taste in the finery of a late-eighteenth-century fop. With one paw the fox held a tall ornamental pole, with which he kept his balance. The other he extended to me. "How do you do, mademoiselle." His pad was soft and sensitive, with a living warmth to it. "I am Renyard von Grimmelshausen, Lord of the Deep City, hereditary keeper of the secrets of the center. Oh, and many other things. I am named, I must admit, for one of my favorite authors. Have you read *Simplicissimus*? I've written a few books of my own, too. I will be your guide, young mistress. At your disposal. Not in this city, of course, which is not mine, but the other city, parts of which *are* mine."

"There's someone wants to shoot you," I said, shaking his paw. "You'd better be careful."

"I am used to it," he assured me. "I am always careful. And you are . . . ?"

"I am Oonagh Beck. I'm hoping to get back to Ingleton as soon as possible."

Lord Renyard frowned, not understanding everything I said. Then he bowed again. "Enchanted, mademoiselle." He spoke in faintly accented English. "You appear to have won the approval of our friends the Off-Moo."

"Who's that, again?"

"Those gentlemen. They are the builders and inhabitants of yonder city. I think it's safe to say they are allies of mine. They'll not harm you."

"But Klosterheim's around!" I looked, but I could no longer see the skull-faced Puritan.

"Oh, he'll not bother us for a while yet, believe me. He cannot come here. How can I help you?" He was serenely confident. I calmed down.

"Maybe you could point me in the right direction for the village," I suggested. There had to be another exit or entrance or whatever. "Or even take me a bit of the way to Ingleton . . ."

"Ingleton, my dear child?"

"It's where I live."

"Is that where you entered the World Below?"

"It is." My granny had told me bedtime stories about the World Above and the World Below when I was a little girl. I'd forgotten all about them. "So? Any ideas about Ingleton?"

He shook his long head. For the first time I became genuinely worried. "Then how can I find my way home?"

"We'll have to look, I suppose."

"Is it possible to stay lost for a long time?"

"Sometimes it's always possible." He was regretful. "But I'm sure I can help. I have a good many maps where I live. A very extensive library on all subjects. I was paying a casual visit to my friends the Off-Moo, so we can leave without risking offense. I come here to relax. They see nothing strange in me, whereas most of your kind and mine are suspicious of a fox who not only wears human clothes but is also educated, as I am, in all the Encyclopedists."

"I don't know much about encyclopedias, Lord Renyard." I felt a bit silly saying that. Had he read them all?

"I am an intellectual child of Voltaire and Montaigne." He spoke with a slight air of self-mockery. "Of whom, no doubt, you've never heard."

"I've heard of Voltaire, but we don't really do much French history or philosophy yet at school."

"Of course you don't." He opened his muzzle and barked several times. It took me a moment to realize that he was laughing. "How old are you, mademoiselle?"

"I'm twelve."

"Another six years before you go to university."

"About that. My sister goes next year."

He asked after my family, and I told him. I said our family name was really von Bek, and at this he barked again.

"Von Bek? It could be I know your father. Or one of your relatives at least. Is his name Manfred?"

"It's one of his names, but they have so many names. I don't think there's been a Manfred first name. Not for about two hundred years at least."

"That could easily be, of course. I met him in about 1800."

"Over two hundred years ago." Was I dreaming or not? Somehow the logic seemed to be that of a dream. "What's the year here?"

"The Off-Moo don't have calendars as we do. But in Mirenburg, the City in the Autumn Stars, where I rule as a prince, it would be about, I don't know, 1820 perhaps. To tell you the truth, my dear, it could as easily be 1920. If I had any means of measuring, I'd be better able to compute exactly what year it was in comparison. When we arrive there I'll be able to help you more."

"Then I suppose we'd better get off to Mirenburg. My mum and dad will be worrying. We can probably phone from there."

"Perhaps they won't be worrying, child." His voice softened in reassurance. "Time has substantial variations, and only a moment or two might have passed in Ingleton while days and weeks go by out here."

For some reason I was reassured by him, just as I had been in my dreams.

"Or several years," added Lord Renyard. Then, realizing he might have disappointed me, he leaned down, offering something like a smile. "But it's generally only a matter of moments. I was just finishing my business here. Would you like to come with me to my home? From there it might be possible to reckon a little more specifically."

"I don't seem to have much choice," I said.

"You could, of course, also stay with the Off-Moo. That gentleman over there is Scholar Ree, their spiritual counselor. He can be very kind."

"I think I'd better stay with you, Lord Renyard, if it's all the same . . ."

"I shall be glad of the company." The handsome fox again offered me his paw and began to lead me back to the larger group of stonelike beings. "First we'll make our adieux."

With grace Lord Renyard bowed to his hosts, then led me out along a narrow trail of smooth rock. Above us the enormous cave widened. The roof of the cavern seemed miles overhead. Instead of stars, crystals glittered and a silver river ran away into the distance, its luminous waters lighting a landscape of stalagmites and stalactites and what seemed like forests of fronds, all pale, shimmering and ethereal.

Reconciled to my inability to contact my parents at that moment, I felt better when Lord Renyard's soft padded paw grasped my hand and we left the Off-Moo city behind. As we walked, he told me a little of the people inhabiting the land he called Mu-Ooria. They had lived here long before the surface of the earth was occupied by sentient beings, he said. Their world was sometimes known as the Border Land or the Middle March, existing on a plane shared in common by many aspects of the multiverse. I was familiar with the idea of alternative universes, so I grasped what he told me fairly easily, though I had never really expected to experience what old-fashioned writers sometimes called "another dimension," and had until now pretty much taken the ideas as fiction. Most of the children's stories that my brother and sister and I read were the kind which describe another world parallel to ours, and I had never thought the idea strange. That said, I knew it might be difficult to escape from such a universe once you had fallen into one, and I remained concerned for my worried parents, feeling somewhat guilty that the fascinating underground world kept distracting my attention.

The Off-Moo had few natural enemies and were peaceful, Lord Renyard told me. The cats I had seen often visited them and communicated between them and certain humans. "Felines often come and go from that city. They have a special fondness for it. I know not why."

Lord Renyard said he found the intellectual stimulus he craved by visiting the Off-Moo. Most of his colleagues in Mirenburg were positively anti-intellectual, he said. "Many are outrageously superstitious. But if they were not, I should probably not rule them."

"You are Mirenburg's ruler?"

"Not the whole city, dear young lady." As we strolled along he told me that he had enjoyed the company of my great-great-great-umpteenth-grandfather and that of another adventurer, his friend the famous aerial navigator, the Chevalier St. Odhran.

"You know the Chevalier St. Odhran? I met him yesterday!" I was excited to have a friend in common with him.

"Indeed? Not his descendant?"

"Only if his descendant is also a balloonist."

He described his friend who often visited Mirenburg. It was my St. Odhran to the letter. And sometimes, I heard, he came here with two friends who *had* to be Lobkowitz and Fromental. This gave me more hope. If the Scot had been able to fly his balloon to Ingleton, then it suggested there was a way I could easily be reunited with my parents and that the Chevalier St. Odhran might also know where to look for me. In that way kids can do, I made up my mind not to worry and to enjoy the experience as much as possible. If a minor earth tremor had opened the world to me, there was a good chance that a similar tremor would get me out.

Lord Renyard had a taste, it emerged, for abstraction. He reminded me a bit of my dad, who was always inclined to wander off the practical point into speculation. I began to lose the thread of the fox's arguments and was glad whenever he paused to point out a spectacular view or describe some flora or fauna of the surrounding world.

I was beginning to get tired and hungry by the time the tottering towers of the City in the Autumn Stars came in sight: a sprawl of tall tenements and chimneys, spires and domes. High overhead I could see pale, bright spots of faded color, rusty reds and dark yellows, which might indeed have been ancient stars. I wondered if I would find my other protector, Monsieur Zodiac, there in the city.

Lord Renyard told me to be careful where I put my feet. "We shall be at my home soon, but the path can still be treacherous." He pointed to the skyline of Mirenburg. "What you observe," he explained, "is a mirror of the city you will find on the surface. Do not ask me how this phenomenon can be. I lack the intellect to explain it. But in a certain place the upper city and the lower city connect and allow us to move from one into the other. I think you will find that upper city more familiar. I cannot be sure, but it might even exist on the same plane as your own."

"In which case they'd have long-distance telephones," I said. "And I'll be able to get in touch with my parents."

He hesitated, doubtful. "Our Mirenburg—*my* Mirenburg—is not an especially progressive city, though she has lately accepted some modest manufacturing reforms."

As we descended towards the city walls, the silence of the huge caverns was broken by a rapid drumming sound. Looking around him, Lord Renyard drew me back into the shadow of a slab of granite. He put his paw to his muzzle, indicating to me that I shouldn't talk. Far away across the ridge, under the dim light of the "autumn stars," I saw two men on horseback. I couldn't make out their features until they rode quite close. I would have called to them if I hadn't remembered Lord Renyard's instructions. When I saw their faces, I was glad I hadn't. It was the mysterious visitor and the other man from the dreams, the Puritan with the pale, gaunt head. Klosterheim. I suspected they were looking for me.

Soon we had reached the high walls of Mirenburg. It was a cold, rather alarming place. I gripped the fox's paw still tighter as he led me through unguarded gates, explaining where we were. "The larger, outer city we call, these days, the Shallow City. But my people inhabit the core of the place. The quarter known as the Deep City. The Shallow City is ruled by the Sebastocrater, descended from Byzantine knights. But I have little intercourse with them. They are very poorly educated, having forgotten their old wisdom and skills. They never leave the city and certainly never venture underground, as I do."

We walked through black, unlit streets and eventually came to a wide boulevard. A single globe of light, very dim at this distance, lit this area of the city. The globe was seated on top of a monolith of black marble, block upon gigantic block, ascending to cubes of basalt.

"The palace of the lower city's Sebastocrater," Lord Renyard murmured. "No threat to us."

Many of the other buildings had the look of public offices or apartments of important officials. Only rarely did I see a yellow light in a window. The buildings were high and close together. I was reminded of New York, except that this city was weirdly silent, as if everything slept. The only time I'd been to New York, I'd been astonished at the noise of traffic and police sirens going all night.

Lord Renyard seemed nervous, murmuring that this part of the city was not one he was familiar with. "Mine is the oldest quarter, what most these days call the Thieves' Quarter."

"Thieves?"

"I am not an entirely respectable person," he murmured, as if embarrassed. "Though I strived to educate and civilize myself all my life, those amongst whom I am doomed to dwell still consider me a monster. Many are deeply conservative. Even their religion is of a very old-fashioned kind. Only in that district, where no decent citizen will enter, can I find any kind of rest."

This sounded rather melodramatic to me. Personally I found a talking fox cool. My guess was that he'd be on every TV chat show there was, if he moved to London. I meant to tell him this as soon as we arrived at his house. After all, if I could travel so easily to his world, he could as easily come to mine.

The big buildings began to open out until we reached a wharf district on what was either a lake or a very wide river. The horizon turned a faint pink as the sun began to rise. Black water glittered. Overhead the stars grew dim. Lord Renyard led me down some watersteps, and then, amazingly, he led me up them again as the sun rose behind us and Mirenburg awoke and began to greet the morning. It was the same city we had just left, but utterly transformed!

Cocks crowing, dogs barking, maids calling from window to window, hawkers beginning to cry their wares, bells ringing, the sounds of carts rolling over cobbles, the bustle of people everywhere. It was the people, however, who rather alarmed me, not because they were sinister in any way, because they were not. They were fresh-faced, round-headed for the most part and of a generally cheerful disposition. They were dressed like people out of another century. Spiral streets wound up towards the town center, where a vast castle tottered. The smells convinced me that I had almost certainly gone back in time.

Now I really was beginning to worry. I blurted out my anxiety. "Lord Renyard, I don't think you're taking me back to my parents. I'm beginning to be concerned about them. I really *do* need to get home."

Lord Renyard paused. Ahead of us were lofty tenements which seemed to sway in a kind of dance. Even the chimney pots hopped and shuddered. "Visitors here sometimes know of ways of going back and forth across the multiverse." He seemed almost sorrowful.

I didn't mean to start crying. Why had it taken so long for the reality to sink in? I had no idea what was happening. I was lost in time as well as space, and however kind Lord Renyard was, he had no easy way of helping me. It was some comfort to be held in his huge paw, to have his stammers and snuffles of sympathy, but it wasn't enough.

I pulled myself together. I was fairly certain Herr Lobkowitz and the others would guess where I was and would find me. I told myself I had every chance of returning home. The fox was greatly relieved when I stopped crying. "It's not too far now, mademoiselle. And as soon as I am in my apartments I promise I will begin the search for those people who can help you."

Again I took his soft paw, and soon we were in the canyons of what he called the Deep City, where tall, dilapidated buildings creaked and swayed around us. Lord Renyard assured me it was in the nature of this part of Mirenburg to behave so and that only rarely did a building actually fall down. "It helps us keep our privacy, however. That and our reputation." His wink included me in a conspiracy whose ramifications I could never hope to understand. To distract myself I changed the subject.

"You said you are a thief, Lord Renyard. What do you steal?"

His big red-furred ears flattened a little, as if with pride. "I am the Prince of the Thieves, as I told you. That is why you are so safe with me. I myself do not steal, but I command as rascally a gang of footpads, pickpockets and tobymen as you've ever had the pleasure of meeting."

"Tobymen?"

"The toby is the highway, my dear. They are highway robbers. Knights of the road, as they're sometimes termed."

"And murderers?"

He was disapproving. "We don't encourage murder."

Among the shadows of the tenements, I began to see shadows lurking. Sometimes I glimpsed a pale, ratlike face, and sometimes I detected a glinting eye in a basement area or heard a scuttling, a shuffling, a sniggering.

Then, outside a tavern whose sign was so weather-stained and peeling I couldn't easily make out its name, Lord Renyard stopped. "Here we are!" I spelled it. "R-A-S-P-A-Z-I-A-N'S."

Raspazian's Tavern was a basement drinking den. The strong smells of alcohol and tobacco roiled up towards us as we descended dirty steps to its door, which was immediately flung open, inviting us to step through.

I heard a sound all around us, as if we had disturbed a colony of rats, but the interior, lit by oil lamps, had an unexpectedly pleasant atmosphere. At the tables groups of men and women dressed in patched and ragged finery, none of it very clean, saluted my friend with their tankards and weapons and called out respectfully.

"Morning, Captain. Who's the chicksa mort?"

"Enough of that, you rogues." Suddenly Lord Renyard adopted a haughty manner. I guessed that was how he kept his followers in order. I was glad to be under his protection at that moment. We stepped through the tavern to a door at the back, and up a flight of steps into a spacious room much cleaner than the one we left.

Judging by the table and chairs, the room was used for dining. On the other side of this was another flight of stairs. Lord Renyard ushered me ahead and up into a comfortable apartment with two bedrooms. It was the quaintest set of rooms I'd ever seen. I had expected a prince of thieves to live in a palace, but these were the simple, comfortable apartments of a gentleman who enjoyed reading. There were bookshelves everywhere. There was even a shelf of small leather-bound volumes next to a spice rack.

The smaller bedroom was for me, he said. There he let me clean up while he sent servants out to find clothes for me. Before long his maid brought me everything I needed, including a mob cap. At least I would look normal when I went out. While I was dressing, I smelled cooking food. At the table Lord Renyard now sat before a pile of various breads, butter and jam, which he offered me while his smiling black-haired maid brought him in a plate of undercooked chicken. Civilized and erudite as he was, the fox remained a fox.

"I have already sent my men abroad, mademoiselle. They seek St. Odhran's friends Herr Lobkowitz and Lieutenant Fromental, who have apparently been sighted and have visited here before. If anyone can discover your friends, my people will."

"What do you know about Klosterheim and Gaynor?" I asked.

"Very little. They are here, too, by now, of course. They work with powerful allies these days, I gather. I have come up against Klosterheim in the past. Although I made a friend of your ancestor, I'm not entirely sure the friendship was beneficial."

"How do you mean?" I asked.

"Well, there were repercussions. It is not something I wish to speak about, dear mademoiselle." He would not let himself be drawn out by me, and I couldn't see much point in questioning him further. The important thing at the moment was to get in touch with my grandfather's friends.

We sat in the cosiness of this strange being's apartment while my brain tried to absorb all that had happened to me in the past hours, and as Lord Renyard talked of where and how his men would be looking for my friends, I gradually fell asleep in my chair. I was only dimly aware of him picking me up in his awkward, delicate paws and putting me into a bed so comfortable it must have more than one feather mattress.

I dreamed again. *I was back in the strong embrace of the albino, his silks and samite swirling about him, his great, growling runeblade pulsing in his right hand. "I battle with a friend!" he declared. He began to laugh. "Come!"*

And in a storm of white we lighted on black crystalline rocks, where the great Lord Renyard, splendid in his ruffles and tailored silks, his beribboned dandy cane in his left paw, his quizzing glass to his right eye, bowed with great respect to us both. Then it was as if the albino had blown me like dandelion flax towards Lord Renyard, with his blessing and his strength.

I looked back, and over my shoulder were the distant spires of Mu-Ooria, the black granite and crystalline landscapes of dreams and enduring illusions. I felt Lord Renyard's paw around my shoulder. The albino was nowhere to be seen, but the great fox's delicate perfume was unmistakable.

Then I was dreaming of Tower House. *My parents were wondering where I'd been, but their pleasure at finding me far outweighed their anxiety. Sometimes I felt I was telling them how protected I felt in the care of Lord Renyard, who sat at the kitchen table, a teacup held between two paws, looking at a brace of unplucked pheasants my mum and dad had given him. His nose was twitching and his teeth were slightly bared, as if he could not wait to begin devouring the succulent birds.*

CHAPTER FOUR

ROM THIS DREAM, I woke up. It was dark. A sliver of light came through my door. I tiptoed to it and opened it a crack. There was no one in the main room, but I heard voices coming from downstairs. Laughter, oaths, the clatter of crockery and pewter. And over it all the sharp, barking tones of Lord Renyard, speaking a language I had never heard before in my life.

"Two pops and a galloper says she's a pike off."

"Dids't challenge the mish of yon dimber mort!"

Out of sheer curiosity I did my best to hear as much as possible of the queer speech which everyone here used. It sounded a bit like English, a bit like Irish, perhaps, but I was lucky if I understood one word in ten. Nowadays, having read my ancestor's book, in which he offered an account of a visit to Mirenburg around 1800 (cf. *The City in the Autumn Stars*), I know that what I overheard was called "the canting tongue," a language which derived from Gypsy and was used, in one form or another, by thieves and vagabonds in England and other parts of Europe.

When I went back to bed, however, I knew they had been talking about me. I had heard my name mentioned. I had a feeling Lord Renyard's men and women were objecting to my presence, partially because they thought he had kidnapped me. I smiled at this until I realized it was quite possible. How could I have been subtly induced to move further and further from my

55

home, where even now our local friends and acquaintances thought I must still be—unless I had been kidnapped? Could the fox be holding me for ransom and merely pretending to help me?

No, I thought as I returned to the warmth and security of my feather bed. If he had entertained such a plan, Lord Renyard would have betrayed himself. If he had been lying to me, I would have caught something of his intention in his face. Yet it was still possible he could be persuaded to hold me captive or, worse, hand me over to the man who sought me and against whom I had already been warned. I was beginning to realize that I could not trust everything I heard or everyone who told me something. If I was to get back home, I would have to rely increasingly on my own instincts and judgment.

I slept, with brief intervals of wakefulness, until early the next morning, when the light through my little window showed that it was dawn. I looked out onto crooked, cobbled streets, swaying tenements, a bustle of people and animals. Seen in this light, the buildings seemed hardly less organic than the people and beasts. The smell of coffee mingled with the smell of smoke from the city's myriad chimneys. The sky behind those tall buildings grew first rust red and then yellow and then blue, until the sun was up in all its glory, shining off windows, milk cans, pitchers of pewter, buckets of zinc, and the steel of swords and daggers stuck in the belts of the men swaggering towards the eating houses and grog shops. If I had been on holiday, I would have been fascinated by all this variety and difference, but now I longed to see something familiar, to reassure me that I could soon be on my way home.

Lord Renyard's pretty maid knocked on my door to tell me the table was laid for breakfast. I washed, dressed in my new clothes, and stumbled out to sit down before an array of ham, cheese, dark bread, butter and jam. Not sure of their customs, I helped myself to bread and butter and made myself a ham and cheese sandwich. I was eating this when the maid brought in coffee and hot milk. A moment later Lord Renyard appeared. He looked a little dusty, as if he had been busy during the night. He explained that he'd had to issue orders to his men who were not all natural early birds. "But I have a habit of rising at dawn, though I'll often sleep during the day. I put it down to my ancestry. And you, my dear, did you sleep soundly?"

"Yes, thank you, Lord Renyard. But I did get a bit homesick during the night."

"Of course you did. Of course you did." He patted my hand with a soft forepaw. "I expect news of your friends at any moment. My men have been everywhere in the Upper, Lower and Middle City. They have reports of the man Klosterheim, who pursues you, but nothing save rumors about any who pursue *him*. Strangers have all been sparing with their names, it appears." Lord Renyard shared a cup of warm milk with me, wiping his muzzle with his napkin. "For the moment it would be wise for you to remain here until I get some substantial intelligence."

I was bound to agree. "Maybe I could borrow a book or something?" I begged. "Since you don't have TV. I mean, I'd like to take my mind off things or I start worrying about my mum and dad."

Lord Renyard was sympathetic. He brightened, glad of something he could do for me. "I will introduce you to my library, though I fear it is primarily in the French language. Are you fluent?"

"Not really. Maybe you've *something* in English?"

"We'll go there and we shall see," he promised. He took a key from his waistcoat and moved slowly towards a room he had not yet shown me. Almost with reverence, he unlocked the door and opened it, walking to the far wall and drawing back a pair of curtains to allow a dim light to shine upon the orderly shelves of a large and impressive library. I loved the smell of old vellum and paper, the faintly glinting titles. I took some pencils and paper, intending to note down titles that interested me. Unfortunately, when I came to look at them more closely, they were all very old or, as Lord Renyard had warned, mostly in French or German. What weren't in those languages were as often as not in Greek or Latin. I eventually found a translation by Henry Fielding of *Gil Blas*, but frankly it was a bit stuffy. I hadn't by that time become a fan of Smollett and Fielding. The only old books I had read were John Bunyan's *Pilgrim's Progress* and children's versions of *Gulliver* and *Robinson Crusoe*.

After going up and down the ladders for a while I gave up. Thanking the fox politely, I kept the pencils and paper and wrote down what had happened since I'd left home. I didn't know it then, but I was starting what became a journal and the basis of this account. While it didn't take my mind off my problems, it did help me focus on the situation and put it in some perspective.

Lord Renyard prepared to leave after a while, begging me to remain, as he put it, under his protection. I promised, though I longed for a telephone just so I could reassure my parents that I was okay. He told me that he was doing his best to get a message to them somehow. "But I would guess your grandparents' friends are here looking for you. I mentioned the rumors." He picked up his elaborate feathered hat, took a firm grip on his long cane, and bent to pass through the low door, closing it behind him.

While he was gone I heard a lot of activity in the tavern below, and a few words, and these sounded like nonsense. I heard a great deal of high-pitched laughter from the women. They scared me. Again I found myself wondering whether Lord Renyard was on Klosterheim's side or Monsieur Zodiac's.

When the fox came back he was in good humor. He hadn't heard that newcomers were looking for me. It was thought they were in audience with the Sebastocrater, the city's ruler. What they intended to do when they left his palace, Lord Renyard didn't know, but he had men watching the palace, and they would contact my friends (if that was who they were) as soon as they could. Meanwhile someone else wished to see me. She might be able to help.

Who else could know I was here? I was baffled. She?

Lord Renyard bowed, offering me his arm. "Would you mind coming with me, mademoiselle? It is only a short way from here."

My head filled with questions I couldn't voice. I replied lamely. "I'll be glad to," I said, "thanks." Hand on paw, we left the tavern and went out into the pleasant evening air. As we walked,

Lord Renyard tried to tell me something of the history of the City in the Autumn Stars, why it was called what it was, who had founded it, who now ruled it and so on. It was a huge city, very well ordered in the main. "The center alone is reserved for the criminal and bohemian classes and all those associated with us. I am the acknowledged chief of those classes. Nowhere else is wickedness allowed to thrive." He seemed faintly embarrassed. "You should know that I am a monster but never had any choice in my calling."

We went down another alley, emerging into a wide courtyard.

On the far side of the courtyard stood a small, picturesque house with two windows and a door. The roof was thatched, and a white lattice supported a huge mass of pink and white roses, which gave the cottage a resemblance to a human face. I had never seen anything quite like it and wasn't even surprised when the windows opened suddenly to reveal two huge blue eyes. Then the door creaked and the house began to speak.

My instinct was to run. I seemed to be able to take a talking fox in my stride, but not a house which behaved like a human head.

"Good evening, child," said the house in a severe feminine voice.

Lord Renyard's paw steadied me, but my voice was shaking when I replied. "G-good evening—um—ma'am."

"I heard you were in the city. Did your friend the fox explain who I am?"

"N-no, ma'am, h-he d-didn't."

"You are not dreaming, at least no more than the rest of us dream, there being no such thing as one particular reality. We pass through the multiverse as best we can, using whatever logic we can, understanding what is possible for us to understand. You are surprised that a house can speak. I would be surprised, for instance, by a box which showed me events on the far side of the world as they happened, yet you take such a phenomenon for granted, if I am not mistaken."

"You're not mistaken, ma'am. That's television."

"I have spoken of them with other visitors. But I did not ask my friend Lord Renyard to bring you here to discuss the nature of realities. I wanted to tell you that you are in considerable danger."

"Klosterheim? Is he close?"

"You have been in danger since the day you were born. You carry fated blood, you see. You carry a power. Have you ever heard of the Graal Staff?"

"No—um—Miss . . ."

"You may call me Mrs. House. I am famous locally as an oracle and have occupied this spot, off and on, for five or six thousand years, though I think the time is coming due when I must move again." Her windows closed for a moment, as if in thought. "I might have to found my own city . . ."

"Thank you, Mrs. House."

"You have not heard of the Blood, yet you are the virgin your enemies believe is destined to carry it. Whether you keep it or not is not yet decided."

"I'm sorry, Mrs. House. You'll have to explain a bit more."

"Oracles aren't especially adept at explanations," she said almost apologetically. "We are best at large predictions, especially if we are bound to one place, as I am so frequently bound."

"Why should I be singled out to take charge of some blood?" I asked.

She seemed almost impatient with me. "If you find the Blood, you or someone you decide upon must take it home and keep it safe forever."

"But I can't find my home. That's the problem!"

"Solving one problem will solve both. The Blood is the blind boy. One will reveal the other."

"Can I find my home first?"

"You will find it eventually, of that I am certain. Unless they put you and the blind boy together. If that happens, you could easily die in terrible circumstances. You must make it your business for them not to catch you."

"Catch me? Who do you mean . . . ?"

"Those who know only the secret of the Blood and the Stone but not their function."

My heart was beating so hard that I was short of breath. I think I had begun to cry. "Tell me who wants to hurt me," I begged.

Her expression quickly became sympathetic. Her roses rustled quietly.

"One, as you know, is called Klosterheim," she declared. "He is here already. But the other is more fearsome. The creature with whom Klosterheim habitually travels. Yes, I see him. Once the greatest Knight of the Balance, now a Prince of Chaos. Paul von Minct." Again her window eyes closed as if in pain. "Ah! He has no face! He has too many faces! Beware of him. Seek your uncle in the fires of industry!"

And suddenly her eyes closed, and I was looking at an ordinary little country house again, with a rather shaken fox motioning for us to leave. I took his offered paw.

"Sometimes, my dear," he said as he led me out of the court-yard, "this world of mine defeats all logic. Its terrors make me speculate whether or not I should believe in a deity, for it seems I am consigned to Hades. I am so sorry you were frightened." We were again in the bustle of the city. "I had only her message. She is known to be very accurate. Yet this time she was also mysteri-ous. Do you have a brother here?"

"No," I said. "Nor an uncle. Not even a cousin I know about."

"Are you by any chance adopted?"

"Of course not! I was just a bit of an afterthought, Mum said. Besides, there was the blood test we did before we went to India, which showed we were all related. Why?"

"Just a foolish idea," he apologized. He was still thinking hard. "The fires of industry she sees are no doubt the many factories on the far side of the river. It is possible that your friends also journey there."

"She said something about getting home. Could there be a way home on the other side of the river? Might it be safer for us there?"

"I doubt it, my dear."

In deep thought we returned to Lord Renyard's apartments.

It seemed to me we were more confused than before we had left.

I was beginning to get used to the miraculous, but it took a while for what I had just experienced to sink in. Lord Renyard wore an air of faint pride as we headed towards Raspazian's. Mrs. House did not send for just anyone, he said. Although she had warned me, she hadn't really told me much that I didn't already know. I was curious, of course, about what she'd called "the Graal Staff," and asked the fox several questions about it on the way back. He had heard of the Holy Grail, he said, and knew of the Black Sword, but he wasn't sure he'd read more than a reference to a staff.

"It could be that it has yet to be found, that you are the one destined to discover it. After all, powerful blood flows in your veins, eh?"

This mystified me even more. When I tried to quiz him about it further, he merely put a paw to his snout in a knowing gesture and winked at me.

To be honest, I was a bit alarmed by Mrs. House's predictions, wondering if I hadn't entered some kind of grand loony bin. It had to be a strain, as Lord Renyard had hinted, being so strange. I wondered if I wouldn't be better off in what they called the "Shallow City," where people seemed more normal.

As we approached Raspazian's faded sign, one of the swaggering, befeathered rogues who served the fox came towards us and, leering at me in a disturbing way, bowed to his master.

"Well, Kushy?" said Lord Renyard.

"Ye've a visitor, my lord. We've seen him before, if I'm not mistaken. Pale cove. Looks like death. Has a cold."

"His name?"

"Didn't mean much to me, your worship." Kushy lapsed into the language I'd heard before.

A brief conversation, and we were on our way again, with the fox frowning and looking down at me. Before we reached the tavern, he had further words with Kushy, who was off like a shot, coming back with a sizable hemp sack.

"What's that for?" I asked.

"For you, my dear. I want you to climb into it."

"I'm not sure that seems like a good idea."

"I don't want this Klosterheim to see you. This way I can get you past him and into my quarters without revealing your presence."

Reluctantly I agreed. The sack didn't smell as bad as I expected it to. In fact it was rather sweet. It must have contained sugar or something similar. Kushy hoisted me onto his shoulders, groaning that I seemed precious heavy for a little girl, and I felt him carrying me into the tavern and setting me down inside the door while a voice I recognized announced itself as Klosterheim.

"I remember you," I heard Lord Renyard say. "You are a friend of Tom Rakehell's—Manfred von Bek."

"The same, sir." Klosterheim's cold tones were also familiar to me. He was the man from the common, all right. "I trust you are well."

"Well enough, after all the damage you and your party caused here. I hope you found what you sought. Too many died in that pursuit. I was forced to take sanctuary in another city for a while."

"Aha! You have been in Tanelorn!"

"That's my business, Herr Klosterheim. What's yours?"

"I fear I call upon you again for help, sir."

Lying still as a corpse in the sack, I managed to get an eyehole parted but, even so, couldn't see much of either Lord Renyard or Herr Klosterheim. But I knew for certain it was the same man I had been warned against.

"I believe you have taken the young countess, Oonagh von Beck, under your protection," Klosterheim said, cutting to the chase. "The granddaughter of Count Ulric and Oona, the Dreamthief."

I'd never heard Grandma described like that, and I strained to listen.

"I was privileged to be of some small service to the child when she became lost in Mu-Ooria. A confusing country for those who do not know it."

"As is the whole world of underground."

"Quite so."

"She journeyed on, I take it."

"You may take it, sir."

"Would you oblige me by telling me where she has gone?"

"I would not, sir." I heard ice in the fox's voice. Plainly he didn't like Klosterheim one bit. Which made me feel a little better since at least he shared this with my grandparents' friends.

"I need to speak to her urgently. She is in considerable danger."

"From whom, sir? From you?"

"I am not her enemy."

"Your allies are not her friends, from what I hear."

"You refer to Paul von Minct, otherwise known as Gaynor the Damned. Why should he and I be allies now?"

"Perhaps I have news that you came to our city in his company."

"Where I learned his true plans. Where, I should tell you, sir, we quarreled and went our separate ways."

"Yet you both seek the girl?"

"I need to get her to safety."

"Where would that safety be?"

"I refer to the city of Tanelorn."

"Until recent times there was no certainty the city was a place of safety. And I seem to recall that Gaynor had something to do with putting Tanelorn in jeopardy."

"Be that as it may, I had nothing to do with that attack. Neither do I mean the child harm. If you could arrange for me to speak to her . . ."

"I must ask her that question. I promise she shall know all that passed between us."

I smiled at Lord Renyard's foxy joke, which he knew I would appreciate.

"She's a high-strung creature with an overactive imagination," said Herr Klosterheim portentously. "We must do our best to protect her from herself."

"Quite so," said Lord Renyard.

Eventually Herr Klosterheim left, and Lord Renyard opened the sack. "Well, mademoiselle? What do you think of that?"

"I was warned not to believe him, no matter what he said."

"And I'd be inclined to follow that warning," he agreed. "Still, it suggests he or his spies will be looking out for you. We must be careful."

"I agree, Lord Renyard. But how can I hide from him and try to do what Mrs. House told me to?"

"She gave you no specific instructions, mademoiselle. She is not a mistress but an oracle!"

I nodded. "But if Herr Lobkowitz can't be found soon, I'll have to do something, don't you think?"

"I understand your frustration, my child." He sighed. "But we should not keep Klosterheim far from our consideration. He has a determined air to him, and I suspect he'll not go far away, even if it's true and he has fallen out with his partner, von Minct. Those two are more than common rogues. They both possess a will towards evil. I sensed it the first time I met him, when he came here with your ancestor."

I wanted to satisfy a question which had been nagging at me. "You speak of the time you met my ancestor, yet he lived two hundred years ago. When did you actually meet him?"

"Perhaps some fifteen or twenty years since. As I said, mademoiselle, time in our city passes at a different pace to the time you experience. I do not know why this is so, though I have heard more than one man attempt to explain it, and I myself once kept an orrery and all manner of astrological instruments until they were stolen from me in one of the wars which occasionally shake our city. It coincides with some cycle of the planes which make up our universes moving at a different rate, much as planets go about the sun according to their own pace. I am not an unlearned being, yet I have been unable to discover any treatise which sets out to explain this phenomenon satisfactorily. Be assured, however, that you are not the first visitor to observe it. It could mean your parents have not even noticed you are missing."

This seemed to cheer him up. It was only then that I realized how my kindly captain of rogues had been as anxious as I about my parents' fears for me. I moved forward and embraced him. His nose twitched; he made a gulping sound deep in his throat, and I thought I saw something like a tear in his big vulpine eye.

The next few days were very frustrating. Lord Renyard's men reported that Messrs. Lobkowitz and Fromental had indeed presented themselves at the palace and had even met Klosterheim and von Minct, though the encounter hadn't been friendly. Whenever one of the rogues of the Deep City had tried to contact my friends, they had failed for a variety of reasons. Lord Renyard wanted to hand me into their safekeeping but thought it unwise to risk a journey across town. We must wait until they come looking for us, he thought.

"They do not know where to search for you. Klosterheim has clearly not shared any of his knowledge with them."

Meanwhile I tried to puzzle out what Mrs. House could have meant in her reference to the one with no face, the Graal Staff and so on. I wondered if the strange oracle was in her right mind. Maybe she was a bit senile. As Lord Renyard had hinted, being a monster, being cut off from common experience, was inclined to make you lose your grip on ordinary reality. I was getting very bored at Raspazian's even though I had now made friends with Kushy and some of the other "tobymen" and "divers" and had begun to pick up a bit of their language.

Lord Renyard eventually, reluctantly allowed them to take me out with them as long as I was disguised, usually as a boy. They showed me their secret routes through the city, even taught me a way of crossing bridges underneath the general traffic.

Kushy called me his rum doxy, which was a compliment, meaning I was a pretty girl, and Kushy's lady friend Winnie said she thought I was a sweet lathy of a girl with a fine little knowledge box, who she wished her own daughter might be. Within a week I became a bit of a mascot to those vagabonds and footpads

and felt honored to be liked by them, even though I'm not sure
my mum and dad would have approved of my spending so much
time in their company. Since I wasn't allowed to leave Raspazian's,
my new friends brought their own children to play with me. To
pass the time, I let them teach me their tricks, including how to
pick a pocket or shoplift without being spotted!

Lord Renyard was gone more frequently, on mysterious business. I guessed he was looking for my friends. Kushy, Winnie and
the other denizens of Raspazian's were careful to look after me,
and I knew that although I was in perfect hands, I couldn't bear
to stay there for much longer, no matter how slowly time was passing on my own plane of the multiverse.

Then one morning the decision was taken out of all our hands
when, without warning, the tavern door burst open and there
stood Klosterheim, his pale eyes glaring in his skull-like face
topped by a black, wide-brimmed hat. The rest of his clothes were
of the same Puritan cut as before, with a wide, white collar and
cuffs. A big belt supported a sword and two pistols, which he drew
as he entered, flanked by soldiers with drawn swords, wearing the
archaic armor of the ancient Greeks but with necklaces of what I
first took to be onions around their throats. They were tall, dark
men with glistening black beards. Kushy and company regarded
them with some nervousness until, with a sweeping bow, Kushy
took off his feathered hat and said with that whining, mocking
courtesy his kind always adopted to authority:

"Good morrow, gentlemen of the City Watch. Your visit's a
rare pleasure. What can we do for you?"

Klosterheim pointed at me. "That girl. She's the one you kidnapped. Kill them all, guards, if they resist. You are safe now,
fräulein. I am here to take you home."

I looked from Kushy to the guards. For a moment I was confused. "He's the one wants to kill me," I said.

Then, instinctively, I raced for the back room and slammed
the door behind me, bolting it as Lord Renyard had taught me.
From the other side came the firing of shots.

I felt fairly certain that Klosterheim, having somehow got the city authorities on his side, would win this round. At any moment they'd come bursting in. With my heart pounding, I opened the window of my bedroom and hopped out onto the tiles of the roof below. I slid down it, grabbed a drainpipe and shinned down into the little paved yard at the back of the tavern. I was hoping to hide somewhere nearby until they were gone. I took the bar out of its lugs, opened the gate and slipped into the alley. By the time I had found a dark doorway in which to hide I heard shouts from the courtyard. Men raced towards me. I had no choice. I crept into the yard behind me and hid among some stacks of crates and barrels. Fortunately their feet pounded past in the alley. Only when it was dark did I risk sneaking out and making my way back to the tavern, just to find the gateway closed again. I would have to risk going out into the street and entering through the front door.

As I slipped into the street leading to the square I saw a glint of armor. The city guards were still there, maybe left behind by Klosterheim. I kept walking, dodging in and out of shadows with no clear idea where I was going. Eventually I came to the unstable black marble that was the river, rows of deserted warehouses, and scuttling rats. I felt comparatively safe by the water if I kept in the dark. Across the river the new town didn't seem so full of soldiers. Sparks and flames gushed up in the black factory smoke. I could smell that smoke from here. A weird hard-boiled-egg smell; it reminded me of Guy Fawkes Night fireworks.

I thought I recognized the nearest bridge, the one Kushy and the others had shown me how to cross. A narrow walkway, used by builders to make repairs, ran underneath. You could get onto it, if you were nimble and small enough, by climbing up some ornamental ironwork and wriggling through a pipe.

Very slowly and carefully I made my way to the base of the bridge. I could hear the rumble of carts, horses' hoofs, marching soldiers. But nobody bothered to look down as I quickly shinned up the ironwork, squeezed through the short section of pipe. I climbed over the protective metal roof and swung down to drop on the walkway on the other side of a locked gate.

Then it was nothing to run softly over the wooden slats until I got to the other side, repeated the operation and found myself beside more rows of warehouses, whose stink, I should add, was not any more attractive than that of the first. I had been right. There were no soldiers on this side at all. They were all concentrating on the far bank.

I kept to side streets. The heat increased as I got closer to the great walled factories. Here Mirenburg made the steel for which, in my own world, she was famous, producing a well-known make of East European car, the Popp. Now she was probably making pikes and swords and cannons and stuff, more suitable for the customers of this age!

And then, as luck would have it, a squadron of mounted soldiers galloped along the thoroughfare ahead of me, just as I reached the middle of a factory wall, with no street I could easily dodge into. They weren't looking for me, I was sure, and were probably on their way to the bridge, but they would recognize me if they saw me. There was a small door in the factory wall, which I fully expected to be locked or jammed; to my astonishment, the handle turned. Without even a squeak of hinges I stepped into the overheated darkness and closed the door behind me. I began to wonder if some goddess had her benevolent eye on me.

The door led into a bleak passage, at the end of which were three more doors. Rather than waiting for the soldiers to go, I let curiosity take me down the passage. Had I been sensible, I would have just hidden for a moment and then gone back into the street. But I walked down the corridor, then opened the middle door a crack. I saw a turnstile and, behind that, people doing various kinds of office work. Apart from their clothes, they could have been in any ordinary office from my own time. Beyond them came the noise and bustle of the factory itself. I saw an occasional bright tongue of flame leaping into the air.

The door to the left was a disused office by the look of it, with a dusty desk and filing cabinets. But there was another interior door beyond it. I had no light once I closed the door behind me, and had to fumble my way across the room until I got to the other side. Again I expected this door to be locked. It was. But as I groped down its face, I felt a big key still in its lock. With difficulty I turned it. Unlike the door in the wall, this one had been badly kept. I twisted the handle, hearing a high-pitched sound. It cut through my eardrums and yet wasn't completely unpleasant. There was a strangely thrilling note to it. Then the noise died away. Something rumbled. Something raced and gushed. Something hissed.

I opened the door wider. It led out onto a gantry overlooking a busy factory. Molten steel splashed like lava from huge buckets hauled on chains by sweating half-naked men, overseen by shouting foremen and other specialist workers, who helped guide the buckets and tip them over a series of molds. The light was glaring, and the heat was like a wall against my body. Flaming liquid steel gushed and splashed.

Through squinting eyes I saw the blind albino boy. He stood in a pulpit made of metal. His head was raised and set to one side, as if he was listening keenly. At a certain moment he raised his slender white hand in the air. All work stopped. He listened again, his crimson eyes reflecting the red-hot metal around him. Overhead more buckets rumbled and hissed; more molten steel flowed down gullies. It was a very hectic factory, but I couldn't really work out what was being made. The molds were at most three inches wide and about three feet long. Were they forging rods of some kind?

I managed to wriggle into a space behind rolls of unused chain and get a better look at what was going on below me. As I watched, one of the workers yelped. A tear of boiling steel had fallen on his shoulder. A medic came from the side of the room and put a patch on him. He went back to work. I noticed that several workers had more than one patch. This had to be a dangerous occupation. Why, I wondered, didn't the factory supply them with protective clothing? I had a poor grasp of economics in those days.

The blind boy fascinated me. He was about four years older than me. Like Monsieur Zodiac, he had long, milk-white hair, while his skin had the sheen of bone. Unlike the workers, he had few patches. Even at that distance I could tell he was sweating. His glaring crimson eyes seemed completely sightless. Had the glowing metal blinded him? His hearing, however, was unnaturally sharp. For it was his hearing, I realized, they were employing.

The men paused so that a bucket of boiling metal was near him, and he listened. Then he spoke to them and pointed in the general direction of some of the molds. The workers finessed the bucket to their molds and again poured liquid metal. Occasionally some kind of boss came along and spoke to the men. They kept their distance from the boy. They carefully avoided touching him.

I watched for over an hour as the albino paused, listened carefully, almost always rejecting the steel, very occasionally pointing and giving directions. As the steel cooled in the molds, the lengths were brought to him, and again he would hold them close to his ears, listening intently. Some of them he accepted, but most were rejected. This seemed to be the norm, judging by the way the workers treated the routine. He was listening for some flaw, I was sure.

There wasn't much doubt in my mind that the boy was related to my grandma and Monsieur Zodiac. Even the way he held himself was familiar. Was he a prisoner in the factory? I couldn't be certain. There were no guards about.

He worked constantly, listening, directing, listening, rejecting. Eventually I realized they were forging sword blades, which would no doubt be polished, honed and decorated by other hands. But he didn't pass many of them. I could tell he was listening to the music within the steel. The blades spoke to him, and he accepted almost none of them, rejecting most.

Suddenly a klaxon sounded throughout the factory. Work was stopped, and men moved away to open packets of sandwiches and eat. The blind boy was led to a spot only a yard or two below where I was hiding. As the men ate, the boy merely drank from a large cup handed to him by a guard. The guards were not rough to him. In their own way they seemed to like him, but they treated him very much as an alien creature, not one of their own. Now I had my chance. When the space was deserted around him I risked calling to him, barely lifting my voice above a whisper.

"Boy! Blind boy?"

He looked up. He had heard me. He did not reply in a loud voice himself, but murmured.

"Girl? Overhead? Yes, she lies on the walkway above, hidden by chains, and—"

"I've seen how clever you are," I told him. "But I'm not here to admire you."

"Why *are* you here? Did McTalbayne send you to find me?"

"I don't know who that is. I'm lost. This is an accident. I have relatives who look like you. Does the name Beck mean anything?"

He shook his head and finished his drink. The klaxon sounded again. The boss approached him to guide him back to his station.

"You must get me away from here," whispered the boy suddenly. "If you are a friend, you must help set me free. What's your name?"

"Oonagh," I said.

"That's like my mother's name! Do you know Tufnell Hill?" A desperate expression crossed his face. "Those two brought me here, but . . ."

"What's yours? What's your name?"

"They call me Onric here," he said. "My father—"

The guard came too close. He stopped whispering.

"I'll try to free you," I said, "but I'll have to get help. I'm only a little girl."

"You have given me more hope than anyone else," he said, his voice dropping so low that I could scarcely hear it. Then the foreman was beside him and leading him back to his post.

I was confused. How could I be related to this boy I had never seen, who dwelled in a different age, in a different part of the multiverse? I stepped out from behind the chains. Somebody shouted. Had they seen me? I bolted for the next door, entered into the darkness behind it, remembered to turn the key and then tiptoed to the door into the corridor, which was still deserted. Where could I get help for this Onric, I thought ironically, when I couldn't even get help for myself!

I returned to the street. Maybe Lord Renyard would find someone to help me rescue Onric and get us both out of harm's way! Were we really related? Was this who Klosterheim and von Minct were searching for? Were they hoping I would lead them to the boy? Did I, after all, have some sort of affinity with him?

In a daze, I managed to reach the bridge and return the way I'd come. Where was I going to find help? Raspazian's seemed the only likely place. I had to hope the Sebastocrater's guards had left, as there was still a fair amount of activity on the bridge.

I crossed over into the warehouse district, found a street I recognized and began to make my way up it. I heard the marching feet of guardsmen behind me. I was so exhausted, I was almost ready to be captured.

Stepping back into a doorway, I felt sick with fear as a hand covered my mouth and an arm encircled my body and lifted me. I struggled until I heard Kushy's murmur in my ear. "Hush, little mort." When we were back in the alleys he let me go. His face was badly battered, and he had a wound in his left side. He seemed ashamed of himself and kept apologizing to me. "His Lordship's still not returned. There's talk he's captured."

I was horrified. "What can we do?"

"Get you away from here," he said. "Get you somewhere safe. I've no idea how Klosterheim has the guards on his side. It probably means he's persuaded the Sebastocrater that you've been kidnapped by us."

"Herr Lobkowitz and Lieutenant Fromental were supposed to be at his palace. They wouldn't have let him do it!"

"We don't know what's happened, missy." He was leading me into the tangle of twitterns running between the buildings. "We need to find the chief. Meanwhile you can hide out here." He opened a door, and we slipped into a poorly furnished room. There was a cot in the corner, a table and some crudely made chairs. "Get some sleep," he advised. "I'll bring you some food in the morning."

I lay down to rest.

When Kushy still hadn't returned by noon the next day, I became sure he was dead or captured. If they tortured him, they'd learn where I was. The plight of the blind albino boy was still on my mind. I couldn't just leave him. He had asked for help. Taking the blanket from the cot, I left the hovel and made my way out into the creaking, tottering streets. First I must find food. Then I must find the Sebastocrater. At least I would be able to tell him that Klosterheim had tricked him, and maybe I could find and recruit Lord Renyard to help save the boy.

CHAPTER FIVE

EAVING IN DAYLIGHT was a risk, but I really needed to eat. At least I was no longer conspicuous. Dirty and poorly dressed, I slipped out into the streets with no idea how I would find food. The Deep City was crowded with frightened people unused to the presence of the city guards, even though the guards kept their distance according to ancient tradition. With Lord Renyard gone, there was no one to demand a return to those old agreements. The guards, in their peculiar antique Greek armor, did not look comfortable. Most of them wore strings of garlic around their necks. Apparently they thought it warded off disease. Only Kosterheim carried pistols. They were armed with swords, lances, shields and bows, while the Deep City's denizens had plenty of guns. Any uprising would be hard to control.

Eventually I applied the bad lessons I'd learned from Kushy and his friends. Feeling rather guilty, I easily pinched a loaf and a pie from a distracted baker in the market. Ravenously I ate them in a quiet doorway. I think anyone as hungry as I would have done the same. But I was very glad my mum hadn't been there to see me! I wondered if I should try to find Mrs. House again. She had foreseen some sort of future for me, and she had mentioned the boy. Then I reminded myself that the best thing to do was to go into the Shallow City and try to find out what had happened to Lord Renyard or Herr Lobkowitz, so I took one of the spiraling alleys, intermittently hiding and walking slowly, getting closer to the wide basalt boulevards.

By midnight I had reached the black marble avenue which ran roughly from east to west with a huge Greek palace in the middle, at the top of which burned a massive single light, illuminating much of the city around it. From a new perspective I was looking at the Sebastocrater's monolithic home.

I had better sense than to walk out into the open, but I kept that great dark dome, glinting with lacquer, gold and silver, in constant sight. Using trees and buildings for cover, I avoided patrols and got much closer to the palace, which was surrounded by black walls lit at intervals by blazing braziers, their flames flowing and guttering in the night air. Overhead the ancient ochers, yellows, browns and deep greens of the Autumn Stars looked down on me.

I heard a sound behind me and smelled something familiar. I retreated into the shadows. Turning, I saw, to my astonishment, that same black panther I had first encountered beneath Ingleton common. I guessed she meant me no immediate harm, because she narrowed her eyes in what, for a domestic cat, would have been a smile. The panther's whiskers twitched, and a heavy rattling sound came from her throat—something which could have been a purr. Her friendly posturing was somewhat at odds with the beautiful ivory saber fangs which grew from the top of her mouth. She lay down in front of me. Somehow I knew she wanted me to climb onto her back so that she could help me escape.

"I can't," I whispered. "I have to get to the palace to see if I can find Lord Renyard."

The cat's purr became a noise of inquiry. Then she stood up and waited expectantly for a moment. I shook my head again. Then, since I would not ride, looking back at me from time to time, she began to lead me through the darkness, closer to the palace. Thinking she might know a secret way in, I followed her until we stood in dense shrubbery beside the great obsidian wall. It was apparently unclimbable, however, and I could see no other way in. Again the panther lay down, clearly indicating that she wanted me to jump on her back, and this time I did what she demanded, wrapping my arms around her powerful neck just in time, before she made a terrific spring. Air rushed through my hair, and I felt suddenly exhilarated as her incredible muscles moved under me. We landed on a broad lawn. A short distance away I could just make out a fountain playing near a summerhouse built like a miniature Greek temple. Not far from the fountain I saw the stiff outlines of about a dozen men, probably guards. The panther loped across the lawn towards the summer house. Another leap and we jumped out of the night, into brilliant day!

It took a moment for my eyes to adjust. Then I saw them. Inside the bright summer house stood not only Lord Renyard but Herr Lobkowitz and Lieutenant Fromental. I think I was only slightly less astonished to see them than they were to see me. I tumbled off the back of the panther and ran to embrace Lord Renyard, who looked delighted and troubled at the same time. I turned to stroke the head of the big black cat, but she had gone. In her place stood a woman who was my grandmother's exact twin, though much younger. She was an ivory-haired, pale-skinned albino with unusually brilliant crimson eyes.

"You're a hardheaded child," she said. She was dressed in a red jerkin and black tight-fitting trousers. There were leather boots on her feet, and on her back was a quiver of arrows. In her left hand was an unstrung bow. "What made you go off like that?"

"Grandma?" I stammered in astonishment.

"Well, in a manner of speaking."

"Are you related to Monsieur Zodiac?"

"I am."

"You—the panther—how?"

"We have a special rapport," she said with a slight smile. "I'm sorry about the mystery, but we knew no other way to find you."

"Are you prisoners here?"

"I am not," she said. "But my men were also caught. Klosterheim has convinced this city's prince that they are to be feared and were responsible for holding you prisoner."

"But why should he be interested in me?"

"Because of oracular warnings concerning the Graal Staff. With the best motives in the world, he wants to take on the burden of guarding the Staff. I suppose he doesn't accept that you're worthy of the job."

"I don't even know what the job is. I don't even know what the Staff is. But I certainly don't have it, and neither do I know where it is." I wanted to ask her about the blind boy, Onric, but I couldn't find a way of starting.

"We understand all that, Oonagh, dear." Herr Lobkowitz stepped forward to kneel down and embrace me. "But Gaynor, the other man you saw in Ingleton last night, is convinced you are the key to its possession. I think they might be misguided, but we let ourselves be captured before we could find you and take you home. You're safe here for a while. It won't occur to them to look for you in our prison, I'm sure."

"How did they capture you?"

"Magic," said Lieutenant Fromental simply and unequivocally. "Powerful sorcery which defeats all our knowledge of such things. None of us, save Oona the Dreamthief here, has any such power. We scarcely know how to defend ourselves, let alone attack it. But you can help us."

Although it baffled me, I suspected that Oona the Dreamthief was my grandmother but at an earlier time of her life. "Help *you?*" I said. "I can't even help myself. I still don't really believe in magic. At least, I didn't until I met Mrs. House, and even she could be just another kind of life form."

"I quite agree with you, dear young lady." Lieutenant Fromental's big brow clouded. "But rationalism cannot entirely explain things I have witnessed in this world they call the Middle Marches. For instance, look outside." He pointed. It was now daylight outside, and the figures I had seen on the lawn were in fact about a dozen American Indians in colorfully decorated breechclouts, leggings and leather shirts. Their heads were shaven, apart from long scalp locks, and their fierce faces were painted. In their hands were various weapons, including stone tomahawks, lances, bows and shields. They looked as if they had walked off the set of

The Last of the Mohicans. Yet each one of them was frozen in mid-movement.

"Who are they?" I asked.

"They are my friends," said Oona. "My clansmen. They came with me to look for you, dear. But since we arrived I haven't been able to communicate with them, and they haven't been able to move. Some spell has been put on them. All the men are under the power of the Sebastocrater, the Prince of Mirenburg."

"Am I a prisoner, too?" I asked.

"Probably not—nor the panther. Nor me. That is how we were able to bring you here and explain what has happened. Our friends came to beg the help of the Sebastocrater. All of us were tricked into entering his grounds and this building. But why he should league himself with such villains as Paul von Minct and Brother Klosterheim, we cannot think. As I say, either they have alarmed him with some trumped-up terror or they have promised him something he can't resist."

"What could that be?" I asked.

"The Stone, I suspect," said Herr Lobkowitz. "He showed an uncommon interest in it when we arrived here looking for you. He asked if we knew where it was. We told him truthfully that as far as we knew, it was lost. He said it and its guardian had last been heard of in Mirenburg. We know, of course, that it was recently stolen from your grandparents' London flat. That's why they couldn't meet us, as they had arranged. Do you the Devil's work, eh? Could the Stone have acquired a new keeper? It determines its own situation, as we well know."

I wanted to ask Oona what her relationship was with me. I was sure she was my grandmother. But there were more urgent questions. "Are they feeding you?" I asked.

"So far we have not been offered food," said Lieutenant Fromental. He pointed to a big pair of saddlebags lying on a couch. "But Prince Lobkowitz packed plenty of provisions before we left Ingleton in search of you. You see, only a few hours have passed in this building since we arrived. I suspect, like the city, it exists outside the ordinary laws of time and space. Try a sand-wich?"

I wanted to ask about Onric, but Prince Lobkowitz spoke first.

He seemed awkward. "We mustn't alarm"—he looked at me—"mademoiselle."

"It's all right," I said. "I know everything here is odd. Well, more than odd. I'm not scared. Especially now I've found you all. There's this boy—"

"You and I are the only ones who can leave," said Oona. "We are the only two not under the spell."

"This Sebastocrater? What's his game?"

"None, I suspect. He means well, but he's none too bright," said Lord Renyard. "It's my guess that Klosterheim and von Minct have fed him lies and have almost certainly frightened him into doing some stupid things, including invading the Deep City, which is protected by so many ancient spells. It could set off cat-astrophic consequences here. If Klosterheim and von Minct have convinced him they are helping you against us, that might be the answer to what's happening. Of course, I don't know him well. He and I never socialized, except at ceremonial occasions. He ruled here, and I ruled in the Deep City. Everything was as it should be. In equilibrium."

"Why is that equilibrium disrupted?"

"It began some years ago," said Lord Renyard. "When Manfred von Bek first visited us. He was not the cause of the dis-ruption, merely an early sign of it. Some serious movement of the Cosmic Balance."

Prince Lobkowitz answered. "I have known this city and her rulers for many years. I have enjoyed conversations here and never had cause to suspect the kind of trick which has imprisoned us. My suspicion is that von Minct and Klosterheim have placed the Sebastocrater under some kind of charm or debt and are using him in their own plans."

"To find me?" I asked.

"I think you either have something they want, my dear, or ac-cess to something they want."

"The Staff which Mrs. House mentioned."

Lord Renyard explained how he took me to see the oracle. Could Onric have been the boy Mrs. House was talking about? I gave up trying to introduce this. Nobody was listening to me. Understandably, they were focused on their own immediate problems.

"Then it's as we all guessed," said Oona. "The Grail has disappeared again. What force works to disrupt the Balance over and over in increasingly close episodes?"

"I believe it is our friend's dreaming that creates the problems," said Prince Lobkowitz. "Yet that dream is due to end very soon, and when it does it could mean oblivion for all."

"No." Oona shook her head. "The dream's merely ending will not bring destruction, of course, but what is in place at the moment of its ending will decide between continuing life or complete annihilation. He will die to ensure that equilibrium, but without our help he might die for nothing."

"And the child"—Prince Lobkowitz glanced at me as if apologizing for speaking of me in the third person—"she carries the secret?"

"Klosterheim and von Minct evidently believe that. This will be their third attempt, however, to gain control of the Grail. Twice we have frustrated their plans. This time they hold more power than ever. A certain mademoiselle here plays a significant role in their machinations. That is why it is important you get to safety, child."

"All I want to do is get home." My response was heartfelt. "But I did promise a boy I'd try to help him. He works in the factory over the river. He said—"

"I don't want to be gloomy," said Oona, "but we could be moving further away from our world, not closer to it."

Seeing my alarm, she softened. "In terms of the multiverse, which is vast and infinitely varied, we are not too far away," said Oona. "All realities meet in the Middle March. You have no doubt already experienced that."

I nodded. Then I paused. "Did you say you had plenty of food,

Lieutenant Fromental, because if you have, I wonder if it would be possible—?"

"Of course, my dear. Of course. Bon appetit!" And he flung open the basket with a grand gesture. I saw now that Mum had packed some of it with my favorite snack foods. I picked out a sausage roll, some salt-and-vinegar crisps, an apple pie and a diet Dr Pepper, consuming them rather greedily. Almost at once I felt like a new girl!

"Now you and I had better get out of here," said Oona. "My warriors lack my particular gifts and were caught in the spell before I understood what was happening. I have to free them. They were loaned to me by one of my oldest friends. I doubt he would be amused by what I have led them into."

I looked at the Indians. "What tribe are they?"

"They're related to the Iroquois," she said. "They call themselves the Kakatanawa, the People of the Circle."

"Who's your friend?"

She smiled widely. "You'd know him as Hiawatha. Do they still teach that poem at school?"

"My granny reads it," I said, giving her what I thought was a penetrating look.

"No doubt," said Oona, with a sudden grin. She was my granny, all right! Every instinct told me she was. I gave up trying to work out the logic of it. That only confused me more. So I stopped.

Again the panther stood regally in front of me. I climbed on her back, and before I could turn and say good-bye to the others, the big cat leaped forward, raced across the lawn and jumped over the wall, into the wide avenue running beside it.

I jumped down and ran into the shadows. Oona, a foot or two behind, joined me.

"What are we going to do next?" I asked.

"Find Klosterheim and von Minct," she said. "It's all we can do, I'm afraid. I'm going to have to use you as bait."

"What do you mean?"

"The only way to lure them out into the open is to have you

return to Raspazian's and be seen there. Then we have to hope that Klosterheim or his companion will seek you out. As long as they don't come with the Sebastocrater's guards, we might have a chance."

"But what will happen if they capture me?"

"I'll be there to rescue you. It's all I can promise."

"Okay," I agreed doubtfully, thinking the plan sounded pretty desperate. Still, I couldn't suggest anything better.

"So let's get back to Raspazian's," she said.

The panther had faded into the darkness. Oona seemed to know how to get to the Deep City the quickest way. We were at Raspazian's before dawn. The Sebastocrater's guards were no longer to be seen. Some of the mobsmen had returned and were hanging around outside the tavern, though they had lost much of their old spirit. Kushy appeared from the basement. He had another bloody bruise on his forehead and was hatless. His clothes were even more torn. But his gap-toothed smile widened as he recognized me.

"'Arry 'Awk be praised! You're in one piece! And free! We thought the watch had you, missy. They only left a few hours gone. You'll have to be careful 'cause they could easily come back anytime. It's you they're after and no mistake, missy. You didn't find Lord Renyard, then?"

"I found him. He's the Sebastocrater's prisoner in the grounds of his palace. Unharmed but incapacitated."

"Kept there by sorcery," added Oona.

"That's it, then, ma'am," said Kushy. "Sorcery's the only thing that could keep the master imprisoned. The Shallow City has broken its age-old compact with the Deep City, has it? The capturing of one king by another was always against our rules, so Lord Renyard told me."

"They say the times are desperate, Kushy," I told him.

"They must be, little missy. They must be," he said bitterly.

"And sorcery's what's needed to free him," said Oona. "Who can help us, Herr Kushy?"

He led us down the steps into Raspazian's. Inside, the place was crowded with thieves and their doxies. All were heavily armed. All looked anxious. They gathered around us, wanting our news, horrified to hear that magic was at work. It was rare enough in Mirenburg. They weren't so much shocked by the evidence of magic as by the use of it. Magic was unsporting, outside the accepted traditions. The Sebastocrater played unfairly. They began to speculate among themselves. Why would he do that? Was he in someone else's power? Were the Lords of Law and Chaos taking an interest?

At last Oona raised her hand. "I can only say that Klosterheim and von Minct are certainly somehow involved. Does anyone here know what power exactly they have over the Sebastocrater's decisions?"

"What do they want?" asked Mrs. Nagel, one of the "diver-divas."

"Put simply, they want this young lady."

"What does she have that they seek?"

"I honestly don't know," I insisted. "I'm just—I'm just a little girl . . ." I had never sounded so pathetic to my own ears as I did then. How lame! I thought.

"Why should we protect you?" someone else wanted to know. "Lord Renyard's already captive. Ancient agreements have been broken, and magic's abroad. Why shouldn't we give you up to the Sebastocrater's men?"

I couldn't answer. I tried but gave up. I felt very guilty, and I was beginning to cry. Oona's arm around me was a small comfort.

She spoke coolly. "Keep her safe and you can bargain. Give her up and you've nothing."

This calmed them. Sharp-featured Kushy stepped forward. He had found his plumed hat. His expression was grim and set. He spoke in a low, desperate voice. "We have our honor. We need magic of our own. We've no choice now. We must ask Clement Schnooke to help us."

I didn't like the sound of Herr Schnooke. Neither, it seemed, did anyone else.

Oona started to speak but then was interrupted.

"I find such confidence flattering, gentlemen."

I turned my head towards the door. A round-faced, cheerful little man stood there. His shiny black hair was slicked down against his skull. His coat was a patchwork of red, gold and green. His brass-buckled shoes were dark green. His neck cloth was bright yellow. He looked like a clown, but the hiss of the crowd and the way they drew back from him told me he was disliked and feared by everyone.

Kushy said in a defeated tone, "Mornin', Clement Schnooke. Talk of the devil, eh, sir?"

"I've been telling you for years that your snotty Sebastocrater deserves a spot of sorcery to put him in his place, Kushy. Now that zoological monstrosity you call a master has failed to save you from the Greek's soldiery, you turn at last to Clement Schnooke. Suppose I refuse my services? Have you some other sorcerer who'll make it his business to represent the interests of the Deep City the moment he gives his word on the matter?"

"Lord Renyard forbade you to practice magic on pain of banishment," said one of those furthest from him.

The harlequin whirled to find him, pointing. "Banishment? Just as well I didn't take my leave when it suited me, eh? What is it I can do for you? Now, I mean? Now I'm needed. Lord Renyard forbade—what was it? Where is Lord Renyard, by the way? Ah, you wish me to free your master from some imprisoning spell. So that he'll return here and punish me for using sorcery? Doesn't seem sense to me, fellow citizens. I'll need a suitably generous stipend, I suggest, if I'm to risk releasing your haughty master. Then I'll ask for a free hand to use black sorcery against the city. 'Tis time that the old arts were practiced here again, and Clement Schnooke given the justice and rewards he deserves!"

Another actor, I thought, whose success on stage had gone to his head. I felt cold and clammy in his sibilant presence as he preened and pranced defiantly in the faces of those who loathed him. He removed his cap and bowed to me. But he addressed Oona, the dreamthief's daughter.

"I've heard of you, dreamthief. And I met your mother once.

She, too, insulted and demeaned me. You show me no respect. Tell me why I should show you any!"

"I don't want your respect," said Oona evenly. "I want your services. What's your price?"

He cocked his wicked head to one side. "Price? A soul or two, perhaps?" He smiled his horrible smile again and danced before us in triumph, wriggling and writhing, pointing his toes and fingers, so that I half expected him to begin shedding his glittering skin. "But gold's more useful. I need enough gold to take me out of here and see myself where I belong. Where I came from."

"Where's that?" I asked.

His cold, sardonic eyes fell on me. "Where's *that*, little miss?" he hissed. "Where's that?"

I looked him back in the face. I knew evil by its eyes, and I knew the extent of its power by the depths of those eyes. "That's what I asked."

He dropped his gaze and sighed. "I was once a prince in Cincinnati. Not the Cincinnati you may know, but a fabulous city, all slender towers and ziggurats, whose cats can speak in complex tongues, where my success as a sorcerer was acknowledged and appreciated, where the fair sex were sweet and plentiful. All I need for happiness is in Cincinnati."

"Why do you need gold to get there?"

"Gold's what I said I'd seek, and gold's what will preserve my reputation. I can find my way on the moonbeam roads but never find my nation. The maps must be bought fresh every six months. And such maps are expensive."

"What if I put you on your way? The secrets of the silver roads are mine." Oona stepped towards him.

"I would still need gold."

"We'll give you gold," said Kushy. "And if Fräulein Oona can guide you to your home, will you free our master and his friends?"

"I'll do my best with my rusty powers," promised Clement Schnooke. "You all know me and what I'm capable of. For in spite of Lord Renyard's repression, half of you have sought me out for potions and spells over the years, and I've obliged."

"At high prices," declared an old woman.

"Reasonable, sister, given the risks."

"You've killed more than one customer," accused another. "You're hated here and you know it. Frau Fröhlich caught the palsy, and Herr Nipkoch shrieked his life away for days before he died. We know Fröhlich the carpenter failed to pay you to harm his wife. And then his *nose* turned black and his head dropped off."

Clement Schnooke smiled and bowed. "I appreciate your endorsements, my friends. They have brought me customers and added to my small savings."

"Well," said Kushy. "We'd be rid of you, so here's a way we can all be served."

Schnooke sneered and postured. "Give me a day or so and I'll have your master free. It will cost you a century in gold."

"By weight?"

"No, fool! By time! Yes, of course by weight. A hundred kilos."

This caused noisy concern among the denizens of Raspazian's. But after a while his terms were agreed to, and Clement Schnooke departed.

"I must return to the Sebastocrater's prison and warn Lord Renyard what's soon to happen," said Oona. "Kushy and the rest will keep you safe."

Soon she was gone; I was back on my own in Lord Renyard's library. But this time I looked for specific books, for what I guessed was the source of Clement Schnooke's sorcerous craft. I found several books and studied them with an intensity I'd never given to my lessons.

By the following evening Oona was back. She brought me another pork pie, some crisps and a pickled onion. I couldn't help suspecting she had stopped off at the pub as an afterthought, but I've always loved pickled onions and was famished. There weren't too many English pubs in Mirenburg.

"How's Lord Renyard and the others?" I asked.

"No change. And my Kakatanawa are still frozen. Horrible as he is, I'm desperately hoping that this man Schnooke can do something, though Klosterheim and von Minct will probably counter him. What would you think of paying a visit to the Sebastocrater?"

"Wouldn't that be dangerous?"

"Maybe. But with Clement Schnooke attacking from one direction, that might distract our enemies enough for us to find out how they are persuading the prince to behave so uncharacteristically."

"What if we fail?" I asked.

"We have my bow. And the panther." Her grin reassured me. "And while I have no desire to place you in danger, I somehow feel you would be safer in my company than if I left you here."

"I know I'd certainly feel safer," I agreed.

"Then let's wait awhile just to see what Clement Schnooke can do."

For the rest of the day I slept and ate or talked to the dreamthief's daughter. She answered many of my questions, but she avoided those to do with her family and her relationship to mine. "And if we were related, you'd no doubt be in greater danger from that pair," she said. "All you need to know is that I'm the dreamthief's daughter."

Laughing, she told me to mind my own business, that what were dreams in one world of the multiverse were realities in another.

"What exactly is a dreamthief?" I asked.

"I'm not a dreamthief," she told me.

"Schnooke said you were."

"I'm a dreamthief's *daughter*. I know some of the simpler tricks of the profession, but I didn't want to follow my mother's calling. I took a small inheritance from her, when it seemed she had died. I became a wanderer across the multiverse, walking the moonbeam paths, looking for my ideal world and a companion to share it with."

"And did you ever find them?"

"I certainly did. But I had to give them up again."

"Why was that?"

"Someone we loved was in danger. Something we valued was threatened."

"You won't say any more?"

"Not yet. I promise I'll tell you more when I can be sure it's safe to do so."

"You have enemies of your own, not just Klosterheim and his mate?"

"I think it's fair to say that you and I have common enemies." She wouldn't be drawn any more. "I've been on your trail since Ingleton. It has taken me almost two years to find you."

"Two *years*! But I've only been away a few days at most."

"Time passes at different rates in different dreams," was all she would say.

"When shall we go?"

"Let's give Herr Schnooke what he needs. I don't know how quickly they will be able to pay him or how swiftly he'll perform once paid. He's working on some sort of rain spell and a creature made of water which will set our friends free. Even if he's not entirely successful, his sorcery will create a diversion. Meanwhile we must be on our guard. The Sebastocrater's men could return at any time."

With some anxiety, though fairly convinced that the dreamthief's daughter knew what she was about, I settled down to wait.

CHAPTER SIX

HE SEBASTOCRATER'S SOLDIERS came back to Raspazian Square in the early light. Still wearing their garlic necklaces, as if they expected a vampire attack at any moment, they emerged from the surrounding alleys.

They didn't attempt to enter the tavern but remained on the outskirts of the square, looking this way and that, gesturing in alarm towards the mobsmen who approached them. The guards were stern but scarcely belligerent. The old lack of aggression between the Shallow and the Deep Cities, which all had taken for granted, was still there. Even the arrival of Klosterheim and von Minct had failed to drive serious rifts between them. Oona and I were both puzzled by it.

"They seem reluctant to be here," she said. "What does this mean when neither side wishes to be at odds? Yet I am sure, if we went out there now, we'd immediately be clapped in irons and dragged off to prison!"

"What have Klosterheim and von Minct told them?"

"We must try to find out. If we can learn that, we'll know better how to act. This is like playing three-dimensional chess, isn't it?"

At nightfall we slipped out into the back alleys and evaded the guards for a second time, but now, with Oona in the lead, we were soon back at the black marble palace, observing it from the

90

shadows of the shrubbery and wondering how we might most easily gain entrance. Eventually she determined the weakest part of the wall and made a short huffing sound. "I'll send the panther," she said. "You first." And she disappeared into the greenery. A moment later the panther, clearly always nearby at her command, appeared and crouched for me to jump onto her sleek back. Again we leaped the wall into the grounds but this time did not head for the ornamental summerhouse, where the frozen Kakatanawa still stood guard, but rather loped up a wide, white path towards the palace itself.

The huge overhead lamp, apparently fired by naked electricity, created deeper and deeper shadows the closer we came to it. The blazing light was blocked by heavily and colorfully decorated stoneworks in the classical-oriental traditions of Byzantium. The deeper shadows were illuminated by flickering firebrands, which in turn created another layer of mobile shadows, suggesting to an overtired mind they might be populated by all kinds of guarding monsters. Once I had dismounted, the panther slipped away, and a few moments later I heard Oona whispering from the shrubbery. As she had expected, most of the Sebastocrater's men were now in the Deep City. There remained only a skeleton guard.

Very soon we were inside the palace, dodging from column to column, seeking out its ruler. We heard distant music. A few servants came and went, but they weren't for a second suspicious. Only in the tall central halls, under a dome inset with gold, precious jewels and mosaic scenes, was there much activity.

A concert was in progress. On his throne sat a slender young, golden-haired man, wearing a circlet of silver inset with diamonds and rubies. The musicians consisted of a harpist, a lute player, a flute player and a drummer. The music was stately and, though not to my taste, surprisingly modern in feel. I was distracted by it.

Then suddenly Oona made a decision. With a bound she was at the young Sebastocrater's side, her sword blade resting against his throat. The music stopped abruptly.

Even I was surprised by this turn of events. Oona had said nothing of threatening the monarch's life.

The Sebastocrater's response at seeing me was spectacular. He jumped up, surprising Oona and knocking her backwards. She barely held on to her sword. Then he, too, fell back again. He was clearly panicked by the sight of me and seemed hardly interested in Oona at all until he looked around and found that she had risen, rescabbarded her sword and now held on her drawn bowstring an arrow directed at his heart.

His eyes darted from side to side, seeking his soldiers. He was breathing rapidly. I moved towards him, and he backed away as if in fear.

"Please," he said, "I beg you. I've done you no harm."

"Well, that's a matter of opinion," I said. He was incredibly good-looking in the typical Greek manner, with a long straight nose and bright blue eyes. "I want to know why you've imprisoned my friends and betrayed your ancient compact with the Deep City."

"For all our good," he said. "Your friends are merely in quarantine. As you should be. At least until a cure is found."

"A cure?" repeated Oona and I in unison. "Cure for what?"

"For the disease you bring with you from your world."

"Is this what Klosterheim and von Minct have told you?" Oona asked.

"Doctor Klosterheim explained how the child carries a deadly plague, which has wiped out Frankfurt, Nürnberg and München and left other great German cities almost without a population, without enough living people to bury their own dead. All those in proximity to her have almost certainly been infected." The Sebastocrater now had the air of a man who faced his own inevitable end. "It is irresponsible of you to bring her here."

"I'm not sick," I said. "There's nothing wrong with me, and I haven't made any other people sick. I haven't even given my white rat my cold this year!"

"They warned us you would say that. You have no signs of the plague yourself, but you have the power to infect others."

I remembered the stories of Typhoid Mary I'd heard from a radio program, and briefly wondered if perhaps I actually *was* the carrier of some deadly virus.

"That's nonsense," said Oona briskly. "The child's as healthy as I am. As healthy as Lobkowitz and Fromental, who saw her days ago. As healthy as Lord Renyard, for that matter."

"It would be irresponsible of me not to isolate them as I isolated your friends. This is an ancient city. I cannot have its citizens infected. That is why we had to act swiftly to occupy the Deep City. If we had not, who knows how swiftly the plague would have spread."

"Then why haven't any of my friends at Raspazian's been infected?" I asked. "Not one of them's ill!"

"It takes time to manifest itself."

"This is ridiculous," said Oona. "You have allowed yourselves to be tricked and panicked by a couple of wicked men. They're responsible for untold deaths. They will kill this child if they need to and are given the chance."

The Sebastocrater seemed only half-convinced. He looked back and forth from the bow-woman to me, to his subjects and musicians.

"Doctor Klosterheim assured me . . ."

"*Doctor* Klosterheim!" she snorted. "He is better qualified as a butcher than a doctor!"

"What do you know of this great medical man? He risked his own life to warn us of our danger."

"Danger? From what?"

At that moment two men had entered the hall and stopped in the flickering shadows cast by the flambeaux on the walls. I recognized them immediately. I could see more of von Minct's heavy, handsome Germanic face, its cold blue eyes and thin lips. Dressed in black, he wore a steel breastplate. Beside him was gaunt, gloomy old "Doctor" Klosterheim, his eyes glistening in their deep sockets. He had a head like a fleshless skull, narrow and vicious. I would certainly never have taken them for a couple of heroes.

"From that child." Klosterheim raised one long, bony finger and pointed at me.

"And how can a little girl offer you danger?" said Oona, settling the arrow on her bowstring.

"She offers the whole world grievous danger." Gaynor von Minct's voice was brutal, coarse.

"I wasn't hurting anyone in Yorkshire." I began to be annoyed. "I hadn't hurt anyone in London. I was perfectly happy at home in Ingleton until you turned up and started laying siege to our house!"

"Trying to avert the danger we foresaw," broke in Klosterheim. "The plague which has wiped out half your country."

I was furious at these lies. "Plague? There was nothing wrong with England when I left."

"You poor girl. After that terrible destruction of Londres, your own grandparents were taken with the plague. Did you not know that?"

A wave of horrified misery hit me. "What?" I looked at Oona.

"That's a foul lie, Prince Gaynor. How low you stoop! And for what gain?" Oona drew her arrow back on the bow as she prepared to shoot him.

The Sebastocrater looked at me with some alarm and raised a kerchief smelling strongly of garlic to his face. Now I understood why the guards were wearing garlic necklaces. They thought garlic was a way of warding off the plague. And vampires, too, of course.

I believed that Oona and my imprisoned friends would have told me if the story were true. "I'm perfectly healthy," I said, "and so are my grandparents."

Oona, for reasons of her own, was grinning widely at the two villains. "They certainly are," she said. "I can guarantee it."

The Sebastocrater frowned. "Who am I to believe? My responsibility is to the people of Mirenburg. Why would Doctor Klosterheim and Prince Gaynor von Minct have come to tell me such a terrible lie?"

"I think they want to kidnap me," I said. "They have already tried it once or twice. That's why I'm so far from home—and so eager to get back there."

"Don't perjure yourself," mumured Klosterheim. "It's not becoming in one so young."

"Agreed," said Oona. "Though it's a habit with you, Herr Klosterheim. You know me and you know my power. You seek what you think this girl possesses. I suspect you have the other half of your recipe already in your power. Fresh caught, eh? But half a spell is worse than none. Either way, the chances are, you'll kill her."

The Sebastocrater's handsome features clouded, and he ran his fingers through his golden curls. He didn't like the thought of being responsible for my death.

"I was already warned about them by my parents," I said. "It's true, your honor. They mean me no good."

"Yet they are so convincing."

"They are clever servants of the Master of Deceit himself," said Oona. "They serve only the Prince of Lies."

"You lie, not I!" cried Klosterheim. But she had struck home.

Oona threw back her head and laughed again. "Ah! Liar! Liar! You no longer *know* what is truth and what is falsehood!"

"What do you demand of me?" asked the Sebastocrater, rather more impressed.

"Release my friends and my warriors, and we shall all leave Mirenburg," promised Oona. "Save for Lord Renyard, who will return to rule the Deep City by tradition, as he has always done."

"And if we should then have an epidemic?"

"You will not. I have told you. Klosterheim and von Minct lie."

"Perhaps you merely wish to rescue your friends. The girl does not show plague. We did not say she did. We know she carries it." Prince Gaynor stepped towards me. "Doctor Klosterheim has explained all this. He was physician to more than one royal court."

"And no doubt poisoned more than one round of royal cocoa," I said, getting a glare of pure hatred from the "doctor" in question. "I've told you. He's a liar."

"Yet *you* could be the liar."

Oona was getting pretty tired of this. She took her bowstring back another inch. "We have no motive. If you give this child up to Klosterheim and von Minct, you almost certainly sentence an innocent to a dreadful death."

I believed her and felt slightly faint. I stared at the two villains. They stared back. They didn't seem to be denying anything.
Klosterheim's cold eyes were angry. Von Minct's face was hidden
again in the depths of his cloak.

Were we at an impasse?

The Sebastocrater sighed. "It would seem that if I quarantined the child, and you, too, fräulein, until such time as we are
certain of the truth, I would be exercising my duty."

"And Klosterheim and von Minct?"

"They, too, shall be quarantined."

Klosterheim hissed his disagreement with this decision, but he
was unsure what to do next. They both glared at me. I felt like a
steak being eyed by two famished men. I moved a little closer to
Oona.

"No," I said, "there's nothing wrong with me, and I should be
getting home. My parents will be worrying."

"We'll take you home," growled Gaynor von Minct.
Klosterheim drew a large pistol from within his cloak. "I believe
this puts you all at a disadvantage," he said.

Von Minct also had a pistol. He cocked it with a heavy click.

Oona did not release her bowstring. She kept her weapon leveled at them as I began slowly to back out of the concert room,
out of the palace, with von Minct, Klosterheim and the
Sebastocrater glaring at me, not daring to follow. I moved towards
the summerhouse where, in the moonlit garden, the band of
Kakatanawa stood frozen.

I hadn't expected it to be dark again. Time was playing the
most peculiar tricks. Once again I was convinced I experienced
some kind of waking dream.

Oona wasn't far behind me.

"Someone is already taking liberties with the machinery of the
multiverse," she murmured. She looked up to where the Autumn
Stars, like blossoming dahlias in dozens of deep, rich colors,
poured down their light. A light which had tangible warmth.

Then a wild, cold wind whipped through the streets of the
city. I heard a wailing command which I was sure I recognized.

Could it be the disgusting Clement Schnooke? He had been paid and was beginning his spell without waiting to coordinate with us.

The voice uttered an invocation, I was sure. It summoned up weather elementals. That was about all I knew. My mother hadn't wanted me to know too much of such supernatural details.

Suddenly a great bolt of lightning cracked down. The light on top of the palace went out. Then came on again.

I felt fine mist in my face. The mist turned to rain, and I shivered with cold.

And then a shot rang out in the night. I looked back. This was definitely Schnooke's work. Rain swept in with long scimitar strokes, and the light from the palace cut through the glinting silver. The effect was almost stroboscopic. I saw the Sebastocrater clutching a wounded arm, with a look of pure astonishment on his face, while von Minct placed a pistol at his head and Klosterheim reloaded.

"The advantage is ours, I believe," snarled Prince Gaynor.

At that moment a huge splitting noise echoed through the garden, and golden light burned all around us, blinding me for a second. I heard a roar like a distant waterfall. A swift shadow moved, and the Sebastocrater went down. Instinctively I began to run.

Soon I heard water pounding on water. A great rush of water. Everything was flooding!

The Indians were suddenly coming to life. Behind them the fountain had flooded.

I had to get above the water. With relief, I felt the ground rising gradually beneath my feet. I was laboring up a slope. For the moment at least, there was a good chance I was safe.

But what of my friends? Were they also managing to escape from the drowning city?

Part Two
Diverging Histories

'Twas moonlight when Sir Elrik rode
His mighty steed from Old Nihrain
With anger such a needless load
Upon his heart; a bane upon his brain;
Yet anger like a plague infected every vein.

—WHELDRAKE,
 THE BLACK SWORD'S SONG

PART TWO

Diverging Histories

INTERLUDE
UNA PERSSON

Then, with joyous heart, Sir Elrik cried,
Why, this be Tanelorn, the Citadel of Peace;
And all the old man did desire and say is true.

—WHELDRAKE,
THE BLACK SWORD'S SONG

T HAD BEEN some years since I had received a visit from my old friend Mrs. Persson. I had reconciled myself to the idea that I might never see her again. In the past her stories had generally involved Bastable, Cornelius or the denizens of the End of Time. Only once had she told me anything concerning Elric of Melniboné, whose adventures I drew largely from other sources, especially from Mr. John D—, that contemporary manifestation of the Eternal Champion, whom I knew best. Mr. D—, as I might have mentioned elsewhere, married a distant relative of mine and eventually settled in the North. It wasn't until a later occasion, when my wife and I spent a year or two in the English Lake District, that I had the pleasure of his company once more.

At the time I met Mrs. Persson again, however, Linda and I had grown rather settled in our rural Texan life and had developed a pleasure in unexpected visitors, the way you hardly ever do in the city.

One late October evening we sat in rocking chairs on our screened porch, enjoying the warmth and watching the sun set over our property's low hills and wide, shallow streams, when a car approached on the dirt road. The machine threw up a great "dust ghost" which rose into the darkening sky like a pale fairy-tale giant. It fell back as the car passed under the tall gateposts on which hung the sign of the Old Circle Squared. My great-uncle had named the ranch when he settled in the Lost Pines area and made his first fortune in timber, his second in cattle, his third in river trade, his fourth in oil and his fifth in real estate. Because of bad advice from accountants, we had made almost no money. Now most of our remaining land is part of the Lost Pines State Park, and for a small tax break we raise a modest herd of long-horns, as much a part of the family as any one of our other domestic animals. We name them all, as they pay their own way like true Texans. The balance of our land, not kept for grazing or in forest, we employ for organic gardening.

Because of the garden we were used to the occasional neighbor dropping by for a bunch of carrots or a pound or two of tomatoes, and so thought nothing of it until the car drew up at our porch steps and a slender, dark-haired woman got out. She had a boyish, startling beauty. She wore a long coat of the kind we call a "duster" in Texas, and her hair was cut in what used to be known as a pageboy. From underneath those Prince Valiant bangs two bright grey eyes smiled at us. I recognized her at once, of course. Mrs. Persson strode up the steps of the porch as I rose to open the screen door for her. My wife let out an expression of pleasure. "My dear Una! What brings you to the back of beyond?"

Linda drew up another rocker for Mrs. Persson while I went to fix her a drink. Still standing, she received it gratefully. Again I offered her a chair, but she said she'd been driving for some hours and preferred to remain standing for the time being. She was in Austin, she told us, to see a colleague at UT, and while she never knew our phone number, she found our address and decided to drive out to see if we were in.

I assured her that we had become lazy; I was pretty much retired and had absolutely nothing to do. I asked after old friends as well as some of those I regarded as friends from her stories.

She said she saw little of anyone except her cousin and someone whose adventures she knew would interest me. "Elric of Melniboné?" She made the words sound delicious, like exotic food. There might have been a hint of irony, the kind a woman gains from living too long in Paris.

"Really? You've been enjoying more adventures in space and time?"

"Not at all. He has only recently returned to his own era. That is, whatever physical manifestation we take with us between one plane of the multiverse and another. What his people know, I understand, as 'dream quests.'"

"You are not now embarked upon any such quest, are you?" my wife asked gently.

Una Persson bowed her head a fraction and winked.

"We are all embarked upon dream quests," she said. "Those of us who are not wholly dead. Wholly dead."

"But your time on the stage, and so on—that wasn't a dream quest," said Linda. "That was a dream come true."

I laughed.

"I wasn't raised to know the difference," said Una, settling at last into the rocking chair beside Linda. "Dreams and identities are there, like the multiverse, to be negotiated, to be tested and tried and sometimes adopted."

"I think I would prefer not to have that choice," I said.

"I know I would prefer not to have it," she agreed vehemently.

"You didn't enjoy your time on stage?" Linda was implacable. She was a huge fan of musical comedy, and Una had for a while a very successful career both in the West End and on Broadway.

"I think I enjoyed it most of all," she said. "It was a long career, because of my peculiar circumstances. I came in with the great dowager halls, the massive palaces of variety like the

Empire, Leicester Square. I went out with revue and the sophisticated topical songs of the 1960s. It was rock-and-roll and satire ruined me, my dear." And she laughed. She had enjoyed it while it was fun, but never seemed to care that it was over. She had done so much more with her life, in political terms, since the mid-1960s. Her main association then, of course, was with Jerry Cornelius and his odd assortment of traveling players, who had been so typical of the situationalist theater which had grown up on the Continent but which had never really caught on in the United States or UK. I had heard that the theater had been a cover for other kinds of more serious activity, but I was never curious about so-called secret-service stories.

Una had, in fact, a new Elric tale—or at least part of one—to tell us. Most of the facts, she promised, came from Elric himself. Others had been verified beyond doubt by various people she had met on the moonbeam roads in recent months.

I mixed her a fresh drink while Linda went into the house to see about dinner. Then, when Linda had returned, Una began her tale.

CHAPTER SEVEN

LRIC OF MELNIBONÉ, Una told us, had embarked involuntarily on what he called the Dream of a Thousand Years. Having arrived in England some years before the Battle of Hastings, in the reign of Ethelred the Unready, he served as a seagoing mercenary against the encroaching Danes until Ethelred, impoverished as a result of his own poor planning, failed to pay him. Therefore the albino took what was his and left for the Middle Sea, where for a while he fell in with a female pirate known as the Barbary Rose, striking merchant ships from the security of her island stronghold of Las Cascadas. Later he went adventuring into the wildern lands of the Moors, beyond the High Atlas into the desert, where, it was said, he came upon a country ruled by intelligent dragons. Little was then heard of him until he turned up as a crusader, becoming the ally of Gunnar the Doomed and sailing with him to America.

Elric, who had used a variety of names, founded a nation. He carved it from the old German and Slavic lands in a place called Wäldenstein, whose capital was the city of Mirenburg. There he and what seemed to be his progeny ruled by virtue of dark magic and a fabulous black sword said to drink souls as readily as it drank blood. Terrible legends surrounded the Princes of Mirenburg until the nineteenth century, when the city appeared to have been abandoned by the crimson-eyed albinos who occupied it. At the early part of the twentieth century, though a few

105

stories still existed in Mirenburg concerning a soul-eating demon called Karmingsinaugen, the old tales of the vampire prince and his vampire sword continued to circulate. They soon merged with those of Nosferatu and the hero-villains of German cinema. Meanwhile an albino resembling Elric began to entertain with a magic act on the English stage. Monsieur Zodiac, as he was called, was a very popular attraction, and his son, who might have been his twin, later took over the act as well as the name.

Mrs. Persson believed that his thousand-year sojourn in our world, where his dream self took on solid flesh, was coming to an end. She wanted to help him return to his world, "where he hangs crucified on a ship's mast," but was afraid he was now too weak to resist the controlling power of his massive runesword, which, she believed, had been stolen and carried across the multiverse. He was desperate to rediscover it and convinced he would die if he awoke from his dream without it.

"Why will he die?" I asked.

"There's a symbiosis between the blade and the man. The blade's the essence of Chaos. It might even have a mind. *His* mind. The blade lends him vitality in return for the souls it feeds upon. Yet the sword could be a holy object associated with the Cosmic Balance itself. We must never forget that the Balance maintains the structure of the multiverse. When it tips one way, Chaos rules ad infinitum across the multiverse. When it tips the other, Law grows dominant. One way lies madness and hideous death; the other, sanity and relentless nothingness. It is the Eternal Champion's fate to ensure that the Balance is maintained. Our fate, I suspect, is to help him in this task."

"Our fate?"

"I'm afraid so. There's also the problem of the Runestaff. Its existence or lack of substance could determine the issue. Many believe the Staff and the Stone are the fundamental components of the Balance itself. Of course, we are also discussing an abstraction." She shrugged. "The symbols of power are not the power themselves. Unless you're a magician, of course."

"I understood the Grail was involved in that equation."

"The Grail takes many forms. One of those could be the Staff. Anyway, the fact is that several people would like to control one or all of these forces represented by those objects, because of the enormous power such possession would give them. This is doubtless why, under great threat, it has again divided itself into its chief components and again gone out of the protection of the family sworn to defend it—the von Beks.

"One of those pursuing the Stone across time and space for his own ends is Gaynor the Damned, a former Knight of the Balance, disgraced and exiled, Elric's most implacable enemy. He goes by many names but is best known in these times as von Minct."

"He's sailed with Elric to America?" asked Linda.

Una nodded. "Gaynor once drew on the power of the Balance, using it for his own benefit. Needless to say, he lost his calling and became an outlaw, the enemy of all who served the Balance. Yet he yearned at the same time to be reconciled with what he had been bred to respect. And if reconciliation's not possible, he'll destroy the Balance and the multiverse with it. This is what fuels his unquenchable hatred. The Balance, of course, is essentially only a symbol of the forces which rule the multiverse. Yet those forces are real enough, created out of the seminal stuff which exists in the place we call the Grey Fees. Forces created by the common will or by an uncommon imagination. That is what we call reality."

"And reality can be destroyed? Is that it? By an act of will?"

Mrs. Persson took a sip of her drink, rocking slowly back and forth, her face turned up to the emerging evening stars. "By an act of extraordinary will, channeled by ritual and superhuman desire. We are dealing with a creature who has honed and channeled that will and that desire for millennia."

"What keeps him alive?" I asked.

"Some believe his very hatred sustains him. Neither he nor Elric is immortal, though their longevity is, of course, phenomenal. Elric is not even conscious of his longevity. Both move from one dream quest to another, though Elric has not often walked the moonbeam roads. It's hard for some of us to understand. How do we count age when so much of your life is spent in dream quests centuries long, in which you scarcely move in your sleep nor grow older?"

Sitting there in the warm Texas twilight discussing the nature of the infinite multiverse was a little odd, but our pleasure in seeing our old friend was more than enough to make us forget the incongruity. Besides, it had been some while since I had learned of any manifestation of the Eternal Champion, let alone Elric of Melniboné, whose adventures I first heard from Una Persson in the 1950s, when I began recording them.

Apparently Elric, in his guise of Monsieur Zodiac, the stage conjurer, was visited by two men he had met during the 1940s, when he discovered himself at odds with various Nazis, including Gaynor, who had transformed himself into a minor German nobleman, cousin to Ulric von Bek. Elric had founded the family line in his first years in Mirenburg. The extraordinary coming together of von Bek and Elric, whose identities blended into a single physical being, was something neither had experienced and which almost defeated description. These disruptions in the order of time had come about, Mrs. Persson had told me, as a result of Gaynor and his ally Klosterheim seeking to use for themselves the power of the Grail and the Black Sword Ravenbrand, sometimes called Mournblade, the sibling sword to Stormbringer.

Meanwhile, Mrs. Persson said, Elric went to Portugal, searching for the Black Sword, which had passed out of his hands sometime in 1974 in the course of an adventure she promised to relate to me on another occasion. Having only a few years left to repossess the blade before his dream quest ended, Elric eventually found himself and his recovered blade in Cintra, outside Lisbon, where the Chevalier St. Odhran in turn discovered him. From there the two men journeyed via St. Odhran's Scottish estates to Ingleton in West Yorkshire, to Tower House, not far from my own ancestral home of Moorcock, near Dent. There they met Prince Lobkowitz and his old friend Lieutenant Fromental and Colonel Bastable, all able to negotiate the moonbeam roads, all Knights of the Balance and members of the

League of Temporal Adventurers, founded in the mid-twentieth century. They had expected to discover the von Beks there. Oona von Bek, a relative of Mrs. Persson, was Elric's daughter and had, like Count von Bek, fought at his side against Gaynor the Damned on more than one occasion.

"What was the reason?" I asked her. "Isn't it unusual for so many heroes to gather in one place?"

"Yes, it is unusual," she agreed. "Indeed there's some danger in it. But it appears they learned von Bek's young granddaughter was being sought by Gaynor, and they went there to protect the little girl."

"They succeeded, I hope."

"Not entirely. The child has a mind of her own and disappeared. It was thought at first that Gaynor and Klosterheim had been successful in their intentions. But the real cause of her disappearance was a weakening in the fundamental fabric of time and space, the Gray Fees, the very DNA of the multiverse. She vanished during a minor local earthquake caused by this chaotic movement. Gaynor and Klosterheim were seen in the vicinity, but it's pretty clear they didn't set out to kidnap her. They are opportunists, and they were lunging after her as clumsily as the rest of us. The presence of so many people from alternate spheres of the multiverse seems to have produced a certain amount of cosmic turbulence.

"Lobkowitz and Fromental set off to find the little girl while the others waited to join forces with the von Beks—Ulric and Oona. Ulric remained with his other children while his wife, who had sworn never to revisit the moonbeam roads—by which means travelers cross between the worlds—took up her old calling. Her mother was a dreamthief, but Oona had been content merely to explore the worlds her mother had once entered with the intention of stealing dreams to sell to her clients. It was in one such world that her mother met Elric and conceived their twin children, as I believe you already know."[1]

---

[1] See *The Fortress of the Pearl*

"And the male twin?" asked my wife. "What became of him?"

"He disappeared before his sister even remembered him. He was kidnapped."

"By von Minct and Klosterheim?"

"As it happens, probably not. They found him later and bought him from his master."

"So what became of Elric? Did he ever contact the child? Or his own lost son?"

"Why don't I tell you the story from the beginning," she said, "as best I can."

Over the next few days, as our guest in Texas, my old friend told me everything she knew of the events concerning Elric of Melniboné and the last months of his dream quest, when his body, suffering extreme pain, hung in the rigging of Jagreen Lern's flagship moments before a mighty sea fight. The naval battle's outcome would be a crucial factor in events which were to change the whole course of his world's history. It would begin actions whose consequences would resonate throughout the multiverse.

How Mrs. Persson knew so much concerning the private lives of some of those featured in this narrative, she would not at that time say. In many cases I have been unable to verify what she told me, and have set it down here without checking.

According to Mrs. Persson this is what happened: Elric, St. Odhran, Fromental and Colonel Bastable, having conferred with the old Count and Countess von Bek, agreed that the countess should set off on her own. They then traveled together to Mirenburg by conventional means, from Heathrow, London, to Munich, Germany, and from there to Mirenburg, capital of the newly independent principality of Wäldenstein, where Germany, Austria and Bohemia came together.

Though still beautiful, the city had yet to recover entirely from the poverty of her Communist past. German had been her official tongue before the Russian conquest, but her people still spoke a Slavic language akin to Polish. Her parliament, however, returned primarily to the German form, so that her seat of gov-

ernment was known as the Reikstagg, and the chief executive of
her elected city council was called her majori, or mayor.

The travelers went immediately to the Berghoff and, thanks
to letters from Count von Bek, received a swift audience with
Mayor Pabli, who put his city's law enforcers at their disposal on
the assumption that young Oona von Bek would be found there.

Meanwhile Elric, who was most familiar with the city's secrets, set about on his own explorations, glad, he told my friend,
to be back in his old haunts. In no time he found his familiar secret back alleys and explored the tunnels only he and a few others knew about, eventually emerging in the underground "looking
glass" city which lay alongside their time and space (an area
known in German as the Mittelmarch), close to the borders of
that exquisitely beautiful land of Mu-Ooria. He found this manifestation of the city largely deserted and in ruins. The Off-Moo
told of a terrible internal war where the people of the Deep City,
the interior of Thieves' Quarter, had clashed with the forces of the
Byzantine Sebastocrater.

Realizing he was not in a place where he was likely to find the
girl, Elric returned to the Mirenburg of the early twenty-first century to report to his friends, only to find them gone, leaving him
a message to let him know they were following other important
clues.

Modern Mirenburg, with its decaying industrial section and
impoverished working class, was not to Elric's taste, but he had
come to love the old city, which still retained much of her beauty
and quaintness. He decided, however, to waste no further time
and employ what little sorcery was still available to him in a world
where the Lords of Law and Chaos exhibited themselves in alien
and rather prosaic ways and where the great elementals, his old
traditional allies, had either disappeared or died.

Unlike his daughter, Elric had only limited experience of the
silver strands of the moonbeam roads, where adepts walked between the worlds, crossing from one level of the multiverse to another, from one alternative Earth to another; but he decided that
if he was to find his daughter's grandchild, he would have to

explore more than one version of the World Below. Thus he gathered his strength, performed the necessary exercises and rituals, and found himself on the roads between the worlds.

Mrs. Persson had described these roads in the past, but much as I longed to see them for myself, I never had the privilege of even so much as a glimpse. To the mortal eye, she said, they appeared like an infinite lattice of silver ribbons, wide enough to take a number of travelers, most of whom walked and all of whom represented an enormous variety of peoples and cultures, some extraordinarily different from our own and some very similar. The travelers reached the roads by several means and interpreted this experience in quite different ways. Most would readily exchange information, and few were antagonists.

Elric had used these roads only in his youthful dream quests, through which his people gained wisdom and made compacts with supernaturals. He was scarcely aware of them in his waking world, where a great fight was brewing between Law and Chaos, waged for control of the Balance, and echoed in many different forms across the multiverse.

After buying himself a horse, Elric made inquiries of his fellow travelers and soon discovered that young Oonagh was to be found in a particular place and had, in fact, not yet left Mirenburg. So he plunged again into the strange, almost limitless underground domain of the Middle Marches, through the infamous Gray Fees, unformed Chaos reacting unpredictably on the imagination. In his wisdom Elric feared his own mind more than he feared any being, mortal or supernatural. Only his need to ensure the safety of the little girl drove him on, and he hated himself for what he considered his own weakness.

Yet in the familiar deep chasms and jagged peaks of Mu-Ooria, following the glowing silver river towards Mirenburg, he was surprised not to see the outlines so familiar to him in his numerous travels. The lake—actually a great widening of the river—had extended itself. The cries of birds, almost deafening, were baffling to him, for they were not the voices of waterfowl but rather were the anxious voices of birds finding what nesting space they could among the towers, eaves and taller trees of a recently flooded city.

The city's phosphorescent liquid had lost much of its luster. Elric felt a vague sense of alarm. When, after several hours' ride, he came to a village of shacks and makeshift houses built from the rubble of more magnificent buildings, he recognized the spires and domes and roofs of that ancient, drowned metropolis, where, in cavernous shadows, naked men dived, disappearing into still deeper darkness, into the faintly glowing silver depths, and occasionally reappearing clutching sodden trophies. Sad, ill-fed women tended sputtering fires outside their dwellings. Elric dismounted beside one of them and asked her what this place was called and what the men were doing.

They were surly creatures, ruined by work that was hard and hopeless. They asked him for any spare food he carried. He gave them what he could, a soldier's rations meant to sustain him for several days, and the citizens fell upon it as if it were a feast. They were willing to help him if they could. Their watery city was all that was left of Mirenburg, where they had once lived under the secure rule of the Sebastocrater and his opposite number, Lord Renyard, until terrible misdirected magic, long banished from the city by ancient treaty, caused a great catastrophe, drawing in both the city and its mirror version in the World Above. Now men dived for whatever food had been preserved, be it in sealed jars or barrels, but the supply diminished daily. They had no way of appealing to any higher being, for they were all cursed.

"How did this curse come about?" asked Elric.

"We have told you," said one grey crone, her black eyes catching faint reflected light from the lake. "Sorcery. The ancient compact made with the gods was broken. The Balance tipped. The result is what you see. A great cataclysm which shook the city to the core and brought the waters pouring in and down upon us. We are all that survived. Perhaps it would have been better had we also drowned with the folk of the Outer and Inner, Deep and Shallow Cities. I saw the towers crumble and collapse. I saw all the people engulfed. I saw the river rush into the craters. Within the hour, this was all that was left of a great and ancient metropolis. Her centuries-old agreements destroyed within a few days, chiefly as the result of fear. Of unknown fear. Of fear of the unknown . . ." And she began to cackle to herself happily. "What destruction we bring upon ourselves, master!" She accepted a useless coin, which she hid in her clothes. "What insects we are! No more able to guard against the future than we can against the day. Time remains our lady, and death our lord, eh?"

Elric, used to such views from the moment he could walk and talk, found her boring and ignored her. She spat at him and cursed him, almost affectionately. He smiled to himself, feeling no insult. She found the coin somewhere in her rags and threw it after him. To both of them the encounter had stirred life. In Klosterheim's hell, he thought, this was what passed for affection. He felt safe enough to dismount and show that he offered them no violence.

Then Elric asked after the child he sought. They told him she had almost certainly drowned.

"As she deserved," continued the crone, "if it's the one I think you seek, master. A little blue-eyed diddicoy, she was. All innocence and winsome manners. It was my guess she was the one what brought this here disaster. Before she came, and those who followed her, we had not known any serious change for two hundred years."

I'm told, said Mrs. Persson, that Elric returned to the more familiar Mirenburg, desperately hoping he had taken the wrong route and that the child he thought of as his own flesh and blood had survived. Perhaps in this aspect of the multiverse, he insisted to himself, she had survived Mirenburg at the time of the city's drowning. He needed expert help.

Where he would find her, where he should begin looking for her, was a mystery. At least he knew that sorcery, though banned, worked on this plane. Should he stay here or attempt to find a world where magic was even more potent? Did he have enough time?

As before, he was welcomed in Mu-Ooria. What language differences they had, what problems were thus created, they accepted in good faith, no matter how outrageous the other seemed. Elric, however, knew no way of asking a direct question of the Off-Moo, or they might have helped him better. Not that it would have made an improvement to the story.

His oldest acquaintance among this people was Scholar Ree, the most widely traveled of the Off-Moo, and his people's spiritual leader. Ree felt something like affection for the albino. With his delicate, elongated lips fluttering, his deep-set eyes glowing with faint phosphorescence, he embraced Elric. It was the strangest experience, like being hugged by hesitant tissue paper.

That wise old creature agreed to help Elric, and together they consulted books and charts while the albino did all he could to curb his impatience, fearing irrationally that time was wasting, that in the meantime the former Knight of the Balance and Satan's ex-servant might be subjecting the girl to horrors he would rather not imagine.

Why they wanted her, Elric was not be sure. Perhaps she was a pawn in a much larger game. Perhaps she had been abducted in order to distract him and his allies while some other plot was hatched, but none of this affected his determination to find her. His bone-white features were tense, his crimson eyes narrowed in concentration, as he bent over Scholar Ree's documents, seeking a road to Mirenburg which would have him arrive before disaster visited the city, where he might consult his own sorcerous allies, most of whom were denied time by the nature of his existing dream quest.

In his whispering voice like the rustling of long-dead leaves, Scholar Ree debated in High Melnibonéan with the albino. It was difficult for the Mu-Oorian to engage with equal passion in pursuit of an answer to his friend's problem, but he devoted his whole attention to it.

At last the two determined the coordinates required for the exercise.

"It will be dangerous for you, Elric, considering your situation," said Scholar Ree. "These worlds have much in common. There is the likelihood of your encountering an avatar of yourself.

Moreover, that avatar could be serving Law and you Chaos, and you'll find him your enemy. Such mighty power does not always work for the common good. These are unstable times, old friend. The Balance tips this way and that; a great Conjunction of the Worlds takes place over and over again as if Creation awaits a final, single action. You could come to great physical harm, or worse."

"Worse?"

"You could *cause* great harm. The fate of millions of worlds is being decided, and you and yours could be lost, unnoticed in such a struggle."

"But I must find her, Scholar Ree."

"I understand that. Pray she is not the catalyst for limitless destruction. That's all I mean to imply."

Elric sighed. "Well, I'll rest a little, then make my way to this other Wäldenstein, this other Mirenburg, where this other empire rules! I heard you give it a name . . . ?"

"The Empire of Granbretan, like your own, is an island nation which has conquered whole continents. Like yours, it's feral yet overcivilized. Like yours, its supernatural compacts are chiefly with Chaos. And, like yours, it is thoroughly hated, ruling by force and threat of bloody violence."

Elric laughed at this.

"Then I shall feel thoroughly at home," he said.

Very shortly he again took his heavy steed in rein and set off through the Middle March.

A rare rain was falling, silver tears against the black fangs of the rock. He held his face up to receive it. It smelled like all the spices and flowers of the world. Just for a moment it reminded him of a garden where he had walked with a child. They had both remarked on it. An extraordinary concentration of scents. And then it was gone.

Elric was careful to follow Scholar Ree's map to the letter.

As it happened, the albino easily found his way to Wäldenstein in the age of the Dark Empire of Granbretan, a world I myself know something about. Of course, there are a million versions of the same era, most of which vary only by the faintest degree, but evidently the world in which Elric found himself did not vary much from those of which I had already heard. In it the oppressive Empire of Granbretan—Britain in our world—had emerged from a Dark Age known as the Tragic Millennium, brought about by conflicts in which terrible, mysterious weapons had been employed. Using a mixture of sorcery and science, Granbretan had conquered Europe and set her sights on the rest of the world. In many aspects of the multiverse she had been opposed by a few heroes, chiefly Dorian Hawkmoon, Duke of Köln, and Count Brass, Lord Guardian of Kamarg. In some they had succeeded in their challenge. In others they had failed.

Elric emerged from the Mittelmarch into a huge cave deep in a mossy forest of old oaks, elms and ash trees. The foliage was so thick, it had almost knitted together to form a canopy, through which the sun managed to cast a green, hazy light, cut occasionally by bright, golden rays through which birds and small mammals moved. The air was filled with a constant fluttering and whistling, an indication of rich life. The colors glowed and gave the canopy itself the appearance of stained glass. Elric found his surroundings restful. He was reminded of the deep Shazaarian woods of his native world. For a moment he almost fancied himself home, until he remembered that the armies of Chaos, guided by his blood enemy Jagreen Lern, had laid that nation waste. Jagreen Lern must soon destroy the lands of the eastern continent unless Elric could summon Stormbringer back and defeat the theocrat.

Mrs. Persson thinks so many shadowy concerns filled Elric's mind in those days, when a thousand realities and the memories of so many men crowded his brain, that only one rigorously trained in the arts of Melniboné, who had undertaken so many dream quests, could remain even remotely sane. I believe that it is less arduous than she thinks, for most readers can keep a multitude of stories in their heads. I grew up reading and watching a score or so of serials a week, at least, and had no trouble separating the threads of my favorite detective tale from a historical yarn,

or a story about a trip to Mars and another involving people fighting some evil genius's attempt at world domination. We are complex and robust creatures, we humans, able to give our attention
to a thousand concerns.

To Elric the forest offered a welcome tranquility after the vi-
cissitudes and setbacks of his journey, and he was tempted to take
his time, but he could not dawdle while the child remained in
danger. At last he found a path, well trodden by horses and vehicles, and followed it until it led him to a tall, moated castle, all
steep-pitched towers and crenellations, flying half a dozen unfamiliar standards, its granite walls almost white against the deep
blue of the sky and the rich greens of the woods.

Elric went forward with his usual arrogant lack of caution,
calling out to the gatekeepers to show that he did not come as a
stealthy enemy.

A rattle of armor and a head appeared in a narrow window at
ground level.

"Who comes?" The language was Old Slavonic, which Elric
knew.

"Elric, Prince of Melniboné, seeking your master's hospitality."

More sounds as guards ran to receive instructions; then, in a
few moments, the drawbridge above the moat creaked, chains
tightened and a groaning winch let down the wide wooden bridge
across to the far bank, revealing an ornate portcullis with just
enough room for a mounted man to pass under.

Elric looked down at the dark, unpleasant waters of the moat
as he dismounted and crossed. From the bubbles rising to the
weedy surface, there were creatures of some size swimming there;
he saw dark shapes darting through the reflective gloom.

A man in somewhat bulky, almost medieval garb stood to
greet him in the cobbled bailey. Clearly an important personage,
he had a rippling scarlet surcoat, chain mail, glinting greaves and
a helmet completely covering his face. The helmet was wonder-
fully molded in the features of a snarling wolf, every detail perfect,
utterly belligerent as if about to charge. Such a helm had been designed to frighten whoever saw it, but the albino scarcely noted it.

He only wondered what kind of creature was insecure enough to require such a mask.

He removed his gloves as he advanced towards the fierce wolf and held out his right hand.

"I thank you for your hospitality, sir. I have made a long journey and would trouble you for some minor assistance."

After some hesitation the wolf unbuttoned his right gauntlet and, removing it, extended his own hand to Elric.

"I am Sir Edwold Krier, Knight Lieutenant of the Order of the Wolf. I rule this province on behalf of our great King Huon, whose throne is in distant Granbretan, at the very center of the world. I fear I am unfamiliar with your rank and station."

"Prince Elric of Melniboné." Elric offered the man a slight bow. "My lands are far from here. Ours is an island nation. We have heard a little of this continent, and I come as an emissary, in peace."

"Then you are welcome, for we of the Empire of Granbretan wish only peace to our neighbors. We fear the aggression of those who envy us our wealth and way of life."

The masked man bowed and signed for Elric to follow some servants into the interior of the castle.

"Granbretan?" Elric pretended to be puzzled. "But that, too, I understand, is an island, some many leagues from here."

"Indeed it is. I miss its sophistication, its pleasures. But I have my duty to do here. Sometimes it is fated that a man serves his nation best in some far-flung corner of a foreign land . . ."

Now they were inside a rather starkly furnished hall, with functional chairs, benches and tables, some wall hangings, a few battle flags, a rather moth-eaten collection of large animal heads, some of which were unfamiliar to Elric. There was a melancholy air about the whole place. Clearly Krier had no family here, but the man was a good host. Wine was called for and brought. Out of politeness, Elric sipped a little, though he had little taste for what these people cultivated in their vineyards.

"I sympathize," said Elric, who missed the complex and varied pleasures he had forsaken when Imrryr had fallen to his own hand. Only as he grew older did he fully appreciate what he had destroyed. "Is there nothing you can do here? Some musicians, perhaps? I take it you are lord of this castle."

"I am governor commander of this province, which they call Raulevici or Seneschal, in the County of Wäldenstein."

"Your nation has conquered Wäldenstein? They attacked you?"

"Europe is full of those who plot against Granbretan. We attacked them before they and their allies attacked us. They are no longer a serious threat to us."

"Very wise," said Elric dryly. "And the threat is now averted, I take it."

"Apart from a few insurgents. Supporters of the old, unjust regime we supplanted. Such terrorists represent only a small fraction of Wäldensteiners, who are essentially a peaceful people with no great interest whether their prince or the protector general rules in Mirenburg."

If Elric expected Edwold Krier to remove his ornate helmet once they were inside, he was wrong. Only local troops went unmasked, it seemed. The wide, Slavic faces of the ordinary guards were visible, but those who commanded them were Granbretanners whose grotesque beast masks were never removed.

Even when wine was poured for them, Sir Edwold sipped his through a specially shaped mouthpiece. Elric felt as if he were being entertained by some nonhuman creature. Yet Edwold Krier was pleasant enough, bidding Elric sit and rest while a female slave removed his boots and bathed his feet. He found this surprisingly refreshing.

"You must stay the night, Lord Elric, and tell us something of your lands. We are starved for news here, as you can tell. Have you traveled through many of our towns? What kind of horse is that hairy steed of yours? I have seen nothing like it. And you are so lightly clad and armed!"

"Thieves," said Elric, "in the Bulgar mountains. I was set upon, my retinue slain, save for those who were able to retreat. It

is possible they made it home. My gold and horses stolen, all but
the one. My horse Samson has a preference to remain with me.
His speed got me clear of the brigands." He shrugged, almost daring his host to disbelieve him. "We wandered a good distance, I
think, before I recovered my senses in your forest."

"My condolences. You have traveled many leagues. I am surprised our border patrols did not help you. Even though we do all
we can to secure this savage land, insurgents still manage to form
bands. Be assured, sir, those who have done this will be hunted
down and captured. They must learn that the protection of the
banner of Granbretan is real. Tomorrow you will, I hope, show me
on the map where you were attacked, and I will send a message.
Your property will be recovered, and justice will be delivered."

"I am grateful, sir." Elric was to some degree amused by such
pompous boasts. He knew that the Bulgar mountains were very
far from here and almost certainly outside Granbretan's effective
jurisdiction.

"Granbretan's laws shall not be broken," continued Edwold
Krier. "From ocean to ocean one rule shall apply in the name of
our noble King Huon, who lives forever, as our power lives forever."

Elric was scarcely able to repress his sardonic tongue at all this
vainglory. He had heard such boasts once made by his own people, who had lived to see Melniboné's towers crumble, her people
slain or in chains and all her power turned to pain in the space of
a single day. He wondered at the hubris of empires and whether
their very size made them collapse so swiftly and decisively when
they did fall.

The two men passed the time in less boastful discussion, with
Elric remarking on the beauty of the woods and the architecture
of the castle while Edwold Krier told him of the original
Wäldensteiner aristocrats who had lived there until they were
unwise enough to rise against the Empire. Then dinner was
served, and Elric was astonished at the ingenuity of his host, who
managed to eat heartily without once removing his helmet.

The hall was lit by tall oil lamps with reflectors of beaten silver to amplify and spread their flames. The light was caught by the bronze and steel of Sir Edwold's wolf mask as, in response to Elric's courteous questions, he explained that it was considered poor manners in Granbretan to remove the helm of one's clan. He had the honor of belonging to what was the most prestigious and noblest, the Order of the Wolf, the same as that of Baron Meliadus, the Order's Grand Marshal, second only to King Huon the Immortal, and the greatest active power in the Empire.

Clearly Sir Edwold Krier hero-worshipped the grand marshal, eulogizing his valor, his wisdom, his influence, so that Elric pretended to be openmouthed with admiration while he sat concocting a plan which would involve some modest sorcery and might get him into Wäldenstein's capital undetected. He had to hope that he had not been misled and that his powers would be effective in this world. He then feigned sleep in his chair and was wakened by Sir Edwold's good-natured suggestion that he retire.

"You are a kind host, sir. I must admit that my energy is not as other men's. Were it not for potions prepared for me by my people's apothecaries, I fear I would hardly be able to move abroad."

"I have heard this is a trait amongst people of your coloration," said Sir Edwold. "You have weak eyes, I gather. And are lassitudinous by nature."

Elric smiled and shook his head. "My albinism is different to any you might be familiar with. My eyesight is no worse than any of my other frailties. Few albinos in your lands have red eyes. Generally they are blue or grey. Just as with your people's albinism, mine is inherited, blood which from time to time recurs in my family. But I assure you, neither true albinos nor albinos of my kind are necessarily unhealthy for want of a little pigment."

"Forgive me—I had not meant to—"

"You made a common judgment, sir. I am not offended."

The wolf rose in his seat. "Then I'll let you restore yourself, Lord Elric. Tomorrow you must, if you will, tell me more of your land. I admit I have never before even heard of a red-eyed, ivory-skinned race with tapering ears. I am a poorly educated man, I fear."

He seemed to have missed Elric's point.

"Believe me, sir, I am as ignorant of your world as you are of mine." Elric got up from his chair to follow a servant to his room. The young fellow was broad-faced with fair hair and pale blue eyes, evidently of local stock. His features also had a closed, self-possessed quality Elric noticed at once, and there was a sense of contained anger, which Elric understood. When they reached his room Elric closed the door. "How long have you served your master?" he asked in the Slavic dialect he had learned hundreds of years earlier.

The man was surprised, frowning. "Since the fall of Mirenburg," he said, "my lord."

"Those Granbretanners seem excellent warriors, eh?"

"The Dark Empire conquers all she makes war upon."

"She's a just empire, is she?"

The man looked him in the eye. "They are the law, my lord, so we must assume they are just."

Elric could tell he dealt with a man of great education and not a little irony. He smiled. "They seem insecure braggarts to me. How did they come by their power?"

"By growing rich, my lord. By building great engines of destruction. By controlling the trade and manufacturing of every nation they conquered. They mean to destroy the world, my lord, and rebuild it in the image of Granbretan." Now there was a glimmer of fire in the young eyes. Elric was sure he had rightly judged his man.

"So it would seem. Do they all wear masks?"

"All, my lord. Only their lowlier slaves and servants go naked-faced, as they call it. This is one of the means by which they distinguish the conquered from the conquerors. To them it is an outrage to go about unmasked. Most wives, for instance, have never seen their husbands' faces."

"Does Sir Edwold Krier have many visitors of his own kind?"

"We are a remote province, my lord, and no threat to the

Empire. I believe Sir Edwold has relatives in his native Vamerin, a town not far from Londra. They maintain a certain influence at court, I understand, and obtained the stewardship of our little province for him. I gather"—the Wäld dropped his gaze to the carpet—"I gather there was no other employment for him. He has few friends. He relies on clan loyalties and his clan's influence at court."

"So few know him?"

"I understand that to be the case, my lord." There were questions in the young man's eyes when he next looked up.

"Do you know Mirenburg?"

"I was educated there, before the conquest."

"It's a rich place, I gather. A manufacturing center. Could you guide me about the city, if I needed it?"

"I think so, my lord. But I don't believe Sir Edwold would permit such a thing. And if I left without his permission, I would be killed."

"Your master will gladly order you to accompany me."

"With respect, I find that unlikely, my lord."

"What's your name?"

"Yaroslaf Stredic, my lord."

"What is your background?"

"I was once cousin to the prince of this place. Now that he is dead, I am its hereditary prince."

"And would you earn a title for yourself again?"

Stredic's face was a mixture of expressions. Elric's smile was thin, questioning.

"Well, Master Stredic, I intend to take you into my confidence. I possess certain powers in what some of your folk call the Dark Arts."

"You're a sorcerer?" Stredic's pale eyes widened.

"I have a few small skills in that direction. I hope to employ some of them tonight."

Now Stredic frowned. For a moment he seemed genuinely afraid. Cautiously he murmured, "I am not sure I entirely believe in magic, my lord."

"I have learned how to call on beings who are invisible to the majority of us, marshal energies which others cannot summon easily. I have gained certain disciplines."

Elric preferred to be counted as a clever conjurer or a charlatan. He was amused by Stredic's mixture of superstition and disbelief, even a hint of disapproval. He took something of a risk by trusting the man but guessed Stredic hated Granbretan enough to cooperate. Swiftly he explained what he intended to do and what the risks were.

Two hours later, when the castle slept, Elric left his room and, led by Yaroslaf Stredic, found Edwold Krier's apartments. Only one armed guard stood on duty outside his door, and the man had no suspicion. His wolf mask turned casually as the two men approached.

Elric smiled as he greeted him. "I wonder if you have seen the twin of this object." He held up his hand to display what was in his palm. The wolf mask looked, and its eyes were instantly fixed on the mirror Elric showed him. His limbs slackened, and his eyes grew dreamy. Then, slowly, he sank to the floor.

Stredic was impressed. He kept silent as Elric opened the door and entered the antechamber. It was empty. A lantern burned from a central chain. It gave off light enough for the two men to pass into the bedroom, where Edwold Krier, his face covered by a Granbretanian "night mask" of gauze, slept the sleep of the just.

This time Elric used what he called "low sorcery" to keep Sir Edwold sleeping. Next he removed the man's mask to reveal a small, sharp face, more like a common rodent's than an aggressive wolf's. The flesh was almost repulsively pallid, kept as it had been from normal sunlight. The brown, sightless eyes, which Elric prized open, were vacant, bovine. The fleshy lips were slack, the teeth dull, yellowed. Elric smiled at a small joke Yaroslaf Stredic made regarding the true nature of the wolf.

Then, with a warning to his companion to step away, Elric began his spell.

Stredic looked on in some fear as the albino's head fell back and his long, milk-white hair streamed out from his head in an invisible wind. Alien words poured from his pale lips, and his crimson eyes blazed with impossible fires. His voice rose and fell, creating mountains and valleys of sound. The bedchamber began to stir with shadows half-seen in the flickering light. Stredic felt the movements of chill breezes upon his flesh, so that he was tempted to back out of the room and seek cover. But Elric had re-assured him that he would come to no harm, so he watched in fas-cination as Elric's own face writhed and warped and his red eyes slowly changed to the color of Edwold Krier's. When he next turned and spoke to the Wäld, it was in the voice and accents of the prone Seneschal.

Then Elric stretched out his hand and touched the sleeping man's arm. Slowly he leached all the color out of Edwold Krier's flesh and took it for himself. When his skin was identical in color to the governor's, and the governor's pale as his own, he next went to a specially constructed stand at the head of the bed and removed the great wolf mask, raising it up and settling it down over his own head.

"It fits. I'll need no spell to change its size." His voice was muf-fled by the helmet. He took it off again and set it back on its stand.

Yaroslaf Stredic noticed how strange Elric's long, handsome skull looked with its brown eyes and darker skin, but he was even more disturbed by what appeared to be Krier's bloodless corpse lying on the bed.

"Now, said Elric, "as soon as we have moved this pale object to my room, set certain checks on his memory and left a few mis-leading clues, we ride for Mirenburg, you and I!"

Yaroslaf Stredic looked with barely controlled horror at Elric as the Melnibonéan flung up his naked head and howled with laughter.

CHAPTER EIGHT

ROTECTOR OLIN DESLEUR, Knight Commander of
the Order of the Wolverine, Governor of the City
of Mirenburg, hero of the Battle of Snodgart, rose
from his great bed of furs and silks, naked in all his manly glory, a
thin helmet of gold and platinum snarling on his shoulders, giving
him the appearance of a waking werewolf. He stretched and
yawned. His boy slaves still lay sleeping in the bed. He ignored
them as women came forward to bathe him with hot towels. He
felt relaxed and sated, having enjoyed a night in which two of his
boys had met their deaths pleasuring him. Their bodies had already been removed. Now he let the women bring his vulpine day
mask, its massive jeweled helm thick with sharp silver teeth in a
grinning muzzle of dark platinum, and place it over his head skill-
fully, on pain of death, as they slipped his night mask from beneath the more substantial one in such a way that his face was not
glimpsed even for a moment. He then strolled onto his balcony to
breakfast while Mirenburg began to move about her business.

Olin Desleur was reasonably content with what he was inclined
to call his exile from the court of Londra, where ancient King Huon,
artificially kept alive in a globe of fluid, schemed further conquest
with his favorite, Baron Meliadus of Kroiden, Grand Master of the
Wolf, conqueror of the Kamarg. While Mirenburg could be boring,
and he missed his native fells, there was a certain security in being
absent from the intrigues of the court.

At court one could die suddenly and in great humiliation merely for taking half a step in the wrong direction or being over-heard insulting the wrong person. With all Europe under the imperial flag, the courtiers took to complicated scheming, unwilling, at least yet, to turn their warlike attention to Amarahk or Asiacommunista, whose alien inhabitants were said to be almost as powerful as the Dark Empire and must surely be the next threat to be averted by striking them before the Empire itself was struck. But for now no one considered it politic to begin much further expansion until the Empire was at peace or, at least, thoroughly under Huon and Meliadus's heels.

The Protector of Mirenburg found the province relatively easy to govern, for it was used to conquerors and had only known brief intervals of independence when it had not had to accommodate them. A few examplary executions, one or two public torturings a week, and the population proved considerably more malleable than some of the other provinces which had fallen under his protection in the course of a successful career. Köln, for example. Then there had been the Kamarg, which had proved so ungovernable under its rebellious Countess Isolda, daughter of the Empire's great enemy, Count Brass, that there had been nothing for it but to deport the entire population to the Afrikaanish mines and install more agreeable Muscovites (always grateful for a little warmth) in their place. The countess herself had come under the eye of the great Meliadus, who had made her a ward, so it was rumored, of his cousin Flana, with whom he was said to keep an exceptionally perverse liaison. But then it was rumored that Isolda of Brass had recently escaped and gone to join her lover with some miscellaneous bunch of raggle-taggle insurgents. Some even believed that her father, though wounded, still lived.

Olin Desleur occasionally missed his wild West Thirding, where he had grown up in the picturesque town of Beury. He was used to hills which shone like copper in the autumn sun, and limestone pavements that formed natural causeways, glinting silver against the summer green. He loved the mingling of snow with the smell of spring at solstice. One day he intended to retire there, to his promised estates, with nothing but a few favorite boys for company.

"And perhaps a little girl or two," he murmured aloud as he looked up from his cheese, "to add variety."

But he would have to earn the privilege first, and that meant keeping the peace in Mirenburg and the province of which it was the capital. A backwater, maybe, but a fairly strategic backwater. They were now producing the majority of the Empire's most advanced war machines.

A sound, half-heard, drew his attention away from his morning meal. From where he sat on a high balcony of what had once been the prince's palace, he could see the city's gates opened for the morning traffic. People and vehicles of all kinds came and went through those gates. His was a rich little fiefdom, he thought with some satisfaction. He watched it all, relishing all the marvelous and quaint sights, from the great steam-powered battle engines of the Empire to the peasants' donkeys. But this morning his eyes were attracted to a party just passing through the gates, the early sunshine glancing off their armor and masks.

Meliadus? was his first thought, voiced to no one. But while the banner was that of the Order of the Wolf, the entourage was far too small. The secondary flags announced the little group as belonging to his provincial governor, Sir Edwold Krier, a man for whom he had little respect but who was far too well connected to be ignored. After all, they were at St. Remus's together. Members of the same club, to this day. Immediately he was on his feet, calling for his ceremonial armor, his helm of state.

As he prepared to greet his countryman, a guard in the mask of his Wolverine Order brought him news that two emissaries had arrived that night by ornithopter and had landed in the east field, having flown all the way from Londra. The emissaries carried letters from the capital. Two Germanians, apparently, in the employ of Baron Meliadus. They were to be treated as honored guests.

The protector gave orders that the emissaries be entertained in the guest hall while he went first to greet Sir Edwold Krier and bid him welcome. Protocol gave more or less equal status to both parties. His fellow countryman had best be dealt with first, however, since it was likely he was here on some business of the province. It was unusual for him to come to the capital on personal business. He assumed, since Meliadus's kinsman had sent no message, there must be some urgency. Or could there be something the matter with the heliograph? The Dark Empire was as proud of her communications systems as she was of her battle vessels. Had some heliographer been drinking at his vanes, or a post or two blown up by terrorists? His captain of engineers would be reporting to him on the matter, no doubt.

Thus, with his own entourage and guards, the Lord Protector of Mirenburg was waiting when the wolf masks came into the courtyard of the great castle, and Sir Edwold Krier's Wäldish servant helped his master from his saddle, taking his banner and following at a respectful distance as he clanked up the steps to give the salute.

"Good morning, Sir Edwold. We are honored to receive you at the capital. Your business, we take it, is of great importance to the Empire."

"Of greatest importance, my lord. You are gracious to receive me thus at such short notice."

"I take it the heliograph is down again for some reason?"

"Sadly, yes, my lord. Three attempts we made to repair it, and even put a new man in. Then the attacks spread to other stations. My warriors are stretched thin, Lord Olin Desleur. But the rest I must discuss with you in private."

"So you shall. Have you breakfasted?"

Sir Edwold said he had eaten at dawn before breaking camp. Once they were together in Lord Olin Desleur's wonderful library, its windows looking out into the gardens of the palace with its ornamental lake and fountains, the spines of the books, dark reds, blues and greens, reflecting the predominant colors of his flowers outside, Olin Desleur's tone turned from one of public courtesy to one of private confidence. He personally shut the door and asked Sir Edwold what was the urgency of such an untimely visit when he, Lord Olin, was needed to entertain visiting dignitaries with letters from Quay Savoy in Londra.

Sir Edwold told him what he knew of the planned uprising.

Olin Desleur turned his back to his books and stared out over the lake. "How did this information come to you, Sir Edwold?"

"I had a visitor a few days ago. An odd fellow, belonging to a race I never encountered before. He was set upon by brigands to the north of us and, while in their power, had heard that a force of men was being raised to attack first our outlying defenses and then Mirenburg herself. It seemed to me that it was my duty to tell you of the danger and perhaps go on to Londra by the speediest route to beg Meliadus for more troops."

Lord Olin gave this some thought. First he had to consider the tranquility of the province and how best to maintain it. If he failed in these duties he would be humiliated, recalled to London, dismissed from his order, even tortured and killed. If, however, he allowed Sir Edwold to take the news to London, he would not be able to present his case, and Sir Edwold could depict him in an unfavorable light if he so chose. He was in a quandary.

"What became of your informant?"

"By now, Lord Protector, he has probably died of his wounds. But I had every reason to believe he spoke truth. There have been rumors of a rebellion in the province for some while, as you will of course know."

"Quite so." Lord Olin had not heard a single rumor, but it would not do to reveal this to Sir Edwold.

"Is there an ornithopter ready, my lord? I believe I should go at once to tell the king-emperor of our need for more troops here."

"Best that I carry the news. They will listen to me more readily."

"But would they not wish to hear the news firsthand—?"

"It will carry more authority if I give it."

"If you say so, my lord." The wolf mask bowed in agreement and some disappointment. "I thought perhaps that your responsibilities here . . ."

"You will have to carry that burden, Sir Edwold, while I warn Londra. I'll make you deputy protector in my absence."

"You do me great honor, my lord." There was still a hint of disappointment in Sir Edwold's voice.

"It will be your duty to gather intelligence and send spies abroad, to watch for any danger."

"Of course, Lord Protector."

Now Lord Olin Desleur recalled the two Germanians who awaited an audience in the antechamber. Politely he took his leave of the governor and hurried through the banner-draped galleries to the room where the two men waited. Normally he would have received them in his great hall, but he needed to know as privately as possible if their visit concerned the potential rebellion. He must have as few available ears listening as possible.

He soon looked with barely concealed disgust upon the naked face of one of the emissaries. The other creature at least had had the grace to mask.

The better-mannered of the pair was huge, heavy and broad-shouldered, much like Baron Meliadus in physique. He wore simple traveling clothes, his homespun britches tucked into riding boots of plain leather. His empty scabbard showed that he had left his sword with the guards. His cloak was pushed back over his shoulders. He carried a broad-brimmed "Bremen" hat in his hand, and his face was covered by a plain mesh mask.

The man's companion was slighter in build and had deep-set black eyes in a gaunt, skull-like face which, to be fair, might have been mistaken for a mask. He was dressed all in black and also carried a broad-brimmed hat. He looked more like the big man's clerk than his squire, thought Lord Olin. They rose and bowed to him as he entered the room, averting his eyes from the bare-faced man and addressing the other.

"Forgive us, Lord Protector. We are Germanians serving the Protector of München and are searching for an individual who offers the Empire great harm. We have been commissioned to seek her out and capture her. There is some understanding that she has sought help in Mirenburg and might be found living amongst your workers in the manufacturing district."

"Unlikely," mused Lord Olin, his busy hands behind his back. He felt just a little less confident about the situation. "Those workers are handpicked. Each of them has more than one reason to be loyal to the Empire. We depend upon them. The Empire's most crucial work is done here in Mirenburg. Our very latest machines are being built and tested here. The fastest ornithopters, the most effective battlecraft. I have made this province the armory of the Empire! We cannot, therefore, afford to let a single sweeper on the factory floor be in any way disloyal."

"Which is why we are here, Lord Olin," intoned the maskless one. "Mirenburg, as you rightly say, is critical to the whole power of the Empire. Because of your efficiency and the need to locate a manufacturing zone near the center of the Empire rather than at the edge, this city is now the *most important* to the Empire save for *Londra herself.*"

Lord Olin's strut became at once less spontaneous and more emphatic as he crossed towards the window to look up the long drive which led from the ceremonial doors below him on the ground floor. "I think the peace of the Empire has come to depend upon us here in Mirenburg," he said proudly. "And be assured, gentlemen, we shall continue to construct machines at the same rapid rate. Already 'Made in Mirenburg' is stamped on the barrels of our latest flame cannon, on the bellies of our mechanical rhinoceri and on the wing levers of our fastest, deadliest ornithopters. We also produce rapid-fire gas projectors and explosives." This, he told himself, was what he had to lose if he failed to keep the king-emperor's goodwill. His success here would give him an opportunity to rule an entire nation within the Empire, enabling him to build up enough power to secure his family from the most arbitrary of King Huon's decisions. And then, he thought, there was his retirement. If he did especially well, some less fortunate aristocrat would be banished from his Lakeland estates, and those lands renamed as Lord Olin's. Olin of Grasmere, he thought. That would be sweet, especially if he could choose which of his rivals to oust.

"You think we are especially in danger here?" Lord Olin asked. "Because others will soon begin to realize what an important center of the Empire Mirenburg is?"

"That is what is to be feared," agreed the naked one. His companion growled something about "focus of attack" and "strategies of terrorism."

"Well, as it happens, I take to the air this very morning. I go to Londra to speak to the king-emperor and ask him for more troops. Your report will give substance to my own request."

"You have heard nothing of a child, then?"

"Nothing. What is she? Some sort of oracle?"

"Just a little girl," said the masked one, "but of ancient blood. Could we ask you, my lord, to put soldiers at our disposal while you go to Londra? They will serve the double purpose of allowing us to continue our search for the traitors and discover the whereabouts of the child, as the king-emperor commissioned us to do. Meanwhile, we have other duties, as these papers will show."

The lord protector unrolled official scrolls and broke the seals off letters of introduction. The two Germanians were Gaynor von Minct and Johannes Klosterheim, loyal servants of the Empire. The crucial message from the Quay Savoy, headquarters of his nation's secret service, suggested that some kind of cult had developed, apparently around the defeated Duke of Köln and his Kamargian allies. Those insurgents should have been destroyed when ornithopters dropped powerful bombs on Castle Brass in the final battle, when Meliadus had brought his troops against Hawkmoon. With a certain aid from the sorcerer-scientists of Granbretan, Meliadus had decisively defeated them, claiming all Europa, from Erin to Muskovia, from Scandia to Turkia, as the Empire's.

"This child holds a secret which could lead us to these rebels," said the naked one called Klosterheim. "The girl," added the masked Gaynor, "is related to a hero these people believe can defeat the Empire."

At this Lord Olin chuckled. While rebellions might occasionally disrupt the Empire's tranquility, the idea of Granbretan know-

ing defeat was clearly ludicrous. They were the most powerful nation on earth. Nonetheless he took their warnings seriously. "I will
inform my deputy and tell him to give you all possible help in trac-
ing this child," he promised. "I have pressing business which takes
me to Londra. The child hides in the factory district, you say?"

"So it's thought, my lord."

"Well, do what you must. But do not slow down production.
If you do, it will be you who will take responsibility before the
king-emperor."

"We understand, my lord."

"No disruption. I will emphasize that to my deputy, Sir Edwold
Krier. You will report directly to him. I will speak to King Huon
about you. He will—"

"This business is secret, my lord. It concerns the Quay Savoy."

"Of course. Nothing public. There is much to be concerned
about. In the last nine months we have increased our ornithopter
and battle-engine production and trained operators for them.
We have modified the Brazilian system, and our steam engines
are now considerably more efficient. We have one of our
Granbretanian scientists working on a powerful bomb. These factories are the most advanced in the world. We are also developing
an aerial battle cruiser—a flying ironclad—together with new
guns. These models will be fully steam powered and considerably
more accurate at long range. Mirenburg's factories have become
the model for others which will spring up all over the Empire as
our might spreads. Once our new ships take to the air, no rebel
will dare defy us. And the rest of the world shall tremble at the
appearance of our fleets in their skies."

"Perhaps the child is part of a plot to sabotage these factories,
great lord," suggested the gaunt Klosterheim.

Lord Olin found the naked man's opinion unwelcome and ignored it, addressing the other, Gaynor of München. "I have business to attend to. My deputy will give you the assistance you
need."

And with that he swept from the room. There was much to
prepare. It would, he decided, be politic not to be in Mirenburg

when any rebellion occurred. His garrison would easily put it down, but it would prove his point and show that without his controlling hand, Mirenburg's factories were in danger. Also, Sir Edwold could be blamed for any failures. Meanwhile he would be gathering a stronger force, bound to defeat the rebellion and thus gaining him credit for success.

When he had gone, the two Germanians exchanged looks of triumph. Their story was believed. They had the run of the city as well as the governor's assistance in hunting down the dream-thief's little granddaughter, Oonagh von Bek. It would be, they were sure, but a matter of time before the girl and her elusive kinsman were within their power. Then they could perform the final bloody deed, which must be completed if the power they sought was to come into their hands. The child's life was the key to control of the multiverse. To eternity.

The two old allies, who had given up so much of themselves to avert the fate they so feared, were determined that whatever threatened their souls now should never threaten them again.

CHAPTER NINE

LRIC WAS AMUSED by Yaroslaf Stredic's astonishment at the success of his plan. Sir Edwold Krier remained entranced in his own castle, his guards sent upon errands into the woods. He could wander where he liked but had been robbed of all his masks and most of his clothes, as well as his memory and his identity. And now Lord Olin had taken Elric's bait. He had left by the latest and swiftest ornithopter, fresh from his own factories, for Londra. He had placed his supposed governor in control of the city. Elric had plenty of time to find his granddaughter without interference.

"We'll have every available guard looking for her," said Elric. His helmet off, his witch-coloring remained intact. He bit into a piece of fruit and looked out over the town. To the east was the smoke and sparks of great chimneys, showing the location of the manufacturing district. To the west rose the domes and sloping roofs of covered markets, where traders displayed their wares. To the north were the steeples of places of worship, where the people of Mirenburg were allowed to confer with any strange gods as long as King Huon the Immortal commanded a shrine dedicated to him and the priests praised him in their prayers. King Huon was not one to deny the conquered their comforting abstractions.

The people of Mirenburg were not especially devout, but more people now attended the temples than before the conquest. So many spies were among the priests, priestesses and congregations

1 3 7

that it was well known the temples were decidedly not places of secret sedition. The most radical hopeful could not have said that Mirenburg seethed. Indeed, superficially, Mirenburg was a city which, with the deaths and disappearances of its ancient families, had pragmatically accepted its return to provincial status under the Empire. Even the kulaks, the landed peasants of the rural communities, seemed to have accepted Londra's rule with a certain philosophical air. Periodically their country was conquered. They judged their conquerors more on the levels of taxes they charged than any other criterion. Granbretan had, in fact, eased taxes a little in the past year. They were still high, of course, and the laws still strict, but a certain security prevailed within those parameters. As is true the world over, the average kulak preferred authoritarian stability to the responsibility of freedom. Even when they had the opportunity to vote, most of those farmers and villagers and tradesmen preferred bellicose displays of strength rather than representation and intelligence in their leaders. No so the industrial workers, however, who shunned the temples and spoke cryptically among themselves, disguising their outrage and anger as a matter of honor.

Stredic told Elric that to the north lay the wealthier suburbs, whose inhabitants liked to complain about Londra but would only support an uprising if one was thrust upon them. Elric was not particularly interested, however, in rebellion, in spite of what he had told the lord protector. If some action of his helped overturn Mirenburg's conquerors, he would not be distressed, but his only real interest was to rescue Oona and leave. If Yaroslaf Stredic chose to use his moment to organize resistance, so much the better. Confusion would help him get her clear. It had cost him much exhausting sorcery to find her, and it would not be long before he began to run out of the much needed serum he had purchased from an apothecary in Brookgate, for a large amount of gold, shortly before embarking upon this expedition.

"We'll initiate an intensive search," he informed his companion. "And we'll help lead it ourselves. The first man to find her will be well rewarded, if not in money, then in whatever else he decides. But we do not have limitless time. Soon the real Sir Edwold must wake from his trance and begin to remember at least a little of who he is, while Lord Olin could return with specific orders from Londra—orders which might not suit our plans."

Yaroslaf Stredic saw the sense of this. He meant to take advantage of every hour his strange new ally had bought him. He was interested in the factories. He knew that the quietly angry slave workers were his most likely recruits. He could also recruit the pilots and many of the auxiliaries to his cause. His planned rebellion would have men to fly the machines and mechanics to maintain them. He coveted the ordnance as much as he wanted to free the workers. It had been these war engines that had achieved Granbretan's conquests, not the unquestioned ferocity of her commanders, or their lust for land and resources.

The same day that Lord Olin left for Londra, Elric of Melniboné, disguised by the vulpine helm stolen from the real Edwold Krier, demanded a marshaling of the city's entire garrison in the sprawling Square of the Salt Traders. In ringing tones he informed the men of their duty.

"A great plot is being hatched beyond the mountains. Some of the intriguers are already here, amongst us. These terrorists and rebels will do all they can to distract us from the nobility of our crusade. They hate us for the very security and freedom we enjoy. They live for strife, while we serve the forces of serenity. They are evil creatures who must be rooted out and destroyed. But we must not kill them. Any suspects must be taken to the dungeons of the Oranesians, the St. Maria and St. Maria, and interrogated by my handpicked investigators. They will soon give us the information we seek. Meanwhile, be alert for the child of whom I spoke. She must not be harmed. She must be brought to me at once, no matter what the time or what else is told to you."

"And what of the youth, my lord?" one captain wished to know.

"Youth?"

"The Germanians wish us to seek and capture a youth as well. They were clear on the matter. If any harm befalls him, or should he escape, those responsible will be publicly tortured and killed."

"The Germanians?" He had yet to meet these other newcomers. "It seems they exceed their orders, Captain. But if an albino youth is found, you must let me know and bring him to me. Under no circumstances is he to be given up to them. They exceed their authority!"

On dismissal the guards broke up into small groups, talking among themselves. Their tone was puzzled, even slightly confused. But they had a feeling in their blood that great events were in preparation and that they would be involved in some historic moment.

Watching this from their apartments in the nearby Martyr's Tower, the two "Germanians," Gaynor von Minct and Klosterheim, glowered in rage. What right had this provincial upstart to countermand their orders when, only an hour before, they had been congratulating themselves on the powerful help they had so easily secured with documents obtained by the expenditure of a few shillings in the forger's art and the aid of certain powerful plotters in Londra? The girl and the youth had been as good as in their hands! Once the children were in the prison of St. Maria and St. Maria (the feared Oranesians), it would have been relatively easy to get them out and carry them off to their ultimate destination. Now this fool had thwarted them!

"It seems we chose a poor moment for our little charade," announced Gaynor, pouring a beaker of fresh wine.

And Herr Klosterheim, nodding slowly, permitted himself a small grimace.

The search of the factory district began the next morning. Soldiers of the Wolverine, Dog and Lynx clans went from tenement to tenement rounding up every girl who remotely fitted Oonagh's description, yet she could not be found. Mothers wailed and fathers groaned as their children were ripped from their arms and inspected. Cupboards were smashed open, and anything hidden in them not a girl-child was discarded, ignored. Floorboards were lifted, lofts were combed and basements disrupted. Overseen by their grim leaders, the soldiers were unsubtle in their methods.

Of course, the guards did not dare to harm any of the girls. They had been warned how they would die if a drop of Oonagh's blood was spilled. At the end of five days, however, they were unable to bring the deputy protector any news.

Meanwhile the frustrated Germanians conducted their own secret searches and failed to be granted an audience with Sir Edwold, who seemed singularly reluctant to see them. They were beginning to feel suspicious of this deputy commander.

Only when Gaynor, unable to restrain himself, demanded that a soldier hand over some poor, shivering blond-headed girl to him, did Sir Edwold's captain-of-the-day challenge him and, in exasperation, put both Germanians under guard. Elric, concerned they might recognize him by his voice, was forced to confront them as they marched arrogantly into the interrogation chamber, surrounded by a detachment of city soldiery and brandishing their documents.

Elric disguised his voice as best he could. He sat well back in his great chair, observing them through the eye slits of his mask, his gloved, beringed hands tapping on the arms as if in impatience.

"What's this? Treachery?" he growled.

Hearing him, Gaynor frowned for a moment, and Elric feared he would be discovered. Then von Minct spoke levelly, a note of interrogation coloring his demands.

"My lord Protector, we carry letters from the Quay Savoy, which serves the emperor directly in all matters of homeland and overseas security. In these letters you are requested"—he spoke with growing emphasis—"nay, *commanded*—to give us all aid we request in this matter. The children whom your soldiers seek are the same as those we came to find. They are crucial to our imperial security, yet your men seem positively to be hampering us. I would remind you, sir, that you challenge the emperor himself!"

"*Commanded?*" Elric feigned anger. He was fairly certain that the documents could not be genuine. Why would Huon or his diplomatic police send these two, who had no credentials as far as he knew? "*Commanded?*" He made as if to give orders to his men. He was acting out a dangerous charade, countering a similar attempt by von Minct and Klosterheim, who might also be play-acting.

Klosterheim, always more of a natural diplomat, stepped between them. "I assure you, my lord, that we acknowledge your station and responsibilities. We have no intention—"

"Show me those documents!" Elric saw a glint of surprise in Klosterheim's deep-set eyes. Had the Puritan recognized him? Discovery at this stage would be extremely inconvenient . . .

"They are in our apartments, my lord."

"Very well! Take these men to the St. Maria and St. Maria," Elric ordered. "And search their rooms for these documents. Our emperor would be seriously angered if we did not show due caution in this matter. Then bring the documents to me and I will inspect them!"

Gaynor von Minct bellowed a refusal, but Klosterheim quickly calmed him, turning to Elric. "We have no quarrel in this matter, my lord Protector. You will see that the documents are genuine. We both seek to protect the security of the Empire . . ."

"Let us hope so, Herr Klosterheim." Again Elric noted a flash of suspicion in the Puritan's eyes as he half-recognized the albino's voice. He fell back silently into his chair while the guards marched the men away. He had gained a little time for himself, but he could not be sure how much longer he could maintain this untypical masquerade.

Now Lord Olin neared Londra. He flew in one of the new, faster ornithopters, fashioned in the likeness of a great dragon, its green, red, blue and black metallic wings clashing, powered by compact, sophisticated steam turbines spreading grey smoke in the vehicle's wake. The pilot, of the Order of the Crow, circled the great machine over Kroiden Field, as much to display it as to find a landing space. From there a massive steam tram, running on bright steel rails, took Lord Olin to the capital. Londra, with her brooding basalt buildings fashioned in the likenesses of beasts and grotesque men, was where the fiercely belligerent Baron Meliadus, King Huon's chancellor, awaited him.

From Kroiden it was already possible to see signs of the capital, the dark green fog which swirled in the sky above the glassy towers reflecting the gloomy fires of Londra, where sorcery and science mingled uneasily, drawn from the half-forgotten arts of the Tragic Millennium, when madness and folly had combined to bring the whole Earth close to destruction.

Now Londra's natural philosophers, her alchemists and masters of learning, all wished to restore the lost arts and discover new ones. Night and day her manufactories poured out their unlikely creations, molded metal and constructions of wood and precious gems, fearsome vehicles, war engines, suits of armor, flame lances, all fashioned in grotesque, baroque shops reflecting the inspired insanity of her masked aristocrats.

Lord Olin, who was familiar with the capital and the court, who had never grown fully used to either, realized, with a pang of anger, how he regretted being posted so far from home. Would he ever know the peace of his native hills again? What was it that drove him to develop his addiction to cruelty, which he had never known before coming here to be trained in the realities of Dark Empire administration?

He was already regretting his habit of intrigue, which had brought him here. He had no love for Baron Meliadus, for the man's kinswoman, Lady Flana (also King Huon's cousin), for Taragorm, Master of the Palace of Time, or for Taragorm's scheming colleague Baron Bous-Junge of Osfoud, Commander of the Order of the Snake, and Londra's chief scientist. He suspected them of treachery but had no proof. And though he would not breathe this to his own shadow, he was actually disgusted by ancient King Huon, who spoke with a stolen voice, who lived off stolen energy, a wizened homunculus maintaining himself in a sphere of life-giving liquid, his long, insectile tongue serving him as hands, his sole desire to preserve his own life, even if whole continents were sucked of their vitality for the purpose.

Yet here he was again, thought Lord Olin, driven by some survival mechanism as warped as those he despised, behaving like any other fearful courtier and now, as it dawned on him how he was acting, hating himself for it.

As the tall ceremonial tram, all black steel and ornamental chrome as befitted his station, bore him rapidly towards the city, Lord Olin seriously considered turning back. But there was no protocol which allowed it. No one would know how to obey him. The tram could not stop to be repositioned until it reached the Londra terminal known as Blare-Bragg-Bellow Station, where ceremonial guards no doubt waited to receive him. He was arriving in state, in all the honor and ceremony Granbretan could bestow upon her great nobles.

The tram was driven by a man in the elaborate helm of the Order of the Ox, whose members traditionally took the levers of such transports. On either side, on upper and lower decks, on seats of brass and polished oak, sat an honor guard drawn from the Order of the Dog and his own client clan, the Order of the Wolverine. These men had always supplied the ceremonial soldiery protecting the great and the good of Granbretan. Their long-snouted masks gave the assurance of loyalty and resilient steadfastness. Red bronze and copper glittered on their armor— ten warriors, a drummer boy, three standard-bearers carrying the flags of their orders, the imperial banner of Granbretan and Lord Olin's own quartered standard, showing his House, his order, his position and his honors.

Seated across from Olin was one of King Huon's own Seneschals, in green iron and the expressionless mask of the Order of the Mantis. To behave eccentrically now, thought Lord Olin, would be to sentence himself to death. He had no choice, if he wished to survive, but to continue into the city, to march through the great palace and the vast doors of King Huon's throne room, and then to stride in full honor through a hall from which hung the flags of five hundred provinces, once sovereign nations, with guards drawn from all but the lowliest aristocratic families lining the long approach. There he must prostrate himself before the great throne globe, that huge sphere of amniotic fluids which hung overhead, and wait until it pleased King Huon to receive him.

Sometimes even Baron Meliadus must wait thus for an hour or more before the king-emperor deigned to reveal himself, a yellowed embryo with a long, flicking tongue with which it operated the controls of its globe.

This morning, however, Lord Olin did not need patience. The globe came to life almost immediately. The mellifluous voice of a god spoke to him.

"Well, my Lord Viscount, what news of Mirenburg, that productive jewel in our skull of state?"

"I am honored, great King, to oversee such a massive achievement. I am here to assure you, as always, of my life and loyalty. Before you beats a devoted heart concerned only with your well-being and the well-being of our great nation, which are one and the same. I came because my underlings brought me rumors of something which has the potential to threaten the tranquility of your realm. I would not bother you, sire, of course, had not you ordered me to report directly to you and not to the noble Baron Meliadus, Your Majesty's greatest and most faithful steward . . ."

"Baron Meliadus is not at court. He pursues certain errands on my behalf. You can save some of your flummery, Lord Olin."

"Thank you, great King-Emperor."

"You have proven yourself a conscientious servant, Lord Olin, and I have no reason to believe you would waste our time . . . ?"

"I would rather kill myself, great King."

"So you had best make haste and tell me why you need more soldiers, for no doubt that is why you are here."

"A planned rebellion, sire. For all I know, it will not occur. The rebels might lose their resolve; we might arrest their leaders; their numbers might dwindle; the moon might not be in the correct corner of the quadrant; their wives might—"

"Yes, yes, Viscount Olin. We are aware of all the factors involved. But it surprises us that the province should offer defiance.

Are we not generous to it, compared to our dealings with Germania or Transylvania, for instance?"

"Very generous, great King. Wäldenstein is a model province, supplying us with many of the raw materials we need, as well as sturdy workers. That is why Mirenburg was chosen to be the site of our most advanced manufactories. Her inhabitants enjoy privileged tax status close to that of our own people here in Londra. In the past five years she has returned splendid harvests, and other revenues have been raised through the sale and trade of her women, who are famously fair and strong, and of her glassware and her china. Her kulaks know rare contentment and would seem the last to offer us trouble. Yet my provincial governor warns me a rebellion is already begun, that a larger uprising against our benign authority could take place at any moment, with armies coming from the East, perhaps from Asiacommunista. Our heliographs have been attacked and destroyed. I have my spies abroad, of course. However, I thought it wise to report this directly to Your Majesty, to beg for more soldiers and war engines that we might snuff out this rebellion before it can inflame more of our territories. Examples must be made."

The arrogant, glittering eyes stared intently down at Lord Olin. "Examples, yes. Wäldenstein is so placed as to be central to our future defense plans. We would not want our armies tied down there while forces from Asiacommunista attack some weaker flank."

"Your Majesty's knowledge of strategy is, as always, acute."

"This is not the only disruption to our realm at present. Indeed, we begin to suspect a concerted plan. Baron Meliadus investigates this possibility elsewhere. And others of Granbretan's finest turn their complex minds to such a problem. How did your man grow aware of this plot?"

"A visitor, great King-Emperor, who was waylaid in Romania. The bandits let slip they would soon be helping in some uprising against us."

"We shall consider your request for troops, Lord Olin, but we must remind you that it is your duty to protect our manufactories at all costs. Even the most minor of failures will carry severe penalties."

"I understand, sire. Mirenburg has become a key city in the defense of the Empire . . ."

"Indeed she has. You are a born manager, Lord Olin. You must tell your king-emperor all your news. What have you heard, for instance, of the Silverskin?"

"The name is unfamiliar to me, great King-Emperor."

"Aha. And what, perhaps, of the Runestaff?"

"The Runestaff, my lord. I—I thought our lord protector had care of it."

"The thing's not what we thought it was. We held a gorgeous fake. Few are familiar with the actual artifact. We hallow it, respect it, even pray to it and swear oaths upon it, yet who truly knows its real function or even its preferred shape? Some do not believe it takes the form of a staff at all. Instead, it resembles a beautiful, golden cup or a block of dark green stone, a giant emerald, some say. So, Lord Olin? Any news of it?"

"I have heard nothing at all, my lord."

"You had visitors from Germania, eh?"

"Indeed, sire. Sent by the Quay Savoy. With letters bearing your own seal. But I thought you had given orders for no mention of that to be made here . . ."

"Fool, those were forgeries!" The voice was like a snake's sudden hiss of warning. "We suspect traitors at court and have been following them. They, too, I'd guess, seek the Runestaff. Did you not have their luggage and clothing secretly searched? Were they not drugged and their bodies inspected? Have you all become such sentimentalists in Mirenburg, my lord, that you pamper these naked savages as if they were a favorite dog?"

"Great King, the scrolls bore the Quay Savoy's unbroken seals of office!"

"Even so, Lord Olin."

"I beseech your forgiveness, my lord." Lord Olin still lay visor-down upon the flagstones. He could not abase himself any further without breaking his own bones, or so it seemed.

"We would suggest, Lord Olin, that when you return to Mirenburg, you be a little more rigorous in your dealings with barbarians and such. You yourself have said how important the city is to our security and tranquility."

"I will return at once and see to it, sire."

"Not at once, Lord Olin." There was a terrible kind of happiness boiling at the back of King Huon's strangely reptilian eyes. "You can only hope your deputy is more suspicious than you are! I want you to confer with Baron Brun of Dunninstrit, and before that with Baron Bous-Junge of Osfoud. They will ask you specific questions. Granbretan will show her gratitude for your speedy decision in bringing your news directly to us. Let us hope you are first strong enough to pay the price for your lapses of intelligence."

An onlooker would have sworn how at that moment Lord Olin merged with the flagstones. From his great mask helm, there came what might have been a muffled weeping.

As the prehensile tongue flicked out, slowly the throne globe dimmed until only those awful eyes were visible. Then all was swirling darkness and silence.

After some moments, when nothing had happened, Lord Olin rose. There was something incongruous in the snarling wolf head which topped that slumped and defeated body as it got to its feet and walked unsteadily down the long hall towards the distant doors. Through them he was directed to another antechamber and another, conscious of the eye of every courtier upon him. Finally he stood in a chamber fashioned of obsidian warped to resemble human figures and symbolic creatures from Granbretan's most distant past.

A servant in the mask and livery of the Order of the Snake signaled to him. With a deep bow the servant led the way to the newly installed moving pavement, which carried them rapidly through miles of palace and many levels of offices until they reached Baron Bous-Junge's apartments, which had an unsavory reputation even in Londra. From inside came screams of such a timbre and pitch that even Granbretan's most jaded courtiers, used to the variety of shrieks and groans achieved through uniquely extracted pain, found them exciting.

On shaking legs, with dry mouth and stinging eyes, Lord Olin dared not pause. He must appear to go willingly to whatever fate Lord Huon had decreed, for if he did not, he would suffer a worse punishment. If he took his punishment as was expected, he might yet live to fulfill his ambitions of a peaceful retirement.

The smell coming from the baron's quarters, a mixture of alluring scents and the most disagreeable stinks, was enough to ensure that most men and women gave the place a wide berth. The main concentration of gases emanated from a low, squat doorway through which the servant led him.

Baron Bous-Junge, leaving his bench, his tubes and retorts, greeted Lord Olin warmly. The cobra mask nodded on Bous-Junge's shoulders, and he moved as if the weight of all his ceremony slowed him down.

"My lord Olin, you honor me. I hear you came to report trouble in your province."

Lord Olin stammered his greetings in return. "A—a—rumor, 'tis all, my lord Baron. We shall s-s-see what develops anon . . . mmmm . . ."

As was traditional in Londra, no mention was made of the punishment, the horrible public humiliation, Lord Olin would soon be suffering.

Baron Bous-Junge took Lord Olin by the arm and steered him through what seemed like miles of benches and equipment, where his specially trained slaves worked, many of them disfigured by chemicals or other forces, some of them probably not even human.

"Let us hope it doesn't have anything to do with this troubling rumor concerning the Runestaff and the men who seek to discover its ancient resting place," murmured Bous-Junge.

But Lord Olin did not want to know anything more than he knew already. He wondered: if he had sent Sir Edwold to Londra, might he have been spared his coming torture? He was suffering complex regrets.

"Many do not believe there is such a thing as the Runestaff," continued Bous-Junge conversationally as they left his laboratories and moved into the rather shabby and neglected luxury of his living apartments. "Even though I search for it, sometimes I myself am inclined to believe it doesn't exist. I have studied all the legends concerning it." Baron Bous-Junge's sinister green mask tipped to one side. Behind it the hard, old eyes seemed amused. "But it is a troubling coincidence that we should hear all those rumors from different sources. The Empire stands for Law, for Balance, for the power of justice and equity. Our Empire is represented by such symbols as the Runestaff. There is always a certain power invested in these symbols. Could we ourselves have willed the Runestaff into existence, out of sheer need?"

"Indeed, indeed, indeed," babbled Lord Olin, his mind on his future.

"After all, our own religion is a matter of ritual and tradition, little else." An almost inaudible hiss of words, and Lord Olin, already trapped, was quick to sense further snares. "We worship our immortal king-emperor, Baron Bous-Junge!"

"Of course we do, Lord Olin. Have you ever sworn an oath on the Runestaff?"

Lord Olin, within his armor, was like a terrified rat in a cage. "Oath? No? Yes! No . . . No, of course not—too—too—powerful . . ."

"Exactly. If we swear an oath by the Runestaff, that oath is binding. We do not invoke the Runestaff lightly."

Lord Olin racked his poor scrambled brains to remember if he had ever lightly invoked the Runestaff. He could not recall. He began to sweat. The sweat soaked into his underclothes, ran along channels in his molded helm and breastplate. He had begun to blubber. His snarling wolverine helm was like a greenhouse.

"Exactly," declared Baron Bous-Junge in answer to his own question. "My dear Lord Olin, I suspect there are plans afoot to obtain power over the original Runestaff and by this means affect the histories of our own realm in time as well as space."

Lord Olin was still unable to utter anything resembling intelligent speech. Baron Bous-Junge did not seem to mind. Equally he threw an arm about Lord Olin's shoulders.

"Are you curious about what gives me that suspicion?" The snake mask lifted to glance right and left. "Have you, I wonder, in your readings and travels, in your conversations, even in your dreams, heard of a creature not altogether human, with red eyes and bone-white skin, whom you might know in that part of the world as Count Zodiac?"

"C-c—?"

"Some reference, I understand, to an ancient Middle European outlaw or trickster. Anyway, he might well be the worst problem we face. Some suspect one of these Germanians to be a disguised Zodiac. Lord Taragorm's oracles suggest it. Are you sure you haven't heard of him? He has other names? Crimson Eyes? White Wolf? Silverskin? Some know him as Elric of Melniboné."

CHAPTER TEN

N HIS ASSUMED identity Elric of Melniboné experienced a frisson he had not known for some time. It had been many years since he had enjoyed the luxuries of so much power, and this was both attractive and relaxing to him. He had been raised, after all, in such opulence, and for a while, as emperor of his own nation, had taken it for granted.

Yet Oonagh had not been found, and he knew his own role must soon be discovered. Every possible man and woman had been set to the task of seeking the girl out, with no success. They had not so much as seen or heard a breath of her. Although the mysterious albino boy might have traveled on, Elric had been certain Oonagh would be found here. All he and Scholar Ree had been able to divine indicated that she hid in this version of Mirenburg. If he had not been so certain, he would scarcely have concocted so elaborate a plot. As it was, he now had to fear the possibility of his sorcery wearing off and of being exposed to the vindictive masters of the Empire.

Even his coconspirator, Yaroslaf Stredic, was growing nervous. Elric seemed determined to alert the Lords of the Dark Empire to the very rebellion Stredic planned. Why anger the Quay Savoy by locking up the two "Germanians"? He began to suspect that all his divinations had been wrong. Yet why would Klosterheim and von Minct, who most wanted to find her, also be looking here? Their presence seemed to confirm Elric's own understanding.

On the fourth morning of the search, Elric was close to calling it off when there was an incident in the factory quarter. Three ornithopters took off directly from the plant, flapping crazily into the air on metal wings, and from just above the topmost roofs, fired down into the city, aiming directly for the governor's quarters and the garrisons. Soldiers returned their fire before the ornithopters lumbered off into the distance and disappeared. They were commandeered by the very slave workers employed to build them. These men learned everything they knew from studying their masters.

Elric was not pleased with this development. Still posing as deputy protector, he now had to pretend to take measures against the factory district. He sent men in with orders to arrest the heads of the factories. When they went in, the guards were met with sustained fire and were driven back. Their captains came to Elric for further orders. He told them that the rebels had taken over all communications, and sent them off to the internal heliograph posts to destroy them. It was his belief, he said, that the rebellion would burn itself out.

Next morning the rebellion had spread across other parts of the city. Rebels were well armed and well disciplined. Elric ordered more of his soldiers into the forests and hills, seeking the girl. He explained that she held the key to their defense.

Eventually, he knew, the Dark Empire would retaliate. But he aimed to give the citizens all the time he could to take control of the city, believing that if the girl was hiding, she would come into the open once the rebels had won. A messenger was dispatched to the border, to the nearest intact heliograph, to signal that all was well with Mirenburg.

By now the citizens had some fifty ornithopters and a variety of battle engines of the very latest design. If Londra attacked, they would almost certainly be driven back until more troops and machines were brought to the war zone.

Elric made one last use of his stolen power. He sent his soldiers marching towards München, allegedly to relieve an even more embattled force there.

And he gave orders for the two Germanians to be brought to him.

The first order was obeyed. The second was not. The Germanians had disappeared. Their cell in the St. Maria and St. Maria was empty!

Elric understood their power. No doubt they had discovered that Oonagh was not, after all, in this part of the multiverse.

He would have given a great deal, however, to know where they had gone. The few spells he could readily cast gave him no further clues.

It was time to look elsewhere for his great-granddaughter. Every instinct told him that she was now in even greater danger.

Leaving the young Prince Yaroslaf in charge of the rebellion, he discarded his disguise, left his helm and armor behind, and set off into the Deep City to discover a gateway through to the roads between the worlds. He would have to begin his search all over again.

Elric had begun to understand how strong were the other forces in play, supernatural forces more powerful even than the two Germanians, the Dark Empire or even the old Empire of Melniboné. He suspected the agency of Law or Chaos, and while he had no certain proof, he was fairly certain that his little great-grandchild and the mysterious boy had in some way been selected to become their means to the ultimate power. Though he knew loyalty to Chaos yet fought for Law, Elric hated both. Too much horror had befallen those he loved as one struggled to gain ascendancy over the other. He trusted none of the Higher Powers. They cared nothing for the mortals they used in their eternal struggle for ascendancy. And as Elric well knew, few mortals could refuse whatever fate the Lords of the Higher Worlds determined for them. His own struggles, even in the thousand years of his long dream quest, had rarely succeeded. The illusion of free will was maintained in spite of the evidence. Even our most private thoughts and yearnings, he suspected, were dictated by some pre-ordained scenario in which Law battled Chaos. The best that we could hope for was a brief respite from their eternal war.

Elric could now do nothing else but search for his young kinswoman and attempt to save her from the worst that might befall her. He shook his fist at the gods and rode off to find the moonbeam roads, leaving his young friend to build what looked to be a substantial force against the infamous war leader Shenegar Trott and the other feared military lords of the Dark Empire. Yaroslaf Stredic might not defeat his conquerors, but he would set an example which might spark further revolutions across Europa.

Meanwhile, Dorian Hawkmoon, Duke of Köln, unknown to Elric, Baron Meliadus, Klosterheim or anyone else, returned to his cave two days after he had left to forage for food. The hero of Köln, still good-looking in spite of his grim experience, his blue eyes like honed steel, his blond hair streaked with grey, had news which might be good. In far-off Mirenburg, many miles from the foothills of the Bulgar Mountains, the citizens had at last risen against the Dark Empire.

Hawkmoon's friend, the wiry little mountain man Oladahn, was skeptical that any rebellion could succeed. The weapons of the Dark Empire were far too sophisticated. He scratched his red, hairy body and shook his head. They had attempted to withstand that final great attack upon Castle Brass and been defeated, in spite of their flamingos, their towers, their flame lances. Only by chance had the defenders found security in the secret marshes surrounding the castle before Meliadus and his forces had ruthlessly destroyed the majority of the flamingos, the horned horses and any human who had resisted them. They wanted no survivors, had completely destroyed the watchtowers, the old towns, every house and shed, bringing in an entirely new population from the Muskovian steppe, intending to ensure that not even a name would survive their conquest of the Kamarg. Neither had Meliadus been greatly disturbed by the probability that a few Kamargian peasants had escaped. They would never be able to rally fighters the way Dorian Hawkmoon of Köln had rallied them. Count Brass's only child, his daughter Isolda, had been plucked by Meliadus from the fires of Castle Brass and, no longer worthy of being Meliadus's wife, made a slave at Meliadus's court until she had disappeared, killed no doubt in Londra by some rival for another slave's affections. Bowgentle, the poet, was dead, as were all other defenders, or so Count Brass believed.

But he was misled. Una Persson herself had visited the survivors soon after they escaped into the great Slavian Forest, where they had lain low for over a year before they felt safe enough to move on. They found refuge at last among Oladahn's folk, the mountain brigands.

Oladahn could not believe the news. "Meliadus, or whoever represents him there, would have swiftly put down any uprising. They are superior in weapons, if not numbers."

Hawkmoon was not so certain of this. His informant had been a Bulgar who had the news from a Slavian merchant. "Apparently they took over a new kind of flying machine and turned it against the Granbretanners."

"Well," said Oladahn, scratching his hairy red arms, "it would not be the first time we've heard such rumors. If we believed them all . . ." His wide mouth clamped shut.

Hawkmoon said he was inclined to believe this. "It seems that many of those outlawed by the Empire are flocking to Mirenburg to strike while they may. At the first sign of Imperial gains they will melt away, to strike elsewhere—and disappear again. If they never attack Londra, they at least whittle away at the Empire." The Duke of Köln had known defeat three times at the hands of the Dark Empire, yet he would fight Huon's people until the end, even if he never defeated them.

Hawkmoon passed a strong, bronzed hand through grey-blond hair. He was a handsome man. The dull black jewel at the center of his forehead somehow enhanced his looks. He frowned as he considered what he had heard. All the power of the sorcerous science he had once employed against the Dark Empire was now gone. He had only his sword, his armor and his horse with which to fight Granbretan, while two of the people he most loved in the world, his wife and his father-in-law, slept under the security of that cave's roof, perhaps destined never fully to recover from the

horrors they had experienced. He regretted refusing the help of
that servant of the Runestaff, the Warrior in Jet and Gold, whose
proffered gift might have given them the chance of defeating
Meliadus when he brought all his force against the Kamarg. But
the opportunity had passed, and Hawkmoon had lost too much.
Now he wondered if he had the courage to risk any more. His own
life was nothing. The lives of those he loved were everything to
him.

With a sigh, the Duke of Köln considered his options.

Should he lend his strength to the citizens of Mirenburg and
the peasants of Wäldenstein, or should he wait for a more propi-
tious moment? What were the chances of such a moment ever
coming?

As he turned to go deeper into the cave system, he heard a
movement outside. He picked up his flame lance from where it lay
hidden beneath a pile of straw. That and its recharger were almost
all he had carried away with him from Castle Brass. He could not
possibly have trusted the Warrior in Jet and Gold. The Warrior
had already betrayed him at the Mad God's court, then returned
at a critical moment, pretending to bring them help against
Meliadus. Yet should he have rejected that? Could he have misinterpreted the Warrior's intentions? Could they have turned the
tables against Meliadus, saved hundreds of thousands, perhaps
millions, of lives, if he had accepted that help?

Warily he returned to the cave entrance. Had he conjured
that strange being back into existence? Riding towards him over
the rolling foothills came the unmistakable figure in armor of
glowing black and yellow, his face, as always, covered by his helm.
This refusal to display his face was one of the things which had always made Hawkmoon suspicious. It was a Dark Empire trait. Yet
here he came again, at another crucial moment. What did he
want this time?

Hawkmoon smiled bitterly to himself. All was doubt these
days.

The Warrior in Jet and Gold might be an agent of the Dark
Empire, though he represented himself as an opponent. Would it

even make sense to let the Warrior know he was here? He shrugged. Clearly the Warrior always knew where to find him. He could therefore have betrayed the survivors of Kamarg many times.

Hawkmoon stepped out into the sunlight to greet his old acquaintance. The Warrior rode up to a few feet below him and stopped, dismounting from his heavy black horse. His arms were scabbarded. His attitude, as always, was casual.

"Good morning, Duke Dorian." There was a hint of concern in his deep voice. "I am glad to see you survived the destruction of Castle Brass."

"Aye, barely. I might have survived it better, Sir Knight, had I accepted your help."

"Well, Duke Dorian, fate is fate. A moment's thought here, a quick decision there, and we might find ourselves in a dozen different situations. I am a simple Knight of the Balance. Who's to say which actions we take are ultimately for the best or not?"

"I hear there's an uprising down in old Mirenburg."

"I've heard the same, sir."

"Is that why you are here?"

The Warrior in Jet and Gold lowered his helmeted head as if in thought. "It might be one reason. Yes, perhaps you guess correctly. I am, as you must know by now, a mere messenger. I obey the Balance and, in doing so, serve the Runestaff."

"The Runestaff, eh? That mythic artifact. And what is this Balance? Another mythical device?"

"Perhaps, sir. A symbol, at any rate, of the whole quasi-infinite multiverse."

"So it is Good against Evil? Pure and simple?"

"That struggle is neither pure nor simple, I think. I suppose I am here to help you make a connection in the cosmic equilibrium."

"Tell me—have you served Granbretan?"

"In my time, sir."

Hawkmoon began to move back into the cave. "A turncoat. As I suspected."

"If you like. But I said things were not simple. Besides, you have trusted other turncoats. D'Averc, for instance . . ."

Hawkmoon knew the truth of this. Even he was considered a turncoat by some.

"Do you serve what you believe in, Sir Warrior?" he asked.

"Do you, my lord Duke? Or do you fight against what you do *not* believe in?"

"They are the same."

"Not always, Duke Dorian. The multiverse is a complex thing. There are many shades of meaning within it. Many complexities. We find ourselves in a million different contexts, and in each situation there are subtleties. In some we are great heroes, in others, great villains. In some we're hailed as visionaries, in others as fools. Were you a man of strong resolve when you refused my help at Castle Brass and allowed Meliadus to defeat you, destroying almost everything you loved?"

Hawkmoon felt something like a knife thrust to his belly. He sighed. "You betrayed us. You stole the crystal when we had defeated the Mad God. What else could I think?"

"I do not propose to tell you what you should think. But I assure you, I am here to help you."

"Why should you help me?"

"I do not help you for any sentimental reason, but because you serve the interests of the Balance."

"And that purpose?"

A pause. Then the Warrior in Jet and Gold said slowly, "To maintain itself. To sustain the equilibrium of the world. Of every world."

"Every world? There are others?"

"An almost infinite number. It was into one of these I offered you the chance to escape."

Hawkmoon dropped his head in thought. "Worlds where our history has taken a different turn. Where the Empire never rose to power?"

"Aye—and where that power has been divided or successfully resisted."

"Where I accepted your help in defense of Castle Brass?"

"Indeed."

"What happened there?"

"Many things. From each event sprang many others."

"But I won?"

"Sometimes at great cost."

"Isolda?"

"Sometimes. I told you. I do not serve individuals. I could not. I serve only the Runestaff and, through that, the Balance. Which determines only equilibrium. The Balance is destroyed and restored as it is needed. In one world you are its savior, in another its destroyer. Now it is needed again and must be remade. But there are those who would remake it and use it not in the interests of humanity but in their own evil interest."

"The Balance is not a force for good?"

"What is 'good'? The Runestaff serves the Balance. Some believe they are one and the same. Equilibrium. The form of justice on which all other justice is based."

"I was once told that justice had to be created by mankind's efforts."

"That is another form of justice. That is within your control. But only fools seek to control the Balance or any of its components. It is no more possible to do that than for an individual to control a whirlwind or the tides. Or the direction in which Earth goes round the sun."

Hawkmoon was confused. He was not an intellectual. He was a soldier, a strategist. For most of his life he had been a man of action. Yet he knew in his bones that he had not best served his cause by refusing the help of the Warrior in Jet and Gold.

"And you have brought me the crystal?"

"A crystal breaks and becomes many crystals. I have brought you a piece of that crystal."

Oladahn, hearing the conversation, crept out of the cave and greeted the Warrior in Jet and Gold with a friendly hand. His red fur still bore some of the signs of the fire which had almost consumed him as he and the others fled Castle Brass through the old underground tunnels. But now he moved with all the energy he had feared gone forever.

"What's that crystal do, Warrior?" Oladahn asked.

"It enables its holders to step in and out of this world and into many others. It enables you to move a whole army from one continent to another in an instant. It enables its possessor to challenge Fate."

"Much as the amulet I lost summoned help from other worlds?" said Hawkmoon, accepting the pyramid-shaped fragment. "I'll need such help if I'm to fight the Empire again."

The Warrior seemed satisfied. "You'll go to Mirenburg, then? With you to lead them, there is a good chance of the uprising succeeding. Mirenburg now produces the most advanced ornithopters and weapons."

"I shall have to seek the opinions of my companions," Hawkmoon told him. "I have responsibilities. We suffered much in the fall of the Kamarg."

"You have my sympathy," said the Warrior, remounting his horse. "I will return tomorrow for your decision."

Hawkmoon was frowning when he went back into the caves, the fragment of crystal clenched in his fist.

CHAPTER ELEVEN

LRIC WAS NOW convinced that the child he sought was not in that Mirenburg where he had helped create a rebellion. He had returned to the Mirenburg he had first visited, which existed contemporaneously with the house in Ingleton where Oonagh's parents waited anxiously for his news. Here he was able to telephone Mr. and Mrs. Beck. He learned from them that his daughter, Oona, had also disappeared into the Mittelmarch, looking for Oonagh.

Mirenburg's beauty had faded under Communism, but she was fortunate in that she had suffered little during the Second World War, having been swallowed by the Nazis with no more fighting than it took to gobble up Czechoslovakia. Her great twin-steepled cathedral of St. Maria and St. Maria continued to dominate the center of the city, which was built on two hills divided by a river. The old city was chiefly on the east bank, and the new one on the west. Its great, brutal monuments to Communist civic planning, tall, near-featureless apartment buildings and factory chimneys, rose above the primarily eighteenth- and nineteenth-century building with its astonishing mixture of architectural styles, including many from Mirenburg's last great shining period. Around the turn of the twentieth century her prince had commissioned some of the great modern architects such as Charles Rennie Mackintosh, Shaw, Wright, Voysey and Gaudí to design new municipal buildings.

Elric sensed an atmosphere of depression everywhere. Civil war had touched Wäldenstein. Rivalries between families of Slavic and German origin flared up as soon as the Communist heel had been lifted. Throughout the Soviet empire and its satellites time had frozen in the 1930s. Civil rights and a radical change in public consciousness had marginalized race and culture as a means of distinguishing peoples. Only in the backward regions of the world did these things continue to inform the views of the majority.

The war had been short; the UN had interceded with help from the von Beks as mediators. The von Beks had goodwill in Mirenburg, though their family had not lived there for many years. Mirenburg had suffered many attacks by would-be conquerors, from the Huns to the Austrians and the Germans and, the last time, from her own people.

It became characteristic of the post-Soviet wars that ancient rivalries, encouraged by those who wished to divide and rule, culminated in the grudges only now being settled. Industrialized, turned into one of the most productive cities in the Soviet empire, exporting the Popp, the only car to rival the VW, Mirenburg had been a showcase. Vehicles, plane parts, light weapons, poured from her factories. Today she produced Fords for the local market. Wäldenstein's labor was cheaper and her pollution laws were not yet as rigorous as Germany's, so the cars were produced at a more competitive price. Thus her great chimneys belched black smoke and glowing cinders into the sky night and day, and her ancient houses grew dark with the soot of over fifty years. Elric had known the city since the fourteenth century, but he had not known it to stink so much since 1640, when the river had run dry and sewage had filled the bed.

Elric employed what skills of divination remained to him in this world, and became convinced that Oonagh had returned to this, her own sphere, assuming she had not been killed in the catastrophe whose realities he had originally witnessed underground.

He had not been pleased to abandon his horse or his clothes

en route to this sphere. Samson would be well cared for, however, in Mu-Ooria. Elric never felt entirely comfortable in the
dress of our own period, which was why he affected evening
clothes so often, but he had no need for secrecy, at least. Here
he was recognized as a member of Mirenburg's old ruling class,
and it suited most citizens to address him as "Count." Not that
they were entirely unsuspicious of him. The local legend of
Karmingsinaugen was still remembered as involving the most
sensational crimes reported in Wäldenstein in the nineteenth
century, and the role was always attributed to him by the tabloid
newspapers, who believed he might share his ancestor's tastes.
He remembered how in earlier centuries they had pursued him
through the narrow streets, brands flaring in their fists, baying
for his blood. In those days he had still possessed his sword, and
on occasions it had suited him to release the power and feed off
their uncouth souls. But of late he found commonly available
medicines to sustain him. His taste for raw life-stuff was only a
memory. He remained amused, however, by the evident fear of
him some superstitious souls betrayed.

Yet for all his familiarity with the citizens, not one could tell
him where the little girl might be. "We would have heard, Count
Zcabernac," they insisted, "if an unaccompanied English girl were
living here."

"But what if she appeared to have her father with her, say, or
a couple of uncles?"

"I'd know. So would many others." This from the overweight
landlady of his pension. She had suggested he return to England,
perhaps leaving an e-mail address or telephone number where he
could be contacted.

Then, just as he had begun to inquire about the availability of
flights from Munich, something happened which made him determined to stay. He was sitting reading the *Mirenburgerzeitung* in
a café not far from his pension when he looked up and saw a tall
man making his way hastily across the busy Ferngasse, barely
missed by a clanking number 11 tram. He recognized the man at
once as Klosterheim, whom he had last caused to be imprisoned

in that other Mirenburg. Full of alarm, Elric immediately set off in pursuit, through the streets and alleys and into the old thieves' quarter, now the home of bohemians and students. Klosterheim disappeared into a traditional hostelry, Raspazian's, and was ordering a drink at the bar when Elric walked in and seated himself in the shadows near the door.

If Klosterheim was in this world, decided Elric, then there was every chance he had come here to look for Oonagh. It was very likely that Klosterheim had escaped from the St. Maria and St. Maria and come directly here. It suggested the girl was not yet in his power. At last Elric might discover why Klosterheim and von Minct pursued the child and why all the omens had been so terrifying.

Elric decided to confront Klosterheim before there was any chance of losing him again. He rose slowly and walked to where the gaunt man stood, paying for a Rottbier.

"Good morning, Herr Klosterheim."

Klosterheim turned but did not seem surprised. "Good morning, Count. I had heard that you were here again. Have you retired from—um—'showbiz'?"

"My family has some old associations with this city. Being a sentimentalist, I visit whenever I can. And you, Herr Klosterheim? Are you here on some sort of evangelical business?"

Klosterheim seemed to enjoy this. "Of sorts, yes."

"I believe I just missed you in Ingleton." Elric said nothing of their mutual deceptions in that other Mirenburg.

"An unusual coincidence. As is this one."

"You were looking for my daughter's granddaughter, I understand."

"We had some idea she could help us find an easy way into the Mittelmarch."

"You have always succeeded before, Herr Klosterheim."

"My capabilities are limited of late." The gaunt man offered him a sour yet oddly humorous look.

"I hope you'll let her parents know when you find her," Elric said. "I spoke to them yesterday. They are naturally anxious."

"Naturally." The grey lips touched the ruby sheen of the Rottbier.

Elric could tell that Klosterheim, his gaunt features tensing, his dark eyes hard and bright in the depths of his skull, would have been quite happy to kill him if there had been some means or excuse. But here the long-undead ex-priest was forced to remain civil. He looked up in some anticipation, however, as a huge man entered the bar and greeted him. It was Gaynor von Minct, of course.

This unregenerate Nazi had pursued Elric through his thousand-year dream since the eleventh century and was now grinning down on him ferociously like a wild beast about to kill its prey. He scowled when Elric offered to buy him a drink. The tension between the three men was so considerable that the barman went over and murmured significantly to the manager, who was serving a customer at the far end of the bar. Elric saw the manager pick up his mobile phone and put it in his hip pocket, as if ready to call the police.

Gaynor von Minct also noted this. "Perhaps we should talk elsewhere," he said. "Would you care to meet later, Prince Elric?"

"Where would you suggest?" The albino was amused. He often felt this amusement when his sixth sense warned him of danger.

"How about the Mechanical Gardens? Do you know them? They are fascinating. There's a little coffee place there, by the Steel Fountain."

"Would four o'clock suit you?" Elric hoped he could get some further clue from Gaynor. The man was arrogant enough to reveal himself by accident.

"Four would be perfect." Gaynor did not wish to be humiliated in public, so did not offer his hand, but he smiled that thin, unpleasant smile of his as he turned back to speak to the glowering Klosterheim.

Mirenburg's famous Mechanical Gardens were public enough to be safe. Making sure he was not followed, Elric returned to his pension. Here he armed himself with an old black, battered

Walther PPK .38 automatic. The two men would gladly kill him if the opportunity arose. He took his lunch at the Wienegatten and wrote the notes he would send to Mrs. Persson at her poste restante in Stockholm. He had developed this habit since they had first met in the early part of the twentieth century, when they had become good friends, possibly lovers, though Mrs. Persson was, as always, discreet about her liaisons.

The Mechanical Gardens had first begun operating in the 1920s, the creation of the Italian Futurist Fiorello De Bazzanno. During the Communist period they continued to function, even if a little run-down. The futurist-deco style of the gardens was reminiscent of a period when the machine inspired a distinctive aesthetic. The large park, on the far bank of the river, covered a number of acres and was filled with mechanical men, trees, flowers and animals, some of them, like the gleaming *Tyrannosaurus rex,* truly monstrous. The park was dominated by an enormous, jovial grinning head made entirely of machine parts, with rolling eyes nodding back and forth as if in approval. Everything moved by systems of cogs, levers, belts and wheels. Most used electricity, though a few were still steam powered. There was a small funfair, with Ferris wheel, merry-go-round, "whip," helter-skelter and a few small roller coasters, though these were not the chief attraction. Everything was mechanical, including the old-fashioned automat, the coffee shop and even the souvenir shop, where big robot "assistants" talked to customers by means of prerecorded tapes and gave change after notes were inserted into their mouths.

With the old spires, domes, roofs and turrets of Mirenburg in the background, the art deco world of cogs, levers and engines presented by the Mechanical Gardens had a quaintness of its own. Great cogs resembling faces flashed and grinned. Massive hands constructed of rods and pistons waved overhead. The watery sunlight reflected off steel, brass and tin, and a mechanical organ played Strauss waltzes and polkas.

Most of the people in the park at that hour were couples who looked as if they had been coming there for years. At the Steel

Fountain, Elric got himself a cup of café au lait and a rum pastry, which he took to one of the green tables overlooking the lawn which ran down to the river. Soon Klosterheim arrived. He wore a black trench coat and a wide black hat. His hands were shoved deep in his pockets. Gaynor was next, his big body swathed in a herringbone raglan coat, a feathered Tyrolean hat on his head. Underneath his coat was a suit of dark green tweed. The two men went to the automat and returned with coffee. Klosterheim's long, bony hand reached out for the bowl and began to place lumps of sugar in his cup. Von Minct sipped his unsweetened. "This place seems changeless. I remember when I first came. It had just opened. Mussolini had completed the March on Rome, and the king had asked him to become prime minister. Splendid days, full of optimism. How quickly the golden years go by! Are you enjoying your pastry, Prince Elric?"

Elric placed his fine, long-fingered white hand on the lattice metal of the table. "You seemed to suggest you wanted to talk about the missing girl," he said.

"My dear Prince, you certainly like to get straight to the heart of the matter. I like that, sir."

"I would guess you have not found her." The crimson eyes narrowed beneath half-shut lids. "You think she's somewhere here, perhaps?"

"You are presuming a great deal, my lord Prince," said Klosterheim. "What if we, too, have only the young lady's safety at heart? Given that she no doubt trusts you, we thought she might reveal herself to you, whereas . . ."

"Indeed?" Elric sat back in his chair. He fingered his chin. He still seemed amused. "So you hounded her through the Mittelmarch in order to ensure her safety? And now you think I'll be bait for your trap?"

"Hounded?" said Klosterheim. "That's a strong word, sir!"

"I am here to warn you to give up your pursuit."

Von Minct became suddenly alert. "You're not exactly fair to us, Prince Elric."

"Perhaps." Elric saw no reason to give them any information.

"So you expected to find her here? And planned to use me as a lure to bring her out of hiding!"

"We were informed we might find her at Raspazian's; that is all. But it was clear she had never been near the place. He said the Fox had her."

"He? Who informed you?"

"A fellow wearing black and yellow armor. He did not leave us his name."

"Where did you meet him?"

"We were lost on the moonbeam roads. We are not entirely skilled in negotiating those roads in this universe, and he helped us."

Elric knew of the Warrior in Jet and Gold. Their paths had crossed once or twice, to their mutual benefit. Why would the Warrior confide in Elric's enemies?

"Did he propose exactly where she could be found?"

"He said to seek her on the wheel." Klosterheim indicated the Ferris wheel. "Can you think what she might be doing there? One or the other of us has watched the wheel most of the time."

Elric was disbelieving. Von Minct and Klosterheim must be lying to him. He said nothing. He had hoped to learn something from them. Doubtless they had hoped even more of him. Leaving his cake uneaten, he finished his coffee and rose. "I'll bid you good afternoon, gentlemen."

They were nonplussed. They had expected to benefit from the meeting.

Elric left them talking to each other in low voices. As he walked out of the Mechanical Gardens he felt disappointed. Had he failed to note an important clue to the child's whereabouts? He glanced back and was surprised to see Klosterheim and von Minct paying their money and pushing through the Ferris wheel turn-stile. Did they expect to find Oonagh in one of the compartments, after having waited fruitlessly for so long? Should he follow?

No. They were as thoroughly desperate as he. Yet he waited and watched them. Eventually they came out through the exit. They had no one with them.

Elric, summoning some of his old witch-sight, did his best to read the air around the giant wheel. It was agitated, possibly populated. He thought he saw other shapes, perhaps even outlines of other cities. Looking around, he could tell that only the great wheel had an unusual quality. He knew it must have some function in this puzzle. But was he going to become as obsessed as his enemies and spend weeks watching the thing?

The park closed at five, and uniformed men on bicycles blew whistles to herd customers out. It would open again in the evening, with the added attraction of a cinema show in what had been the park's original kine-theater.

Elric returned to his pension. He had an unconscious sense of what was happening to Oonagh and why Klosterheim and von Minct were here. Nothing was clear, but his instincts told him that there was something wrong. Something that wouldn't save Oonagh, however, because that pair would act on whatever erroneous idea they had. She was still in mortal danger. The problem remained how to find her and get her to safety. That was going to be a difficult task, he admitted, smiling to himself as he changed for dinner. He tied his bow tie, adjusted it at his throat, straightened his sleeves a little and was again the dandy who had once graced the boulevards of Mirenburg and Paris in the Belle Epoque. He had been acquainted with half the great poets and painters of the day. All the artists wanted to paint his portrait, but he had allowed only Sargent the privilege. The painting now hung in a certain apartment in London's Sporting Club Square and had never been exhibited. It had been reproduced once in the *Tatler* for July 18, 1902, in a general photograph of the artist's studio. It showed a man no older than Elric seemed now, adorned almost exactly as he was, in superbly cut evening dress.

In this costume he had once gone upon the town. But he had not always been found at the parties of the rich and powerful nor in the boulevard cafés for which Mirenburg was famous in that era before war had disrupted her pursuit of pleasure. Sometimes he might have been glimpsed in the cobbled alleys of the Deep City, or even climbing up the narrow gap between buildings to make his way easily and with great familiarity across the rooftops.

But those days were over, Elric reflected with a little self-mockery. Tonight he would dine conventionally enough, at Lessor's in the Heironymousgasse.

And then, he thought, he might make a visit after hours to the Mechanical Gardens.

He dreamed. This time he led an army against a powerful enemy. All the beasts of Granbretan were massed against him, but in his mirrored helm he rallied his troops to attack. And he was Corum—alien Corum of the Vadhagh—riding against the foul Fhoi Myore, the Cold Folk from limbo . . . And he was Erekosë—poor Erekosë—leading the Eldren to victory over his own human people . . . and he was Urlik Skarsol, Prince of the Southern Ice, crying out in despair at his fate, which was to bear the Black Sword, to defend or to destroy the Cosmic Balance. Oh, where was Tanelorn, sweet Tanelorn? Had he not been there at least once? Did he not recall a sense of absolute peace of mind, of wholeness of spirit, of the happiness which only those who have suffered profoundly may feel?

"Too long have I borne my burden—too long have I paid the price of Erekosë's great crime . . ." It was his voice which spoke, but it was not his lips which formed the words—they were other lips, unhuman lips . . . "I must have rest; I must have rest . . ."

And now there came a face, a face of ineffable evil, but it was not a confident face—a dark face. Was it desperate? Was it his face? Was this his face, too?

Ah, I suffer!

This way and that, the familiar armies marched. Familiar swords rose and fell. Familiar faces screamed and perished, and blood flowed from body after body—a familiar flowing . . .

Tanelorn? Have I not earned the peace of Tanelorn?

Not yet, Champion. Not yet . . .

It is unjust that I alone should suffer so!

You do not suffer alone. Mankind suffers with you.

It is unjust!

Then make justice!

I cannot. I am only a man.

You are the Champion. You are the Eternal Champion.

I am only a human being. A man. A woman . . .

You are only the Champion.

I am Elric! I am Urlik! I am Erekosë! I am Corum! I am Hawkmoon! I am too many. I am too many!

You are one.

And now, in his dreams (if dreams they were), he felt for a brief instant a sense of peace, an understanding too profound for words. He was one.

And then it was gone, and he was many again. And he yelled in his bed, and he begged for peace.

And it seemed his voice echoed through the entire city, and all Mirenburg heard his sadness and mourned with him.

CHAPTER TWELVE

WASN'T SURE exactly what happened after the Sebastocrater was shot and it started raining, except that Lord Renyard, Lieutenant Fromental and Prince Lobkowitz all left the summerhouse and ran after me at the same time with Lady Oona. As I labored for the high ground, Oona's Kakatanawa (suddenly awake) began yelling what I guessed were their war cries just as a ball of bright silver light appeared over the ornamental lake, where von Minct and Klosterheim fell back, blinded.

There was a horrible roaring noise in the distance, and it began to rain more heavily. Oona picked me up and set me squarely on her shoulders. Everyone was shouting. Then suddenly there was silence, stillness. I looked back. The whole scene—summerhouse, Kakatanawa, Sebastocrater, guards—had frozen, as if something had stopped time again. But Oona was in a hurry, and she and I were unaffected by whatever spell had been cast. I saw the panther trotting ahead of the others, leading the way through the narrow streets of Mirenburg. The whole city was frozen. We sped on through the gates, racing in moonlight towards the heights above the city. Only when we were looking down on the towers of Mirenburg did Oona pause and lift me from her back.

Any barmy notion I might have had that Oona and the panther were the same had gone, of course. Yet I still had a sneaking

1 7 3

suspicion in the back of my mind that they were more closely related than most would think credible.

Below us I saw a ball of golden fire approach the still hovering ball of silver fire through slicing bursts of rain. They quivered together in the air, as if sizing each other up. They expanded, growing brighter and apparently denser at the same time, and did not touch until, in the blink of an eye, they had merged, become the same thing, a single iris the color of polluted copper.

"Stay there!" cried Oona above the noise of the rain, and ran back down towards the city.

"Don't leave me!" My shout was impulsive. With a wave she was gone, racing back towards that baleful eye which began to grow larger as she got closer. She disappeared through the gates as I waited anxiously, watching little stars and sparks descending on the roofs, chimneys and steeples of the City in the Autumn Stars. Then the globe became a red, glowing coal and dropped earthward again.

Was Herr Clement Schnooke working the magic he had promised? Or was something else going on, maybe started by von Minct and Klosterheim? I waited nervously. Suddenly I heard the rush of water from somewhere. I looked down through the starlight and saw the glint of the river, which was rising with terrible speed. I was so fascinated that I couldn't move. Then the panther was there, pushing at me with her nose. It was wet and warm, just like an ordinary pet cat's. She seemed to want me to follow her. Reluctantly I turned and climbed to higher ground. The water had already risen above its banks and spread out through the city streets. I began to hear distant shouts when the remains of the fiery ball fell back towards the Deep City and plunged down to where I guessed Raspazian's to be. Now I was certain this was Herr Schnooke's magic at work. I had a sinking feeling that the spell had gone seriously wrong, that Schnooke had been destroyed by his own magic. How many of my friends had he taken with him? I guessed that the spell had clashed with all the other magic at work that night. I know I witnessed a genuine disaster. All the inhabitants of Mirenburg were in serious danger.

At last Oona stood beside me again as her Indians crept out of the darkness with Lord Renyard, Herr Lobkowitz and Lieutenant Fromental.

"I have to go back there," I said. "I made a promise."

"You can hope the majority survive," said Oona very wearily. "We are only minutes away from being swallowed by the thing . . . Damned amateur magicians!"

Which suggested it was definitely Schnooke.

But I had to get back to help Onric. I babbled. I insisted. I struggled to make them let me go.

Oona continued to speak softly and kindly to me, but her attention was elsewhere. In the end I had to hope the boy had saved himself from the flood. His coworkers, after all, had seemed to value and respect him.

"We must stick together," Oona insisted. The others agreed. She turned to her Kakatanawa to speak to them in their own language.

I gave it one last try: "But there's a boy back there. He's like you, Lady Oona. Like Monsieur Zodiac!"

She didn't really hear me. "We can do little here. We must assume our friends are still in pursuit. This has much to do with them, I suppose."

I felt sick as I watched the city fill with water. I now clearly heard shouts, screams and the noises of panicking animals. Oona said something again to the Kakatanawa.

I found it hard to turn my back on the flooding city. I still had friends down there. When I mentioned this to Prince Lobkowitz he put his hand on my shoulder and squeezed it. I looked up into his kindly, miserable eyes. "What we have to do is more important than the fate of those poor souls, my dear. We must get away from here as soon as possible. We have to consider the wider good."

"I would have thought Onric could have been included in the wider good," I said.

"What name?" She frowned at me through the rain. "What name?"

"Onric. An albino. Looked a lot like you. He had a job in a factory down there. Well, he'll probably be out of work now." I was a bit fed up that nobody had listened to me.

"A factory?"

"A steel-making place. Where everything's white-hot, you know, unless it's red-hot."

She turned to look back at drowning Mirenburg. Some factory chimneys still smoked, but it was easy to see that their fires had been dampened, flooded and were choking. "Was he my age?" she asked in a strange voice.

Lord Renyard came over to us before I could reply to her weird question. "The moon," he murmured, and looked up.

My heart began to beat all the harder, for through the rain a full moon glowed, bright, clear and blue. The rocky landscape ahead of us was bathed in a faint blue light.

Behind us on the road below we saw people and animals plunging in panic out of the city gates nearest us, heading towards higher ground. We continued on the rocky paths well above them as my friends clearly tried to gain as much height as possible above the still rising waters.

Oona cursed the incompetent magician Clement Schnooke from time to time. I felt that more than one kind of magic had met here tonight, without actually managing to do anyone any good.

"We can't be certain how far the river will rise," said Oona. "For all we know, it won't be much. But we have to get up into the mountains if we can. They are using quicksilver against us."

I had no idea what she was talking about, and I was almost in tears again, imagining my new albino friend drowned in his factory after I had promised to help him.

"Are we going back home?" I asked.

"As soon as we can, dear," murmured my grandmother.

"You might say we have lost the path through." Lord Renyard was looking longingly back at the flooded city. I felt so sorry for him. All his people had been left behind, everything he loved, including his prized library. At least my own home was still in one piece. Or so I supposed.

The Autumn Stars were appearing over the city, forming al-most a pattern around the still glowing blue moon. I tried to look up in the sky and see where they began and ended, but I couldn't tell. I focused on a big rent in the black clouds, almost as if the light itself had created it.

Wet, miserable and tired, we kept walking all that night and by dawn were well into the mountains. Only then did Oona sign that we could stop and shelter in the pine forest while she and the Kakatanawa went off to find food for us. Prince Lobkowitz and Lieutenant Fromental built a fire. Lord Renyard, having spent much of the night in low conversation with Oona, was definitely depressed. He went over to some mossy rocks and sat down. I joined him. He seemed pleased.

"What's going on, Lord Renyard?" I asked. "I'm sure your peo-ple must have been able to save themselves. They're very re-sourceful. Not too many will have been hurt."

"Some, at least, are safe. Perhaps all of them. The worst flood-ing appears to have been in reverse. In the mirror city. In the world below. Our path was between the worlds."

He didn't seem to have seen what I had seen, yet I believed him.

"What happened?"

"A clash of magics, almost certainly. Those men who seek you are ruthless. They'll risk anyone's life to capture you. But nobody expected them to try to flush you and Oona out with a water spell. That went wrong for them when their spell clashed with Clement Schnooke's. You saw the result."

"What was Schnooke's spell?"

"His was a time spell, with elements of fire and water spells, intended to release us and divert our captors. But two kinds of magic being wrought at the same time—well, people will always suffer." He sighed. "And it is always the innocent who suffer most. Had I been free, I might have prevented this."

"Isn't there somewhere else—some other . . . you know . . . world—where you can go, where things are more or less the same?"

"I am something of a monster, my dear. Few places on the sur-face find me acceptable. I must eventually seek either fabled Tanelorn or return to Mu-Ooria and the Off-Moo, who seem to appreciate my company."

"Where are we going now?"

"To find a new gateway to the moonbeam roads, the old one being blocked for us by von Minct's cruel and bloody sorcery."

"What do all these people want from me, Lord Renyard?"

"They think you can lead them to what they seek."

"Which is?"

"Well, ultimately it amounts to what someone from a pre-Enlightenment culture might describe as power over God and Satan. Whatever you call it, that's what von Minct and Klosterheim want. Power. Immense power. Power over all the worlds of the universe. What Prince Lobkowitz calls the multi-verse, that is, all the versions of all the worlds."

"I know what it means," I said. "I read a lot of comics, and my dad gets *Scientific American.* What, billions of them?"

"Oh, billions of billions—we call this quasi-infinity because while it is not an infinite number, we cannot know a finite number."

"Why would they want so much power?"

"To rival God and Satan, as I said."

All my family and most of their friends were of a secular dis-position, so I was inclined to be amused by the ideas of God and Satan as such. "Isn't that Satan's job?" I asked.

"It was," said Lord Renyard seriously. "But Satan no longer wished to be God's rival. He sought and found reconciliation with God. This reconciliation was not in our enemies' interest. They want, if you like, to take the job Satan renounced. To return to a state of cosmic war."

"So if they got what they wanted, they'd rule an infinite num-ber of worlds of evil?"

"They would not call it evil. They believe that an ideal uni-verse is one in which their priorities are uppermost. It is almost impossible for us to understand. Perhaps someone else can understand them better. They are not like us. They have no self-doubt. They believe that what is best for them is best for everyone. For everything. At least, they think that every 'normal' person wants to do what is best for von Minct and Klosterheim. Anyone who disagrees with them or resists them is abnormal and must be re-educated or eliminated. If they have God's power, they can set the cosmos to rights."

"Even though God created it?"

"Even so."

"They're mad," I said.

Lord Renyard laughed at this. "Ah, the directness of children. How I envy you!"

I found this condescending. "So how are you planning to get them sorted?"

"We can only oppose them. As effectively as possible. And protect those they would harm."

"How on earth could I give them that kind of power?" I was even more baffled. "I'm a little girl."

"A rather brave and clever one," he said gallantly. I wanted to hug him.

"But still—"

"We need to discover what it is you have," he said quietly. "We do know that the Sword, the Stone and two cups are involved. All the things called 'objects of power.'"

Oona and her men were returning through the woods. They carried several game birds. Lord Renyard began to salivate. "Here's our breakfast," he said. "I wonder if mine might be a little more underdone . . ."

I realized that I was very hungry, too.

After we'd eaten we packed up and moved on across the hills. It felt like Yorkshire again. I was enjoying the smell of the heather, the glint of the sunlight on limestone, the cool shade of the woods. Hunting hawks sailed high above us. Every so often we passed streams and groves of wildflowers. I began to hope we might already be on our way home.

I had to give up that idea when we reached a well-trodden

road and saw an old-fashioned coach drawn by six black horses, pounding along at a dangerous speed, with its driver cracking a whip and yelling at the top of his lungs. I recognized the crest on the coach's door. It belonged to the Sebastocrater and must have come from Mirenburg. It went past too fast for us to catch up or see who was in it. If it was Klosterheim and von Minct, they might have seen us. Prince Lobkowitz frowned. "That's the Munich road," he said.

"How long will it take them to reach the city?" asked Lieutenant Fromental.

"Another three days if they can get changes of horses."

"Must we follow them?"

"Of course not," said Oona. "Our first duty is to protect the child. In doing that we shall also thwart their plans."

"So which way should we go?"

She hesitated. "I don't know, but we should try to get home before this gets any worse."

"That would be my preference," I said.

One of the Kakatanawa who had been scouting ahead of us on the other side of the hill came running back. He spoke rapidly to Oona, who shook her head in disbelief. Then she and the others followed the Indian. I ran after them.

We stood looking down on a pleasant valley with a stream running through it and a few cows grazing. Nestled between a small copse of elder trees and may bushes was a house.

The others did not know what it was, but I did. So did Lord Renyard. He put his large, warm paw on my shoulder. He could probably tell how frightened I was.

The house was the twin of the one I had first "met" in Mirenburg. With blinds down and shutters closed, it had the appearance of being asleep.

"This could be good news, you know," murmured the fox. "Mrs. House is not your enemy." His tone was reassuring, but I could sense he was as mystified as I was.

"How could it—she—get here from there?" I asked.

"Well, first you should consider that the same builder put up more than one house of the same type, mademoiselle," he suggested gently, as if preparing me for disappointment.

"No, it's the same," I said. "Same windows, doors, blinds, slates, chimneys. Same patches on the walls. It's her face, all right."

"Her?" Prince Lobkowitz came to look down at the house with us. "Face?"

Lieutenant Fromental fingered his prominent chin. "I've always thought of houses as having faces, too." He chuckled at his own whimsical imagination. "What children we are, eh?"

"I *am* one," I said. "And that house does have a face. That's Mrs. House, I'm certain."

"Mrs. House?" Oona drew her brows together as if summoning an old memory. She brought her Kakatanawa to a halt. The tall, bronze-colored men murmured among themselves, occasionally laughing. They were as surprised as the rest of us at finding such an old, seemingly well established house in this countryside.

"Mrs. House—should it indeed be her—is an old friend of mine," explained Lord Renyard. "The little mademoiselle also met her before."

"She's the one who mentioned the Staff and the Stone," I said. "And talked about the blind boy. It was all a bit vague, but I'm pretty sure that's what she was saying. That's why I was asking you those questions."

"Someone you met inside the house?" asked the burly legionnaire. His big face frowned, as if he did not quite understand what was being said.

"No," said Prince Lobkowitz patiently. "You mean the *house herself*, do you not, Miss Oonagh?"

"That's what I mean," I said. "That's what I remember."

As we continued to approach her, Mrs. House opened her eyes.

The effect on my friends, apart from Lord Renyard, was almost comical. They came to a stumbling stop. The door, which was Mrs. House's mouth, moved. Her rich, slightly echoing voice sounded through the valley.

"Ah, it's good to see you're still safe, dear girl. You escaped the floods, as did I. I knew in my bones I would soon be on the move again, but I did not think the journey would occur so soon—and what's more, under threat of flooding. It's folk with basements I feel sorry for. I know Lord Renyard, of course, but I haven't had the pleasure of being introduced to these others."

Stammering, as I had done originally, I introduced my friends. All, including the Kakatanawa, returned respectful greetings.

"Hmm," declared Mrs. House, turning her smoky eyes towards Oona, "the famous dreamthief's daughter. I heard you were retired."

"So I thought, my lady," said Oona. "But circumstances dictate—"

"Explain no more. Circumstances dictate most of our recent actions. I understand. And you, little girl?" she returned her attention to me. "Did you come by the Staff or the Sword yet?"

"Not yet, madam."

"No blind boy?"

"Almost, but . . ." I shook my head. "I found him, then lost him again."

She sighed. "Time falls away. Falls away. You must try harder."

I found myself smiling. I liked Mrs. House better since she had left Mirenburg. I wasn't sure why. "I'm not sure how."

"My girl, sometimes we must give Fate a nudge in the right direction."

"Do you know the right direction, ma'am?"

"Well, I suppose I do. I have some experience in these matters. I'm not sure I'd say it was *exactly* the right direction. Where are you off to now?"

Most of my party were pretty stunned by this dialogue. I tried to explain a bit more, admitting I didn't have the faintest idea where we were going. After I'd done my best, I added, "So you see, we're escaping from Mirenburg, like you, and have no clear idea where we're going. I'd like to get home, of course, as soon as possible . . ."

"Our gateway was blocked by the flood," Oona told her. "But you think we should have found the Staff there, do you?"

"The Staff preserves itself. That is its essence. If it was in Mirenburg when the flood came, it would not be there now."

The Kakatanawa had seated themselves in a row and were regarding Mrs. House with some respect while Prince Lobkowitz puzzled and Lieutenant Fromental scowled thoughtfully, as if they might, by concentration, come up with a logical explanation for the phenomenon.

From the heights above came the sound of a familiar voice. Turning, we saw the outlines of Herr Klosterheim and Gaynor von Minct, and they had a small army of cutthroats with them. Men with dark olive skins, wide-brimmed hats, bandoliers of cartridges and big boots, so evidently mountain brigands that we did not need to see their brandished pistols and muskets to know who they were. They lined both sides of the valley and had crept closer to us while we talked to Mrs. House.

"You'll note that we have you covered," called Gaynor von Minct in a mocking voice. "It would be unfortunate should you resist us and harm come to the young lady."

"I'm a fool," said Oona through her teeth. She looked from one end of the valley to the other, unable to find decent cover. "I should have guessed they'd find help and return after they saw us on the road."

At a word from her, the Kakatanawa rose and surrounded me. Prince Lobkowitz, Lord Renyard and Lieutenant Fromental laid their hands on their weapons.

"Any bloodshed will be unnecessary." Von Minct and Klosterheim were now astride large horses. They came cantering down the slope towards us.

Oona whispered to me: "You might have a chance if you could get into that—house—somehow. Is that possible?"

Mrs. House's voice spoke softly from behind us. "You might *all* have a chance if you came inside. The door is open. All you have to do is step into me, you know."

For a moment I wondered what the consequences might be.

Then I had backed towards her mouth, her door, and skipped inside. It was cool in her dark hall, but the vivid floral wallpaper was
comforting and it was only a little damp, rather as if I stood in
someone's throat. Quickly the others all tumbled in after me. I
looked to one side and saw another door. A few more steps, and I
was in a pleasantly furnished front parlor. There was richly colored William Morris paper on the walls, big easy chairs with
Victorian floral prints, a lovely old horsehair sofa matching the
chairs, even a potted aspidistra. Carpets were also floral, including that which covered the stairs, disappearing up into comfortable darkness. I was soon joined by Oona, some rather baffled
Indians and my other three friends.

"This is most unusual," said Prince Lobkowitz, walking over
the soft, yielding carpet to part the dark velvet curtains and look
out at our pursuers. They were still standing there. They had
clearly not decided what action, if any, to take. They looked,
every one of them, dumbfounded.

"I rarely have guests these days," said Mrs. House from somewhere. "People have poor manners and can be so destructive. But
I suppose I have little choice in the circumstances. You had best
leave by the back door, as soon as you get the opportunity."

Outside, the brigands were approaching cautiously.
Klosterheim and von Minct stood with pistols in their hands,
looking up at the windows.

Quite suddenly the scene changed subtly. The landscape was
almost identical, but our enemies were no longer there, and the
trees in the copse looked slightly different.

"It has been quite a while since I have done something like
this," said Mrs. House. "I'm afraid you will have to forgive me for
any mistakes." I almost thought I heard her giggle to herself.

The landscape changed again. And again. Trees and shrubs
appeared. Rocks were differently placed. "I have no very clear
idea where I'm going, my dear," came Mrs. House's rather exhilarated voice from the roof. "But it seemed wiser not to wait until
those violent men tried to come in as well. I have always disliked

violence, haven't you? And I never look forward to repainting afterwards."

Once again the scene outside changed.

"She's moving through the multiverse," whispered Prince Lobkowitz. "She's taking us to safety."

"Are we going home, Mrs. House?" I asked.

"We are escaping from danger, my dear," she replied. "I can promise you nothing else for the moment."

"We're grateful," said Oona. "But do you know where we are?"

"I do not move with any direction in mind, I must admit," said Mrs. House. "Just through time and space. As I always do when threatened. But I believe I will bring you a little closer to the blind boy. Or so my seventh sense suggests."

My friends were obviously disappointed, even though they were relieved for the moment to be out of harm's way. "By the back door," Mrs. House reminded us as we prepared to leave. "To be on the safe side. You never know who's watching."

"Is it the back door to the past and by the front to the future?" asked Lieutenant Fromental, with some curiosity.

"Quite often," replied Mrs. House. "Good-bye, all of you. I hope you stay safe and well. Keep looking for the blind boy. He will be expecting you now, dear."

Some of the others were already through the door. "Where shall I look?" I asked.

"Where you've looked before," she said. "Where blind boys work."

At these references to the blind boy, my friends grew alert. Significant looks passed between them. They were at once puzzled and suddenly keyed up.

"I've been trying to tell you," I said.

Prince Lobkowitz made as if to speak to me, then changed his mind. Instead, he uttered a long, deep sigh. He laid a hand on my shoulder.

The sun was setting behind the hills. Large-winged birds as big as cranes sailed against the crimson light. It was getting colder.

There was now a deep, green wood at the back of Mrs. House. Reluctantly I left her strange embrace and stepped out of the door. It creaked as I left, almost a human voice. Cautiously we entered the peaceful gloom of the trees, walking slowly in single file. When I next looked back, Mrs. House was out of sight. She had saved us from our worst enemies, but I felt in my bones she would not be able to help us again.

CHAPTER THIRTEEN

ARKNESS CAME BEFORE Oona decided it was safe to
stop and make camp. Her Kakatanawa still had
plenty of game in their bags, so we ate well before
we were ready to sleep. I curled up with Lord Renyard, who removed his elaborate jacket, waistcoat and shirt and allowed me to
cuddle against his ample red fur. I don't think I've ever known
anything as soft! I slept better than I had since I had first found
myself underground.

We woke in the morning to the smell of a fresh fire and roast-
ing meat. I felt far more relaxed and certain of seeing my mum
and dad again. Lord Renyard's protective paws had kept me safe
and warm, and the soft sound of his breathing had made me feel
almost like a baby. I smiled at everyone and even got responses
from the normally laconic and stern Kakatanawa.

We were camped on a hillside near a freshwater spring bub-
bling out of the ground to form a stream and run over rocks to
join a river in the valley below. The trees were in their first full leaf
of summer, and the whole of the hillside bloomed with blue, yellow, red and purple wildflowers like a brightly colored map. I don't
think I've ever seen so many flowers together in one place. In the
valley were copses of dark green oaks and cedars casting dawn
shadows. The pale blue sky flushed with gold as the sun rose, and
a single large hawk hovered overhead, to the consternation of

thrushes, blackbirds and finches. The place was idyllic, a fairy-land. The sense of security was all-prevailing.

Prince Lobkowitz whistled as he dressed himself. Lieutenant Fromental buttoned up his rather battered uniform jacket and glowed with the pleasure of his cold dip in the river.

"All we need to do now," Oona said, "is to find out where we are and then see if we can discover a town where we can make a fresh orientation."

"We could be anywhere in the multiverse," said Lieutenant Fromental. "Even in a world where humans do not exist at all. We might have to begin our species all over again . . ."

Lord Renyard remarked that this would be rather difficult for him. As it was, he had abandoned one of the best libraries in Europe, with many first editions of the finest Encyclopedists, some personally signed to himself. He was not sure that he could re-member every single word they had written, though he had mem-orized Corneille and several of Voltaire's shorter works. Lieutenant Fromental admitted that Lord Renyard was indeed the best-read gentleman he had ever met. "You would have to tell everything you know to our children!"

"My point . . . ," began Lord Renyard.

Oona interrupted this fantasy, arguing that she would remain faithful to her husband and I was far too young to get married; and in the circumstances we had better not spend the day talking but push on in the hope of finding a human settlement!

So we were soon on our way. I had the privilege, with my short legs, of being carried on the backs of every one of the Kakatanawa as well as the other men, while Oona, with an arrow nocked to her bow, trotted ahead looking for a trail.

She soon picked up a good, metaled road, which suggested we were in the twenty-first century or at least the late twentieth. I began to look forward to civilization again. We rested for lunch not far from the road we hoped would take us to a main thor-oughfare.

Then, just as we were preparing to move on, we heard a roar-ing, clanking and hissing noise so loud it threatened to burst my eardrums. We ran rapidly for the relative safety of the rocks. Over the horizon flew the strangest plane I had ever seen in my life. As it sailed above us, with great wings beating steadily, it threw out a trail of ash and cinders stinking of sulphur, like the old-fashioned steam train my family had taken from Settle to Carlisle on my last birthday. Shaped like an enormous bird with a beak of brass and steel, clashing metallic feathers, enameled green, red and yellow and seemingly about the size of a jumbo jet, its vast wings lifted and fell, creating a downdraft nearly flattening the lot of us!

I caught a glimpse of what might have been the crew. Goggles and masks gave them an equally birdlike appearance. The plane flew low and was lost from sight over the nearby northeastern hills.

"An ornithopter!" declared Lieutenant Fromental in some delight. "Can their power source actually be steam? Such a vessel's never been made to work before. The power-weight ratio problem is thought to be insurmountable. You know Leonardo's designs?"

"It appears to be steam," agreed Prince Lobkowitz. "Eh?" He looked at Oona. "There's only one culture I know of in the multiverse which successfully used steam and ancient science in combination to produce a working ornithopter . . ."

"The Dark Empire," murmured Oona with some concern. "The Empire of Granbretan." She sighed. "We appear to have escaped the frying pan and landed in the fire."

"The Dark Empire?" Lieutenant Fromental was curious; his big, dark eyes looked from face to face. "Grand Bretagne? Britain?"

"In this world," said Prince Lobkowitz, "London—or Londra—is the hub of one of the most evil empires history has ever known."

Lieutenant Fromental said nothing, but a look of peculiar satisfaction crossed his face for a moment.

"So how did they get here?" I asked.

"I think the question is, how did *we* get here?" answered Oona.

"I've never accidentally stepped into this world." Prince

Lobkowitz seemed concerned. "Still, there have been more histories of its particular culture than any others I've come across. Perhaps in this one they have learned the error of their ways."

"We must hope so and make the most of things. That ornithopter does not necessarily mean they actually rule this part of the world. At least we can be fairly certain we're in Europe!" Oona was anxious, I could tell, and trying not to alarm me.

"We have more chances of finding someone who can help us. Remember, the Dark Empire arose after the Tragic Millennium. Before the Tragic Millennium, people had more knowledge than almost any other culture."

"A wisdom King Huon and his sorcerer-scientists perverted," murmured Prince Lobkowitz. "They are a mad, cruel, stupid, unpleasant people. Their sadism is infamous. They have tortured the populations of whole provinces to death. And with refinement, too."

He looked at me and seemed to regret what he had just said.

"Prince!" Lord Renyard glared at him, indicating me. I was worried and fascinated at the same time. I must admit, my stomach had turned over a bit. On the other hand, I don't think I was as scared as they expected me to be. Now I've been through that whole thing, I know what's involved. Then I couldn't imagine what really, really evil people could be like.

That night we kept a low fire and put it out as soon as our food was cooked. We would eat the rest of it cold in the morning, when the Kakatanawa went hunting and scouting.

At dawn the massive clanking, booming, smoke-spewing ornithopter flew over low and took a look at us. We were in open country, with no chance to hide before the flying machine saw us. This time it swooped down and circled before disappearing over the ridge ahead.

We had no choice but to move on. The Kakatanawa were alert, with arrows on their bowstrings. Oona explained that if this was only a scouting craft it would probably not offer any special danger. However, if we had wandered into one of Granbretan's conquered nations, they might see us as a threat to be eliminated.

A little later our questions were answered. We saw two more aircraft soaring into the sky overhead and attacking the first ship we'd seen. Their guns gushed and smeared fire over one another's fuselages. The pilots, protected by transparent canopies, were apparently unhurt and continued to maneuver. The two new planes, with their clanking wings and clattering rotors, were much less maneuverable than the first one, which outflew them, sending shot after shot into their armored hulls until at last one suddenly lurched sideways and descended rapidly towards the ground. Seeing this, the second ship turned and limped away through the sky. The first screamed down to land, with a massive bellow of steam, on the rocky side of the hill and turned over slowly, rolling sideways. Its rotors and wings flopped crazily, finally buckling and coming loose as it fell, metal screeching and groaning, until the whole contraption burst into flame.

The wreck was unapproachable, and Lobkowitz shouted at all of us to get back and get down. We barely made it into a shallow dip in the ground as the thing blew up and fragments of red-hot metal showered around us. Lieutenant Fromental's jacket caught fire but was swiftly put out. There was a faint smell of singed hair. Lord Renyard flicked something away from his foreleg.

Nearby, the victorious machine descended to land. We wondered what the fight had been about. Rather than run, we thought it best to wait and see what would happen. The plane extended hydraulic legs and sank down onto them, for all the world like a settling bird. She stopped her engines and emitted a massive hiss of steam. The canopy slid back, and the crew of heavily suited and masked pilots and gunners climbed out. Once on the ground, they took off their masks and, shading their eyes against the noon sun, stood waiting for us as we approached.

"It's all right, I think," said Prince Lobkowitz. "No Granbretanner would ever take off his mask in public. They seem to be the Dark Empire's enemies."

After a quick discussion, we decided to send Prince Lobkowitz forward. The rest of us watched as the men talked. I breathed a sigh of relief when Prince Lobkowitz and one of the pilots shook hands.

The prince came back smiling. "They are insurgents," he said, "based in Mirenburg. They've driven the Granbretanian armies back beyond München, and hundreds of thousands of mercenaries have come over to them, along with large numbers of recruits from all the conquered territories. Well-trained soldiers." The rebels, he said, had taken control of the factories and were turning out their own improved war machines and weapons in large numbers. Granbretan, fundamentally decadent, was being forced back to her heartlands. The Empire was too used to relying on its superior weapons. When they were met with weapons of equal or better power, they were confounded. They were, however, by no means defeated; they might never be defeated, but at last their conquests had been successfully resisted.

In a German I didn't really understand very well, Prince Lobkowitz and the pilots talked at length. Eventually he said in English, "They want us to come back to Nürnberg and then go on to Mirenburg with them. I think it's our last chance to resume our journey and try to get"—he indicated me—"this young lady reunited with her parents."

So that's why we turned around and began our journey back.

It was, as it turned out, a pretty iffy decision.

We were rather knackered by the time we arrived in their version of Mirenburg. This city was totally different from the one we'd left. It was half-surrounded by huge chimneys belching out smoke, just like the first one, but there were so many more of them! Each chimney was carved in some grotesque representation of humans or beasts or both. The buildings were like something out of a Gothic movie, all weird shapes and sizes, and the streets were full of people in the most bizarre costumes and armor! I had never seen anything like it in a book, game or movie. The colors were mostly dark and rich. Many people rode horses, while others were carried aboard big rail-traveling trams driven by steam and also shaped like various animals. It seemed that no human artifact should be allowed to resemble itself! It was the coolest place I'd ever visited. Better than the best theme park, a mixture of London during the Notting Hill carnival, a big funfair and a fancy dress party. I had the feeling I was enjoying it more than my friends, apart from Lord Renyard, whose long mouth grinned and whose eyes glistened. I held his big paw while he loped along, using his tall dandy cane for support. Some of the people seemed a bit surprised by him, but most gave him no more attention than the rest of our party. Maybe they were used to seeing six-foot-tall foxes in eighteenth-century finery eyeing them through an ornamental quizzing glass.

"I was only aware, mademoiselle, of the *theory* of parallel or 'alternate' worlds," he said as he strolled along. "But this demonstration is incontrovertible, is it not? I must admit that while I miss my home and my library, our expedition is providing me with a considerable amount of intellectual stimulus. I continue, naturally, to be sympathetic to your terrible situation, but find myself fascinated, especially when it occurs to me that this could be a world where the superior species resembled myself, and your own—forgive me—might be considered monstrous, eh?"

I told him that he had been such a kind friend to me that any pleasure he got cheered me up. If I knew that my mum and dad weren't worrying, I'd be enjoying the adventure a lot more myself.

His large, warm pad closed gratefully on my fingers. I realized at that point that we'd become real friends, and I felt rather proud of it. I wished everyone at school could see us together. There wasn't anything much cooler than having a talking animal as your best mate, especially when he was probably the most intelligent person you'd ever known—and a king of thieves to top it all off!

Later we found an inn for the night. I asked if I could share a room with him. No one objected. Oona seemed almost relieved at my choice.

We were greeted as friends by the people of Mirenburg. Their morale was high. They had driven back a force said to be unbeatable. They had word that Dorian Hawkmoon, a local legendary champion against the Dark Empire, was heading their way with an army. They had never before believed they could defeat their conquerors, but now it seemed highly likely they were going to drive them back to the sea and beyond. They had by no means destroyed the threat—they might never entirely destroy it—but they now knew it was possible. They were determined to do their best.

Tomorrow, we were told, we would be granted an audience with Prince Yaroslaf Stredic, who had recently become protector of this city and the province it commanded. He was also chief of their armies. His destiny was to save the whole of Europa from Granbretan and confine the perverted, sorcerous evil empire to her own shores. She would be contained thereafter by the superior arms Mirenburg now possessed.

Meanwhile there was a feast to attend, an affair hastily thrown together by the mayor. I apparently fell asleep halfway through and was carried back to the hotel by Lord Renyard, because I woke up next morning in a beautiful little hand-carved bed with roses painted all over it, and found that the fox was already dressed.

"An important day for us, mademoiselle," he said, handing me a cup of tea. "I have ordered your breakfast. This morning we meet the savior of Mirenburg."

And that was how I found out how this revolution had effectively been started by a red-eyed albino who bore a strong resemblance to the man I knew best as Monsieur Zodiac.

Soon we were back at the palace, seated at a big formal table. There was a bit of a preliminary ceremony while we were greeted officially as friends of the revolt, and then we started this lovely lunch. Most of the ingredients were unfamiliar to me, and some I really didn't like much, but I did my best with it, sticking mostly to salad and hot veggies. I noticed also that most of the Kakatanawa didn't look too happy with the food, which seemed unfair since they had supplied us with so many delicious meals on the trail.

Prince Yaroslaf Stredic, according to tradition, was at the head of the table, and we all sat clustered around him while various other officials and notables spread out along both sides. At the far end of the table, clearly taking an interest in us but refusing to join in any discussion, was a monk. He wore a cassock with a deep hood, and his face was impossible to make out. His broad shoulders could not be disguised by his habit, however. Prince Lobkowitz wondered if he was a renegade from Granbretan, whose people couldn't bear to have their faces exposed.

The prince was a pink, round-headed, good-natured young man with an air of confident power and was full of "Lord Elric's" praises. We learned how they had met, the trick played to get them here, Elric's cleverness, his support for the revolution, the flight of Klosterheim and von Minct, and Elric's following them in the belief that they meant me harm and might lead him to me.

I felt incredibly important when Prince Yaroslaf told me of Elric's concern, of his having the city turned upside down in search of me. We asked if Elric had left a message for us, but of course our coming hadn't been anticipated.

"Clearly," said the prince, "your friend didn't expect you to follow him. He'll regret not having stayed longer, but he has been gone for a year now, at least." He concentrated as he calculated the length of time Elric had been gone. "He is a brave, noble man, if an unusual one. Sorcery has always made me uneasy, I suppose because I associate it with Granbretan."

I wondered what spell the albino had cast that disturbed Prince Yaroslaf, but clearly the Protector of Mirenburg didn't want to discuss it anymore.

Elric had told them nothing of where he was going, Prince Yaroslaf said, but moments before he said farewell, he had mentioned the "moonbeam roads." Everyone in our party knew what this meant. "He has crossed between the worlds, still searching the multiverse for this young lady," murmured Oona a bit doubtfully. "I hope he is careful. He lacks much experience of the roads themselves . . ."

Great! The one man who seemed to have some chance of getting me home had not only disappeared but had put himself in extraordinary danger as well. I did my best to remain positive when I heard this news. I was flattered that so many important people cared about me, but all I really wanted in my heart was to see my mum and dad again and then mooch off down to the stream and mess about looking for crayfish. On my own. With them to go home to. Would I ever see them again? *Don't think about it!* warned my inner voice. I knew it was pointless, but that was the level of depression I got flashes of from time to time.

"Tomorrow," promised the Prince of Wäldenstein, "we will be able to talk more casually." He apologized for the formality and the brevity of our time together. He was delighted that we were comrades of the albino, he said. "That man will go into our history as the hero who began the revolution against the Dark Empire. Without him, none of this could have happened, and we should never have sounded the trumpet call which brought us our other great hero—"

I followed his eyes, and I saw the hooded man shake his head very slightly as Prince Yaroslaf changed the subject. The mysterious lunch guest didn't want to be known to us. I tried to work out why he was so familiar to me. Surely this wasn't another trick of Klosterheim's. But Klosterheim's shoulders were narrow.

I had another thought: Gaynor the Damned?

Once again I was suddenly alert. If there was something going on here, I wanted to know about it. I kept my own counsel, though. I trusted my friends, but I didn't know these new people. I decided to bring the subject up later and see if anyone else had ideas.

"How I long to hear your stories," said the Protector of Mirenburg. "I look forward to learning how you became friends with the albino. He remains a mystery to me. Yet without him—" Again he stopped, as if he felt he was saying too much.

Meanwhile, he added regretfully, they were coping with a fresh counterattack from Granbretan in the region of Lyonne, and he had to oversee the battle plans. "The momentum of this war has been unbelievable. So ill prepared was Granbretan, so careless in not creating defenses against their own latest war machines, that a revolt in one key city set off a chain reaction. Those who had once compromised with the Dark Empire, as Count Brass began by doing, learned to trust nothing they were promised. Almost everyone had lost a loved family member to the savage cruelty of those neurotic masked warriors. They wanted revenge."

After a bit more ceremony at the end of the lunch, I looked down the table and saw that the cowled man had already left.

We returned to our inn, and Oona disappeared into the city. She came back a while later with a little more news of Elric. She had talked with other citizens. "My father was certainly here," she said. "And he seems to have instigated the revolution almost by accident. His chief motive was to find you, Oonagh. They all mention how he constantly asked after you."

"Your father?"

"Didn't I tell you?" she asked.

I hadn't quite put it all together. Of course, there was every chance she and Monsieur Zodiac were related, but I hadn't realized how closely. I was starting to get a dim idea why some people didn't seem as old (or as young) as they ought to be. We were all in danger of meeting grandchildren who looked older than we did! Not that it made complete sense. For instance, if there were millions of possible versions of my world, there were millions of possible versions of myself—or Oona, or Prince Lobkowitz, Klosterheim and, indeed, Elric! Or was that what set us apart from most other people? The fact that we were *not* reproduced on every "plane." Was that why we could move so readily between the worlds, while others couldn't?

I would like to have explored this very different Mirenburg, but everyone else felt it was too dangerous for me to go out on my own. Our inn was called The Nun and Turtle. A very well known place, I was told. I was sure that if we had enemies hiding in the city, they would be bound to know that we had arrived. There was even a chance they were staying at the same inn!

Even when they explained the old folk tale behind The Nun and Turtle's name I didn't understand it any better. But the inn was clean and comfortable, a bit like an English B and B. Eating at communal tables seemed the rule here. We all sat down to supper together in the dining room, and it was then I put my theory about time and the multiverse to Prince Lobkowitz.

"Is that it, Prince?" I asked.

He nodded seriously.

"It's something I've considered myself, Miss Oonagh. It could be that we are somehow separated in time as well as space. The Dark Empire of Granbretan, for instance, probably exists in our distant future. Lord Renyard's Mirenburg seemed to be about two hundred years in your past. We might accidentally be meddling with, or even changing, history, or perhaps we are being changed by it. We know that time is by no means as simple as we were taught it was—neither linear nor cyclic. Some even argue that time is a field, acted on to produce a whole sequence of events occurring coincidentally and thus producing divisions, changing directions, new dimensions. Why does the multiverse have to be in a permanent sense of flux, for instance? What would be gained from a perfect and constant balance between Law and Chaos?" He went on a bit longer and rather lost me, but I understood the general drift.

I was very sleepy, but when, before bedtime, Lord Renyard asked if I wanted to go for a walk, I agreed. He was fascinated by how like his own city the older buildings, the layout of streets and so on, were. However, the differences were what commanded his attention. He found most of it, especially the fashion for creating buildings which looked like grotesque creatures, absolutely vulgar and was relieved that next to a more modern building called The Oranesians, the old cathedral of St. Maria and St. Maria was still standing. We climbed twisting cobbled stairway streets to reach it. Once at the doors of the ancient Gothic church, Lord Renyard took off his hat and bowed his head as if in prayer while I looked around, seeing the whole city spread out below, its huge factory chimneys, with their glaring or tormented faces, like besieging giants.

Mirenburg was clearly on a war footing. The city walls were lined with guns and ornithopters. They squatted on every available flat space, on roofs and in squares. People told us that

Wäldenstein had successfully driven back the Dark Empire and that its armies were now in Franconia and Iberia, trying to drive the Granbretanners back into the sea. Already—to serve a strategy, most suspected—the Empire troops had retreated back across the Silver Bridge that spanned thirty miles of sea, and were now massed in their land stronghold. But the enemy would not give up its empire easily. So far they had not begun to take stock of their old knowledge or set their sorcerer-scientists to work.

Two names, Bous-Junge and Taragorm, were whispered. These were apparently the Empire's greatest sorcerer-scientists, who both studied the old lore and added new.

"This is a dark world, mademoiselle," said Lord Renyard. "Darker, I think, than my own."

"You believe some worlds are darker than others?" I asked. "I mean naturally darker and more evil?"

"I suspect it. Where evil has had longer to take root, in soil more conducive to its growth. Surely only the first universe, the first world, where all the avatars of all our heroes dwell, was innocent. No new worlds begin afresh. They are developments of earlier worlds. So therefore it could be possible that some universes develop a kind of *habit* of evil . . ."

CHAPTER FOURTEEN

HE INTERIOR OF the church was disappointing. Clearly it had been a thousand years or more since Christians had worshipped there. Now it was full of strange pictures and even stranger idols. I began to understand a little of what Lord Renyard said. Neither of us wanted to stay there. We both preferred the building's familiar exterior. As we came back out into the fading sunlight I asked him if he thought this world had developed that habit of evil. It was possible, he said, but he hoped not. The forms people worshipped or used as channels to their own souls were not always what we would regard as beautiful or artistic. "Taste," he said. "I had considered a scholarly discourse on the subject. *Sartor Resartus?*"

"Law and Chaos?" I said. "They're not the same as good and evil, I'm told."

"Merciful heavens, no! Not at all. Not at all. Evil is a cruel and selfish thing. Chaos can be wild and generous, and just as some Lords of Law are self-sacrificing and concerned for others, so are some Lords of Chaos. Did you never hear of Lady Miggea of Law or Lord Arioch of Chaos? Both are selfish and calculating. Both would sacrifice anyone else to their ambition. Yet Armein of Chaos is jolly and openhanded by all accounts, as is Lord Arkyn of Law. They would be friends in other circumstances, I'm sure, those Lords of the Higher Worlds."

"Then why on earth are they at odds?" I asked.

"Their duty demands it. We all serve Fate in some way. We all have loyalties and predispositions. We all have different remedies for the world's pain."

"Do these lords and ladies fight all the time?"

"Some do. Some do not. They do their duty. They are loyal to their cause. Only rarely do you hear of a renegade like Gaynor."

"And does anyone serve these lords and ladies from choice?"

"Certainly. The Knights of the Balance. Born to struggle in perpetual battle."

"Have you met any of these knights?" I was beginning to wonder if Lord Renyard's faith in the so-called Balance, which my mother had talked to me about as well, was as needy as that of the people who had filled St. Maria and St. Maria with such hideous idols.

"I believe I have met some. I believe you have, also."

"My grandmother? Can women . . . ?"

"Absolutely. There are many great champions, I hear, who are women. There are some who are androgynous. All colors and tastes." He uttered that strange, barking laugh. "Your grandmother, Oona, is a quasi-immortal. Her blood, of course, is that of champions."

"But she isn't a champion herself?"

"I do not know, and it is not my place, dear mademoiselle, to speculate. Her father, who calls himself Count Zodiac—"

"Which would make him my great-grandfather. He seems immortal."

"By no means. Only in his dreams, from what my friend Lobkowitz tells me!"

"Is Prince Lobkowitz a champion? Lieutenant Fromental?"

"They carry the wisdom which sometimes helps a champion. Or so I'm told. Companions of the Order, perhaps? Like their friend and, I hope, mine, the Chevalier St. Odhran. But Colonel Bastable is almost certainly a knight, as well as a member of the League of Temporal Adventurers."

"And what's Gaynor, then?"

"Like Klosterheim, Gaynor allowed his selfish greed and

egomania to possess his whole being. Both once served nobler causes. Both renounced those causes. You know, my dear, that I am a rationalist. I am of the Enlightenment. It is my whole being. Much of what you are asking should best be asked of Lobkowitz himself. Or your grandmother!"

I knew I was pestering him as we walked back down the steps. It was dusk and he wanted to get back to the inn. He had my hand in his paw as we hurried along. But I had a lot of questions. "Herr Klosterheim was once a Companion of that Order?"

"Yes, but not loyal to Chaos or Law. Now he embraces Evil, which is a much lesser thing. A petty thing, though dangerous and often powerful. Yet I suspect that he, if not Gaynor, serves the purposes of Law while not necessarily sharing its ideals."

"I heard someone mention the Lords of Hell, the Lords of Entropy. Who are they?"

"Names, nothing else. Lords, like Arioch, who are greedy and cruel, are sometimes called the Dukes of Hell by humans, but they are a miscellaneous crew. Lady Miggea, though she be a corrupted servant of Law, is called by many who have confronted her a Duchess of Hell. And some of the great elementals are also mistakenly identified with Lucifer."

"So does Lucifer exist?" I asked.

Lord Renyard looked troubled at this. "We no longer know," he said.

The shadows were gathering. We had walked further than we realized, and it was a long way back.

"So who's the most powerful?" I wanted to know. "Law or Chaos?"

"Neither," he said after a little thought.

"Okay. Then what single quality do you associate with them?"

Perhaps to keep his mind off the potential dangers of the city at night, Lord Renyard gave my question some thought. At last he answered, "Love is one."

"And the other?"

"Greed."

We had taken a wrong turn. Lord Renyard paused as we came

out of an alley. Across from us was an old bridge. We were down where the river made a radical curve. Lord Renyard set out for the bridge.

"But the inn's on this side," I said.

"It will be quicker if we take this bridge, cross through the old factory quarter, and then cross again. A shortcut."

"How could you get lost in your own city, Lord Renyard?" We were both becoming nervous.

"I thought I recognized landmarks, streets. I was wrong. I do apologize, dear mademoiselle. Sometimes I wish I were a mere fox and used my nose a little better."

"Why don't you?"

"Snobbery. I used to think such means uncivilized. I think I'm a little wiser now. Too late, you might say."

He was right about the shortcut. We were hardly in the industrial part of the city for a few minutes before he spotted another bridge. Below it and to the left and right along the embankment, presumably for the factory workers, was some sort of recreation park, with a menagerie and sideshows. I love fairs and carnivals, though I find it hard to enjoy old-fashioned circuses. There were even a few mechanical rides. A big Ferris wheel but no roller coasters, and some really funky steam-operated bumper cars made in the form of wild animals. A sinister-looking helter-skelter stood beside an oddly fashioned merry-go-round, whose riding beasts were totally fantastic and like nothing I'd ever seen. We had to traverse the park to reach the bridge. I didn't complain. I knew I couldn't ask to take some rides, but it was hard to pass them *all* by. The Ferris wheel overlooked the river and turned slowly to the music of a distant steam organ. It reminded me of the London Wheel, which I'd already ridden several times. If we were here for a while, I'd definitely ask someone to take me. But it wasn't fair to ask Lord Renyard, who clearly found it very distasteful.

More and more people came into the park, cackling and grinning and laughing themselves silly. Evidently they came to enjoy themselves after work. Dressed in their best finery, they looked as strange to me in those odd clothes as I did to them. The park's lights had come on. The gas jets spread a warm, yellow aura.

Suddenly I thought I saw Monsieur Zodiac disappearing into one of the sideshows. I remembered he had worked in the theater in England. Maybe he hadn't left Mirenburg, after all. Maybe he had been waiting for me.

With a quick word to a startled Lord Renyard, I broke free of his protective paw and ran into the booth. Pushing past the grubby white flap, I found myself in the gloom of the tent's interior.

I saw someone ahead of me. Someone with long white hair who could be Monsieur Zodiac, though he seemed too short as I got closer.

I called out, "Monsieur Zodiac, is that you?"

The figure looked up, as if he heard me. Then he was gone again. But there was a strangeness about his stance which alarmed me. Was it the blind boy? I became suddenly frightened, and when I heard Lord Renyard calling my name I went outside again and found him. The last thing in the world I wanted to do was worry that kindly beast. He was greatly relieved to see me and begged me not to do that again, especially in the dark park. I told him what I'd seen.

"Could Monsieur Zodiac only have pretended to have left, to confuse Klosterheim and Gaynor, maybe?"

Lord Renyard fingered his long muzzle. "I did not think he was in this realm. He traveled on, across the moonbeam roads. I thought his business was . . . elsewhere. Yet Fate could have sent him here as readily as we were sent. But would he not have sought us out by now?"

"Only if he knew we were here. Maybe he didn't want to be spotted."

"We are not close acquaintances, my dear girl. I know of him, of course. But our meeting was only brief and underground."

"He would have known me if he'd seen me. He's looking for me."

"But you are rather small, mademoiselle, if I may say so."

"Well, you're not likely to blend in with the crowd," I pointed out. "He'd surely have remembered you."

It was now completely dark. Flares and lamps were burning orange-yellow against the night. Lord Renyard grew agitated, his long whiskers quivering.

"We must hurry," he said. It was hard for him to tug me. "We must rejoin the others." He led me back through the thick press of the evening. There was a peculiar vibrancy to the busy crowd as we made our way to The Nun and Turtle. Lord Renyard sensed it, too. He had noted how, in wartime, people were inclined to make the most of their leisure. He might even call it a kind of madness, a lust for life and its pleasures because they could be taken away forever at any moment. The atmosphere actually made me slightly uncomfortable. I was glad to get into the warmth and relative peace of the Nun, where old Herr Morhaim busily took orders for supper, apologizing in his thick Turkish accent that his menu was limited somewhat by the exigencies of war.

For all that, we ate very well. We had another audience scheduled with Prince Yaroslaf the next day. We hoped he would allow us to remain in the city and pursue our own quest. We were a little afraid he might decide to enlist us for the war effort.

I had a lot on my mind and was surprised I slept soundly and peacefully. Once again my friends had thrown a great invisible shield around me. Lord Renyard came to his bed at some point. He didn't wake me in the process. Then, in the early part of the morning, I had some alarming dreams which did wake me. I'd seen the white-haired man again, only this time he wasn't a man but the youth who looked so much like my great-grandfather, and he smiled, beckoning me towards him. I wasn't frightened by the boy, but I was suddenly filled with a sense of dread—a sense that he was in great danger and that only I could save him. Then I felt both Lord Renyard and Oona standing nearby.

The dream faded. It was dawn. I could see Lord Renyard fast asleep, his long legs sticking off his bed at an angle. Observing him more closely, I realized he was sleeping perfectly comfortably, like a large dog. He had drawn the quilt over him for the sake of propriety. His clothes were all neatly folded or hung on hangers near him, and his dandy pole lay alongside the bed. Very occasionally he snored and his whiskers twitched. Affection for him welled up in me to see him there, so vulnerable and peaceful.

Though the fox's presence was reassuring, I could not go back to sleep.

I saw that someone had left a set of clean clothes for me. This was luxury. I got out of bed and went along the passage to the bathroom to use it first. I pulled the cord which would bring up a maid with some hot water, and though the water was cool by the time it arrived, I had a delicious and uninterrupted bath. I got into my fresh clothes and went down to breakfast on my own. I knew we had to be ready to meet the protector at his palace, and I felt an obscure pride in not having to be hassled along, as usually happened at home when we were going out early for some reason.

I had the satisfaction of seeing the look of surprise on Oona's face when she came down. She laughed. "I was giving you a few more minutes. I thought you were still in bed. Did you sleep well?"

"Mostly," I said.

Our carriages arrived while we were still eating. We tried to hurry, straightened ourselves as best we could and got into the waiting four-wheelers, which set off at a clip over the cobbled streets, threatening to bounce the life out of us.

It was the kind of grey, drizzling morning for which I'd always had a perverse taste. I enjoyed the ride through streets now packed with vendors and soldiers. The soldiers had the grim, staring look you saw on the news where they showed people who had been fighting too long in places like the Middle East. Quite a lot wore the masks and goggles of airmen, while others carried huge, thick-hafted, platinum-tipped flame lances on their armored shoulders. A few wore the baroque animal armor identified with the clans and societies of Granbretan. It felt very odd for your own country to be the enemy; it was hard to get my head around the idea. I'm not saying Britain always behaved herself properly, and I knew a fair bit about empire, but these people seemed to have come up with the ideas and methods of Adolf Hitler combined with the imperial instincts of Cecil Rhodes.

I shared a carriage with Lord Renyard, Prince Lobkowitz and Lieutenant Fromental. Oona followed with some of her Kakatanawa, who, of course, hadn't been able to fit into one carriage. My companions weren't very talkative this morning. They explained the normal protocol for visiting Mirenburg's royal leader at an audience rather than at a meal. It was quite different, they said, to how one would behave, for instance, in the presence of the perhaps now drowned Sebastocrater.

"Possibly more formal," said Prince Lobkowitz. "New states set high store by such things, as do new statesmen." He had already approved of my dress, which was very nice, given that I hadn't even shopped for it. In the carriage I worked on the hairdo Oona had tried to give me on the run. I thought I looked pretty good, all in all. Not that I usually cared.

The carriages moved up a wide avenue to what Oona called the Krasnya Palace, although the drivers called it something else. It was much fancier than the Mirenburg I'd left. The palace had a French rather than a classical style and reminded me of Versailles.

We left the carriages and ascended the wide steps up to the front doors, which were guarded on both sides by women in very bulky armor, with flame lances held at the slant. Next we were greeted by an elaborately dressed majordomo with a magnificent black beard shot with grey, who asked us to follow him through the marble corridors, past freshly painted walls. The entire place had been elaborately redecorated from top to bottom. It smelled of paint throughout. The predominant color was now vivid green. Most vivid of all were the curtains, drawn back from the long windows, but the trim on the wood was a pretty violent green, too.

Door after door opened, was entered, then closed behind us until we stood in a small throne room filled with people. Sitting on the white alabaster throne itself was the nice-looking gentleman who had entertained us to lunch the day before. He had the same straightforward, almost naive manner, and we got the impression again of an honest man of action. He had been elected to his position of protector, but apparently the right was his by blood. He rose from his throne and came down the steps to greet us, standing on the lowest step while the majordomo introduced us one by one. He had the most trouble with getting his tongue around the Kakatanawa names and in the end resorted to letting them introduce themselves, which they did with all the grace and style of born diplomats.

"Good morning to you, honored visitors," he said. "We are especially glad to greet gentlemen from far Amarahk, who do not disappoint us, for our legends say the Amarahki were great warriors and handsome people." He spoke in a low, respectful tone.

It was an odd understanding of America, but I rather liked it. I realized there had been a time, and possibly was still a time somewhere in the multiverse, when Native Americans governed their own country. He seemed to have the idea that we were all from America, and nobody told him otherwise. He might as well think we were from there as from anywhere. In this "brane" or "realm" of the multiverse America had not been colonized by Europeans except in certain isolated places.

"Any friends of the great Lord Elric, of course, are friends of ours. You already know this, and I am again glad to welcome you here." He had climbed a few stairs and now sat down again. "He alone is responsible for what was begun here."

"It is a shame he left no forwarding address," said Lieutenant Fromental rather sardonically, without insulting the young protector.

"I agree," said Prince Yaroslaf. "But he had already done so much for us, I could ask him no more. It seemed clear to me that he did not wish to tell us where he went, save to find the 'moonbeam roads' he spoke about."

The conversation lost me after that, but the others seemed to be getting something out of it. In the end I gave up listening and decided to enjoy myself as best I could. About the only interesting bit was when we were shown a display of captured armor and weapons from Granbretan. It really was weird stuff, especially the mantis armor of King Huon's guard, which looked as if a whole lot of giant insects had been wiped out. At some point refreshments were brought in, and I had the best glass of lemonade I'd ever tasted. Yet I still couldn't help thinking of the white-skinned boy I'd seen. I really wanted to get back to the fairgrounds and find him. I wondered if, later on, I could persuade Lord Renyard to help me.

Meanwhile I continued to find Prince Yaroslaf's formal court rather funny. In their padded clothes they were like a hall full of Renaissance Michelin Men. I knew it was wrong to laugh, but it was hard to keep from giggling sometimes. These people were fighting for life and freedom against a terrible evil, and all I could do was laugh! I decided I must be shallow. And this made me even more amused. The guiltier I felt, the more I wanted to giggle. In the end I asked a footman where to find the bathroom. This turned out to be a sort of inverted pyramid in the floor. At least I didn't really need it. Once inside, I almost exploded with laughter, giggling myself silly.

The door had a kind of grille in it so that people inside could see if someone was waiting outside, without anyone being able to see in. After about ten minutes I was all right. I put my eye to the grille and watched the people coming and going along the passage. No one needed the toilet, so I relaxed and collected myself. The next time I looked through the grille, however, I got a shock.

Passing the door, as bold as brass, was Herr Klosterheim! So the man in the cowl *had* been Gaynor! I was totally astonished and almost fell backwards. When I peered out through the grille again he had, of course, gone.

For a while I was too terrified to leave. Yet I knew I had to warn my friends. Was Klosterheim in league with Prince Yaroslaf? I had no way of knowing. And now I felt sick with anxiety.

Eventually I pulled myself together, left the bathroom, and hurried to look for one of my companions.

Fortunately Oona found me before I found her. She, too, seemed scared, and I had another reason to feel guilty.

"I'm really sorry," I said. "But I've got something important to tell you. If I hadn't gone to the bathroom, I'd never have found it out." I was panting. "I saw Herr Klosterheim and had to wait until he was gone. Then—"

"We thought you'd been kidnapped," she said. Then she paused. "What? You've seen Klosterheim? Where?"

"In the hall. Passing the bathroom," I told her. "In that corridor. Back there. He didn't know I saw him. Did you know he had followed us?"

"The prince thinks they left with Elric following *them*. What can this mean? My guess is that they're working for the Empire and don't even know we're here. Yet Prince Yaroslaf knows them both. He knows they are probably his enemies. Why hasn't he had them arrested?"

"Perhaps he's playing a more complex game than we think," I said, feeling a total idiot.

She nodded absently. "The sooner we get out of here, the better."

Since the reception was in our honor, it was some time before we were able to leave. Our carriages hurried through the late-morning streets of Mirenburg. I was hungry, as I hadn't even had much chance to look at the buffet. That lemonade had improved my expectations of Wäldensteiner food.

Back at the inn my friends conferred. One of us must find out if von Minct was here and if he and Klosterheim had the confidence of the protector, who had declared that Elric was his enemy. We feared, of course, a repetition of the events in that other Mirenburg.

"And repetition," said Prince Lobkowitz, "is very much a norm in the multiverse. It's a sign of order, as in music. Our lives, personalities and stories all tend to repeat themselves, as do the composition and arrangements of the stars and planets."

"Surely such repetition is the natural state of Law," suggested Lord Renyard.

"And the antithesis of Chaos?" said Lieutenant Fromental.

"So does Klosterheim serve Law or Chaos now?" I asked.

"In truth, he makes the alliances which suit him, but he and von Minct tend towards a corrupted form of Law," answered Oona.

I still couldn't see why those two would have anything to do with me. As far as I knew, I had no understanding, affiliation or interest in Law, Chaos or anything else supernatural. All I wanted was to get home and be able to tell my mum and dad about my adventures. I was pretty sure that was all Oona wanted for me, too.

"We need to get in touch with the man who essentially got this whole war going," said Prince Lobkowitz. "Hawkmoon and his people recently retook Kamarg, as you have heard. We should contact him. He is a manifestation of the Champion Eternal, a seasoned Knight of the Balance, who understands the nature of the multiverse rather better than most. Hawkmoon is bound to know a scientist who can help us."

"Are they still in Kamarg?"

"I assume so. But his army moves with supernatural speed."

"How far is it?" asked Oona.

"We should have to cross a fair bit of Europe," said Prince Lobkowitz. "Parts of which are still at war, as we have seen. Our journey would take us across the Switzer mountains, which are full of bandits, or via Italia and Frankonia. A dangerous path, for which we should need a guide, I think." Prince Lobkowitz was shaking his head. "Even if we were loaned enough ornithopters to fly us there—and we know they have none to spare—it would be a long journey."

"Is there no other alternative?" asked Lord Renyard. I had the feeling he didn't want to leave Mirenburg, however different it was from his own city.

"There is only one solution which makes sense," said Lieutenant Fromental after a while. "Some of us must go to Kamarg by land, and the rest must take the young lady there by air."

I didn't want us to separate, but I *did* fancy the idea of having a ride in one of those weird planes, so before anyone else could say anything I cried: "I like the idea!"

"I'm not sure . . . ," began Oona.

"It would get me to safety quicker, wouldn't it?" I said. "And Mr. Klosterheim and Mr. von Minct would be less able to follow."

"You speak sense, I think, little mademoiselle." Lord Renyard put his two red-furred paws on the table to emphasize his assent.

"But what if you did not see Klosterheim?" said Oona. "What if you only saw someone who resembled him?"

"Then who was that monk at lunch yesterday? I'm pretty sure it was Gaynor."

"I saw him, too," she admitted. "But I didn't assume it was Gaynor. Hmmm . . ." She sighed. "We must wait," she said, almost to herself. "We must wait."

"Oh, please!" I lost my cool altogether. "*Why?*"

"No spare flying machines, for a start," she said. "Our best hope would be to get you and someone else onto an ornithopter already bound for Kamarg."

"We haven't time to see how the war goes," said Prince Lobkowitz. "I've talked to people here. They say there are still battlecraft in the area. The Dark Empire makes raids. They've been driven out, but they're not defeated. There's every possibility of a flying machine being attacked. It would be too risky."

"But my mum and dad will be worrying," I said. "I don't want to miss a chance of getting home."

"I understand." She looked so worried, I felt sorry for her. "Traveling to Kamarg, however, won't necessarily get you all reunited sooner. It would just be a chance that Duke Dorian or one of his people could help. If, for instance, they have the crystal which gives them access to other dimensions, they could offer us real protection. While I can travel the moonbeam roads, I need to find a route through before I can try to find Elric or a way to your home that's reasonably safe. If Mirenburg hadn't been flooded by that fool's spell . . ."

"I know you will do whatever you can," I told her. "But if there's *any* way of getting home . . ." I was repeating myself and stopped.

"Hawkmoon has his own concerns," she said. "He won't sacrifice them for our interests. Only if those interests coincide with his duty. Like us, he has enemies all around him. We have to stick together. Watch one another's backs. That's how we'll survive until we get that chance you want." Suddenly, affectionately, she had reached out to me. I realized how carefully she was guarding her emotions. I knew then how much she loved me. I knew she had to be my mother's mother, no matter how impossible it seemed. I so badly wanted to ask her how she had kept so young, but I knew it wasn't the time.

My emotions began to roller-coaster again. I forced myself to calm down. I felt suddenly better. Now all I could do was enter the safety of my grandmother's embrace.

CHAPTER FIFTEEN

EXT DAY I sat in my room trying to make conversation with Lieutenant Fromental, who had obviously been left on guard in case Klosterheim came looking for me. By now none of us was completely sure I had actually seen him.

Fromental was a kind, gentle giant who took his job seriously, but he wasn't very good company. He knew a lot about French comics and American thrillers, especially the Jack Hammer mysteries, but we had almost nothing in common. We didn't even like the same movies. He had been in the French Foreign Legion and had wandered into Mu-Ooria years ago while exploring in Morocco. There he'd met Prince Lobkowitz, but he didn't like to talk of their adventures fighting what they called "the Lost Nazis." I needed something to take my mind off everything, like a trip to the pictures. How *did* these people relax? I wasn't as much worried about Klosterheim as they were. I was thinking of those pleasure gardens, wishing they had TV in this weird world and consoling myself that it would probably be totally weird TV anyway. There wasn't even a book I could read. Some of them seemed to be written in English, but the spelling was all different, and I didn't understand a lot of the words. I tried translating, with Lieutenant Fromental's help, but he was puzzled, too. He thought some of the language was more like French than English. Even the books with pictures didn't make much sense, so I asked Lieutenant

Fromental if he felt like going to the fair. He was very serious when he apologized, spreading his huge hands.

"Little mademoiselle, we have to be sure no harm befalls you. If Klosterheim is in the city, you are in considerable danger. Considerable danger. I cannot impress on you enough how much danger . . ."

"I understand," I said. "It's dangerous. I know." The problem was that the dreams were beginning to fade again. I knew I couldn't put myself in peril and frighten my friends, and I wasn't about to let boredom get to me, but I was also thinking of the person I'd seen in the tent who so resembled both the missing Monsieur Zodiac and the blind boy, Onric.

Another day dragged slowly by. And another. I waited eagerly for news of the war, hoping someone would tell us it was over. Everyone else went out whenever they wished. Once a week the whole Kakatanawa troop stayed with me. They had a game with beads and a large hollowed-out piece of wood which one of them told me was called the "canoe," and I became obsessed with playing it for a while.

My friends had begun to think I had made a mistake about seeing Klosterheim in the palace. Prince Yaroslaf had clearly not invited him to court. The prince remained adamant that he considered Klosterheim and von Minct enemies, who would serve themselves at every turn and serve the Dark Empire if it suited them. They had been seen elsewhere, however. One report placed them in Kamarg itself, fleeing shortly before Hawkmoon's army retook the province. Another put them on the northern coast.

I think I eventually wore Oona down. She finally came to the conclusion that Klosterheim and von Minct had moved on, if indeed they had been here at all. I didn't get my ornithopter ride, but she did allow me to go to the fairgrounds as long as all the Kakatanawa and Lord Renyard went with me. It was better than sitting inside.

Thus, in the company of twelve Americans and a gigantic

fox, I found the tent where I had seen the boy, only this time I went in the front entrance. Bright yellow and black displays announced something translated into English, I assumed, as a "Cornucopia of Thespian Skills." Lord Renyard paid for all our entrance tickets. None of us could read the rest of the sign, which was in a language about as far removed from the English I understood as Chaucer's, but we were all pretty sure it *was* English. It reminded me that I was still puzzled about how people, admittedly with some very strange accents, seemed to know a more or less common language. Lord Renyard said it was the lingua franca of the multiverse, which, through a series of very peculiar circumstances, was spoken by people who could walk between the worlds.

Under the canvas, a medium-size pit had been dug into the ground. It was surrounded by long benches, and an old man was standing in the pit, telling a story whose point I missed entirely.

I waited patiently, hoping that the albino boy would be next to perform, but the old man was replaced by actors wearing animal masks and doing something called *Adalf and Eeva*, which made no sense at all. Lord Renyard, who seemed pretty bored, said they reminded him of Greek players. The scene went on for hours, it seemed to me, and in the end we had to leave. I didn't see the boy anywhere. By the time Oona turned up to take us home I was actually looking forward to getting back to the Nun and Turtle.

Oona laughed at my expression and comforted me by saying how she and Prince Lobkowitz had been trying all day to find a way underground. She was now pretty certain this version of the city didn't have a mirror image, and she had decided that it was time for us to move on. In München, Barkelon or Parye, she said, we might have better luck. But not here.

Everyone seemed a bit down. All of us there preferred action of almost any kind to no action at all. As we left the tent we found ourselves surrounded again by revelers in fanciful costumes dancing in a long line, their hands on the waist of the person ahead of them. People were laughing and singing, and some staggered a bit.

We stuck together but couldn't avoid getting caught up in the cheerful crowd enjoying the ritual dance.

And then, as we danced by a gap in the tents, I at last spotted the albino boy again: a young man with glittering red eyes staring straight out of hell and straight into mine. I tried to wrench myself free of the crowd and wave to him. I had a clear view of his face this time, and though they were clearly related, it was not Monsieur Zodiac. It was Onric!

I wriggled out of the mob and ran back to the tent to find him. All of my friends were shouting and following, but the youth had disappeared. I stopped running to let everyone catch up with me. But before they could do so, a figure wearing a papier-mâché Red Riding Hood wolf mask darted from the crowd and grabbed me. I don't think the black-clad man had any idea how strong I was as I kicked and bit him, clawing for his eyes and dislodging the mask to reveal the cadaverous face of Herr Klosterheim.

I had been right! I felt triumphant even as he tried to drag me away and Oona, Lord Renyard and the Kakatanawa converged on him. Uingasta, one of the Americans, got hold of Klosterheim, who had dropped me, but the man, abandoning his mask, slipped free and ran off into the crowd, pursued by everyone but Lord Renyard and me.

The dancing people seemed entranced as they re-formed their ranks and danced on, as the Kakatanawa and Oona straggled back, disappointed.

"So I wasn't barmy, see?" I declared.

"You weren't barmy, dear, that's true." Oona was out of breath. She kept her bow strung and an arrow nocked on it. "We've got to get you out of the city. He knows you're here. He's been waiting his chance. I'm sure he's told von Minct, and one of them is sure to try this again. We can guard against *him*, of course. But what about those others? Klosterheim is bound to resort to supernatural aid at any moment, as soon as he can, and that will endanger the city and all of us—including what the city represents to those who oppose Granbretan." She spoke in low, urgent tones. "We'll leave as soon as we can. Come on. Let's get back to the inn."

I couldn't work out why she was reacting like this. Had she never believed Klosterheim was here? Had she been humoring me? Perhaps she thought Klosterheim had lost the power to travel through the realms. Perhaps his desperate attempt to kidnap me indicated that something else was going on, that our enemies were becoming more desperate and therefore more dangerous.

Next morning we put our affairs in order and, with help from the palace, slipped out of The Nun and Turtle, through a private gate in the city, taking the München road. Oona and Prince Lobkowitz had tried to get the use of some ornithopters, but none were available. Though they were producing new machines all the time, those factories were having to be moved and, wherever possible, hidden. They were the main target for any squadron the Dark Empire sent over. There was some chance Granbretan would be trying again to destroy the factories, perhaps in the next night or two, so we accepted his need and made other arrangements. Prince Yaroslaf, respecting our danger, sent some of his best guards with us. He did everything he could to accommodate us.

Oona and the Indians rode in carriages, because the Indians didn't know much about horses. I sat inside with her part of the time, and the rest I had a pony I could ride, so long as I remained close to Prince Lobkowitz or Lieutenant Fromental. Lord Renyard, of course, also rode in the coaches.

While seated in the carriage with Oona I told her what I'd been thinking about the desperation of our enemies. She leaned over from the seat across from me and rumpled my hair. "You're a smart young lady. Our enemies grow increasingly less subtle. That means there's a clock ticking somewhere for them. You're right; they're losing time and patience and becoming more dangerous."

"And yet you still have no idea what they want me for?"

"I'm getting a bit of an idea, but nothing too clear yet." My grandma's ivory beauty continued to amaze me. She was like one of those stunning 1920s figurines fashioned in ivory and bronze. At night her skin had a faint, pale glow, and her red eyes carried an expression not entirely different from her father's when he seemed troubled. In the light of early morning she was like a Greek statue come to life.

"I wonder where he is." I spoke without thinking. "Your father—Monsieur Zodiac?"

"Elric? I fear he might be lost, or that people might even be deliberately misdirecting him. Somewhere in his own world where he was born, he's suffering horribly. He's the prisoner of a cruel enemy who would bring the unchecked reign of Chaos down upon them all. He has seen Chaos in all its aggressive variety, and he fights it, though he is also dependent upon it for his very life. Should he be killed in this, his dream, then he dies in his own world, too. Every action he or his enemies take in one realm, he takes in a million others, save that these selves, as substantial as you or me, are the creation of a particularly powerful form of dreaming. Every other world but his own is a dream to him. He hangs, dreaming even now, on the yardarm of a ship, desperate for that one thing which sustains him, which will free him."

"Which is?"

"A sword," said my grandmother with weary bitterness. "It has taken him a thousand years to earn that blade. And now, to save us, he risks everything, when salvation for him could be hours or days away." And she fell into such a silence that I couldn't bring myself to ask her another question.

Later she began talking again. Elric, she said, was clearly her father, as I'd guessed, and not just an average multiversal adventurer! His destiny was somehow linked to the destiny of every world he had touched in his thousand-year search for his sword. There was some trouble with the carriage, and we had to get out while someone saw to it. We were still less than half a mile from the city, and the walls remained in sight. Prince Lobkowitz brought up a pony for me to ride.

"What's so special about my great-granddad's sword?" I asked him.

He looked at me in complete bafflement. "Elric's sword? Aha! The Black Sword. There is an aspect of it in every world I know, yet the sword itself, capable of generating hundreds of versions of itself, is elusive. Without it, our work can never be completed. Elric's destiny in this complex equation is to use the sword to bring a halt to a multiversal phenomenon which has grown out of control."

"Which is . . . ?" My persistence made him smile. He guessed that this was all Oona would tell me.

"She knows how important it is for Elric to reach the end of his thousand-year dream with that sword in his hand. That has been the whole point of his dream. Yet so strong are his feelings for those he regards as his descendants, that he is risking his own chance of salvation. A noble thing to do, but in the scheme of things, it is a very dangerous thing to do, putting many at risk. He does not, of course, know what he risks, save his own life and soul. Yet you are also important to him because you are his great-granddaughter, and Klosterheim and von Minct and those they represent would gain a great deal from diverting Elric and capturing you. I am beginning to guess that they deliberately led the albino on a wild-goose chase while going back to Mirenburg, perhaps knowing you would return. Yet," he mused, "you also have something they desire. As has that boy."

"So von Minct was the cowled man at the table?"

"We could presume so. But remember, there are many players in this game, and not all of them are fulfilling the roles they seem to have been assigned . . ." He laughed rather bitterly.

The carriage fixed, we were off again. My pony was used to a different kind of handling, I think. Every country has slightly modified habits of riding, so the pony and I took a while to adapt to each other. Still it was a pleasure to be riding again, even if there was no chance of a gallop or even a canter. We had to stick close together, said Prince Lobkowitz, especially at the moment. If we needed to scatter, then we could enjoy a gallop!

I think von Minct realized too late that we were leaving. Behind us I saw a single cowled figure which ran frantically in our wake before abandoning the chase. We had escaped the city just in time.

For the first fifty miles or so Prince Yaroslaf's guards accompanied us until we were well into the mountains and on our way to München. This whole country, they said, had been taken from the Granbretanners, who were still making attacks on Mirenburg's factories from bases on Jarsee and elsewhere. Sometimes nonmilitary parties would be attacked or bombed just because the enemy ornithopters failed to reach their targets and preferred to lighten their machines before returning home. Also some defeated groups of Dark Empire soldiers and their supporters lived now as bandits, preying on anyone who looked weak enough to attack safely.

I had asked Oona why we were taking these risks, but she had been too busy to answer. Now I had no opportunity. She assured me that we should be safe enough when we arrived in München in two or three days' time. The ancient city had sustained some damage in the fierce fight to free her, but her old spirit of defiance lived on.

During one of the spells I spent in the carriage we rode by towns which were in ruins, some from the recent battles and some from earlier conquests of the Dark Empire, whose policy was to attack from the air, killing anything that moved before landing its troops. I had only ever looked at scenes like these on the TV. And then it had always been our side making most of the ruins, and I'd felt differently about it—often angry, sometimes guilty, but not like this. This was a feeling of furious frustration and a deep hatred of the cowardly people who did this, flying out of the clouds to bring destruction to whole families. You could still smell the smoke and ash. There was something stale and disgusting about the way it clogged up your nostrils and lay on your skin. Oona put a scarf up to her mouth as we passed through a valley where the country people were doing their best to rebuild their villages, putting up frames and walls, reslating their roofs. They waved to us as we went by, and appeared cheerful under the circumstances. They obviously assumed we were a war party, and cheered us on, urging us to give back to the Dark Empire the hell they had experienced themselves.

Once or twice an ornithopter bearing the black and red roundels of those opposing the Dark Empire flew low to take a look at us, but we flew the same banner on a long spear carried by Shatadaka, another of the American warriors. The ornithopters would rise, their pilots waving to us, and go on about their business. We were careful, however, not to wave our flag until we saw the aircraft's markings first.

When a machine bearing no markings passed overhead, we felt sure it was an Empire ship. It flapped down to identify us, then soared up again, rotors roaring, and disappeared, heading for Mirenburg. I could tell Oona was alarmed by the way she tensed in the carriage and called for one of the spare horses. I think she felt more in control when mounted.

We made camp that night in a wood near the road. Oona posted extra guards and would not let me move a foot from her. To be honest, I didn't much feel like moving. I slept, as before, curled up beside Lord Renyard's soft red chest.

In the morning we hurriedly saddled our horses, hardly stopping for breakfast. The Kakatanawa had become better at handling the carriages and harnessed them in no time. Oona was suddenly in a great hurry to get to our destination. We ate lunch on the move in the carriage: bread and sausage with some water from a nearby stream. Emerging from a sweet-smelling pine forest, we rode beside a small lake rimmed by hills and distant mountains. Again there were flowers everywhere, though not the same as I'd seen earlier. I tried again to ask Oona about the albino boy. Did she know who he was?

"I'd like to talk to him as much as you would," she said rather noncommittally.

"Do you think you might be related?"

"It's entirely possible." She grinned. "Since you say we're so alike. And it's obvious I'm my father's daughter. I do, after all, have a long-lost twin." Then her mood changed rapidly, and she fell into that frowning silence again, staring out of the window at the faraway peaks. At the next break, I switched again from the carriage to the pony.

The country, though bearing terrible scars, was absolutely beautiful. Occasionally I spotted a tower, and sometimes an entire castle, among the trees and rocks. One stood on the very edge of the lake, completely desolate. Like so much of the ruin Granbretan left behind her, it was a monument to the evil which had destroyed it.

I wondered if there were people in Granbretan who hated what their own country was doing. You heard a lot about the evil ones but not much about the good ones.

"That's because there are so few good ones left," Prince Lobkowitz told me. "That culture has bred to particular traits, and they don't allow much sentiment about 'Do unto others as you would have them do unto you'! Naturally there are those over there who hate what Granbretan is doing, who hate wearing masks and all the other aberrations they encourage. Would they dare as much as breathe criticism of the Empire and King Huon? I very much doubt it. Would they nurture a revolutionary movement? With spies to betray them at every turn?" He looked thoughtfully at the surrounding landscape. "It would require many brave and intelligent people to overturn the Empire from within. No, the best we can hope for is that it will collapse as quickly as it arose. The nature of empires, whether they be Roman, British, Russian or American, is that they are expensive and uneconomical to maintain, requiring a vast standing army and its equipment. It only makes sense if you are fond of lists, codes and filing cards. There are so many better ways of investing your time and money, most of which do not involve so much noise, violence, bombast and cruelty."

"And Elric—Monsieur Zodiac—does he come from that empire or another one?"

Prince Lobkowitz smiled and stood up in his stirrups to stretch his legs and give his bottom a rest.

"Your great-grandfather is from a very different kind of place, an ancient civilization which gradually compromised with Chaos to give it power over the whole world. But it had not always compromised, as Elric learned. Once it had been an enemy of Chaos, a respected trading nation, famous for its probity. But as trade spread elsewhere, Melniboné became increasingly inclined to maintain her relationships with sword and fire rather than honest coin. So she kept her empire, at the cost of many of the softer mortal qualities. For Melnibonéans, though mortal, were not human. They belonged to a race which had come to our world many thousands of years earlier and made compacts with the great elemental Kings of Fire, Water, Earth and Air, compacts with supernatural entities we have no means of describing. And they were supported by their dragons, the Phoorn, who spoke the same language as they did—flying monsters impossible to defeat, with venom that became fiery poison when exposed to the air. Dragon venom alone sank many a Young Kingdoms ship."

"Wow! Dragons? Really?"

"All this sounds very exciting to you, young lady," said Prince Lobkowitz, "but believe me, it's no fun to be terrorized by a living creature the size of a sperm whale, which can fly and spit venom on you. It's like being attacked by a really big, heavily armed military helicopter, only the thing has a vast tail, which can knock the mast off a good-sized ship and destroy a house in a single flick. How does it fly? How do those ornithopters fly? They fly, I think, by different logic to a jumbo jet, but we know they fly."

"I'd still like to see one of those dragons," I said.

"Pray you never get the chance!" Smiling, he reached over to clap my shoulder. He was smiling. But like most of the smiles I saw these days, there was something else under it. I guessed they had enough pieces of the jigsaw puzzle now to realize the kind of game being played by our enemies, and how much danger we were in.

Again I'd been politely cut off before I could ask all my questions. I wanted to know what the Black Sword was, if it was some-

thing more than just a sword. A kind of magic blade, was it? Like
Excalibur?

Our road now wound along the shores of yet another lake. In
the far distance at the very end of the flat stretch of water, surrounded by hills steep and high enough to be small mountains,
was what looked like a good-size town.

"Oona told me he was looking for some sort of sword . . ."

"He already had the Black Sword. I imagine he left it behind
in Ingleton for a reason. Perhaps its magic is so powerful it can be
detected anywhere, or perhaps he doesn't trust it . . ."

"Trust it?"

"I'll not add that to your burden," he said firmly. Then to me:
"That's right."

"So why do Klosterheim and von Minct want me? Oona
doesn't really know. Have *you* worked that out yet?"

"I can't be sure. I think they believe you to be some sort of key,
perhaps to the Sword itself, possibly to the Grail, given your name
and background. The best thing is not to get caught by them and
never find out. The less you know about any of that, the better off
you'll be."

"Now you've made me even more curious," I said.

"Well, you'll have to live with that for a while. We tell you
what we think you need to know in order to survive. These are secrets usually much better kept to a few of us."

"All right. Then what about my mum and dad?" I asked.
"That's mostly what's on my mind. How are they mixed up in this?
And Gertie and Alfy? And my grandma and grandpa?"

"You know your grandmother is Oona, the Dreamthief's
daughter. She's the only one actually mixed up in anything with
us, and she's trying to make sure all of us are kept safe. But since
the enemy has focused on *you*, you are her chief concern. You
should never have been involved, and honestly I have yet to work
out why you are."

"Have they mistaken me for someone else?"

"That's my guess. Not, of course, that I'm in any position to tell them so or be believed by them. I don't know how the misunderstanding began . . ."

"You mean everything's been an accident—wandering into the caves and everything?"

"I don't mean that. Not at all. There's the boy, after all . . ." Again a sense of something shutting down.

"So who are they really after? You sound like it's someone in a witness protection program!"

He laughed heartily at this. A moment later Ujamaka, who was driving the first carriage, lifted his lance and pointed with it. There in the distance, from the far shore of the glassy lake, a shape could be seen descending between twin peaks. A big ornithopter.

My saddle became suddenly uncomfortable. The flying machines scared and fascinated me at the same time. I wanted to down and walk but decided to ride back to Lord Renyard's carriage and travel with him rather than go with a silent Oona. The Kakatanawa made room for me as we watched the big flying machine descend. I was terrified and hugely curious. All kinds of conflicting emotions roiled inside me. The thing was *huge* and very noisy!

The sun was getting low in the sky, its light diffused by thin, white cloud, as the powerful machine turned against its disk and skimmed the water, steam shooting from its curving exhausts. The prow was in the glaring shape of a hawk; its rotors turned slowly as the jointed wings beat with relentless rhythm. It had no roundels and was by all appearances an Empire ship. We did not raise our own flag but came to a halt as we watched the thing circling us. There was no way we could find cover against its guns now. We hoped they wouldn't waste fuel or ammunition on people they couldn't identify.

"Damn!" cursed Oona, looking out and up. "And München not fifty miles from here!" She looked back at the woods. She knew we couldn't make it. Even if we got there, the ornithopter could burn us out of the forest.

"We'd better keep going," she ordered. "The town's our best

cover. But don't go too fast or they'll *know* we're enemies." At that, the dark bulk of the clanking flying machine flew over again, steam and cinders spewing from those exhausts. Oona smiled and waved at it as it passed so low we could see the mask and goggles of its pilot glaring down at us, the heavy heart of its engine pumping. The ground vibrated as it went over. I held my ears.

Then it was gone, back the way we had come. We picked up speed and entered into the relative safety of a ruined house. That terrible stink of ash and death was everywhere. Nothing was alive. No paper or cloth had survived, so there was no record of what had happened. Just another passing victim of Granbretan's efforts to bring order to a world it found disorderly and therefore threatening.

"They know we're here," said Oona. "So there's no point in trying to hide at this stage. Lord Renyard, get out of sight as soon as you can. The rest of you look as if you're setting up camp. If they see we think they're no threat, they might assume we're at least neutral!"

The massive, clattering, hissing thing was overhead again, blotting out the sky. Oona waved a second time. This time she was answered by a burst of flame from a turret. The flame splashed against a nearby wall. The air was filled with the smell of burning kerosene.

"Flame cannon," said Lord Renyard, who automatically lifted me behind him with his powerful paws.

"We're sitting ducks," said Lieutenant Fromental. From the depths of a voluminous overcoat he produced a pistol. We had no long-range weapons with which to retaliate.

"It's almost as if they were tracking us and picked the best place to ambush us," said Prince Lobkowitz, checking a revolver of his own. "Klosterheim was in Mirenburg! He was able to get word to this aviator!"

"But he won't want to risk killing me, will he?" I pointed out. "Not if they want me alive."

It was a good argument, they all agreed. The Kakatanawa prepared their spears and bows. Their expressions told me that if there was any way of destroying a steel ornithopter with those weapons, they would find it!

At Oona's instructions the Kakatanawa formed a tight circle around me, their war boards used like a Greek shield-wall. Then we watched as the ship took another turn about and again came in low—even lower this time than the last—its huge clawed feet dragging the water and setting up a wake which lapped at the town's remaining pier. I felt horribly sick. The craft made a third turn and seemed to be preparing to land on the water. I thought it was bound to sink, but maybe it was wide enough and boat-shaped enough to float. Water hissed all around it, and steam shrieked as it spewed from the vents. Then, almost on cue, two more Dark Empire ships came thundering over the horizon, and Oona gave the order to seek any cover we could!

We darted desperately through the ruins. From ahead came a sudden blinding flash. The two aircraft were dropping bombs on us!

Some of the horses were better trained than others and held steady, but most of them bolted, threatening to drag the carriages to destruction. Oona yelled for her men to cut the traces, letting the horses run from the explosions. It probably saved their lives.

More bombs. All around us blazed the same white, blinding light. None of us could see anymore. There was an acrid stink, and my throat began to burn and my eyes water. I blundered on through the confusion. There was shouting and clanking of arms and armor, jingling horse gear, the guttural voices of the Kakatanawa and the Dark Empire pilots yelling through the flares.

In the confusion I lost contact with the others. Now I was really scared and started calling for Oona. I could hear her somewhere nearby. I knew that if I stayed where I was, I might be better off, but it was very hard to do in all that chaos. When I grew dizzy and found it hard to keep my balance I began to realize that they weren't just using flares. There was something else in those bombs: poison gas.

I tripped. I fell. I tried to get up. I became dizzier. I lost all sense of whether I was rising or falling. From my knees I looked up. Was the brilliant mist clearing? I heard sounds, saw shadows moving. I tried to rise, but I was even weaker. I saw huge, black eyes, a snarling muzzle.

And then I passed out.

PART THREE
THE WHITE
WOLF'S SON

Near six foot tall was Lord Rennard,
All dresséd in silk and lace,
Walk'd he prowde into the farmer's yarde
Filléd with cunning courtesy and grace.

—"THE BALLAD OF LORD FOXXE"
   Coll. Henty, *Ballads of Love and War*, 1892

From corners four rode our bold heroes
No self or selfish meaning to their muse
To meet again in Mirrensburg
Strong justice there to choose.

—HENSHE, *THE GREAT BATTLE OF MIRRENSBURG*,
   1605
   Wheldrake's tr., 1900

CHAPTER SIXTEEN

Across the Silver Bridge that spanned thirty miles of sea came the
hordes of the Dark Empire, pigs and wolves, vultures and dogs,
mantises and frogs, with armour of strange design and weapons of
obscene purpose. And imprisoned in his Globe of Thorns, curled like
a foetus in the fluid that preserved his immortality, drifted the great
King Huon, all his present helplessness symbolised by his situation.
Hatred alone sustained him as he schemed the punishment he would
bring upon those who refused the gift of his logic, of his sublime
justice. But why could he not contrive to manipulate them as he
manipulated the rest of the world? Did some counterforce aid them,
perhaps control them in ways he could not? This latter thought the
mighty King Emperor refused to tolerate.

—THE HIGH HISTORY OF THE RUNESTAFF
   Tr. Glogaeur

 FELT TERRIBLE when I woke up and realized that I
was aboard one of the Dark Empire aircraft. The
whole thing shuddered and shouted as the metal
wings beat at the air and the rotors labored to help keep us aloft.
Inside, the ship was much noisier than outside, and the stink of
whatever chemicals fired the boilers was very powerful. I found I
was not tied up but just very stiff from lying in the cramped space
behind one of the pilots' seats. Two pilots and, I supposed, a gun-
ner and a navigator shared the cockpit. When the unmasked
"navigator" turned to look at me, I wasn't surprised to see
Klosterheim.

He sported the air of a man who had seen all his schemes and
plans reach fruition. How much had our recent actions actually
been manipulated by him and Gaynor? And not only *our* actions, of
course, for there were many players in this game. More, probably,

2 3 3

than we knew. Klosterheim and Gaynor had tricked Monsieur Zodiac into pursuing them. Rid of him, at least for the moment, they let us escape from the safety of Mirenburg, then pounced. Surely Prince Yaroslaf hadn't been in league with them! Yet at that moment everything stank of treachery to me.

Where were my friends? Had they been killed? There wasn't room for anyone else in the plane's cabin. Lieutenant Fromental wouldn't have been able to get in at all.

I felt sick.

I felt awful. Not just physically, from the fumes and cramp, but mentally as well. I wanted to vomit, but if I was going to throw up, it would be, if I could manage it, all over one of my captors. I didn't say anything, in case I sounded too feeble, but I glared into Klosterheim's eyes and was rewarded with a sense of endless vacuum, as if the entire multiversal void were encompassed within that gaunt, unhappy creature. Strangely, I felt a kind of sympathy for him. What must it be like to live with that emptiness?

By now I'd picked up a bit of his history from my friends. If he wasn't immortal, he had lived for a very long time and survived more than one experience of death, unless, as Prince Lobkowitz had told me, he had an avatar in a number of multiversal realms, who knowingly carried on the agenda of his dead selves. Was *that* what immortality might be? Not one body living forever, but one personality living through hundreds or millions of versions of the same body? Herr Klosterheim had seen scheme after scheme fail. He had been defeated more than once by those who Prince Lobkowitz had referred to as being on "our side." Indeed, defeat of one sort or another was almost all he had experienced. Why didn't he give up?

I think he read something of this in my eyes, for he turned away, muttering and snarling to himself. The ornithopter banked sharply, and for a moment I thought I wasn't going to be able to keep from throwing up. Then I sank into unconsciousness again.

When I next woke we were on the ground. I was alone. The engines had stopped. I heard distant voices and looked up to see a crow mask peering down at me. I stared back. I tried to hear what was going on outside the cockpit. Klosterheim was talking to someone in the guttural tones of Granbretan, a strange mixture of French and English. I wondered if, at some point, the French had conquered England again and left this language as their heritage. Or was I hearing Norman English from a world where William the Conqueror's speech had come to dominate Anglo-Saxon rather than compromise with it?

Then Klosterheim and the others came clambering back in. I think we had stopped to refuel.

"What did you do with my friends?" I asked him. I was hoarse. My eyes still burned. I don't think he even understood my words. He settled himself in his seat as the canopy closed and the pilot began to get the machine's steam up. The rotors whirred, and the wings began beating as we lumbered up into the air.

After a few minutes in flight the ornithopter banked suddenly, its wings laboring, and I caught the flash of something that could only be the sea, and a wide silver arc which might have been a bridge. I think it was dawn. As the light increased, my eyes hurt even more. Whatever they had gassed us with was powerful stuff.

I think the altitude had something to do with my dizziness, because I soon passed out again, still feeling sick and still determined to vomit, if I could, on Herr Klosterheim.

If this was his last chance to gain whatever it was he wanted, he deserved it, given the cleverness of his deceptions. But needless to say, his success didn't bode at all well for me.

The journey had already taken more than a day, I guessed. I woke and passed out again intermittently. I did have the momentary satisfaction finally of throwing up over someone's boots, and by their dull, cracked blackness I have a fairly good idea they belonged to Herr Klosterheim. Of course, given his history, it couldn't be the worst thing that had ever happened to him.

The last time I woke up, someone or something was lifting me out of the narrow space behind the pilots' seats. I felt fresh air slap me in the face. I opened my eyes, shaking my head as if I'd surfaced in water. It was dark again but a substantially different kind of darkness. I felt it all around me, populated, unquiet and encroaching. I glimpsed slimy greens and browns, ocher and murky blue, shadows which revealed cruel, mad eyes full of suppressed glee. I had a strong impression of flames billowing blackgrey smoke. Suddenly there was a gushing roar, and I was blinded by a light again, though this was a vivid red and yellow flame, almost healthy in comparison to the other.

I heard more oddly accented voices. Klosterheim replied in the same dialect. Grunts, snuffles, barks and growls sounded as if we were in some sort of menagerie. I realized the animal noises came from various masked people who surrounded me, looking down at me. A hand stroked my body, and I shuddered.

A brazen-headed wolf spoke. A familiar voice. "She must not be harmed."

That, at least, was reassuring.

"Until the time is ready," the same wolf added. "She must stay a virgin or she's no use to us at all. The Stone is ours. Our friend has brought us the cups as a sign of his good faith. She'll bring us the Sword, and the boy will bring us the Staff. But only if we are careful to follow every aspect of the ritual. Blood for blood, cup for cup. The law of like to like . . ."

"Bah! That's mere superstition. Her only use is as bait for the albino and his pack." A high-pitched, unfamiliar yap. They spoke a form of English which was becoming easier to understand.

"They won't take the bait." That was Gaynor von Minct. I knew his voice well. "They'll have guessed what we're up to." Cynical, brutal, bleak, its tone mocked his companions. "No, there has to be more to the child's power."

"Let us first discover if the worm attracts the fish." Another voice I didn't recognize at all, like the sharp hiss of dry leaves. "If it does not, we shall investigate the nature of the worm."

"Do as you will." The voice came closer. I opened my eyes and looked into the face of a huge cobra, its stylized mouth open as if to strike, its fangs at least a foot long, its crystalline eyes winking and sparking in the darkness, its metallic scales flashing bright green and red. "Awake, is it, little worm?" This last to me.

"Bugger off," I shouted. It was the strongest swearword I knew at the time. "You can't hurt me—"

"Oh, but we can, little worm." The cobra drew back, threatening to strike me. "We can. It is only our restraint that saves you sweet, exquisite pain. For you have come to the capital of the world's pain, the land of perpetual torment, where your kind is privileged to know the very rarest of agonies. We possess a special vocation for turning pain into pleasure and pleasure into pain. And we shall turn your courage into the most abject cowardice, believe me."

He was trying to frighten me, I think, but there wasn't any real need. I was already so terrified, a false calm had settled over me. It made me appear braver than I was, because I laughed, and the cobra reared back again, raising a green-gauntleted hand, then letting it drop to his side.

"We must not hurt her," Klosterheim said urgently, "not yet. Not yet."

"There's no entertainment in frightening children." A woman's voice. I looked for the speaker. A bird in steel, gold and rare gems; a stylized heron. "Your triumph is unseemly, gentlemen."

"My lady," returned the cobra, "we are, of course, your servants in this matter. She shall be placed in your charge, as Baron Meliadus has ordered. However, if she fails to bring us our prey, you understand that she will become our property . . ."

"Naturally. I assure you I have more slaves of her age and sex than I can afford. The war effort has forced us all to make sacrifices."

"Sacrifices," repeated the cobra. I expected to see a forked tongue come flicking out of that gaping mouth. He savored the word.

"These days, dear Baron Bous-Junge, it is our duty to make as many as possible," said the woman. She sounded quite young. Her voice had a cool, mocking edge to it. I think I was more afraid of her than of the others.

They were all wary of her, I could tell. I guessed she was more powerful than the rest of them. I was probably in Granbretan, but of course in those days I knew nothing of their social structure. I had heard that King Huon was hideous and that Baron Meliadus, his chancellor, was ambitiously cruel. Baron Bous-Junge was some sort of court alchemist. Details of their lives were sparse on the Continent. Few of our kind who crossed the Silver Bridge from Calais to the city they called Deau Vere ever came back to speak of what they had seen.

Intellectually I knew all this, of course, and I seemed to have reached a point where I couldn't feel any more fear, although there was plenty to be afraid of.

I began to see more details in the gloom. The room had a low, domed roof and smelled of something rotten around its edges. In a brazier suspended from the ceiling by brass chains, incense burned with a faint glow. Judging by the waft of musky air, it had only recently been lit. Outlines of armored, beast-masked figures moved around the walls and congregated near the door. The swirl of colors came from the walls, which were made of glass. As I got more used to them I realized we were inside an aquarium. What I was seeing through the glass was liquid and the shadows of water creatures. I thought I glimpsed a mermaid, or something that might have been a shark with arms. I guessed they were genetic experiments or maybe clones gone wrong. What I hadn't realized was that this was also to be my prison cell!

Von Minct and the others began to talk among themselves. They dropped their voices so I couldn't hear. I felt they were talking in code. But why would they be doing that here, in their own capital city?

How many elaborate plots, I wondered, were being hatched in Londra? I had the sense that they relished scheming, in spite of the risks! Some people are like that. I was pretty much the exact opposite. I liked everything straightforward and aboveboard, but I suspected that I was going to have to learn a bit of cunning quickly if I had even the slightest chance of surviving. I was probably on my own now, since I couldn't see that Klosterheim and company would have left Oona, Lobkowitz, Lord Renyard and the rest alive. Monsieur Zodiac had gone off on a wild-goose chase, and everyone else was simply too busy fighting their own particular battles to have much time for me.

I was puzzled why I wasn't grieving the loss of my friends. In the past I had been upset by a lot less. I suspect when your own life is at stake, you're inclined to defer emotional outbursts until you can afford them.

I didn't want to look too closely into the aquarium. I slept again, and when I woke up my eyes had adjusted so that I could simply sit in the middle of that strange, domed room and look at the water swirling and churning with what appeared to be a merman, with a great fishy tail where his feet should be. He put his odd, grey-green face to the glass and peered at me blankly without attempting any kind of communication. When I rose and walked towards him, he darted off. Something with huge teeth and brilliant eyes replaced him in a flash, and I recoiled. I decided to stay in the center of the room and watch. I sat on the floor, although there were plenty of chairs. The chairs were carved with even more grotesque creatures than I saw in the aquarium. I actually felt slightly more secure on the floor. I also had a feeling that it wasn't only the merman watching me, though what those people thought they could learn from me, I wasn't altogether sure!

Hungry, I wondered if they planned to starve me until I was too weak to run. That way they wouldn't have to worry about me escaping. Not that I knew where to go if I *did* escape!

Almost as soon as I'd thought of food something moved, and a young woman in a red woolen one-piece suit, a blank mask hiding her face, her head closely shaved and embedded with what looked like precious jewels, appeared behind me with a tray in her hands. She had passed straight through the aquarium walls to reach me. There must be a door there, but I couldn't see one.

"This is certainly the best prison I've ever been in," I told her as she set the tray down on a small table beside one of the chairs. Of course, I'd never been in any prison before that. "What's your name? I'd like to be able to thank everyone personally when I write my memoirs."

That sounds ridiculous to me now, but I distinctly remember saying it. Bravado? Sheer terror, probably. "Why don't you take off your mask and have supper with me? Or maybe it's breakfast . . ."

I made myself stop talking. I was on the verge of hysteria. The girl bowed. The wall began to move; one section of the aquarium slid past another. She bowed again as she stepped through. Another shimmy of watery light, and she was gone.

The food was delicious, and I don't think it was just because I was hungry. But I probably would have eaten it no matter what it was. Only afterwards did it occur to me that it might be poisoned. Sure enough, as soon as I put down my spoon, having cleaned a plate of what I assumed was a sweet dessert, I felt sleepy again.

The next time I woke up I was no longer in the aquarium room. A white light, bright enough to blind me, hit me full in the eyes. I couldn't easily see outside the circle of light as my eyes tried to adjust, but it was clear I was being observed again. I had the impression of more shadowy beast masks and a murmur of conversation. I got to my feet and found I was dressed in a filmy silk frock. I had on fresh underwear and was wearing thick tights. Everything was a shade of soft green. Someone had obviously cleaned me up while I was knocked out, because even my hair had been washed. Then a big man walked into the circle of light and hauled me up bodily before I could object.

The substance in the food also served to calm me. Either that, or I was in total denial about the fate of my friends and the fact that I was unlikely ever to see my mum and dad again.

The man carrying me was dressed in armor. It was like being lifted by one of the robots out of *Star Wars*. My clothes weren't heavy enough to give me much warmth, and I shivered against his metal-covered body. I was carried down a short corridor and then out into a street, where a tall wheeled machine, hissing and puffing out steam, waited for us. Shaped like an animal and about the size of a double-decker bus, it had a single huge wheel in the front and several small ones at sides and back. In what I assumed was a driving seat, on the top and at the rear of the thing, sat a figure whose armor and livery were identical in design and materials to the carriage. His head was enclosed in a snarling horse's head with sharp-filed teeth like a dinosaur's. He could just see over a tower in the roof made of copper and brass and glass. It looked like a mobile observatory with a telescope to me!

The driver signed to the man who held me. A door opened in the windowless side of the vehicle, and I was put in rather gently before the door was closed and locked.

A dim light was produced by gas jets. I could hear it hissing faintly. I was in a compartment with seats arranged around the sides. In the center of the floor was a circle of light in which I could see a busy street, people riding horses, and even what looked like a kind of huge motorbike. These were dwarfed, how-ever, by buildings erected in the shape of ugly, squatting hu-manoid figures with beast heads. They reminded me of something I'd seen in *The Egyptian Book of the Dead*.

Watching the scene immediately outside, I found that by moving a wheel near the big circle of light, I could see everything around me for some distance. It was a mobile camera obscura. I had come across something like it in Oxford, when I visited my uncle Dave, also in Bath, where one of my mum's sisters lived. But they had been fixed versions. Like many of the Dark Empire's in-ventions, it was a very awkward way of achieving the privacy they seemed to crave, but science had obviously developed very differ-ently since that period they called "the Tragic Millennium." Their economics had to be radically different, for a start; but I suppose when you are bent on looting everyone else's goods and land, you don't have to worry too much about efficient costings.

As we moved, I turned the wheel, trying to get as good a pic-ture of the city as I could. I was sure it was London—what they called Londra—though there wasn't a single familiar building or street. A busy, baroque city, with everything anthropomorphized. Slaves, naked but for masks, hurried on errands. Shops displayed their wares, most of them pretty ornate and many of them impos-sible to identify. Groups of warriors marched together along nar-row thoroughfares over which those same grotesque buildings loomed. The bus was soundproofed, so I could hear the street noises only faintly.

We were soon joined by a guard of mounted soldiers in the livery and masks of what I guessed to be the Order of the Dog. They were heavily armed, though I wasn't likely to escape, since the door I had come in by seemed to be the only way out, unless you were the size of a mouse.

Ahead of me was a riot of statuary the size of the Empire State Building, all of it populated, judging by the windows and doors and the tiny figures I could see leaning over balconies or crossing walkways. It was very impressive because it dwarfed the tallest of the other buildings and dominated the city with its various towers, ziggurats and domes in a crazy profusion of quartz, obsidian, marble and ebony. This could only be King Huon's palace. When the carriage drew up inside a covered courtyard lit by naked flambeaux I saw mantis masks of rank upon rank of warriors, carrying the banners and insignia of the "king-emperor." I recognized them from trophies which Prince Yaroslaf displayed in his own palace. But on living men, the armor and masks truly resembled the carapaces of insects.

Huge as the courtyard was, I still had a strong sense of claustrophobia. One of the leaders stepped forward. I watched the door open from where I sat inside, and there he was, just as he had been in the camera obscura, only, if anything, a bit larger. He reached in and signaled me to come to him. As soon as I stood beside him, he picked me up and took me out to a four-wheeled sedan chair, pushed and pulled by slaves. He put me into this, then joined the entire legion, who surrounded me to march us through King Huon's palace. We finally came to a set of doors, very tall and studded with jewels, bas-relief, painted panels, all depicting what seemed to be the mythical history of Granbretan and stories of her more recent conquests. The guards divided, each section pushing on one of the doors, which moved gradually open, revealing an even more fantastic scene inside.

It was a hall you could have placed a small city in, with room to spare. From the distant heights of the vaulted ceilings hung great woven sheets embroidered with all kinds of brilliant and grotesque devices. Judging by the proliferation of animals on many of them, I guessed they were the banners of Granbretan's leading clans, interspersed with the insignia of the conquered lands.

Their backs against the richly decorated walls, hissing, murmuring soldiers and courtiers intermingled, showing a strong interest in me. I pretended I couldn't see them. I wasn't there to entertain them but to offer my defiance.

It must have taken half an hour to move all the way to the end of the hall. There in midair hung a large globe, rather like a Christmas tree decoration, its insides swirling with murky colors shot through with sparks of gold, silver and emerald. I saw the faintest suggestion of eyes staring out at me. The coldest, hardest, nastiest pair of eyes I had ever seen, they contained the malice and greed of ten thousand years.

We reached the steps below the globe. As one, the mantis guards flung themselves facedown with a deafening crash. I looked around and saw that everyone was in the same prone position. I sat there, refusing to join in, watching as the contents of the globe gradually eddied and swirled, became agitated, began to form a shape. At first I thought these people were more insectlike even than the guards, because what I saw was a sort of egg, and within the egg was an incredibly wizened and wrinkled homunculus, the owner of those terrible eyes, who curled a long, prehensile tongue from its disgusting, toothless mouth and touched something within the globe.

A voice, startlingly beautiful and sweet, came from the floating creature within the globe.

"Good morning, child. Few of your kind are as honored as you. Are you aware who I am?"

"You're King Huon," I said. I had nothing to lose by being polite to this disgusting thing. "And you used to think you could conquer the world."

A vast susurration and clucking arose behind me. The sound was immediately silenced, presumably by a gesture from Huon's captain. Almost in amusement he said, "You seem aware of your importance to us, little creature. Or are you mad, like so many of those we make captive?"

"It could be both," I said. "I know I'm some sort of bait for a trap you're setting, and I know you're going to try to win back the power you've lost."

Now there was nothing but silence in that incredible throne room.

Courtiers waited to see how the king would react.

An unpleasant, beautiful chuckle came from the throne globe. "You are our route to the Runestaff. You understand, at least, that you have no more personal worth than a grub on a fisherman's hook. Or do you hope to deceive Huon, who sees and knows everything?"

The tongue flicked again, and the curtain to the right opened to reveal the shape of a man pinned against a board. His skin hung in strips from his body, which resembled the pictures you see in an anatomy book. Only his face, still masked, was not a bloody map. From within the wolverine helm came a whimpering groan.

Gloating, greedy, full of a glee I found more horrible than anything else, King Huon whispered, "Here is one of our favorite subjects, who came to warn us of your revoLieutenant His name is Lord Olin Desleur. This is his reward."

The curtain closed. "We are less kind to our enemies," he said.

My stomach turned over. I couldn't erase that image from my mind. I tried to control my breathing and contain the sense of horror I felt, the pity I had for the crucified man.

King Huon remained amused. "I gather you have met your brother, young Jack D'Acre, only recently. We await his arrival with interest. Yes, yes, our servants have found him. Do not fear, my dear. You will be reunited with him soon. And when that event takes place, we shall be conquering far more than a single continent or even a single world. When that happens, my dear, sweet child, the entire multiverse will be ours."

I was completely baffled. This was the last thing I'd expected.

"Who on earth is Jack D'Acre?" I asked.

CHAPTER SEVENTEEN

ING HUON DID not reply. His insect tongue flicked out to touch what I supposed was a control panel. The globe grew murky, as if it filled with dirty blood, and then he was gone. They wheeled me out of the throne hall again. This time, when we reached the first anteroom, we turned in a different direction, into unfamiliar passages and halls.

Could I really have a brother I didn't know about? A dark secret of my mum's? Impossible. Mum just wasn't that mysterious. She and Dad had met at university and become sweethearts; then they'd separated for a bit because my dad got a Mellon Fellowship to study at Yale, and she'd had a few boyfriends, as he'd had girlfriends, but they always said they were made for each other, they got on so well. And who was Mr. D'Acre, anyway? Not *my* brother! Jack had to have another dad.

Needless to say, the masked guards wouldn't respond to any of my questions. Though I put a brave face on it, I was beginning to have a distinct sense of dread. Something especially nasty was being planned. Luckily, my imagination couldn't summon up the dimmest picture of what was in store. Even the sight of that poor, dying Sir Olin Desleur aroused pity and horror in me, rather than fear.

Did I secretly hope that somehow the armies of Europe would come pouring over the Silver Bridge to rescue me? Even though they were winning, it wasn't unlikely their famous hero Hawkmoon would arrive in time to save me, and it would be a very long while before Granbretan itself fell. They would fight to the death to defend their capital. There was every chance, in fact, that Granbretan was already planning a counterattack. I suspected I might be involved in that plan. Was I a hostage, maybe?

The odd little four-wheeled carriage rolled and bumped its way through a series of tunnels. They were low, dank and smelling very strongly of perfume, which didn't cover the stink of mold. It reminded me of those really strongly scented candles you could buy in tourist places. In fact, the flambeaux and other sources of light had largely been replaced by big, fat scarlet candles, guttering in their holders as a hot breeze blew through the tunnels. The walls here were painted with faded hieroglyphics rather than being carved or molded, and I was again reminded of Egypt, the only other culture I knew which had so many beast-headed men and immortals in its mythology. Yet how could a mythology like that ever have come to Britain? In a way, the masks and obsession with personal privacy made some sort of ghastly sense, but nothing else did. Dark, internalized, repressed and aggressive, these people reminded me more of twentieth-century Nazis than twenty-first-century Brits. For a moment I thought of football rowdies, wearing team colors, decorating their faces, supporting teams with names like Wolves or Lions. But I still found it difficult to believe I was in London. Maybe England had been conquered by aliens, and my own people killed!

At last my transport stopped, and I lurched forward in my seat. Through the window I saw we were outside a door made of lumps of sparkling granite and slate. It creaked and whistled as it opened very slowly to admit the carriage. The mantis guards stood to attention while guards in other masks, resembling the hoods and heads of rearing cobras, took over. The naked slaves strained to drag the chair through the door as it thumped shut behind us.

Even murkier passages, lit by dim red globes of some kind. I couldn't work out what powered them. They displayed that bizarre mixture of advanced science and backward medievalism which characterized Granbretan.

We were now in another hangarlike building. This one was crammed with a profusion of very odd-looking machines. Many of them were monstrous, with snouts, dials, levers, wheels, cogs and engines whose purpose was totally unfamiliar to me. Some of the machines glowed faintly; others pulsed with color through layers of thick dust. The place resembled a museum more than a working factory. Perhaps these were some of the machines found since the end of the Tragic Millennium, and no one had discovered how they were used. It wasn't hard to arrive at that conclusion. My logic was that if they could use them, they would have used them. I would have seen them on the streets. The ones which looked like weapons would have been used against Hawkmoon's Continental army.

I took a long look at the things as we rolled by. The metal was all in weird colors: electric blues, glowing reds, vibrant greens. There was that smell you sometimes get from old wiring when it overheats. It was so strong, it stung my throat and eyes. I started to cough. The sound echoed through the vaulted ceilings high above and bounced off the metallic monsters on both sides of me.

The little vehicle stopped again. I peered out. A group of men stood in the shadows at the end of the hall. They wore cloaks made of snakeskin, mottled, dry, stretching from head to foot. Deep cowls hid their heads, but I caught a glimpse of eyes and the faint outline of the masks they wore, a dull sheen of dark metal.

A brusque command sent the slaves running from the place, and I was left, still sitting in the sedan chair, wondering what was going to happen next.

The door opened. One of the cowled men reached out an old, skinny hand, covered in papery yellow skin, and signaled for me to get out. I did. My knees were trembling. The cowled men then surrounded me, and I was led through several more doors until we entered a laboratory of some kind, with benches, retorts, smoking test tubes, all of very unusual shapes. Miles of twisting glass pipes ran with evil-colored liquid and issued thick, smelly steam.

Now we were in a much smaller room, and the door closed behind us again. One of the figures sat on the far side of a desk and signed for me to sit down on a three-legged stool with thick padded arms.

"Good afternoon, my dear," said the cowled one who had been taking the greatest interest in me. "I hope you are enjoying your time as our guest."

I made some sarcastic remark. He chuckled at this. "I am Baron Bous-Junge of Osfoud. No doubt you have heard of me. I am the chief of Granbretan's scientists."

The first thought that came into my head was *Vivisection!* They were going to cut me up!

He came closer, dry cloak rustling, snake head peering, snake eyes glittering. "We shall have to make some tests, but you seem very healthy. Are you a strong little girl?"

"Stronger than you think," I told him. "And I've never had a day's illness in my life." Which wasn't remotely true. I'd had dozens of the usual complaints, from chicken pox to flu.

Again I heard a certain sort of amusement. "We were told you were a child with a mind of its own. Do you understand why our great king-emperor was so tolerant of your rudeness, little girl?"

"Because you need me," I said bluntly.

"Has anyone told you what you are needed for?"

"By the look of things here, I'd say you want some fresh ingredients for a stew. I haven't seen past those masks you wear, like cowards, to hide your faces, but I'm beginning to suspect you file your teeth."

There was a moment's silence. Maybe Baron Bous-Junge was collecting himself. Had what I said struck a chord with him?

"Do you know where you are?" he asked, and then answered his own question. "You are in my quarters. This is where we perform some of our most useful experiments. Many are on living captives, from the youngest baby to the oldest man, and very, very few survive, sadly. It is all in the name of science. They gladly contribute to the great sum of human knowledge, without which we should never have risen above the animals."

I almost laughed at that. "You seem bent on getting lower than the average animal," I told him. "I mean, you're dressing up like them and behaving worse than them. Hasn't anyone ever told you what idiots you look in all that gear?" I sniffed. "I'm not surprised how bad you smell, either."

Now his hand spasmed, as if he controlled himself from striking me. All this was proving that for the moment, at least, I was safe. Either they needed to keep me in one piece for use in a planned ritual, or something else was stopping them from doing what I guessed they would normally do to someone who gave them that amount of cheek. A reedy, nasty chuckle came out of the mask. "I doubt if we have made a mistake. I have heard of your family's arrogance. You Germanians have given us a great deal of trouble, one way and another, what with Duke Dorian and the rest. It will be a relief to me to bring this matter to an end at last, though I must say I have not been bored by your escapades. I gather, your grandmother and her father have already been neutralized. Just as well. Just as well. They had become impure, what with one thing and another. Now only you and your brother remain. The blood is strong and clean and will be best suited for our purposes."

"So you really are a bunch of blood-sucking vampires, are you?" Why on earth did he think I was German? They seemed to have a lot of confused information! Their confusion could get me killed.

"I don't recognize the word. But the expression is crude. Have you eaten?"

"As much of your rotten food as I can stomach!"

"Go through that door." He lifted an arm. The ranks of cowled figures parted. I knew they had the power to carry me through if they wanted to, even though I felt that for every door which shut behind me, my chances of escaping became less and less, so I walked through with as much dignity as I could.

The room on the other side was rather surprising, reminding me of some old professor's study. Pictures of sorts on the walls, a fireplace, a mantelpiece, a big, high wooden desk, wooden bookshelves, all carved with those same grotesque faces and creatures. Every surface was covered in books, notes, scraps of paper, scrolls.

There were even some clay tablets covered in hieroglyphics not dissimilar to those on the walls. There were two big, comfortable armchairs and signs of other creature comforts, like a pot of what looked like tobacco, a long-stemmed pipe (presumably for smoking while wearing a mask), several more or less identical cloaks on hooks, what were probably spare masks, a conical hat with a wide brim, which reminded me inevitably of an old-fashioned wizard, and what appeared to be a string of desiccated rats hanging from a central hook in the ceiling and rotating slowly above the flames from the fire, which smoked in the grate and heated the room to an almost intolerable temperature. He indicated that I should sit down and then, to my great surprise, reached up with both hands and removed his mask.

The face I saw was pale, of course, and not very wholesome. He was younger than I might have believed from his hands alone, but still getting on. There were little branches of veins under his eyes, and his lips were an odd blue color, as if he had been chewing blackberries or something. He had a white beard almost to his chest, which appeared to have unrolled from under the mask, and white hair falling almost to his shoulders. Yet the face actually had quite a kind look to it, and his eyes had wrinkles I'd have sworn were laughter lines. When he did smile, his eyes twinkling, I responded almost with a joLieutenant I was getting used to sinister threats in ordinary gestures.

"Do you have children of your own?" The words came without my really thinking about them.

"Ah," he said, settling back into his own chair. "Children. Now, there's a thing. It is a century or two since my last child died, young lady."

"So you're older than you look!"

"If you wish. How old do I look?"

"About sixty," I said.

He huffed at this, the way a cat does. "Sixty? That must seem very old to you."

It didn't, particularly given my grandma's age, but I wasn't going to tell him. "What did your children die of?" I asked him.

"Oh," he said vaguely, "old age, mostly. They lacked the genes, you see."

"Why was that?"

"Because I needed them. We maintain ourselves as best we can. That is why so many of us have children. They keep you young. They have kept me young for several hundred years. But sadly, the time is coming when not even the genes of my own progeny will help. I suppose I must reconcile myself to death."

"That would probably be a good idea," I said, "since my friends aren't likely to want you alive for any reason."

He chuckled. "Oh, I doubt that. I doubt that. I have so much wisdom they could use. Not, of course, that I am offering it. My loyalties are to my king and country."

I wasn't sure if I believed him, but I let it go. Baron Bous-Junge picked up a hand bell from the table beside him and rang it twice. Immediately one of those poor, naked slaves stepped smoothly in. She was a pretty woman, but she wouldn't look at either of our faces, as if she had been trained to avoid direct eye contact. He murmured something to her, and soon two more slaves, who might have been related to the first one, brought in trays. They placed them on a table erected for the purpose and began pouring something into two beakers, while placing what looked like cakes and big, fat crumpets on irregular-shaped plates. Everything smelled good, just as if we were having tea at home. My mouth watered, and then, to my own astonishment, my eyes began to water, too. I wasn't going to let him see, but I think I was crying. Again I was suddenly missing my mum and dad, and I wished I weren't, because it made me too vulnerable. I did what I could to stop the tears.

Almost sympathetically he handed me a plate with some pastries on it and a beaker full of what I'd swear was ordinary tea. But I found it hard to eat or drink at that moment.

"They are not poisoned," he said.

"I can't see why they would be," I replied. "You or one of your soldiers could kill me easily."

He seemed to like this answer. "You have all the spirit I

expected. You are your mother's daughter. And you're intelligent, too. Your people must be proud of you."

Alfy was the smartest in our family. "You should meet my brother," I said. I began to eat, partly to disguise how I was feeling.

"I hope to, quite soon. Our allies have gone to seek him now. We're sure he's in the building." This really did startle me. Then I remembered enough to keep my own counsel. Was this the "brother" Huon had already mentioned? Jack D'Acre. A funny name. I hadn't seen it spelled out then. Huon might have been saying "Jacques Dacra" as far as I knew. It sounded vaguely French. But then, everything they said sounded vaguely French. I really wanted to find out what they thought they knew. I had already given away too much in the throne hall. I couldn't resist one chance to misdirect them.

"So they haven't found my brother yet?"

"Perhaps you know where he is hiding. He would need someone like you to help him. Those barefaced incompetents tracked him down in Mirenburg, I hear. More than once. Now he's gone again. He can't be far. We need to move more swiftly, given the state of affairs elsewhere in the multiverse."

Alfy had never been to Mirenburg and wasn't likely to be going in the near future. Bous-Junge had to be talking about the mysterious Jack D'Acre. But how could all of them have got that so thoroughly wrong? Was this whole thing a horrendous mistake on everyone's part? Were they hoping to find this Jack in Ingleton? Did they plan to trade him for me?

"He won't cooperate with you any more than I will," I said.

Baron Bous-Junge chuckled. "Oh, that's not the problem at all. Everyone cooperates with us when we persuade them. The problem is that he is elusive. Given what a peculiar little chap he is, I suspect your twin has help from more than just you."

It was beginning to dawn on me that they really did think this Jack fellow was my twin brother. Realizing how far off the mark they were and that this perhaps gave me a certain power, I started to smile, then checked myself. "Who, for instance?" I asked.

"Oh, I think you know, my dear. Your grandmother, your

great-grandfather, no doubt your father. There's a whole clan of
your kind here, who never ventured to Granbretan before. The
Austerite, the Frankonian . . . We have trapped prisoners. They
have eagerly told what they know. Baron Meliadus took charge of
them and used his special skills to extract that information. No
doubt King Huon will persuade him, in turn, to share with us."

This alerted me, too. So there were rivalries here. Factions. I
could tell by his tone.

"Baron Meliadus is still in Europe, eh?"

"Leading our soon-to-be-victorious forces. Hawkmoon took
us by surprise. We did not know he had learned the secret of multidimensional travel."

Was that it? Were they trying to find out how we moved from
one "realm" of the multiverse to another? Of course! If they had
that power, they could contemplate conquering endlessly, com-
bining forces with their alter egos on all the other worlds, threatening the structure of existence itself. They knew some of us had
the power to call upon the powers of Law and Chaos. Presumably
they thought my brother could do it. They didn't seem to know I
had absolutely no means of doing it myself, that I needed help
from someone else.

"And then there is the other albino, Zodiac. Evidently a relative, also? He could help us. There is some indication, from my
own readings of the multidimensional skrying globes, that he
might be induced to join forces with us. That would be ideal. And
might save your brother's life, as well as yours."

"You'll never get him to help you," I said.

"I think that's a little optimistic of you. His interests lie just as
much with us as they do with you. We understand how to unite
the swords. We have discovered the emerald stone. We know how
to divide the cups. Our science has achieved this. All we require
now is the agent which will bind them and make them re-form.
Then we control everything."

"I thought only God could do that."

Again he chuckled, his round, rather jolly face lighting up.
"Oh, dear! What makes you think God has any power? Or Lucifer,

for that matter? It has been a very long time since those two forces had any means of exerting their will upon the Dark Empire. They died, you see, when so many died, during the Tragic Millennium. Some believe that the Millennium would never have occurred had it not been for those deaths. I think you must accept, young lady, that King Huon is the greatest power in the universe!"

I didn't understand exactly why this depressed me. I'd never known any sort of formal religion. I thought of God and Lucifer as ideas, representing certain human and spiritual qualities, not real entities. If I'd given them any consideration at all, it had been in response to the self-involved, anxious, miserable evangelicals who turned up from time to time at airports and railway stations to ask if I "knew Jesus." Those poor, desperate individuals caused so much harm in my world. Those fundamentalists, with their suspicion, their sentimentality, their anxious superstition. They constantly thank God for helping them win gold discs or gold medals (apparently accepting that God favored them over any other contestants). This was the antithesis of the kind of rigorous selflessness I associated with my family. Their motto in Germany had always been "Do you the devil's work," which had something to do with protecting family relics, lost, as I understood it, during the Second World War, recovered and sent to America for safekeeping. Granddad kept something at his London flat, but I'd never seen it. Certainly for several generations we hadn't taken any of that stuff very seriously, except as rather funky stories with a vaguely Wagnerian ring. Yet I had the sudden feeling that I was actually sensing some great revelation, something important about the human condition, about mankind's relationship with the supernatural, and it seemed to involve not only my family's honor and survival, but everyone's—and many of the things I most cared about. If it wasn't a religious feeling, it was definitely profoundly mystical. Maybe that was what real religious experience felt like.

I was in no doubt, however, that the Dark Empire represented something close to pure evil. I just wasn't so sure that our side represented anything like pure good! And surely one was needed to combat the other.

"I wouldn't reckon any of your chances once my family find out where I am," I said defiantly.

This amused him even more. "My dear child! My dear child! Do you really expect Monsieur Zodiac to come whirling to your rescue with his mighty black blade?"

"It's a possibility," I said.

"I scarcely think so!" He chuckled again. "I understand Monsieur Zodiac finds it rather difficult to walk across the room without that sword's support."

"Which is hardly the point." I put down my beaker and finished my cake. I thought I had a sense now of what they feared. "Since he possesses the sword."

"Ah!" His eyes twinkled. "You have not heard?"

"What?"

"The albino no longer owns the sword. He left it behind when he went looking for you."

"It won't be much for him to go back for it!"

"I'm sure he's a very skilled traveler between the worlds, my dear, but you see, Messrs. Klosterheim and von Minct already have it. That was why they were able to come here and negotiate with us. The sword was their payment for the aid and special skills we gave to them."

"Klosterheim's got it?"

"Not at all. The black sword is now in our safekeeping. I think it highly unlikely your great-grandfather will want to risk very much."

Emotion suddenly flared in me. "He'll get it back. He'll show you he's not so easily tricked! He'll be here!"

"Oh, my poor child. Of course he'll be here. He's bound to try to help you. That is why we have let slip where you are. But without his sustaining hellblade, I fear he will not be of any great advantage to you."

And suddenly I knew that white-bearded wizard for what he really was: a conniving, cruel, disgusting man.

Our eyes met. He saw what I thought of him. He threw back his head and began to chuckle heartily.

"He'll be here, my dear. He'll be here. But whether he arrives in time to find you fully alive, I very much doubt. You see, the sword needs special food if it is to be useful to us. Special food . . ." He looked up at me, and now there was an indefinable lust in his eyes. "Young and fresh."

And as his cackle rose and his shoulders shook, I understood how thoroughly my friends and family had been defeated by his and Klosterheim's cunning.

I flung my plate and cup at him. Again I was close to tears, but I turned my fear into anger. "You nasty, dirty old man!"

The liquid from the beaker stained his beard, so that it looked as if blood ran down his chin and chest. His eyes hardened for a second, and then he burst into laughter again.

"I must admit," he said, as he dabbed at himself with a napkin, "that this is certainly one of the most complex and successful traps I have laid in all my many, satisfying centuries. We have you. We have the sword. Now all we need is young Jack. And I am certain he will join us again soon."

He cast a calculating eye over me and once more was all avuncular twinkles and chuckles. "You're a spirited child, my dear, and will take some keeping, I can see. We have allowed for that. You will be put in the custody of Flana Mikosevaar, Countess of Kanberry. She is of the blood royal, a possible heir to the throne, and the widow of Asrovak Mikosevaar, the hero who died by Dorian Hawkmoon's hand at the first Battle of Kamarg. She has had twelve husbands, several of whom met bloody ends, not always in war, and one of whom was Baron Meliadus, the King's Chancellor. She has no love for mainlanders, though she keeps the name of that infamous Muskovian renegade, her most recent spouse. Best you curb that tongue with her, since she has been given permission to begin punishing you in certain ways not permitted to the rest of us. Do not expect her to be lenient because you are of the same gender. Countess Flana is famous for the pleasure she takes in inflicting pain on others."

Baron Bous-Junge's features now beamed in a fat smirk as he replaced his mask and summoned the slaves. A sigh like escaping steam came out of his mask, as if he was already tasting the revenge he would have on me.

The old-fashioned hand bell summoned his slaves as he turned his back and pored over some old books. He had forgotten me entirely. That might have been my chance to try to get away, but I left it till too late. The slaves surrounded me. They escorted me back to the same carriage, and I had no choice but to climb in again.

After another incredibly long journey through passageways, halls and tunnels, arcades and covered streets, we finally arrived at the Heron Palace, home of Flana Mikosevaar, Countess of Kanberry, who was to become my jailer. The Heron Palace was built around a beautiful courtyard. Unusually for the Dark Empire's taste, it was open to the roiling sky. Its water garden fed green lawns and richly scented flower beds full of blossoms I had never seen before, as well as roses, hydrangeas and lupines, familiar from home. The garden was comforting in spite of the bizarre blooms. I had the impression that given the complete absence of insects and birds, the plants were flesh eaters.

I was left alone in the small antechamber looking out over the garden and, since I had no other way of calming myself, took an intense interest in the flowers. Although the windows were wide open, they were covered by screens so that it was impossible to go out.

After what seemed hours, Countess Flana and her entourage entered the room. She was tall and slender. She covered her head with a magnificently wrought heron mask, with a long, sharp beak and a half-raised crest, all in silver and ebony. From it two large golden, cool and unreadable eyes regarded me.

"I hear you have strong opinions of your own, Mademoiselle von Bek." The voice was humorous, vibrant. If I hadn't been warned by Baron Bous-Junge what she was really like, I might have thought I would find sympathy there. I kept my own counsel. I was still planning to escape. I felt it was almost my duty to try, since I seemed so crucial to whatever Dark Empire plan was in place to conquer the multiverse.

Of course, I hadn't taken them and their plans seriously, but even their reconquering of the Continent would be bad enough. I might manage to stop something if I escaped.

I decided to pretend to be deceived by Countess Flana, who sent her slaves from the room and came to stand over me where I sat on an uncomfortable, asymmetrical couch facing the garden.

"You like my little private garden, child?"

"I love it," I said as innocently as I could. "Do you work in it yourself?"

This brought a soft laugh. "As it happens, I do, when I am alone. Which is all too rare."

Slender-fingered hands reached to remove the elegant mask, revealing one of the most beautiful women I had ever seen, on or off the screen. She had a fair, glowing skin, platinum hair and dark red lips. There was a kind of wondering, dreaming quality to her as she turned those eyes, the shade of sunflowers, upon me. Her color was higher than I would have expected, and the flush took time to leave her cheeks. It was very hard not to trust and like someone who looked so beautiful, even vulnerable. I wondered how she had handled twelve husbands. Twelve. She seemed to belong to the wrong order. Was there an Order of the Spider? She contradicted everything I knew about her. I wondered about her kind's potential longevity. She looked twenty-five, but she must be more than one hundred.

For all her reputation, I found myself warming to her as she drew back the screens from the French doors and led me into the tranquility of the water garden. The sky above was awash with speeding dark clouds, which flung their shadows over black towers, domes and turrets. Once a big, black ornithopter flew over the city, its engine pounding, throwing out the usual trail of smoke and sparks.

"So you are Jack D'Acre's sister?" We walked among the flower beds and the streams of water. "There is little family resemblance."

"I agree," I said. "You'd never know we were related."

She frowned at this. "Oh, no, I think the prophecy was accurate. I miss little Jack. He lived with me, you know. An odd experience, no doubt, for us both." She stared into the fountain. A tribe of stylized bronze merpeople rose onto rocks, water spewing from their metallic mouths. They rode dolphins and carried tridents and nets, yet, for all their classical origins, they were distinctly Granbretanian: faintly grotesque, faintly aggressive and possibly alive. Her voice became distant as she remembered something. She raised her head and watched the disappearing ornithopter as it flew between the towers. "Then he ran away."

If I hadn't known better, I would have thought she recollected a lover who had left her.

"But now I have you," she said. She reached to stroke my hair. "Poor Jack. Poor Jack."

"Were you the one who blinded him?"

"He sang so beautifully. And he knew the future. He was a seer, as you know, my dear. And you are aware, I'm sure, of the fate of such folk."

I couldn't stop myself from repeating, "How was he blinded?"

"By the light. They needed him to listen for the demons in the steel, you see." Her voice faded and became almost inaudible. "They didn't know his true value. They took him off to Mirenburg. My informants tell me they were trying to make a particular kind of sword." Perhaps she was thinking back to when it had happened. I couldn't be sure. I had never been with anyone as mysterious, as impossible to read. "Taragorm, you see, had these machines . . . But originally I bought him for his voice."

"*Bought* him?"

She frowned, puzzled. "Taragorm had other purposes for him, and no sense of his talents. He cost me the fortune of one of my husbands." She laughed softly. "But he was worth it. Until he went away." She sighed. "The king's orders, of course. Now this . . . I'm sure he'll be discovered eventually. But this time they will tear out his tongue. If he is lucky. They'll ruin him."

I knew a second or two of hope. "I didn't think anyone could escape from Londra."

"Oh, he hasn't escaped the city," she said. "He is still here, somewhere. He must be. I can almost smell him. After all, he can't go back to Mirenburg now, can he? I'm told your presence will make him reveal himself, once he knows his sister is in our power. What do you think?"

"I think he'd be an idiot to risk it," I said.

She found this amusing. She smiled and reached for me again. I let her stroke my neck and shoulder, but she could tell I was tense. She withdrew her hand. "I miss him. I suppose you do, too."

"Not as much as you, I think."

Her expression became strangely grateful. I found it very difficult to believe her a husband-killer, but I could have been seeing only one side of her. Or maybe all these Granbretanner aristocrats were like that. I had the impression that half these people only barely repressed hysteria. Something about their taste for masks and enclosed spaces was associated in my mind with that kind of madness. I had read the expression "my blood ran cold" and had never really thought what it meant. Now I knew. In spite of the warmth, I found myself shivering in her water garden as she led me down crazy-paving paths, staring thoughtfully into vivid, fleshy blooms and pretending, I supposed, to frame her thoughts.

"You didn't know him as I knew him," she said. And she sighed deeply, then laughed. "Who could?"

"You really think he'll come back to you just because I'm here?"

"Oh, no, my dear, he won't come back to me because of you. In fact, because of you he is even more likely to stay away."

She looked at me blankly for a moment, then turned away. "That's absurd. Jack is my adopted son. I intend to make him king-emperor someday."

"But King Huon's immortal, isn't he?"

She looked at me in surprise, as if I had overheard her speaking to herself. "Of course he is." She smiled as she stopped to point out an especially magnificent variety of lily: purple caps, not dissimilar to deadly nightshade.

We wandered back to the French doors, and she again surprised me when she asked, "Have you any preferences for food this evening? There are certain shortages, because of the war, but I can have almost anything prepared for you."

I shook my head.

Her voice softened. "You're not enjoying your stay in Londra. Why is that?"

"I miss my mother and father."

"They turned you out?"

"No. That Klosterheim and his friend chased me all over the place. Underground. All through the dimensions. Across half of Europe. And as a result I lost touch with them."

"Where are they? Still alive?"

"In England," I said. "In Yorkshire."

"Oh!" she exclaimed, brightening. "What a coincidence. We have provinces here in Granbretan which bear very similar names."

"I shouldn't be surprised." I yawned. It had been a long, long day. The sun was in its final quarter, spreading red, agitated light across the rooftops and domes. Maybe I liked this woman because she *was* unstable. It suggested a kind of vulnerability. "How long are they going to keep me here?"

"Not long, as I understand it. They have the Sword; they have the Cup; they have the Stone. Now they need the Blood and the Staff to perform the ritual. And you and Jack, of course, will provide those."

"Why is that?" I hardly wanted to hear her reply.

"Male and female fluids are needed, and of course, they must come from your veins. For you traditionally guard the Grail. Keepers of the Stone, as they say. The Blood must come from twins of that old von Bek strain. Taragorm, who is still a good friend of mine though we were married once, told me all about it. To gain control over the Balance, virgin blood of the twin Grail children must spill and mingle, while the essence of what is male and female must combine in ritual bloodletting . . ."

"Ritual bloodletting?" I was beginning to get a clearer picture. Not a very pleasant one. I shivered.

"Yes, of *both*. That is very important. I'm sure you understand, being of that blood. But much of this is new to me. I have never studied magic, you see, and know few who do. Taragorm has machines which speak to him. They are perfectly clear about what has to be done. Like to like. Same to same. Shape to shape. Blood to blood. It is the absolute fundamental of their science as well as their magic and medicine. We follow the principles of similarity. The principle of the Balance itself. Opposites in balance. The principles upon which all life is based. But Taragorm explained this to me and will no doubt do the same for you."

"Taragorm?" I wanted to know more about him.

"He is the master of the Palace of Time. He can travel in time, they say. At least he can see into the past and future. The world's greatest scholar in the Doctrine of Signatures. What our ancestors called *Signatura Rarum*. Like affects like. The fundamentals of science. He searches the dimensions, back and forth through history, seeking to restore all the wisdom we lost when the Tragic Millennium descended upon us."

"And what brought that disaster?"

"Who knows, child? Perhaps a similar sequence of events. What is done in one time and place repeats and repeats, yet with each repetition comes a subtle change. There is a legend of a sword, a stone, a cup, I understand, which no doubt dates from the same period. It would be ironic, would it not, if we repeated the same mistakes which brought that long, dark age from which we so recently emerged." Her laughter was sweet and light but with an edge of weariness to it. "How boring if that turned out to be the truth."

I must admit, a lot of this magic stuff went over my head. Countess Flana didn't seem to notice.

"When does this ritual take place?" It seemed reasonable for me to ask a question about their plans for my death.

"When all the worlds are in conjunction," she said. "Smaller conjunctions appear fairly regularly. A hundred spheres. A million spheres. Over the past two or three centuries there have been a series of such conjunctions. Repeating and repeating. And at every repetition, Taragorm tells me, an opportunity has been lost. On this occasion they intend to be certain. They will preserve the Balance, and they will control it." She smiled almost tenderly at me and reached out her hand to me again. This time I avoided it. "They intend to gain control over both Law and Chaos."

"Isn't that a bit overambitious?"

"It seems so, doesn't it, my dear? What is in such men that they must control so much?" She smoothed her dress over her legs. "They say Hawkmoon or some avatar of his is destined to destroy the Balance. But if they control it, they will take control of the Grey Fees . . ."

"The DNA of the multiverse?" Wasn't that what someone had called it? I hardly knew what they were talking about.

"You are a well-educated child. They believe they can re-create the multiverse in their preferred image. When the main-landers Klosterheim and von Minct came to them with the plan, they were skeptical. However, they were at last convinced, partly by the ease with which those two moved between the various realms of the multiverse. Our people only had the vaguest of notions of such worlds, though they have been working on a means of traveling to them for some time. In the *Signatura Rarum* there's evidence our ancestors had this power and lost it. If Granbretan is able to pass between one world and another easily, we will find and kill those who conspire against us. Until now, the ability to travel at will between the dimensions has belonged only to others. That is why you and your brother are so valued, of course, as are your great-grandfather and your grandmother. Not only does your blood possess the magical properties required to perform the ritual, but your physical capture will bring the others to us at the right time. And they'll reveal their secrets because we'll be able to experiment on them in the optimum conditions."

Something nagged at the back of my mind. There was a flaw somewhere in her logic.

"So you want half my family in on this. Are we all going to die?"

"Your bleeding," she said, "would not mean your dying in the conventional sense. But, of course, it will not be pleasant. I almost feel sorry for you."

I suddenly had an image of Mrs. Ackroyd, the farmer's wife up at Chapel-le-Dale, hanging the pig and slitting its throat in order to make black pudding. The poor thing squealed horribly while its blood poured into a big bucket. I remember her pushing her hands down into the bucket, stirring the blood and pulling out strings of some impurity. Even my friends the Ackroyd girls thought it was gross. I ran away. I didn't wait for a lift. I ran almost three miles nonstop and was in a bit of a state when I got to Tower House. My mum and dad were furious when they heard I'd seen this. They very nearly refused to let me go and play with the Ackroyds after that.

I had this image of myself hung like Mrs. Ackroyd's pig, and I suddenly felt sick. I asked where the toilet was. One of the slaves took me to a similar cubicle to the one in Mirenburg, and I threw up some bile, but I wasn't really that ill. I stayed there for a bit, just trying to collect my thoughts and wondering how on earth I was going to escape. It might have seemed hopeless, but it really never occurred to me that I really was in extreme danger. The image of that pig prepared me for it, though.

I opened the cubicle grille to look out. The young slaves were waiting for me. I couldn't see a way of escape at that stage, but I was beginning to get an idea, based on these people's psychology. The mysterious Jack had got away. He must be very clever to have done it, considering they'd blinded him. Or did he have friends among the king-emperor's lackeys?

For the time being, until I got a better idea of my surroundings and my chances of escape, I decided I'd better just go back. When I returned to the courtyard, Countess Flana was wearing her silver, gold and platinum heron mask again. She had a visitor. The man had his back to me but wore no mask. I recognized him at once.

She was saying, "The boy is lost again. Would the girl know where he is? If so . . ."

I heard him reply, "That's what I came to warn you about. Don't even break her skin, if you can avoid it. She must stay a virgin or the blood's no use to you. With luck, the albino and his bitch-whelp will lead us to the boy. The boy will bring you the Staff. Without it, the other objects are useless." He turned as I came in. His eyes narrowed and hardened.

I looked into the handsome face of a man I had thought our friend, who had been so charming and delightful when we first met, who had brought Elric to Ingleton and enjoyed our hospitality. A man I had liked and trusted. The balloonist bowed in that exaggerated way of his, and his smile was hypocrisy itself.

"Good afternoon, young mademoiselle. So pleasant to see you again." The Chevalier St. Odhran doffed his elaborate bonnet.

CHAPTER EIGHTEEN

*Now Hawkmoon, Count Brass and his daughter Isolda, Oladahn of
the Bulgar Mountains, all dressed in mirrored, flashing armor, again
led their forces against the armies of Meliadus and his barons.
Meliadus fumed. What power did these rebels have that they could
appear and disappear at will, forever choosing the place and time of
the most crucial battles . . . ?*

EANWHILE, AS LORD Taragorm and Baron Bous-
Junge contemplated the ritual which was to end in
Oonagh's terrible death, Elric, searching the worlds
of the moonbeam roads, determined for himself that Klosterheim
and von Minct had tricked him. He returned to the world in which
the Dark Empire forces were at bay, and learned from Yaroslaf
Stredic that his daughter and the others had arrived and headed for
München. He arrived at the lakeside ruins and found his friends
only a few hours after the Granbretanian ships had left.

The stink of the ornithopters was still in the air. The party had
been raided with poison-gas bombs; Elric recognized the kind. The
bolting horses had escaped the worst of the gas. They now stood
some distance away from the ruins, cropping the grass, carriages
abandoned. Two of the party were gone: Oona and Oonagh. The
rest had been left to die. Using his own considerable skills in sorcerous alchemy, Elric quickly revived his friends, learning from
them the possible fate of the others.

Lord Renyard was the most agitated. He blamed himself for

what had happened. Elric was able to reassure him. "Plots and counterplots, Lord Renyard, are in the nature of this particular game, where even the loyalties of one's closest friends are tested. We have all been deceived by that pair and their allies. I understood Bastable tried to reach you and failed. This complicates our game. Given the way in which all the realms of the multiverse now arrange themselves in conjunction, I would guess Granbretan plans to begin their blood ritual very shortly."

The great fox scratched himself behind his left ear. "Why is that so important to them? Do they serve Chaos or Law? What do they want?"

"Oh, they're playing for pretty high stakes, I think. They play for more than either Chaos *or* Law."

"There's something more than that?"

Elric turned for help to his friend, Prince Lobkowitz, who walked slapping at his clothing and wrinkling his nose against the smell. "Something more indeed. They seek the 'consanguine conduit,' bringing together all the scattered manifestations of the Balance itself."

"The Cosmic Balance? It's broken?" The fox found his hat and licked at the dusty felt until he was satisfied it was clean enough to readjust on his head.

"The Cosmic Balance can't be broken, though perhaps it can be destroyed. It is an idea. But those elements which represent it only rarely come together. Frequently they take unfamiliar forms." Prince Lobkowitz watched as the Kakatanawa rather inexpertly rounded up the horses and, helped by Lieutenant Fromental, harnessed them to their carriages. "Of course, the Balance itself *is* merely the symbol of the forces which work to control the multiverse, but it is a useful and powerful symbol. Control the symbol, many believe, and you control both Law and Chaos. Since rational people have never wanted such control, and irrational people were incapable of achieving it, the theory has still to be tested."

"It has never been tested? Never? What is this Balance, then? How is it comprised?" Lord Renyard looked on intently as Elric began to pick through the ruins where the ornithopter had landed, perhaps hoping to find concrete clues to where his daughter and great-granddaughter had been taken. It seemed obvious that they had been carried off to Granbretan. Probably to Londra. Few escaped that island, he guessed. He cocked his gloomy head to hear Prince Lobkowitz's reply.

"Traditionally the Balance comprises a stem, a crosspiece and two bowls suspended on golden chains from the crosspiece. It combines the essence of both Order and Entropy. The stem is rooted in a great rock sometimes popularly called the Rock of Ages. Others merely call it 'the Stone.' In some parts of the multiverse these elements are themselves individually venerated, even worshipped. One found its way into legend as Excalibur, Arthur's sword, which was embedded in a rock before he pulled it free. Other tales speak of the Stone as the Grail, a giant emerald—not always a magnificent cup—which has the power to cure the world's pain. Some believe it is the same thing as the Runestaff, which appears to have the Grail's properties and can reveal itself in many forms."

The fox opened his mouth in a puzzled grin. "I fear, sir, that as a rational creature, 'tis hard for me to understand such strange logic . . ."

Prince Lobkowitz nodded slowly, watching the others and mopping at his neck. Like them he was sweating, probably as a result of Elric's potions. "Throughout the multiverse, intelligent, imaginative beings ascribe differing powers and forms to these symbols," he said. "The cups, the swords, the rocks, are merely the more familiar forms we choose. Manipulation through representation is the quest of every alchemist, for instance. That's the peculiar logic by which we control the elements, which some condemn as sorcery. Represented by elementals—sentient beings with the power of the tornado or the forest fire, the earthquake or the storming heavens—these forces are far stronger than anything we can invent or hope to control. Even those above the elementals, the Lords of the Higher Worlds, who represent our vices and virtues as well as our ambitions and temperaments, our intellect, our courage, even our morality, would not challenge the power of the Balance. They, too, understand how they must perpetually struggle, Law against Chaos, in order to maintain the life of the multiverse, to ensure that it grows neither moribund nor too fecund. Either state is antipathetic to our existence. What's more, we are ourselves manifestations of those conditions. That's perhaps why we exist at all. Through our stories, which are formed from our desires and fears, we create order and ensure our own existence. The multiverse protects her own security and her own continuing growth by creating those forces which will, in balance, sustain her. We represent such forces in symbols which we use to interpet and organize that small part of the multiverse we inhabit and understand."

Elric came back, having found nothing. "And then," he said, by way of augmenting Prince Lobkowitz's explanation, "there are the Grey Fees." He allowed himself a thin smile, to which, by way of acknowledgment, Lobkowitz responded.

"The Grey Fees, it's believed, is the primordial matter which can be given shape entirely by thought and desire," he said. "Some who have studied the magical arts are convinced that control of all other elements is as nothing if you control the Grey Fees. The Balance is the regulator. Destroy that regulator and you personally become regulator, with control of all creation."

"Aha!" The fox was at last enlightened. "You become God!"

"And that, we are convinced, is the obscenity which the Dark Empire and their allies, von Minct and Klosterheim among them, wish to manifest, believing that both God and Satan, in their reconciliation, no longer have interest nor the power to manipulate and control."

Lord Renyard found this easy to understand. He murmured something about epicurianism and stoicism. "And there will always be those, too, who by creating conflict manage to take advantage of all sides."

"This began some centuries ago," Prince Lobkowitz concluded, "when Prince Elric's distant relative, Ulric von Bek, was commissioned by Satan to seek the Holy Grail and thus cure the world's pain. Your friend, Manfred von Bek, got himself involved in a plot by the Duchess of Crete and her associates, who wished to find the ultimate alchemical power over nature, which involves, of course, the ability to control the elements, thus turning lead into gold and so forth. Still later, the present old Count Ulric forestalled a Nazi plot to gain that power. But Klosterheim and Gaynor, who cannot easily die, because of their own experiments and skills, continued to seek control of the Grail. That is what they believe they are doing now, but I suspect Bous-Junge, Taragorm and all those other brilliant, poisoned minds of Granbretan have even more ambitious plans."

"If they gain that control—"

"Then we all cease to exist, I fear. However, they are more likely to fail and bring catastrophe down upon themselves. But even that prospect does not greatly concern our friend Klosterheim. It is *oblivion* he desires, I suspect, and this is his means of finding it. *Annihilation.* Even Gaynor has decided that he would rather die than lose his chance at controlling the very life-stuff of existence. Not that he fully comprehends what that death will mean for him: an agony of 'now' in which he relives the moment before his death for eternity. For if you would abolish time, you abolish all that makes you a living creature, as opposed to an atomic particle, which has no history but is re-created over and over again." Prince Lobkowitz let out a melancholy sigh. He could tell that not all the assembled party followed his reference to physics. But the expedition was re-assembled at last. He looked to Elric. "What now, old friend?"

Elric was troubled. "Apparently, we've been outmaneuvered by our enemies. Granbretan and her allies now possess at least two of the elements they seek, and will do everything they can to gather the rest. Even the Black Sword isn't safe from them. We gamble everything on this game—as, I suspect, do they."

"And our time grows short," said Prince Lobkowitz. "Now every Knight of the Balance, in every manifestation of our world, comes together to defeat those greedy forces, the combined power of the Dark Empire, Klosterheim, Gaynor and the rest. We must outwit them, as they have just outwitted us. They have a habit of cunning, which most of us lack. And that little girl's well-being, her very life, depends upon what we do next."

"I would give my life for the child," said Lord Renyard simply.

"As we all would," agreed Prince Lobkowitz. "But we do not wish Prince Elric, for instance, to give his life, for that would mean that he could not fulfill his destiny elsewhere. So you see, dear Lord Renyard, we act out of necessity, not sentiment, nor always decently, nor always courageously, in a highly complex conflict, full of subtle attack and counterattack. Imagine a large orchestra, in which every instrument must be in perfect tune if a particular piece of music is to be played, also perfectly and at a specific moment. Yet each member of that orchestra can be separated by thousands of miles or even thousands of years, scattered across the multiverse, which, if not infinite, appears to be infinite. If only one of our heroes does not act as he is supposed to act, if events do not happen exactly when they are due to happen, if Elric and his avatars do not do what they must all do precisely at the right moment, then there is no hope for any of us. Life will be extinguished. The multiverse will collapse into inchoate primal matter, *and there will be no intelligence, this time, to give it form.*"

"You refer to the death of God. The death of an idea. Even so, it takes a certain courage to continue to live in such circumstances," said Lieutenant Fromental, his open, friendly face graver than usual. "Any fool can throw up his arm with his fist around a sword and cry 'Liberty or Death!' but it takes a special kind of hero to know that it is not for him to choose the time of his death, or even choose his own weapons. You know that, I think, old friend." He came up to the others, dusting his hands and smiling sympathetically at Elric. "But what I am seriously curious about is, who betrayed us? Too often, it seems to me, our enemies have anticipated our moves, known where we were going and what we planned."

Elric ran his pale hand through his milk-white hair. "Aye. As if we had a spy in our midst. Yet the idea is anathema. Everything we do and say is based on mutual trust and mutual hatred of a common enemy. Who would have either the motive or the means of betraying us?"

The albino paused and shrugged. He rubbed his chin. "I have come from a world where betrayal and lies are commonplace, where anything is said and done in order to win at all costs, where people have grown used to hypocrisy and deceit and regard them as natural, legitimate instruments of trade, politics and daily intercourse, unable to distinguish truth from falsehood. They embrace the sentimental lie with the enthusiasm others bring to religion. Indeed that habit of mind has *become* their religion. Yet those of us who came together so recently to avert this plot are all habitual enemies of Gaynor, Klosterheim and their kind. We must reject the Prince of Lies. It is in our self-interest to remain loyal to one another." He sighed. "Well, there is nothing to do now but go to Granbretan and see if we can find the children before those creatures begin mingling their blood with those sacred objects."

"Children's blood!" The fox was shocked. "They are sacrificing children? How disgustingly barbaric! But why?"

"The corrupted practices of sorcery," said Prince Lobkowitz. "You begin by believing that like affects like. Like then *becomes* like. Therefore, like *controls* like. Pure blood of near-immortals is the material they hope to use to produce their new reality. When the multiverse melts and collapses into its unformed and uncontrolled fundamentals, they will absorb the blood, making it their own, and ensure that they survive to re-create the multiverse to their own design. Even if they fail, as I suspect they must, it will destroy all that regulates the multiverse. Meanwhile many heroes will die for nothing, believing themselves to be dying for a cause, dying to re-balance the elements, dying in defense of God himself. Every avatar of the one we call the Champion Eternal will perish."

"The destruction of the Knights of the Balance," murmured Lieutenant Fromental. "Even Satan did not seek that." He spoke with strong feeling, as if from experience. "We must go there. We must save our little mademoiselle."

Prince Lobkowitz drew his greying brows together. "But how on earth can we reach Granbretan undetected?"

"That is not our chief problem," Elric told him. "We can scavenge masks from the many corpses Duke Dorian has left us. I'm told the Dark Empire forces have retreated back to their Silver Bridge which spans the sea between Karlye and Deau Vere. Even if

Colonel Bastable cannot help us, as I believe he intends to, it would be easy for most of us to join groups of refugees. It will be considerably more difficult to find and rescue young Oonagh and my daughter."

Lord Renyard was a little perplexed. "I must go with you, gentlemen. How do you propose to disguise me?"

A new voice chimed in from behind them. "At last! Thank the Lord we are still to some degree synchronized. I would have been here sooner, but I had some minor problems with a timing device. I am sorry I was unable to keep our appointment in Mirenburg, Monsieur Zodiac. I simply couldn't leave the job at that point. The machine shops and factories are the only ones in this extraordinary world where I could find the engineers and craftsmen I needed. And as usual, they were behind schedule. Anyway, she's ready now. I gather you got my message."

Elric turned, recognizing the voice, but it was Prince Lobkowitz and Lieutenant Fromental who spoke first, together. "Good afternoon, Colonel."

The strong, open features of the newcomer brightened in a grin. "Good afternoon to you, too, gentlemen!" He stepped forward to embrace Prince Lobkowitz and shake the hands of his fellow Knights of the Balance. With heavy goggles pushed back over a military cap, he wore something very close to a uniform, in light blue and scarlet. In certain worlds he would have been recognized immediately as a member of His Majesty's Imperial Merchant Air Service.

Colonel Oswald Bastable was glad to see his old friends. He told them quickly of his time in Mirenburg, how he had thought it unwise to reveal himself to the party there, because he, too, had seen Klosterheim and Gaynor in the palace. "I decided to let them focus on you, gentlemen, whom they had already detected. This allowed me the time I needed to complete my 'infernal machine.' Of course, without Prince Yaroslaf's help, nothing would have been possible. Your word, Monsieur Zodiac, went a long way with him.

"I tried to tell Countess von Beck to wait, that I was preparing a better means of travel, but she left precipitously while I was at the factory clearing up some details of my ship. Young Oonagh almost recognized me when I joined you briefly for that first meal at Prince Yaroslaf's reception. The prince was sworn to secrecy, but I couldn't resist making brief contact with you. It was a bit of a toss-up, you see. I could have told her who I was and risked old Klosterheim and company guessing what I was up to, or I could keep my identity secret and risk your party, Prince Lobkowitz, leaving before I could contact you. That, of course, is exactly what happened. When I heard you had gone, I ran after you, but you were already some distance from Mirenburg. I was a little too late, it seems. I guessed they were waiting for you to leave the safety of the city, where they'd be able to take a crack at you. I tried to warn you, but unfortunately you misinterpreted me. Anyway, she's completed now and at your disposal. Training the crew was the hardest part. They have a very different theory of aeronautics. They're not British, you see. However . . ."

With a modest gesture of his gauntleted hand, Colonel Bastable pushed back his cap, turned and indicated low hills behind them.

Flying low, casting a long shadow on the ground, her engine droning softly, hull glittering with newly doped canvas, bright metal and fresh paint, flying a Union Jack from her aftlines, came a slender airship, the glass portholes of her armored gondola winking like round, innocent eyes.

"Gentlemen, may I present HMAS *Victoria*. She's our prototype. A nifty little bus, though I do say so myself. Carrying some pretty powerful ordnance. And I think we can slip across the channel in her tonight, what, and do what we need to do."

Prince Lobkowitz nodded gravely, staring hard into Colonel Bastable's face. "I suspect, sir, that you have a personal agenda in this matter."

Wide-eyed, Bastable returned his stare. "To protect the well-being of this world, sir? How does that sound?"

Elric, unable to determine the nature of their exchange, turned away in some impatience, leading the party towards the airship as she began to settle in the air a few feet above the ground.

CHAPTER NINETEEN

HE SIGHT OF the Scots balloonist made me feel suddenly sick and helpless. St. Odhran's crooked smile told me all I needed to know. He had betrayed us. We were as good as finished. I remembered how Monsieur Zodiac had trusted him, even leaving his sword in the traitor's hands!

"You rotten . . ." I couldn't come up with a word bad enough. I was close to tears.

Countess Flana had better things to do. She had grown bored with me. Asking the chevalier to sit down, she summoned slaves and ordered them to wheel me out of her little sanctuary. Before I had the chance to recover my composure, I found myself in a set of apartments which, the slaves told me, had been prepared for me.

Certainly it looked as if my capture had been anticipated for quite a while. There were changes of clothes in my size, a neat little bed with a fluffy down comforter, and everything was made for a person of my height. Everything but the doors and windows, that is. They were, if anything, oversize, and all discreetly locked, barred or both. The windows were so high, I couldn't see out of them. Only when I managed to clamber on top of a piece of asymmetrical furniture (which vaguely resembled a hippopotamus) could I see a few roofs, the odd chimney against a black and scarlet sky full of perpetual, restless movement, clouds of smoke creating sinister half-familiar shapes. The glass was thick and blemished. It helped produce the effect of warped menace. I was glad to get down and have a look around my cell.

As prisons went, it was luxurious. There was a little sitting room with funny-looking chairs and another of those weird toilets. The cupboards revealed more clothes, many of them really beautiful, a couple of plain masks, which fit me, some books made of light, silvery stuff which was neither paper nor plastic. Pictures in the books gave the impression of movement. The script was in a language I could scarcely understand. I tried to do a bit of reading, but the strain was too much.

At some point a slave brought me my supper, which consisted of a cup of salty soup, several different kinds of fish in thin strips laid on the plate in rows, some fruit and a very sweet drink which reminded me of that apricot nectar which Mum would never let us have because she said the sugar in it would rot through bone, let alone our teeth. I felt quite a lot better after I'd eaten, though. I was ready to face, if not the worst Granbretan could throw at me, then something close. They had shown me that poor, ragged creature, his skin hanging in ribbons from his body, so that I could sit and think of the similar fate in store for me, but in spite of the evidence, I refused to believe they were going to do anything so cruel.

I think I was in shock or denial, because I had become pretty unemotional, in spite of all I knew of their intentions. I shed no more tears. I had a cold hatred for St. Odhran. My duty was to get away from him, to spoil his plans as much as possible. I exercised by running around the room shouting pop songs to myself, then jumping up and down on the bed, then trying some of my mum's tai chi and yoga positions. By the time I stopped I had worn myself out and lay on the comfortable feather bed, panting and staring up at the heavily decorated ceiling, which had masked, naked people doing things which were not so much obscene or sexual as impossible to interpet, which was probably just as well. The walls, too, were decorated. They showed a painted forest through which a procession of people and monsters marched. All the colors were the usual dark greens, browns, reds and purples. Pretty oppressive.

As I looked around my room, I found myself nodding off in spite of my determination to try to stay awake and think through my situation. I was soon fast asleep, dreaming of cows with animal heads, of Lord Renyard dressed like an old-fashioned Victorian nanny, of Elric/Monsieur Zodiac carrying a huge black sword, which I thought at first streamed with blood until I saw that there were glowing letters engraved in the metal, red as the albino's eyes. Then came my grandmother, Oona, with her bow and arrows, loosing one shaft after another into the carcass of a monstrous wolf which pranced and snarled at the edges of my bed, gathering courage to pounce.

It was very dark in my room when I heard a scratching at the door, which swung open at my mumbled greeting. I didn't see anyone come in until a large face with green-yellow eyes was close to mine. A rumbling purr broke from the throat of the beast I recognized as our black panther. Then the door opened again. A female slave stood there, holding a tray on which was a steaming beaker of liquid like tomato juice. This slave was masked and naked, like all slaves of the upper orders. She had a really lovely body, all rounded muscular curves, and her soft, glowing skin seemed unnaturally pink in the faint light coming through the high windows. I realized I didn't know how to turn a light on in the room, and was surprised by the soft radiance which slowly filled it.

The slave made no attempt to offer me the tray but put it on the nearest surface and crossed back to the door. Was she checking to see if she'd been followed? Meanwhile the panther sat down between us. I felt sudden relief, a sense of gratitude. I wasn't really surprised when the panther's companion stripped off her mask and revealed herself as Oona, wearing what I now saw was a flesh-colored body stocking. She had obviously worn it to hide her albino skin, which would have been easily detected even in the murk of corridors lit primarily by flaming torches.

"I thought they'd left you behind," I whispered. "How did you get here?"

My grandmother smiled. "By ornithopter, the same as you. I didn't inhale much of the poison gas which knocked you all out. I was able to hold my breath and pretend to be overcome. Both Empire ships took off at the same time. One carried von Minct, and the other left with you. But they had forgotten our ship, which returned and found us. I flagged it down and persuaded the pilot to fly me to Karlye, where a major battle was taking place. In the confusion I disguised myself and joined troops retreating over the Silver Bridge. Things were so confused on the other side, with soldiers and fighting machines everywhere, that I easily made it to Londra." She grinned. "So unused have the Granbretanners become to attack by those they conquer that they have few defenses in the city. With a little help, I slipped through the gates and reached the palace."

"But you didn't have any keys . . ." I looked at the door she had entered by.

"I am not above using the odd manipulation." She reached down to pat the panther. Another vast purr rumbled in the cat's throat as she looked up at my grandmother, who answered her with a kind of *huff* which the panther responded to by half closing her eyes in a friendly way.

"Where did she come from?" I asked. The panther hadn't been with us when we fled Mirenburg.

"Oh, she always knows where to find me." My beautiful grandmother smiled. "We have a rapport. Sometimes we might almost be the same creature. Come, get dressed quickly. I'm taking you away from here."

"Escaping!" I was excited. Maybe this was why I had not felt total terror at the Dark Empire's plans for me. Maybe I had always known she would come for me. "Do you know about that traitor, St. Odhran?"

"Oh, yes," she said, "I know all about St. Odhran." She seemed too disgusted to say more.

The Heron Palace was alive with sound. Were we under attack? The building itself was moaning and whining, and the fluttering flames of the overhead flambeaux made the corridors seem alive, organic. Oona and the panther trotted swiftly over the uneven flagstones, keeping me between them. We went past doors from which came all kinds of animal noises, suggesting this was some sort of private zoo. It smelled like the zoo, too. In reply to my whispered question, my grandmother put her thumb up, indicating I had hit it in one.

When she got the chance, she murmured into my ear, "This is the menagerie of Asrovak Mikosevaar. He was a keen collector. Many powerful people here keep menageries."

"I'm used to barred cages and all that sort of thing. Or at least big ditches and glass!"

"These are not for public view," she whispered, "but for private pleasure."

Before she could tell me more I felt the warm night air on my face and smelled that mixture of soot, scorched metal and burning coke which was the predominant smell of the city. "This brings us out near the river, which is exactly where we need to be."

"Won't they be looking for me? I mean, you might be able to disguise yourself as a soldier, but nobody would believe I was one. Not even a little Gurkha."

She smiled. "We're not going back the way we came. I'm hoping to follow the trail of Klosterheim and von Minct. I found their prisoner."

"The boy? Jack?"

"Yes."

"How did they get Jack here? He wasn't with them in Mirenburg."

"They know a way of traveling between Mirenburg and Londra," she said. "But I can't use it. The wheel. Anyway, Jack's out of harm's way for the moment."

While we held that whispered conversation we hurried along the galleries. Only once was our way blocked, by a couple of masked male slaves who weren't really suspicious of us but were curious. Oona's response was to reach out and bang their heads together so that they slipped gently to the floor. I was very impressed.

"You'll have to show me how you do that, Grandma," I said. I was taking a perverse pleasure in using the term to this attractive young woman, who really was my grandmother!

"Later," she said. "When we are all safely back in Ingleton, there's a lot I do want to show you. Wisdom that has to be passed on."

I was no longer certain we'd ever make it back to West Yorkshire, but I was heartened by her promise even though I suspected she made it to reassure me. The galleries were getting more populated, busier, with slaves bustling back and forth, carrying everything from trays of food to furniture. I was surprised they didn't notice the panther, but when I looked for her she had disappeared.

"Where are we?" I asked the first time we paused.

"We have left Mikosevaar's and are now approaching the apartments of Taragorm, Master of the Palace of Time."

"Isn't he one of our worst enemies?"

"Which is why we went this way rather than another," she said. "I'm guessing they'll first try searching the streets surrounding Flana's when they find you gone in the morning."

"What happened to your panther?"

"Oh, she's become absorbed in someone else, don't worry." It was the only answer she gave me. I wondered just how much magic was around. I caught a distinctive odor I associated with both electricity and the sulphur stink that matches make when you strike them. For some reason, I thought of it as the smell of magic.

We descended, by steps and slopes, lower and lower into the palace depths. This part was deserted. Then Oona opened a small door in the side of a very narrow passage, and even I had to duck to enter. She closed the door carefully behind us. She felt around in the dark. I heard something rustling, and it scared me. I stuck close to my grandmother. "What's that . . . ?"

A Bic sparked. A conical yellow candle burned with a smell like fried fish.

Gradually I made out a small room. It seemed to have been used as a sort of store cupboard. In the far corner, a figure stirred.

He yawned as he turned over on a dark grey mattress, blinking awake.

It was the young man I had seen before, whom I'd tried to track down without success in Mirenburg's Mechanical Gardens. I saw his face clearly now. He had the same high cheekbones, almond eyes, strong mouth and chin, the gently tapered ears, that I had seen on Oona and my great-grandfather. The young albino turned his head towards us.

"Jack," murmured Oona. "I've found her. You must lie low here for a day or so. Then we'll try to get away."

He nodded. He hardly seemed interested in what she said. "My father . . . ," he began, then stopped. He frowned. "Who are you, girl?"

"My name's Oonagh," I told him. "Are you Jack D'Acre?"

"That's close," he said. "It's what they call me at home. I know your voice. The girl in the factory . . ."

"That's right." I wondered where his home was, and was about to ask him when Oona said, "Jack's from London. Not Londra. He lived in Clapham before Klosterheim and von Minct got news of him." She moved back towards the door. "I must find some clothes and a better mask or I'll be of no use to anyone. I'll return as soon as I can. Should something happen and I don't get back, let me show you this." She went to the far wall of the little room and pulled away some boxes and sacking. She pointed to a short door down in the wall. "You'll have to lead Jack to safety, Oonagh. If you are in danger, go through there. It will take you to the river, where I think you'll be able to find a boat. The panther will help. It's the only way to escape the city now."

Then she was gone. When I next looked, I saw that the panther was sitting guarding the door, her eyes closed, her head hanging slightly as if she slept on her feet.

"Are you the female principle they keep talking about?" The boy stood up, came towards me. He stumbled, almost fell, his hands grabbing at air.

His red eyes stared at me without seeing. I remembered Mrs. House's oracular remarks: *"You have been in danger since the day you were born!"* He was the same boy from Mirenburg. I racked my brains to try to think of what else Mrs. House had told me. *"The Blood,"* she had said. *"You have the Blood."* Well, I knew that from the Countess Flana, too—whatever it *meant!*

I didn't know what a female principle was exactly. "I spoke to you in the factory. Then I saw you later in a sideshow. Aren't they still looking for you? What happened?" I went up to him and reached out my hand and took his. His soft, gentle fingers followed the contours of my face.

"You're young," he said. "Younger than me. The one who helped me. I heard Klosterheim talking about 'the female principle.' They seem almost scared of us."

"I kept my mouth shut. Did you say anything?"

"No," he said, "but then, I have no secrets. Klosterheim and Gaynor have been holding me prisoner off and on for quite a while. They found me in London and then brought me here. That was ages ago. Then they took me to Mirenburg, where the wheel is, so they could move through various different versions of our world. That's how we managed to escape the big flood. Did they take you to Mirenburg?"

"No," I replied. "I think they were using you to try to trap me, as well as your father. After I talked to you in the factory, I saw you a couple of times, in different places. They almost captured me once, but Oona saved me."

"She's a saint, that woman," he said. "Were you part of McTalbayne's gang?"

"I don't know the name."

"Worst bastard that ever was on the street," he said. "Charged you rent for the cardboard box you lived in."

"You were homeless?"

"I told you. I had a home. A decent-sized box." He grinned to himself as he felt his way over to a small chest which had been placed against the wall. "Want something to eat?"

"No, thanks," I said, watching him open the chest and take out what looked like a pie made of green pastry and bite into it.

"These are good," he said. "Meat. Sure you won't have one?"

"Maybe later. I'm not that hungry. So when did they first capture you?"

"First? A while ago. I don't know exactly. McTalbayne had us up west on a run. I was always used as the diversion, see, because I'm blind and look sort of funny. So that was my job. I was in Marks and Spencers, having a bit of a fit, while the rest of them stripped the racks near the door. We'd done it a hundred times before. Then, suddenly, I felt myself grabbed. I thought it was the Old Bill, the cops, but it turns out to be Klosterheim and that filthy wanker von Minct. They pretended they were police. Only when I was in the car I realized they were bullshitting me. They got me down to the river and over the bridge, and before I knew it, it was 'Three, please' for the London Wheel."

"You've been on it?"

"Well, only that time. A waste of money in my case. Next thing I knew, I was in Mirenburg. Weird place, isn't it? Are you a Londoner, too?"

I was fascinated. "Yes," I said hurriedly. "What? You mean the London Wheel took you to Mirenburg?"

"That's how they travel," he said. "What part of London?"

"Well, I was born in Notting Dale, but we moved to Tufnell Hill. Near the old windmill."

"Oh, I know it," he said. "McTalbayne used to take us up there on the way to Hampstead. We did the fair and that. Apparently it's the last working mill in London. Owned by a recluse of some sort. I know McTalbayne had his eye on the place but got put off when he went to see if he could break in . . ."

I had the strangest sensation, talking to that blind albino boy who looked so much like my grandparents and Monsieur Zodiac. The panther was still sleeping by the door.

"Do you know who your mum and dad are?" I asked him.

"I'm told my father was Elric and my mum was a dreamthief. Then there's my sister."

"They think I'm her."

His hand came out again to explore my face. "Oh, no," he said. "There's no resemblance at all."

"So it's mistaken identity, is it? Because we've got the same relatives?"

He shook his head. "Don't ask me. That pair didn't tell me much. I found out from my real sister almost everything I *do* know. Which isn't much! How are you related?"

"Oona," I said, "is really my grandmother."

"Oona?" He burst into laughter. "Oona? You mean the woman who brought you here, right?"

"Right." I was a bit upset by his response.

"Well, I don't know what she's been saying or what anyone else is telling you," he said, "but we can't be *that* many years apart." He spoke in a coarse, rather aggressive tone. Maybe, I thought, he is just defensive. He must have had a terrible time since he was a baby.

"Eh?"

"Oona just can't be your grandma," said Jack D'Acre. "She's far too young."

"Well, that's what you'd think—"

"I know it. Far too young. You've got it *completely* wrong. Oona's my *sister*." He put his hand to his mouth. "Oops. I wasn't supposed to tell anyone that. Keep it dark, okay, or we could be in trouble."

 DECIDED JACK'S ordeal had addled his mind, so I didn't press the subject. A bit later my grand-mother returned briefly with a further warning to lie low. "Hawkmoon's made impressive advances. They say he has supernatural help. A crystal whose facets resemble the multiverse itself, the light representing the moonbeam roads. He is capable of moving whole armies across space and time. His army vanishes for a while and then reappears hundreds of miles deeper into enemy territory. Meanwhile the Empire makes finding you two its prior-ity. Huon has offered rewards and punishments. Some of the pun-ishments have already started. Flana herself, I understand, is suspected."

King Huon had ordered an intensive search for me and the blind boy. The biggest operation Oona had ever seen. We were more important to the Dark Empire than the defense of its city. I tried to ask how Jack D'Acre could be her twin brother, but she had no time to explain, she said. "It's to do with the relationship of one world of the multiverse with another. The closer they are in conjunction, the closer their time lines. We grow used to these discrepancies when we travel the moonbeam roads. I suspect that is the secret Hawkmoon has. Klosterheim seems to know some-thing about the duke's source of power. The Empire wants to find anyone who has the ability to travel in that manner—you and Jack in particular."

At least I now understood how she looked roughly the same age as her father. So it really was possible, for a special few at least, to go back into history and meet their own parents before they were born! Did it mean you could manipulate events? Change the course of history? From what she said, this power was granted to you only if you were one of a kind, or at least a manifestation, like Elric, of a recurring hero called the Champion Eternal.

When Oona left to scout out our escape route, she took the panther with her. She had given me plenty to think about.

Those resonances began to make sense of so much that had been a mystery to me. If I ever got back to school and passed my A-levels, I decided to specialize in mythology and anthropology at university. Then came a fresh anxiety: Had the school holidays ended? Was I being missed at Godolphin and Latymer? It's stupid the kind of things you think of when someone is threatening to hang you upside down and bleed you to death like a pig!

Jack D'Acre wasn't Oona's brother's real name. He had been homeless, hanging out in Covent Garden and Longacre, when his mates called him that as a joke because they thought he had a French accent. He didn't know where he was from, though he vaguely remembered a time before he was blind. He might have dreamed that he'd lived in a cottage in the country, he thought, with woods all around. He remembered "a kind of brilliant darkness," he said. He had lived there with Oona, his sister, and in those days they had been exactly the same age.

It was odd talking to my great-uncle who was probably no more than five years older than I. He still seemed more like a brother. He had a restless, boyish manner. His white hair was cropped short, and he wore a pair of sunglasses to hide his eyes, but his resemblance to Elric and Oona was uncanny.

"They also called me Onric," he told me, "in Mirenburg. A weird name. I prefer Jack, don't you?"

"Well, it's easier to remember. I'm a bit inexperienced at all this between-the-worlds traveling. I'm not sure I'd be able to do any of it without help. How did you go blind? Were you always on your own?"

"Oona says it was during the Empire's first experiments. I was only little when I was blinded. Some agent of Taragorm's found me out on the moonbeams apparently. I must have been abandoned there. After that I was never on my own for long. I don't know how I got away from Bous-Junge before. There was always someone offering to help me who I could be useful to. One bloke in Oxford used to take me out with him as a leprosy victim."

He laughed. "We got a lot of money thrown at us—from a distance. McTalbayne wasn't the first by a long shot. I've done worse than he wanted me to do. At least I got regular food and my own box." He chuckled again, his whole face opening up into an honest and at the same time very sad expression. Then he withdrew again. "All I had to do was be myself and create a diversion, wherever we were. Sometimes it was shops, sometimes streets. Mostly it was stealing from institutions, big stores, those who could afford it, though I didn't really like doing *any* of it. After that bastard Klosterheim found me again he took me to Bous-Junge, as I said. Then to Mirenburg, where they were trying to forge that sword. Then back here. They know how to get onto the moonbeam roads, though they find it hard to use them. Klosterheim knew who my mum and dad were, he said. He claimed he would make it his business to get us together again. I think they might even have bought me from McTalbayne. I suspect money changed hands because I heard them talking later. I've got this very sensitive hearing. Five hundred quid, maybe? Only a couple of hours after we got off the Ferris wheel we weren't in London anymore, as I said. That bloke Gaynor met us in Mirenburg. For a while they had me in the local fairground. I guess it was a way of hiding me from anyone else who might be looking for me. It wasn't a bad scam, all in all. But things got more and more restrictive. They wouldn't let me go anywhere without at least two minders, and not very far, at that. I heard them talking. The Dark Empire wanted to find out how to use the moonbeam roads. Klosterheim and Gaynor let them use me to listen to the sword blades. They wanted some other bloke to see me. They called him "our mutual friend." Never said his name. They made me work, testing those swords by their resonances. They were trying to make this one special blade, see. For a special customer they hoped to trick. At least that's what I guessed. Anyway, we spent some time in that weird-smelling city, and then they brought me back here and locked me up in a filthy storage room of some sort. I think it had been a warehouse. I couldn't get out. Mainly wanted me as bait for their trap . . . I didn't know what had happened to my sister then, and I didn't, of course, know about you or my father. Then I met you and guessed it was you they were after next."

"Do you know why?"

"Some big war or science project they've got on? What would your guess be? Human bombs? I've heard lately that the Empire's losing ground every day. They were so confident of their own superiority, they never expected their slaves to rise up. They certainly didn't realize the momentum that revolt would give Hawkmoon and the others. I heard Klosterheim talking about it just before Oona found me. Hawkmoon's got a secret weapon, I think. That crystal my sister mentioned. The armies were actually fighting on the sea bridge, last I heard. Whatever it is they want from us, they want it *bad*."

"They want to kill us for our blood," I said. "At least they want to kill *me*. Maybe they'll let you live; I'm not sure. They're falling back on witchcraft as they lose battles. Not human bombs but human sacrifice. Which, I suppose, is much the same thing in the end. And they don't have any game plan for failure!"

Jack nodded. "That makes a lot of sense. It's all the new weapons they're producing in Eastern Europe that's nobbled 'em. Weapons they designed themselves but were too busy and conservative to build in their home factories, where they're still turning out the old models. It's all they're tooled up for. When that chap Hawkmoon turned up he was still alive, he gave heart to millions. He must be a pretty amazing person. Everyone but the Empire thinks he's the cat's meow. Even Meliadus is scared of him."

Jack's features were expressive. He had learned to hate and to control his hatred in a way I'd never had to. "From what I heard before my sister got me away, he's got them off balance. They're still trying to get their breath back. A year ago they wouldn't have believed they would have to worry about all these guys banding together against them. Up to then they'd had a lot of success with their divide-and-rule policies."

"How do you know all this? Just from listening?"

"Sharp ears, I told you. I've been luckier than you. Because I'm blind, even Klosterheim, von Minct and Taragorm talk in front of me. They think I'm deaf, too." He grinned. "But they keep quiet about meaning to sacrifice us to one of their gods, if that's what they're up to. Funny. I thought they were atheists."

There wasn't any point in telling him more of what I knew. At least, not yet. Why scare him? But it was on the tip of my tongue more than once to reveal the grimmer truth. Of course, I was also a bit mixed up about their motives. "Anyway," I said, "we're valuable to them. They could have killed us at any time. How did *you* get away?"

"Oona found me eventually and brought me here. The London Eye's the secret, all right. I don't think I ever want to ride another Ferris wheel again. You wait for hours to get on, and then there's just a mild sensation of going up and down. Then you get off and you're in Mirenburg or here or somewhere. I suppose it's cheaper than running a plane of your own. I'd love to find out what that was all about."

"Well," I said a bit harshly, "we might soon. I know they are ruthless and cruel. They'd kill us at the drop of a hat if they felt like it, but right now they need us a lot more than we need them."

"I wonder why," he mused. "I mean, apart from throwing fits in the middle of Oxford Street shops and hearing voices in swords, I'm not exactly much good for anything." He grinned into the middle distance. "They don't think I've got royal blood, do they? Why sacrifice *us*? We're not especially important. Apart from Oona, I haven't got any family. All my friends have been killed. My sister's the only one looking out for me." He laughed again. "Klosterheim really didn't expect her to turn up. He thought she was dead. She must have followed him here. Now we'll wait and do what she tells us. If anyone can beat 'em, she can. She's playing a tricky game, I reckon."

"So are they," I said. "She's a brave woman, isn't she?"

"A bloody diamond," he agreed.

After that, neither of us had any clear idea how much time passed. When we got hungry, we ate from the small store of food and water Oona left us. We slept on piles of old fabric and talked about our lives. Jack said that Oona had called him Onric when she first recognized him. Their mother had gone off, he said, though he was unclear why and where. He repeated how he and Oona had lived together in a country cottage for a while, when they were little, in the days before he was blinded. It had been some sort of explosion, he thought. For a while he remembered only darkness and confusion. "It was like I was blown out of one world into another. One time into another." Maybe his father had rescued him . . . He next wound up in Bristol, adopted by a junkie named Rachel Acker, who kept him as a sort of talisman. She claimed he was her son. They both knew she was lying, but he got his food and keep, and she got her heroin. He said she was sweet to him when she wasn't totally out of it. Then Social Services discovered them and wanted to take him in, so she took him and ran off to Oxford first and then London. He and Rachel worked out a reasonably unambitious little shoplifting scheme, which kept them going for some time, but eventually Rachel disappeared, probably overdosing somewhere. And that's when McTalbayne had recruited him.

I asked him what he thought of being part of a gang run by a modern Fagin, and he laughed. "It beats being banged up in some orphanage. I've heard about those places, and I know what they do to you. At least I was my own boss. Well, partly. It's important to be your own boss. McTalbayne says it's the secret of the British Empire's success, our will to entrepreneurism." He shook his head. "What do you reckon? Is this lot here"—sightlessly he lifted his head and waved his arms to indicate, I supposed, the whole of Granbretan—"I mean, are they the best the British can be?"

I think this was an argument he had been having with himself. He didn't seem to mind that I couldn't think of an answer.

"Don't worry, kid," he said, lowering his arms. "I'm not barmy. I'm just getting bored and sick of this smelly hole. Do you think she's been caught and isn't coming back?"

I had to admit I feared the worst. We were running out of candles. What food there was didn't taste very good anymore, and by the next meal we would have no water. "It's got to have been a couple of days, at least," I told him. "Maybe we should do what she told us to do and head for the river. She seemed to think we'd know what to do. But there's no Ferris wheel anymore, is there?"

"I'm not sure. Maybe she has friends who'll know us." He felt his way to the far wall and cocked his head, listening as I dragged stuff away from the little secret door. "Where does that lead to?"

"Somewhere better than this," I said. "It couldn't be worse, could it? I don't want to starve to death in here, do you?"

He agreed enthusiastically. Since we didn't know where our next meal was coming from, we decided to wait until there was nothing left to eat or drink. "I think our best bet is down there, from what I've heard," he said. "It's supposed to be full of escaped slaves, crooks and old con men, but I bet it's not a patch on what I was used to . . ."

"No cardboard boxes?" I asked a bit nastily. And he laughed.

I took his hand.

I became increasingly convinced that my grandmother had been captured or dangerously delayed. Soon after I made up my mind that she probably wasn't coming back for us, there was a thump on the outside door. Nobody came in, but I heard guttural voices, the clank of armored men. A search party! The snuffling of large dogs. Another thump. Guards in conference. They were going to find a key and come back. We now had no choice.

I took the two remaining candles from the shelf. Jack held them while I wound as much spare fabric as I could around both of us, in case we needed to keep warm. Then I opened the tiny back door, pushed Jack through and clambered in myself, pulling

it and other stuff behind me. I hoped the searchers wouldn't necessarily guess we had been there.

The passage fell away steeply. It was dank, smelling strongly of
foul water. From the fresh scrapes on the walls and floor, probably
my grandmother had been there at some earlier point. The path
was so slippery that we found ourselves sliding quite rapidly downwards, almost like a helter-skelter, as the corridor curved and
twisted radically. It must have been some kind of old garbage
chute, as it still smelled of what had been poured through it.

We were a long way down before I heard a hint of voices
above. They came closer. Men were shouting over the menacing
noise of growling dogs. At last we hit fresh air, so cold it made us
gasp and shiver. We stood on cobblestones. High overhead were
the restless clouds which sat forever above the towers of Londra.
Before us was a maze of little alleys, some of them blocked with
rusted, rotting bars which were easily pushed down.

Jack stood there shivering, wrapped in rags, listening and staring around with his unseeing eyes while I kicked in several different grates, on the basis that if we were followed we didn't want to
give them an easy clue to the way we had gone. Those dogs
sounded businesslike.

I grabbed Jack by the hand again and pulled him through the
nearest alley, imagining I could already smell the river. But the
maze was endless, twisting back and forth on itself, even though
the river, surely the Thames, was only a few yards away some of
the time! Every so often I heard distant explosions and saw whole
squadrons of big, old-fashioned ornithopters lumbering through
the air.

Dimly I realized that a battle was taking place somewhere,
though not directly over us. Jack's ears were superb. He heard the
different notes of engines and described air fights he thought must
be happening over on what he called "the Surrey side" of the river,
the South Bank. Were the Dark Empire clans breaking up under
threat? Fighting among themselves? Were we witnessing the
opening engagements in a civil war?

The Empire must have been rotten through and through to

have collapsed so thoroughly. Or had it always been stretched too thin, its power maintained by illusion, its victims too used to its dominance to realize their own numerical strength?

We finally reached a small cut in the river, where a couple of old, filthy rowboats were tethered. Everything looked as if it hadn't been used in years, and the Thames was dirtier than I had ever known it, with bits of nasty-looking debris floating in it. The water, reflecting lights and far-off explosions, was a murky crimson.

As I pulled Jack onto a slippery little jetty a shadow rose from one of the skiffs. Our black panther! Now I knew which boat to use. "Good girl," I whispered, rubbing her broad head as we climbed in with her. She looked expectantly towards the far bank. Maybe from there we could make our way to the coast, in the hope that Dorian Hawkmoon's army had already invaded.

It was not something I knew much about, but Jack couldn't believe it, either. "What did my sister say about a crystal helping them?"

"That's all she *did* say. What is the crystal, anyway?"

"I only know what I overheard Klosterheim and Gaynor saying. There's some sort of crystal shard which allows you to move yourself and sometimes whole chunks of real estate through the dimensions. What purpose that has, I don't know. Most of these people don't seem to need a crystal to get from one world to another. Maybe it's what allows you to bring something enormous through with you. Like an army. You know, not just yourself but tanks and planes or houses or something."

I could see how it would help Hawkmoon's cause, at least in minor ways, to own such a device. With my grandmother almost certainly killed or captured, I should be grateful for any advantage. If we could keep out of their hands for a while, maybe Hawkmoon would save us. Gingerly I tested the rowboat, bouncing the end of an oar in the bottom to see if it was still riverworthy. The panther moved to the prow.

The boat was sounder than I had any right to expect. All those years rowing on Grasmere were at last proving useful. I helped Jack sit down, put the oars into the rowlocks and maneuvered slowly down the cut, which was thick with filthy, smelly flotsam and jetsam, steering us in the shadow of a long wooden jetty. The stink of the river made me feel sick.

Jack sat holding the tiller ropes, tugging them left or right at my command, so we got out fairly easily. I rowed under a series of jetties, making as little noise as possible. It grew pitch black quite quickly, except for the sky, illuminated by the flickering red glow from the Surrey bank, the occasional spurt of flame or a gouting explosion. The sky was thick with flocks of flying machines, their metal wings clashing, their clawed landing gear stretched out as if they stooped on their prey, but we saw no direct fighting. I had the impression the battle order had changed. Perhaps Hawkmoon's people were being forced back as the Empire rallied its strength.

Eventually I judged it safe to push out into midwater and attempt a crossing. A horrible fog was rising, but I had spotted a potential landing place under cover of the jetties on the other side. As I crossed, the river would carry me down, and with luck I would wind up where I wanted to be. We were nearing the opposite bank when suddenly a white, brilliant light illuminated the whole scene. I thought we would be spotted for certain, but nobody shot at us.

We landed and went ashore, scrambling to a low, narrow landing platform, up some steps to the main jetty, the panther leading and me pushing Jack as he groped for handholds. A narrow lane ran between two sets of tall warehouses, which looked as if they had fallen against one another and were now offering mutual support, like old drunks.

And then the panther vanished again! All around us were chimneys and factories, just like in Mirenburg, and if anything, the stench was worse. We moved between rotting tenements, where not one person gave us a second glance. We were still bundled in our rags and looked just like everyone else on this side. This must be where they kept the drones of the Dark Empire anthill, without masks and, by the look of them, without hope.

I led Jack deeper and deeper into the mass of wretched apartment buildings and thundering factories. His bone-white face was turned to the sky, which still raced red, and his skin reflected the flames. His hair was the color of cream, and his eyes were the color of blood. In the weird, sluggish, wavering light, he looked as if he were on fire. He sniffed his way through the swaying build-ings, his head cocked for any threatening sound, but he missed the danger when it eventually came.

Suddenly Jack stopped.

"Soldiers!" he hissed.

Too late. "Oh, bugger!" We turned instinctively. Behind us crept half a dozen warriors in the snarling war helms of the Order of the Vulture, Asrovak Mikosevaar's own legion.

I heard a stomping sound in front of me. Rounding a corner came a score of hounds bearing flame lances. They were led by the Chevalier St. Odhran, in all his bizarre Scottish finery. I dashed into another alley, dragging Jack, but there was no way of escape.

They seemed to have known where to capture us. St. Odhran recognized us both. We couldn't hope to fool them. We were trapped. At any moment we'd be back in the hands of enemies who planned to kill us in the most disgusting and painful way imaginable.

Oona *had* to be dead or captured! I had led her brother into a trap! All our efforts had brought us no advantage. I felt that I deserved what they were going to do to me, that I had betrayed my friends in a profound way.

Jack yelled a warning.

St. Odhran put his hand out towards me.

But instead of grabbing me—he pushed!

Suddenly Jack and I were falling.

CHAPTER TWENTY-ONE

E FELL SLOWLY for what seemed a mile or more. I could see Jack's white hair standing straight up from his head, just below me as he sank in slow motion. Once he turned, staring upwards. His blind eyes had an expression of pure pleasure.

In other circumstances I might have enjoyed the sensation, which was like riding in a hot-air balloon—a cushioned weight-lessness.

It was impossible to judge the time. We could have fallen for hours. My mouth was very dry. My heart stopped pounding from the terror of the encounter with St. Odhran. I was determined to get my nerve back.

Someone *had* to have known where we were. Had the traitor deliberately set things up so that he could push us into the pit? But who had warned them? The panther?

I heard Jack land first. I drew a deep breath. He grunted with surprise, sprawled flat on his back. "Bugger! I was enjoying that. What's happening?"

I came down with a thump beside him. The ground yielded slightly, like a sponge. But it wasn't grass. Deep moss? I got up and helped Jack to his feet. All the stench of the city had disappeared. The air was clean, sharp, even a little bitter. I took big gulps of it, the way a near-drowning person might. I tasted it on my tongue.

After all the horrible, suggestive smells of the city above us, this air was a welcome relief.

I still had a candle in my pocket. I decided to risk lighting it.

"That was awesome!" Jack said enthusiastically from nearby. I saw his pale skin in the fluttering yellow light. "A lot better than the London Wheel! I wouldn't mind doing *that* again." He treated the experience as he had treated a ride in a theme park. He hadn't seen St. Odhran. He didn't even know how profoundly we'd been betrayed. Again, it seemed churlish to spoil his moment. He wouldn't benefit from any outburst of mine.

I was thirsty. I thought I heard water running somewhere nearby. The candle illuminated what appered to be a ventilation shaft or maybe, in an earlier epoch, a goods chute for whoever lived down here. Hadn't there been something like it in *The Time Machine?* A sort of gravity regulator. Of course, I half-hoped we had accidentally returned to the land of the kindly, courteous Off-Moo, who would surely know how to help us. But St. Odhran wouldn't have sent us into the arms of our allies.

I held the candle up as high as I could. There was glittering dust in the shaft. Magic? Vestiges of an older science, as Flana and most of her kind believed? Another invention from before the Tragic Millennium? The surrounding walls were the same spongy, pink-red rock as the floor: tough, elastic and made of no material I had ever experienced. It felt faintly damp. Its smell was almost familiar. Fishy yet pleasant. I put my palm on the wall and brought it to my nose. What *was* that smell? Skin? Hair after you've washed it? Definitely something organic.

"Over there," said Jack. "The air's different."

Ahead of us I saw an even smaller passage leading off to one side and poked my candle in so that I could see where it led. It gleamed back at me, reflecting the light, but I couldn't easily tell if it went anywhere or had been blocked off.

"I'm not sure. If we got stuck . . ." I began nervously.

"We won't." He was totally confident. Now Jack took the lead. Anything was better than just sitting around, so I followed him. I told him to let me know if he needed my eyes, and blew out the candle, squeezing after him through the slightly yielding rock, along a short passage until I breathed a sigh of relief as we emerged into a much larger cavern, full of thin, spiky stalactites and stalagmites, with a rather beautiful, pastel-colored luminous fungus growing over everything, enabling me to see quite a long way in all directions. Strangely familiar territory. Could this really be the way to Mu-Ooria? Or, in this world, had Granbretan conquered so thoroughly that all the Middle March was theirs, too? No. The Middle March, by its definition, was common territory to all. Once there, we'd be free.

I described it to Jack, and he nodded. "I've been somewhere like it, I think. God, doesn't it smell clean after that horrible crap?"

I felt we needed something more than "clean" to reassure us, since St. Odhran had deliberately pushed us down here and I couldn't see a friendly, elongated Off-Moo face anywhere. We appeared to be on our own.

"Have we lost 'em?" asked Jack.

"I doubt it," I told him. St. Odhran had surely known what he was pushing us into. Where exactly were we?

I took Jack's hand. The floor of the cavern was unusually smooth. An underground river had once run this course. As my eyes became used to the soft glow I saw the walls of the cavern rising in a sequence of terraces and ledges. The cavern was a natural amphitheater, with the terraces forming seats and walkways. The perfect place for a bit of human sacrifice. The Dark Empire had certainly been here. Many of the outcrops of limestone were carved in their typical designs, of animal faces and grotesque, bestial figures, only partially human. I was surrounded by an audience of gargoyles, their stone eyes glaring, their stone lips curled in cruel, triumphant sneers. I could hardly believe we hadn't been deliberately lured into a trap.

My hand tightening on Jack's must have alerted him. He turned his sightless eyes on me. "What's up? I can't hear anyone."

"We're still in Empire territory," I told him. "And I have a horrible feeling this is where they've wanted us all along. It's some sort of theater or ceremonial temple." I didn't speculate further for him.

"Are we the first act on?" He was trying to make light of the situation, with the dawning understanding that we might not get clear. "Or are we the grand finale?"

"They want our blood, remember? Mumbo jumbo, but that doesn't make it any better for us!"

"Well, if it's only a pint or two, they're welcome to mine. Let's get the transfusion over and go home. I fancy a nice big plate of Dover sole and chips. How about you?" Jack had become unnaturally amiable.

It wasn't really in my nature to make jolly quips as the great big saw drew nearer and nearer, but I could not be irritated with him. I knew why he was doing it. I was pretty nervous, too. I thought that our only hope of getting out of this cavern alive was to leave at once, before the people chasing us realized we were down here. Again, as we made our way along that ancient riverbed, I was impressed. These images, corrupted and warped as they were, reminded me of what I had seen when we had gone with my parents and grandparents on our trip to Egypt. Strangely, I wondered if we were on the inside of a pyramid. The walls did slope slightly inward as they disappeared out of sight into the gloom above. Heads of birds and fish, reptiles and mammals, stared down. But they lacked that peculiar integrity which you found in Egypt. Perhaps they had derived their ideas from a more barbaric source. History and the human imagination being what they were, maybe they'd come up with it all themselves, developing it out of the football tribes, as I mentioned before, who had once ranged urban England and the Continent, looking for trouble.

I had another thought. Was this, in fact, an old sports arena? Were we going to be pitted against real lions or gladiators or something? Was this reserved just for football—only with our heads as the balls?

"Should we be keeping quiet?" Jack's voice was just audible in my ear.

Whispering back, I told him what I thought. "I can't see how they would have made a mistake, given what's happened. St. Odhran pushed us down here deliberately."

"Who's St. Odhran?" he asked.

"He used to be a friend of mine," I said. "Turns out he's the worst villain of all."

"Scottish bloke, is he?"

"Why, yes!"

"He's been around for a while. He's the one got me the original job in the forge testing those swords, I think. 'Our mutual friend'? I heard him talking to Klosterheim before Oona got me out of there. Something about a sword, now I come to think of it! They seemed to be bargaining. I was part of the bargain, though I wasn't always sure it was actually *me* he was talking about. What's the Stone?"

"I've heard them mention that, too. A religious object of some kind. With a lot of jewels in it, which is why it's so valuable. The Runestaff?"

"That's the word. Only I thought they said 'Moonstaff.' I guessed they'd lost it and thought I could find it for them."

I explained what little I knew. The whole time I talked I scanned our surroundings, trying to see if anyone else was here. In this part of the amphitheater, the rock had a more volcanic appearance, as if lava had poured over the terraces and hardened. They gleamed, reflecting all the grotesque heads, reminding me of my first impressions of the World Below. Maybe we weren't just underground, but in a bizarre mirror image of the World Above. We were definitely in a riverbed. Or maybe even a lake bed. Were our pursuers going to flood the place, as Mirenburg had been flooded? It seemed an unnecessarily elaborate plan, even for the baroque tastes of Granbretan.

I was desperately looking for another tunnel like the one which had brought us in here, but the closer to the ground things were, the harder they were to see. Eventually I gave up and began looking for a way down into those terraces. It didn't look as if anyone on our level was meant to climb up into the seating areas. We were definitely the performers, rather than the audience.

There didn't seem much point in trying to retrace our steps. I decided to move us closer to the smooth side, so that we'd be harder to see in the shadows. I honestly felt sorrier for Jack D'Acre at that moment than I did for myself. At least I hadn't been blind most of my life.

"Aaahhhh!" It was a hiss of pleasure from above. I looked up. I couldn't see anyone.

I stopped. Although I found it hard to tell, we seemed to have reached roughly the middle of the amphitheater. Out there, at the center, was an enormous square block of green stone, taller than me. It might have been a monstrous emerald. Slightly opaque, it reflected the light from the pastel mold growing in patches along the rising tiers of that inverted cone. And now at last I saw eyes glittering, too. Not many. A pair here. A pair there.

A wet snuffling, a grunting, a whine or two. It was truly horrible, as if we two were about to become entertainment for a bunch of salivating beasts. Wet, slobbering noises. Little cackles and croaks. None were sounds I'd ever heard in the throats of real animals, for they still had a trace of human origin.

Was the theater filling up with the nobles of the Dark Empire? I still couldn't actually see any people. I drew Jack with me to the side, into the deepest shadows. I surveyed the frozen lava of the tiers for signs of those beast-headed Granbretanners, but only saw the odd shadow which, blending with the carved figures, might have been a household god, might or might not have been human.

An echoing voice confirmed the worst.

"No need to be shy, my dears. All that we have sought is at last in place, save for the Runestaff. But that will manifest itself soon. Like answers to like. Child answers to child. Blood answers to blood. You will bring it to us. The Staff cannot remain hidden, just as you are now unable to remain hidden. That much we know. We have waited what seems centuries for this moment. Now the Consanguinity is assured. See!"

A yellow light played over the great block of emerald stone. On it, laid out like an altar with its vestments, sat two shallow golden bowls. And what I had not immediately seen was the huge black broadsword piercing the glowing green stone from left to right. Scarlet symbols twisted and turned in the blade near the hilt, like somber neon. Like smoke trapped inside a jar. The colors were incredibly vibrant, as if the objects had not just a life of their own but a soul as well.

Around me, overhead, I heard a creak, a jingle, a suppressed cough. There was no doubt we had a small audience.

I heard Jack sniff. "Ugh. Bous-Junge's here."

"We can smell you, Mr. Bous-Junge," I said. A cheap shot, but I had a feeling I wasn't going to be up for anything much better.

"And that other one. I can smell him, too. What's his name? Taragorm? They're thick, those two." Jack had some difficulty speaking. His mouth was dry. "He's just as bad."

But no King Huon? I thought. No Baron Meliadus? Was the Countess Flana still a prisoner? And what about St. Odhran? Shouldn't he be here to relish his triumph?

I heard a sort of *phut*, a swish. I looked down at a dart sticking out of my arm. Another sound, and Jack was similarly shot. Quickly I pulled the thing free of my arm, then yanked the other dart from Jack's. But I was already feeling woozy. I leaned against the wall, trying to hold steady. Those cowards! We might as well be feral cats!

"Bloody hell," I heard Jack say. "The animals are shooting us." And then he crumpled to the hard, smooth, glassy surface of the amphitheater.

A moment or two later I went down, too.

Was I dreaming it, or did Bous-Junge's unpleasant, tittering laugh fill the auditorium until the sound drowned out everything else, including my consciousness?

When I came to, I thought I heard the last vibrations of that voice, fading away. But I guessed more time had passed than that, because I was tied up, spread-eagled on one side of the stone itself. I guessed Jack must be on the other side. My arm was very sore but not in the place where the dart had gone in.

Baron Bous-Junge wasn't wearing his mask. His round, sly

face smiled at me as he held up two glass vials with something red in them.

It was blood. And I had a fair idea whom it belonged to.

"We are in time. We are in time!" This was an unfamiliar voice. Beyond Bous-Junge I saw a really peculiar, globular mask, with four different styles of clock face, one like Big Ben, the famous London landmark. Hanging from it, extended over the wearer's body, was a wide pendulum, moving backwards and forwards so steadily that I thought they might be trying to hypnotize us. The legs and arms extending beyond it were skinny and mottled with brown spots, like those of a very old person.

Baron Bous-Junge giggled. "What? I can see it in your eyes, child. Did you think we'd be wasteful with your blood? That which flows in your veins makes you what we wish to be. When your blood flows in *our* veins, we become something of what you are. We take on your inherited power. We become guardians of the Grail. First we try its potency *without* killing you. We'll bring the Staff to us. We have read all the appropriate books. The Staff heals all wounds and resurrects the recently dead. We have to keep you fresh. You're good for another few pints yet."

"That's the smelly bastard talking." Jack's voice came from the other side of the stone. "But who's the ticking bastard with him?"

"He means me." The voice was curiously bleak, without nuance. "I'm Taragorm. We saved you from the moonbeam roads, didn't we? Onric, isn't it? Or do you prefer Jack?"

"I don't remember you!"

"Oh, you saw me once, Jack. Just the once."

"You're the bastard who blinded me!"

Taragorm's silence didn't deny the accusation.

"What did you do that for?" Jack wanted to know. He sounded calm.

"We needed to be able to find you," said Taragorm. "If you escaped, you'd hardly get far blind. Our mistake. We had no notion how many clever friends you have! Ah, here are our *own* clever colleagues at last." There came a faint boom as if he struck the hour.

A little behind him I saw Klosterheim. His frame was dramatically thin compared to that of his bulky companion, Gaynor von Minct.

"You are late, Prince Gaynor." Bous-Junge sounded disapproving. "The time is near. There's not a moment to be lost. We must test the Stone and the Sword. Then we must fill the bowls. One with the male blood, one with the female. All countertypes are prepared for the Balance. The intellectual"—he bowed to Klosterheim—"and the practical brute." He bowed. "Greetings, Prince Gaynor the Damned."

"I wasn't always this brute," muttered Gaynor dully. I thought he mourned some other state, some time in his life when he had fought nobly with us, rather than against us. This rogue Knight of the Balance glared over at me. Something unreadable shone in his eyes. He sighed. "I have just come from the surface. It was difficuLieutenant I think we shall be safe for long enough. And then it will be easy for us to reverse our losses."

"Losses?" Bous-Junge raised an eyebrow. "They had crossed the sea bridge. Are they now in the capital? There can be no doubt the crystal aids them. Yet I thought it smashed . . ."

"They have a fragment. They only need a fragment. The fraction is as great as the whole, remember? Hawkmoon's killed or badly wounded. He's disappeared, but Count Brass has taken Londra," Klosterheim told him. "They summon armies from nowhere. And so many of your own have gone over to his cause! King Huon is destroyed. Meliadus pronounced himself king for about half an hour. The little red-haired brute, Oladahn, killed him. The last I heard, they were trying to find where you'd imprisoned Flana. They wanted to make her queen."

"She'll not be queen, that traitoress. Her mask sits on a spike at the river gate, and her head's food for her dead husband's pet beasts."

"Then who—?" began Taragorm.

"We'll form a republic," said Bous-Junge. "And rule without responsibility . . ."

Prince Gaynor the Damned gave out a great snort of laughter.

"Aye. Kings and queens have a habit of carrying the blame for whole catalogs of injustices."

"Count Brass will not have long to relish his victories," sniggered Bous-Junge. "Within the hour we'll be masters of the multiverse. Merely with a thought, any one of us will be able to destroy entire worlds and create fresh ones. We shall each of us take the four quarters of our stations and rule those quarters by agreement. And by agreement, none shall enter nor seek to influence the quarter of the others. So we maintain our own balances, without need of that thing . . ."

He pointed towards me. Obviously he meant the rock Jack and I were slung over like two parts of a saddlebag.

The square emerald rock grew noticeably warmer, and I could have sworn I heard it give a faint moan. It felt like flesh against my own skin. It quivered in time to the sword vibrating within its green depths.

Klosterheim came to stand, regarding me, his cold eyes full of unreadable despair. He uttered a deep sigh. "Now do you still think my colleague was wrong in refusing to accept the reconciliation of Heaven and Hell? Look what has become of it all. Hysteria of self-knowledge, monotony of self-analysis, introspection spreading like a disease. What is all that but the infection communicated over the unpurified borders of death? The spirits of the mortal world were never meant to be so neighborly with the spirits of the other. I have done all I can for you now. You have used my knowledge to ensure not only the death of God but the death of Lucifer, too. So be it."

With a grunt of impatience, Prince Gaynor reached towards the hilt of the black sword, which I could just see from the corner of my eye. Even as he began, Baron Bous-Junge's hand moved out and laid itself on Gaynor's wrist. "You know that only one of their blood can handle the damned blades. First you must *become* of their blood. That's why drinking their blood is so important for other reasons. Bide your time."

St. Odhran stepped jauntily into the arena. He was, for all his treachery, very attractive.

"All you wanted was to trick the albino. Bring him underground." St. Odhran was smiling that mocking, crooked smile. "You have almost all you seek."

"We're grateful to you, sir," Klosterheim said.

"You'll be well rewarded, Scotchman," said Prince Gaynor, his big face full of other thoughts. "But you'll not get a fifth of the power we share. That's divided between us. We concocted this scheme together from the beginning, Klosterheim, Bous-Junge, Taragorm and I. Years it took. We knew the Conjunction of Conjunctions would come. We knew we could gather together all the elements of the Balance. We found the Stone, which some have called the Grail, and brought it from von Bek's in London. Down here. Waiting. You, St. Odhran, supplied the Sword. You, gentlemen, brought the two golden bowls. The children will give us the blood of twin immortals to represent all the opposites and complementary elements of the world, Law and Chaos, which must be taken from twins who share shamanistic ancestry. All we lack is the Staff. I know in my bones that the Staff will be inexorably drawn to the other elements, for it cannot exist without them. It will manifest itself as a result of our ritual. Yet what form it takes, we do not know."

"It will come. When we bleed the twins, it will come. It will be drawn to heal its defenders."

"Twins?" I said. "What on earth makes you think we're twins?"

And this *did* stop them in their tracks! I think they realized for the first time how unlike each other Jack and I were. Not twins. Not even the same age. How had they rationalized that? Then I remembered my grandmother. Could she actually be Jack's twin, and could he actually be Zodiac's son? In all the convolutions of the multiverse, I suppose it was possible . . .

Shaking his head, as if to say it was too late to consider this now, Bous Junge drew his long knife and advanced towards me. I had made a serious mistake in speaking out. I had caused him to change his mind. I knew he was going to slit my throat, let my blood pump all over that rock and then test its properties.

I closed my eyes, trying to be brave.

"You have made such wonderful mistakes, gentlemen." I heard a new voice, edged with irony. I recognized it. I strained to see where it was coming from. "I was almost inclined to let you play the farce through, but sadly your threat to the child's life means there's too much at stake to let you run unchecked any further. First, Baron Bous-Junge, perhaps you would oblige me by releasing the girl and my son. You'll find I'll be a little more lenient with you if you obey quickly."

I peered into the shadows of the lower tiers of the amphitheater. There, looking relaxed and almost cheerful, with a peculiar light in his eye which said that he was enjoying himself, was my mother's grandfather, Monsieur Zodiac, otherwise known as Elric the albino.

"Damn you, Silverskin!" Disdaining ritual, Gaynor tossed back the vial of my blood into his throat, swallowed it and ran for the black sword, which vibrated steadily in the stone. He emitted a shriek of triumph that echoed throughout the cavern. It pierced my head. I wanted nothing more in all the world than to see what happened next, but as hard as I tried, I could not remain conscious.

Gaynor's hand closed around the hilt of the sword. The scream intensified. And I fainted.

CHAPTER TWENTY-TWO

WAS NOT unconscious for very long, because when I woke, Gaynor was still screaming. The sound of the sword had somehow combined with his voice. He was glaring down at his right palm. Across it was a raw red welt, as if he had gripped a bar of white-hot metal.

He looked utterly baffled. "But, the blood . . . ," he said.

Elric drew an identical black sword from his scabbard. He held it aloft in both hands. The thing moaned and muttered; scarlet writing blazed out of the black steel and reflected on his ivory skin, in his own crazed, laughing eyes. His long, fine white hair rose and floated in a misty halo around his head, and I understood at last why he was feared. *I* feared him. And I was on his side.

Gaynor grabbed the other vial of blood from Bous-Junge. The baron made a halfhearted effort to hold on to it. The dirk forgotten in his hand, he looked up at Elric and the black sword. He was fascinated by something he had probably only ever heard about in legend. The two Granbretanners, as well as Klosterheim, shared the same attitude of astonishment. They had never encountered Elric or anything like him before, and they no doubt saw their defeat in that laughing apparition with his shrieking weapon, threatening everything they thought already theirs. They had been so triumphant, so certain that their great game had been played and won. And now it became apparent that Elric and his friends had anticipated them. I saw St. Odhran step back to join

308

the albino. I still didn't trust him. Was he going to try to wriggle out of his involvement in our capture?

Gaynor narrowed his eyes, steeled himself and drew his own sword, a long, silvery blade with a plain hilt. He forced his wounded fingers around it. "You know this blade, too, do you, Lord Elric? It is Mireen, Lord Arkyn's Sword of Law. I paid that Scottish traitor a high price to possess her. With Taragorm's help I turned back time. All this I did to defeat you and take possession of the Balance. I shall own both, once I have dealt with you. One of those blades is counterfeit, forged in Mirenburg. I suspect it is the one you hold, since the other pierced the Stone when St. Odhran brought it here." And he put both hands around his hilt and moved forward as my kinsman vaulted down into the arena to confront him.

"The Sword of Law against the Sword of Chaos!" chittered Baron Bous-Junge, almost with relish. "I have yearned to witness this for so long. It is perfection. The Balance is doubly personified. Thus we shall make it our servant!" He moved closer to me, the long poniard drooping in his hand. He had not forgotten me. He meant to draw more of my blood, even if it killed me this time. That blood had to be absorbed by the stone if his sorcery was going to work. Even I knew that. Taragorm was out of my line of vision. I guessed he was preparing to spill Jack's blood.

Gaynor gulped down the second vial of blood, seeming to relish it. He wiped his lips on the back of his hand and examined his palm with evident satisfaction. The wound had healed. "Ah," he said. "It tastes so pure." And he cast a crafty eye towards Jack.

Then Elric was on him, the black sword howling and screeching with a voice all its own, like a live thing. His thrust was parried by Gaynor. Another thrust. Another parry. A counterblow from Gaynor, which sent the physically weaker Elric stumbling backwards. The white sword had no voice but possessed a blue radiance. Blue letters in the same foreign alphabet flickered along its length. Then, as Gaynor aimed another massive swing at him, Elric flung up the black blade to block it.

"Ach!" swore the big man as the white steel shattered and bouncing shards clattered to the floor of the arena.

"The forgery! It could not even hold its color, eh?" Elric grinned into Prince Gaynor's twisted face as Gaynor flung the remains of the sword behind him.

"One of 'em must have the right blood. What's simpler than that consanguinate sorcery . . . ?" The brute stamped back to the emerald stone, reaching for the black sword still embedded in it. He put his hand back on the hilt, and this time, although there was pain, as I could tell from his face, he had the strength to pull the thing free. "Ha! Now we are evenly matched, Lord Elric. I know this sword. She is called Ravenblade, the Black Sword's sister!"

Gaynor had charge of the sword in the stone. He wrapped his two hands around it, gritting his teeth as he did so.

"Mournblade I call her." A terrible half-smile was still on Elric's lips. His eyes flickered like furnaces. "Well, not for the first time have the sisters fought, though you master your blade with borrowed blood. We must hurry, Prince Gaynor, for I have another appointment with these swords I would not wish to miss."

My ancestor's lunatic laughter was something I hope never to hear again. It was the humor of a man who relished the taking of life and staking his own in the process. As if risking death and dealing it had become his sole pleasures.

Gaynor grunted, and he hefted the sword, watching the scarlet letters squirreling up and down the black iron.

Then this sword, too, was moaning and yelling like a living creature. Two black swords! One pitched against the other. What did it mean?

Gaynor renewed the attack. From where I hung, helpless against the stone, I watched the two men make flying leaps over the barriers, fighting back and forth, up and down the tiers of the amphitheater, sometimes in the light, sometimes in shadow. Often it seemed to me that the swords themselves fought and the men were merely adjuncts to their battle. I knew I watched four sentient entities up there.

I was not the only one fascinated by the fight. All other eyes were on it. Beast-masked warriors had entered the upper tiers and were poised above the combatants, watching them intently.

Elric went down, and Gaynor pressed his advantage. Stormbringer flew free of Elric's hand.

Gaynor stood over his opponent. "Here's blood for the block!" he snarled. "Enough for a dozen rituals!" And he lifted the yelling sword to bring it down on the albino. "Miggea!"

He would have cut Elric in two if the blow had landed, but Elric rolled clear, regained Stormbringer and staggered to his feet as Gaynor recovered himself.

Elric began shouting weirdly accented words into the air, in a language that sounded a bit like Hindi. I guessed the words were represented in the letters on the blades.

Gaynor glared around him, suspecting some other kind of attack. He lumbered down on the albino, swinging Mournblade in an arc which left an aura of black and crimson light streaming behind it. The two were shouting almost in unison.

I heard Gaynor say, "Would you rather have the Balance destroyed, Elric? Would you rather there were no control at all? Merely the Grey Fees, the abolition of time, the destruction of space?"

Elric was still smiling. "The Balance is not for us to use, but for us to serve, Prince Gaynor the Damned, as well you know. It is an idea and can never truly be destroyed. Anyone who has ever attempted to enforce his power over its constituent elements has only failed. They have gone to the ultimate hell, never free of themselves or their own frustrations. Put down that other sword, Gaynor. I demand you obey me. Mournblade has no loyalty to your own blood, only to that you have stolen. You temporarily deceive her. Do you think she is not aware of that? She will soon lead you further towards your own just fate."

Gaynor was jeering. "Weakling! You betray everything. You betray that which makes you strong! You are *all* Betrayal, Elric of Melniboné."

Elric's expression changed, and he took up the attack, just as Gaynor had hoped he would.

But Elric was tired. It had cost him dearly to get here in time, to confront them and hope to rescue us. Still, he *was* here to save me; I knew that. If he lost this fight, whatever happened to him in that other world, I was almost certainly finished. As was this world. Maybe all the worlds.

Then I saw another, much older man standing above Elric. Another albino. Who . . . ? A strong family resemblance. He could have been my grandpa. Elric in a different time? Impossible.

Then I realized it actually *was* my grandfather. Ulric von Bek reached out and touched Elric as he backed away from the relentless Gaynor. Then Granddad had vanished. Briefly I thought I saw still another white face staring out of the shadows. Then it, too, had gone.

Elric had more vitality now. I knew the older man had given it to him. Elric used it to advantage. Back Gaynor went against a blinding flurry of sword strokes. I couldn't believe the speed. All I know about is fencing, which we do at school. This was like fencing with claymores, those massive broadswords the Scots liked to slaughter one another with. How did they achieve that speed of reflexes, let alone the strength needed to swing so many pounds of steel with such ease? My respect for both antagonists increased. This was no ordinary medieval bludgeoning match.

And there was no clash of metal in the air, just that sickening vibration, the moaning and shouting of sentient, living steel.

Again the opponents drew apart, panting, eyeing each other, the blades resting on the glassy surface of the seats. They spoke to each other, but their voices were too low for me to hear. I strained forward.

Suddenly Bous-Junge of Osfoud fell to his knees, squirming onto the floor of the amphitheater, clutching at his back. He dropped the long, greenish knife he had planned to use on me. Sticking out between his shoulder blades was the feathered shaft of an arrow. I looked to one side. Oona, my grandmother, stood in the shadows on another tier of the amphitheater, her own skin grey rather than white, her eyes held steady by sheer effort of will. She smiled at me, dropped her bow, and fell sideways onto the slippery rock. She had anticipated Bous-Junge's intention to throw the knife into Elric's back and had killed him first. But the action had obviously cost her dearly.

I wanted to run to her. I struggled to get free. "Oona!" I shouted, but of course, I was still tied up and could do nothing.

Then I saw the Chevalier St. Odhran coming straight for me, his own dirk in his hand, a weird smile on his face.

In panic I looked around for help. I screamed. I've never screamed like that before or since. St. Odhran reached me, raised the knife and cut my bonds. As I sank, sighing, to the ground, he took my weight. I was numb and weak, but I knew that sensation would come back soon, since I was uninjured. Leaving me to re-cover, St. Odhran moved around the other side to free Jack.

At this point Klosterheim hissed his hatred and frustration and, seeing that I was helpless and unprotected, drew his saber to take advantage of my situation. "Your blood *must* feed the rock, child. There is still time for us to succeed. See how they weaken by the second."

He was two steps away from me before St. Odhran came back. Klosterheim glared at the Scotsman, muttered an insult, and then began to run, hauling himself up over the barrier and beating an erratic path up into the darkness of the heights. St. Odhran made no attempt to follow him. Was he giving the German a chance to escape?

Klosterheim had been wrong. The fighters didn't look partic-ularly weak!

Elric and Gaynor clashed again. Muscle against muscle, flesh against flesh. I smelled the particular stink of predatory animals, mingled with something altogether less familiar.

Down went Gaynor, spinning wildly to avoid the weaving runesword, blocking Elric's long, slashing blow to his torso. Up he came again, his own runesword gibbering and squalling down at Elric's unhelmeted head. He caught the albino a glancing blow as he slipped to one side. Unwounded, Elric drove back his attacker.

Gaynor grunted and cursed yet grinned at Elric's skill, just as Elric smiled respect for his opponent's proficiency. So familiar were they with the nearness of death, or worse than death, that they actually took pleasure in it. Their only alternative, after all, was to fear it. And fear wasn't there in either of them.

This was a horrible game and one I would have stopped if I could have, but the glee of the fighters, the noise of the swords and some understanding of the stakes which they were dueling for overrode my repugnance. I was fascinated.

Thump! Thump! Their bodies were like battering rams in ordinary traveling clothes. Neither man was armored.

Grunting, breathing in high, painful gasps, the two separated again, rested again, clashed again.

Gaynor lifted his head and took several steps backward.

Elric frowned, staggering.

Taragorm had intervened! I saw it happen. Chimes boomed from his body, from somewhere within his architectural mask, and they were totally out of sync. It was like watching a beautifully choreographed ballet whose music was a cacophony, one element absolutely at odds with another. Elric and Gaynor were each thrown by the sounds, just enough to increase the risk of being cut by the other. Gaynor was ready. Stuffing something into his ears with his left hand, he backed away. He had anticipated this.

The sounds from the clock mask grew more jangled and out of tune. Taragorm was using a prearranged strategy, formulated no doubt long ago to help Gaynor in some other battle. The air around him spangled and faded, and I recognized magic at work.

Elric's movements became increasingly disorganized, yet he kept his grip on the sword. His glance towards Taragorm told me he knew what was happening to him. I struggled to get up, yelling that I was coming to help. The circulation had not yet returned to my arms and legs. At the same time I feared I might still be in danger from St. Odhran. I watched, probably a bit like a hypnotized rat, as Taragorm disappeared around the rock, presumably to dispatch Jack.

Elric stumbled.

St. Odhran reached me, lifting me up to put me on my feet, caught me as I fell, and then pushed me down onto the ground so hard that I was winded. "Stay there," he said urgently. "For your life, stay there!"

Big Ben's hammers bounced against her bells. Boom! Boom! Boom! Boom! The familiar sounds of the Westminster chimes hideously off-key. It was madness. Elric wobbled and fell as the still grinning Gaynor moved in swiftly beside him, with Mournblade raised again to strike. This time Gaynor would not be distracted, and I still could scarcely move.

All at once Elric rolled, sprawling spread-eagled on his back. Stormbringer was still in his left hand while his right tried to find purchase on the glassy rock as he willed himself to stand. Gaynor took his time as he stalked forward, his huge mouth open in a roar of pleasure.

Then Elric pointed upwards with his right hand, and lights streamed out of it. Green, red, violet, indigo, the colors poured from his mouth and fingertips. His lips writhed and snarled, uttering incomprehensible words. Morbid shadows formed around him.

Gaynor was openly contemptuous. "Conjurer's pranks, Lord Elric. Nothing more. You'll not deflect my attention as you have that of previous enemies, who lacked defenses against you. I can match you spell for spell, Sir Sorcerer-King!"

The tentative smile on Elric's face broadened. He raised his head and called out in his own language. He called on the ancient gods of his people to help him save his soul.

With a noise like bursting rockets, Elric was suddenly plucking at the air, as another might pluck at the strings of an instrument. A red glare surrounded him. Blue fire continued to pour from his mouth. In response to his spell making, sword after sword began to appear before him. And every one of the swords was black, pulsing with runes, identical to those grasped in the fists of the two fighters. Yet even now, with so many identical sentient swords, Stormbringer and Mournblade were subtly different, subtly more powerful. Stormbringer had an extra quality to it, impossible to identify. It was clear that there was only one true Stealer of Souls.

A forest of swords surrounded Gaynor now. Hundreds of them, all rustling and clashing together in their eagerness to engage the former Knight of the Balance.

Gaynor had no doubts about what was happening. His eyes held a bleak understanding as he spat on the floor, glaring at Elric, who stood with folded arms on the other side of that mass of swords. "Well, I reckoned without your particular powers, I suppose, Elric." He sneered at his own folly. "You didn't spend all those thousands of years on your dream couches in order to learn a few entertaining magic tricks for the provincial stage. I should have considered better what I was facing. Still, one symbol is destroyed and another takes its place. You'll perish yet, Lord Elric, if it's not at my hand. You have death all over you."

"I welcome it," said Elric, still gasping for air, "but I'd prefer to *choose* where death comes to me and what price I pay."

The black swords hovered over and surrounded Gaynor. At first the blades took tiny nicks out of him as he attempted to fend them off, like a man swatting at insects. Then the nicks became deeper wounds, and blood began to pour from him. His clothes fell away in tiny shreds of rag. Even his boots were cut from him like that until he stood there, blood coursing down every part of his head and naked body, his mad eyes still glaring defiance. The blades then carefully removed his skin and filleted his flesh, leaving his head until last. As he watched himself being cut into tiny fragments, piece by piece, his screams became no longer defiant but terrible in their desperate pleading for Elric's pity.

Elric had no pity.

Perhaps he alone knew it wasn't over. For each piece of flesh the black swords cut off Gaynor, a new Gaynor grew before our eyes. Gaynor after Gaynor, every one of them wielding a black sword and attacking Elric. An army of shadow Gaynors, each becoming gradually harder to see, fought against the albino and his army of supernatural swords.

With the same little smile playing around his handsome

mouth, Elric fought on steadily. Like someone who has found the comfortable rhythm of a walk, though I'm sure he knew he could not yet anticipate Gaynor's defeat.

I watched in relief as one by one, Elric began to defeat his shadow enemies, who drew on the decreasing resources of the multiverse. With each sword cut, an aspect of his enemy, a fragment of Gaynor's soul, was taken into Elric's blade. The original Gaynor grew rapidly older and feebler even as his many avatars continued to fight on around him. Elric drove slowly forward until he stood before that proud revolutionary, that renegade Knight of the Balance, his lips working as if he found no suitable words, until, by its own volition, Stormbringer lunged forward and pierced Gaynor in his ambitious heart, making him drop his own sword and grasp at the black steel which entered his body. He cast one final horrified look at Elric and whimpered one last time. His huge body then dissipated to nothing. All the other Gaynors raced inward to rejoin him, to give him substance, even as that substance was drawn luxuriously into Elric's greedy Stormbringer.

I was horrified. Elric visibly bloomed and grew stronger before our eyes.

At last Gaynor was gone, in all his aspects, and Mournblade had blended with Elric's own sword. All those other swords, with their stolen souls, had blended with their great original, and Stormbringer howled out her wild song of triumph as Elric's crimson eyes blazed and he opened his mouth wide in a bloody victory grin.

"*Stormbringer!*" he cried.

And then it was very quiet.

I saw a shadow slip away through the upper tiers. Klosterheim! I opened my mouth to warn them of his escape, but then I closed it. The beast-masked warriors were throwing off their helmets, revealing themselves to be the Kakatanawa who had traveled here with Elric. Silently the warriors surrounded Klosterheim. He died without noise.

Those of us left standing didn't move. A moment later, tiny animals started to scuttle out onto the cavern floor, pouring from unseen holes in the rock. A kind of rodent smaller than voles, they chittered around our feet, utterly oblivious of us, their tiny twitching noses leading them to the blood. I wondered what else had gone on down here, and for how long, if a breed of vermin had developed dependent on the blood and flesh of tortured human beings. Snuffling and squeaking, they found those little morsels of Gaynor which now could never be reunited, at least until the whole multiverse turned upon its axis, mirror into mirror, blending and becoming one for that brief moment of complete coupling. The animals scuttled and peeped and squabbled over the tiny bits of flesh and bone that were their anticipated feast. An hour or two earlier and it might have been Jack and me whose scattered morsels fed the scavengers.

Taragorm, Master of the Palace of Time, lay crumpled over the body of his colleague, with whom he had schemed to take the power of God. The vermin found him next. His mask had fallen forward, revealing his wizened features. The tower of Big Ben hung broken on the floor of the amphitheater. Perhaps St. Odhran thought he'd redeemed himself by killing Taragorm.

Like a character out of *Macbeth*, the Scotsman leaned, panting, his bloody knife dropped to the ground, his back resting against the emerald stone, which continued to agitate internally. Jack D'Acre stood beside him. St. Odhran had his arm around the boy.

"The Stone could have brought them back to life had it not been for the schichis," he said. "Now we'll never see that miracle. That's why they chose this place, I suppose."

Having betrayed and killed his companions, was the aeronaut trying to pretend that he had been on our side all along? I wasn't about to forget what I'd seen and heard him do at the Countess Flana's or what he'd done later in that alley. He had shoved us down the chute to be sacrificed. Only after Elric arrived did St. Odhran see the tide turn and change his mind.

I glared at him to show I knew what he was up to.

He looked back at me, grinned and bowed, absolutely unrepentant. I refused to look at him or Jack but went over to where my grandmother had fallen, on the other side of Elric, to try to help her.

She wasn't injured but rather weak from hunger. They had been starving her to death after catching her on her way back to us. They had planned to torture her, but Elric, dropped from Bastable's airship with the Kakatanawa, had found and released her while trying to find us. She had led him to the amphitheater. In turn she had done whatever she could in her weakened state to help Elric.

Elric barely glanced at either of us. He was making his way back down to the floor of the amphitheater, to the great block of emerald stone. The sword was still held purposefully in his hand, and I could tell that what he was about to do was unpleasant to him. St. Odhran continued to lean back and watch Elric dully, his arm still about Jack's skinny frame.

With a shout and a grunt, Elric leaped into the air and plunged the sword into the top of the rock, where it then rested with a foot or so of its blade buried in the stone. Stormbringer vibrated gracefully now and sang to itself an utterly different song from the one it had sung while in Elric's hands. The albino released the hilt and, overcome at last with weakness, staggered down to the floor of the cavern.

Oona got up, suddenly invigorated, and moved towards him.

"The rest of you must finish this," Elric panted. "I've done what I must, and the Sword will serve me again, never fear. This is my bargain with it. But I will try to destroy the Balance. Erekosë—Hawkmoon—all that I am, was or will be . . ."

Those were the last words I would hear him say.

Oona had reached the great emerald stone. She took first one bowl and then the other and hung them by their chains from Stormbringer's guard. They were in perfect balance. She smiled, her skin bathed in the light from each of the components. She looked towards her father.

Before our eyes, Elric fell stiffly backward through a circle of crystal pillars, whose tops formed into elongated icicles racing ahead of him as he fell up an infinitely growing circle, whose slopes became increasingly angular, turning from white to dark blue to deep, pulsing green. I myself desperately wanted to follow him, to go with him into his own vanishing dream. But he faded and disappeared, as if he had never existed.

I stumbled. A hand was on my shoulder. Refusing my wish to follow him, Oona held me back. "Let them go," she said.

"Them?"

I looked up into her face. It was a mask of grief. Then I saw her grief change to alarm. To determination. I followed her gaze.

Two more men had appeared from nowhere. They were standing on either side of the Balance. One was black, handsome, massive. The other was white, wiry, grim. Yet both looked like brothers—twins, even! Were these the real siblings von Minct and Klosterheim had discovered in all their magical scrying? Both bore huge black broadswords like Elric's. The white man had a black, pulsing jewel embedded in his forehead. Slowly they turned to regard the Balance. Then, as if for the first time, they saw each other!

With a terrible cry the black man lifted his sword. Not against the white man—but against the Balance itself!

"No!" cried Oona. "Erekosë! Now is not the time!" Staggering towards the ghostly pair, she lifted her hands. "No. The Balance is needed. Without it, Elric dies for nothing!"

For a second the black man turned, frowning.

This gave the white man his moment. He drove his own sword deep into the black man's heart. Erekosë gasped. He struggled, trying to tug the sword from his body. The jewel in the white man's skull blazed with dark fire as the black man died. But there was no joy or triumph in the victor's face. Instead, he wept. And Oona wept with him.

Oona leaned back heavily against the sides of the amphitheater, clearly relieved. I watched in astonishment as slowly the black man seemed to be drawn up the length of his enemy's blade, drawn into the metal and then into his body until there was nothing of him left. Then the white man collapsed to the ground, the black jewel growing dull, as if it died with him.

St. Odhran walked slowly and stiffly to look down on the corpse. Then he knelt, reaching for the white man's left hand, which clenched something. St. Odhran pried the fingers open and took something from them. Whatever it was, he put it in his own pocket. Robbing the dead, I thought. But this was all over my head.

"It's done," said St. Odhran. "For now, it's done."

"Who is he?" I whispered. "What is he?"

"Merely another fragment of the whole." St. Odhran sighed heavily as he knelt, cradling the dead man in his arms. "He's served his turn. As most of us have." He looked down at the dead man. "Eh, Hawkmoon, old comrade?" And then, to my further amazement, the white man began to fade until St. Odhran's arms were empty. I felt I would never understand fully what had gone on here. The Balance pulsed, alive, it seemed to me, with the souls of those who had died in its restoration.

St. Odhran stood up and went over to Jack. The look in his eyes seemed to be one of pity.

Turning her eyes from the Balance, Oona led me over to Jack and St. Odhran. We were all exhausted, and I was aching horribly. She took St. Odhran's hand.

He bowed and kissed her fingers. "Madame." They seemed to share a secret moment.

"What's this about?" I said. I suppose I was showing my "usual impatience," as Mum and Dad call it, with other people's intimate moments.

"I'm sorry, little mademoiselle, if I appeared to disappoint you." St. Odhran drew a deep breath and smiled with all his old, sunny charm. "We told you, I think, that each and every one of us had a specific part to play if we were to succeed in restoring the Balance and defeat those who'd use it for evil.

"I elected to deceive our opponents by pretending to make a forgery of Elric's sword, because a sword had to be introduced into their equation. But the black sword I brought here was Mournblade, the twin of Stormbringer. The other, the white blade, was the forgery. We had to make them think they were winning, or those four would never have gathered in this place for their ceremony. We might never have been able to forestall 'em as we did. It was a dangerous chance, of course, but we had to take it. Everything was done according to careful calculations, considering all the risks. I couldn't let *you* know the risk, or you would not have responded in the genuine way needed. There's been nothing that's happened, nothing that's been avoided, that wasn't planned either by their side or ours. Our only grief was that while we tried to protect you at all times, we gambled with the lives of our children. A very hard decision.

"We are engaged in a momentous war, and this has been the subtlest part of our strategy. We needed to make them become self-assured and unguarded, to believe the real power was all theirs, before we could strike in unison. Hawkmoon's advance, Colonel Bastable's aerial voyage, your capture, our arriving in time—everything was planned. Everything but that final scene. Those men—"

But I didn't want him to tell me any more. I just couldn't take it.

"I told them I wasn't Jack's twin," I said lamely. I wasn't entirely happy to hear I'd been used as a cat's-paw.

"That's right, you're not," said my grandmother. "I am. But those fools never did discover the true nature of time. They would have done irreparable damage. Of course, I am not your mother's mother, as you doubtless know. Your mother is one of our *adopted* childen. Your grandfather and I wanted to lead normal lives as ordinary people. But I'm almost immortal, and your grandfather was not. He was, however, the most courageous man I ever knew, and the sanest. And I'm proud of your father. We never planned to have our own children, because we hoped to lift the family curse."

"And did you?"

"Not really," she said. With the same grieving air, she reached towards Jack and embraced him. "You're my brother, Jack, as you know. A near-immortal like our own mother and father. In time it will be impossible to tell us apart by our ages. Whatever curves we followed in the moonbeam roads brought us out at a time a shade different from our original birthplace at the edge of the Grey Fees."

I saw then that Jack's blind eyes were full of tears. I was so touched for him that I didn't realize myself that I was beginning to fall in love.

"Now Gaynor's soul is trapped in the Black Sword," said St. Odhran, "and the sword is more powerful, ready for the task it is to perform in Elric's world. The rest of Gaynor's physical substance is scattered and transformed. Yet it must be recognized that another Gaynor will come eventually, and another, to be first an idealist, a champion fighting for our great cause, and then a renegade, prepared to commit any savagery, any cruelty, any treachery to win power over that which he once served. But for the moment our business is done. Now only Elric lives on in his own world, to call upon his sword for that one final time, when he will bear it against the overwhelming forces of Chaos and seek, with the Horn of Fate, to herald in the dawn of another age."

I was still wary of St. Odhran. I'm not one to bear a grudge, but I do have a strong sense of justice when someone's done me a wrong. "You pushed me," I said. "Twice."

He shook his head and straightened himself. "God love us, mademoiselle, but I'd relied upon you staying put. So then I had to come searching for you in the hope I'd find you before someone else did. Then, when I did discover you near one of the old elevator shafts which acts these days to ventilate this place, I had all those troops around me and was watched from afar by Taragorm as well. All I could do was push you into that shaft, knowing that at least I'd know where to find you. I was trying to buy time. I had not thought you'd escape the city, certainly not that you'd get across the river which runs overhead now. You showed more resilience and courage, the pair o' you, than anything I credited you with. And that was a fair bit."

"It's true," said Oona. She smiled, but she was still sad. Perhaps she missed her father. "We were in league. That, of course, was how I was able to rescue Jack and come and go from Countess Flana's apartments."

"Why was Flana involved with Klosterheim and the others?"

"In her case, a certain ambition to be queen, but mainly nothing more than boredom. She found solace in intrigue, since she never found it in human company. She paid a high price for her distractions. Don't grieve for her, young lady. She'd never known love and had seen twelve husbands come and go. Some of them went painfully and reluctantly. She would never have known what love was, I'm sure." Oona looked up, shrugging. "She might well have welcomed her death as another adventure."

It sounded a bit morbid to me. I had liked poor Countess Flana in spite of her part in my imprisonment.

From out of the shadows came a familiar and welcome figure. Lord Renyard looked flustered but highly delighted. His dandy pole clutched under one arm, he put his paws around me in an awkward, strong, and entirely affectionate embrace. His expression changed, however, as he addressed the others. His tone became urgent.

"We must leave here," he said. "We have only a few hours at best."

"But Londra's defeated," I said. "Isn't it?"

Lord Renyard shook his shaggy head. "Far from defeated. The diversion we created here allowed Londra's troops to remarshal against their enemy. Seeking you proved a useful distraction, which is another reason I didn't want you to be found. The death of this lot and of King Huon allowed the soldiers to rally under fresh leadership. Lobkowitz and Fromental are gone, vanished from a world they helped create. We can only hope they're safe. Hawkmoon's dead, and his dimension-shifting crystal lost. A badly wounded Count Brass has fallen back across the Silver Bridge.

"The Dark Empire controls the city again and will defeat us if we cannot give the Balance time to restore itself. Huon may be dead, but Meliadus has merely disappeared. Some believe he'll return and make himself king. Count Brass is content to leave the Empire confined within her island home and reach an armistice. Like most old soldiers, he wants as little bloodshed as possible. He was always given to seeing the Empire as a bringer of order and justice to disparate nations."

"But that's a mistake," I said.

"That's what Colonel Bastable thinks," declared Lord Renyard with a frown.

"He still means to bomb the city?" St. Odhran demanded urgently.

"I believe so, sir. That's why he let me and the Kakatanawa off the ship. So we could tell you and help you get away if necessary. A mighty infernal machine, I gather."

"Oh, mighty indeed," said Oona, suddenly alert again. "He's going to drop an atom bomb on Londra."

"There has to be a way of stopping him," I said reasonably as my mind reeled. Sorcery and atom bombs? How were they able to accept all this at the same time? "Can't you get an ornithopter up there to signal to Colonel Bastable?"

"It would take too long," said Oona. "Besides, they'll be at a far greater altitude than any ornithopter could reach." She frowned. "That's what he was building in Mirenburg. In case our other plans failed. As Count Brass retreats, he believes we face defeat. We can't contact that airship . . ."

"The HMAS *Victoria*," said St. Odhran softly to himself, and shook his head.

"A nuclear blast will stop them forever," I murmured, overawed.

"I doubt it," said St. Odhran, "but by Bastable's logic it will give Europa time to recover thoroughly and ensure the Dark Empire does not threaten others for many centuries to come. You'll recall what brought about the Tragic Millennium? And it was after that the Empire emerged . . ."

"Come, my dear friends. Colonel Bastable was adamant. We have to leave at once." Lord Renyard's yap was shrill with anxiety. "He insists we couldn't possibly survive such a blast. If nothing else happened to us, the river would flood in and drown us. Hurry, my friends. Hurry!"

"What about the Balance?" I asked. "Who's going to look after it?"

"The Balance has gathered all its elements together," said Oona. "And they are, anyway, primarily symbolic. The blast will only facilitate its restorative powers. He's right, young lady; we'd better get moving."

"But it *hasn't* got all its elements," I pointed out. "They never had the right twins, and there's still the Runestaff! Am I the only one to see that? What about our blood? Taragorm and Bous-Junge would have won if they'd had everything properly sorted."

"I doubt that, dear." Oona sighed and reached out her hand to me. "The Runestaff doesn't exist, you see. It's a myth, that's all. A myth common to many of the worlds where the Dark Empire has had an influence. Just another image and a word to describe the Grail, which takes many forms. We were hoping to delay them a little further by letting them think they needed it, but my guess is, they knew instinctively they could go ahead without it." She smiled at me. "You were in even greater danger than you ever knew! Most of us were."

"Look," murmured St. Odhran. "Will you look?"

There, growing before our eyes, hung the Cosmic Balance, the sword embedded in the great emerald, the cups suspended from the sword's wide crosspieces, an aura of pale blue-green fire flickering around it. A sight so profound, so awesome, I almost felt I should kneel in front of it, the way you do in a church.

Oona interrupted this reverie. "Quickly," she said, "I promise you the Balance is now beyond harm. We have done our work. Come."

Then, with Jack's help, Oona led us back the way she and Elric had come: a series of winding tunnels, below Londra. But we didn't go back into Londra. Eventually we entered another system of caverns, untouched by the artistry of the Dark Empire, where the walls were entirely illuminated by moss and slender streams of phosphorescent water running between high banks. Jack had an instinct for the best places to ford, listening carefully and then leading us forward. Patches of pastel moss glowed here and there in the distant roof, giving the impression of ancient stars.

Soon we had left that awful amphitheater far, far behind. I, for one, was relieved it was going to be destroyed.

"This is beginning to look familiar," I said as we stopped to rest and eat. Oona nodded. "You *have* been in Mu-Ooria before, haven't you? We've reached the borders of their land. They are not the only folk who live underground, but for the most part they exist in peace with the other inhabitants. Peace, they find, ensures their longevity. Generally speaking, it seems fair to argue that those who live by the sword generally do die by it as well." And she sighed. She seemed to be recollecting her earlier sorrow.

Lord Renyard hadn't noticed any change in her expression. He came and stood beside us, looking out over the eerie planes of that extraordinarily beautiful nightscape. "I will lead you from here," he said. He pointed with his pole. "That way lies Mirenburg, drowned beneath a lake of mercury, where once I studied the French." He pointed in another direction. "There lies the road I took when I was a cub, seeking a route to Paris, where I might discourse with my heroes. And this way"—again he pointed in a new direction—"lies Ingleton."

So I *was* going home. At last! I could hardly believe it. In fact I would not *completely* believe it for a while!

As I babbled my thanks to Lord Renyard and to Jack, Anayanka, one of the Kakatanawa, stepped forward and spoke to Oona. It was clear they had decided to leave us. "They know the way home from here," she told us. After a dignified and affectionate leave-taking, they made their way across a glowing field of moss and disappeared into darkness.

A little later we saw a herd of white buffalo being stalked by a pack of equally white panthers. I thought I caught Oona casting a wistful glance towards the panthers. What had happened to her own companion? Had she been left behind? I asked.

"No." Oona smiled. "She's perfectly safe."

Led by Lord Renyard and Jack, who was well adapted for the

World Below, we traveled on foot for at least a couple of days, when suddenly the big cavern we were in shook with a long tremor which I feared must be another earthquake. Was I really never going to reach Ingleton?

A spear of rock detached itself from overhead and, whistling like a shell, landed ahead of us. More rock crashed from the impact. We dived for any cover we could find. Another huge fragment fell, and another, but none too close to us. I was relieved when at long last the shaking stopped.

"Bloody hell," said Jack. "What was that?"

"Bastable's bomb." Oona paused. "So he's done it at last! Targeted the seat of Empire and blown it to bits. Whether he survived or not, I guess we'll find out later."

"How do you mean? Wouldn't a blast like that just wipe an airship out?" said Jack.

"Not if it's Bastable's," she replied mysteriously. "He has a habit of being blown sideways, away from the result of his actions."

This made St. Odhran smile, but it only baffled me and Jack.

"This isn't the first time he's done something like this," said the Scottish aeronaut.

Lord Renyard still wanted us to hurry. We stopped and rested several more times, and although I tried to count the number of days likely to be passing in my own world, I lost track somewhere.

Eventually Jack lifted his head, hearing something the rest of us did not, and pointed. Shortly afterwards we came again in sight of that gloriously ethereal city of the Mu-Oorians, its pale, spiked towers rising into the cavernous gloom. Here we were greeted as long-lost friends and treated to the best which that strange people could offer us, including their scholarly conversation. We described our adventures, much to their awed approval. And then Lord Renyard announced his intention to spend the rest of his days among this gentle people. "I pray you will not think me ungrateful for all the offers you have made. But it would be best, I feel, if I remained with folk who see me not as an exotic sport of nature, but rather merely the last of his race."

The Off-Moo became agitated by the tale of the airship bombardment of Londra but accepted that an unspeakable evil had been forestalled. How strange, they said, that so much energy was wasted on negotiating war, when peace could be negotiated with exactly the same amount of effort and to far more profitable ends. They mourned all Londra's innocents.

Invigorated by their integrity, we took our leave of the Off-Moo. We all found their world attractive. It offered a kind of tranquility without loss of intellectual stimuli, a tranquility which could not be reproduced elsewhere. Lord Renyard was happy to be with these old friends, he assured us. He promised to lead us to the surface and then would return to their city after he had delivered us safely aboveground.

In our final journey we crossed underground hills and valleys washed by that peculiar silvery light. Sometimes, in the distance, we saw herds of animals, pale descendants of creatures which had once roamed the surface of the world.

Less than a day later Jack lifted his head and pointed, sniffing the air, and we began the steep upward trudge to the surface. I had hoped we might emerge just above Tower House on Ingleton Common, where I had first fallen into the World Below, but that route was closed to us. Any caves which had temporarily opened up were filled in again. We finally squeezed into one of the old mine shafts and crawled out through abandoned workings that the quarry blasting had closed off as dangerous. We eventually got to the surface, emerging into one of Mr. Capstick's fields, to the irritated surprise of his sheep. I forgot my own happiness when I looked at Jack's face. I never knew anyone who showed his joy so obviously. He took a deep breath of that good dales air. "Are we home?" he asked.

I was blinking back my own tears. "It certainly looks like it," I said.

Then Lord Renyard and I parted. I didn't want him to go. He was just as upset. He gave me a lot of advice, most of it to do with reading Rousseau and the Encyclopedists, and then he was gone, loping back into the darkness of the Middle March to continue his lonely life among a people even stranger than himself. I was never to see him again.

We walked into a perfect dales morning, bright, crisp and clear. It was good to get some healthy northern air into my lungs.

"Come along," said my grandmother briskly, stripping off her weapons and bits of her costume so she looked as if she were wearing a fancy tracksuit, "let's get down there, then. Your parents will be wanting to see you."

A mile or so down the hill we soon spotted the grey granite tower of our house, where Mum and Dad were waiting for us with some very bad news.

CHAPTER TWENTY-THREE

Y GRANDFATHER HAD died the night before. He had waited in London to see if there was anything he could do to help, my parents said, but they thought the anxiety had been just too much for his heart. Strangely, when they found him, he had seemed very much at peace and had written, perhaps to cheer himself up, a note on his scratch pad. "She's safe." Nobody was entirely sure who "she" was. He'd lived a fine life to a good age.

My grandmother, of course, took the train to town at once. She was very sad but soldiered on and made all the funeral arrangements herself. It was amazing how many people came to old Count Ulric's memorial service. The funeral picture appeared in most of the papers, and they had it on TV. Grandma didn't come back to Yorkshire. She had some family business to sort out in Mirenburg. She said we weren't to worry if we didn't hear from her for a while.

Jack D'Acre was living with us. Oona had asked my mum and dad to make him part of our family. She left it to me to offer them what details seemed relevant, but they were happy to have him. They assumed he was homeless, an orphan, the natural son of some distant relative. He certainly had the family looks, they said. Alfy and Gertie came back with us from London. They got on well with Jack.

Colonel Bastable had missed the funeral. He phoned from

331

London later, then caught the train the following day. Dad picked him up at the station. Bastable's big Bentley tourer was still parked under canvas on the common. Red-eyed and laconic, he asked if it would be all right if he stayed overnight and then drove out early the next morning, after he'd helped St. Odhran inflate his balloon and get airborne. He needed a break, he said. Mum and Dad fussed over both men while they were at our house. As they understood it, Bastable and St. Odhran had contributed enormously to my rescue when I was lost underground.

My parents were sorry they had missed Monsieur Zodiac, who had an engagement, St. Odhran told them, and sent his apologies. They were glad to hear we wouldn't be bothered by Klosterheim and Gaynor again. Those two had clearly been dynamiting new routes down below.

Privately, I still missed Lord Renyard, but he had probably been right. My parents, though broad-minded and sophisticated, weren't ready for a man-size, talking, eighteenth-century-educated fox.

Colonel Bastable had apologized on behalf of Messrs. Lobkowitz and Fromental. He said some important national business had taken them away.

I had one last conversation with St. Odhran. We went for a walk together over the tranquil hills above the house. I wanted to know a bit about the Balance.

"The Balance was destroyed. Both sides wished to restore it for their own reasons," he told me. He looked down at me. Those eyes, which had managed to deceive me, were now frank, serious.

"Who destroyed it?"

He smiled sardonically and looked away up the fell. "The Champion," he said.

"And the Champion restored it?"

"It looked that way, didn't it?"

"Is nothing permanent? Even the Cosmic Balance? I thought it was the ordering mechanism for the multiverse!"

"It's a symbol," he said. "A useful one, but a symbol. Sometimes we fight to restore the Balance, sometimes to maintain it, and very occasionally, to destroy it."

"What point is there in all that? What logic?"

"The logic of context," he said simply. "Context is all-important. One set of views, one faith, one idea, can be useful and good for us at a certain time. At another, they threaten our destruction. The Eternal Champion fights to maintain equilibrium between Chaos and Order. But his fight is not always a clear one. Not always sympathetic to most of us."

St. Odhran was graceful as always in his leave-taking. A small crowd of locals and tourists gathered around the balloon. He left as the sun got high, scattering what looked like golden confetti down on the cheering crowd. It turned out to be handfuls of the little fake gold coins they throw over the bride and groom at Egyptian weddings. A few hours later, Colonel Bastable made his excuses. He had another appointment he was bound to keep, he said. He roared off in his Bentley. And then it was just us, the family. I think we were all a little glad to be together again with no one else around.

That next night was Midsummer's Eve, and St. Odhran had told us to expect a great battle as Law and Chaos fought for the Balance across all the realms of the multiverse.

From our Ingleton tower we watched the War among the Angels, as it was described in our part of the world. All of us were crammed into those few square feet with windows all around, so that we could see inland up Ingleborough and across the rolling hills out to sea at Morecombe Bay. The glaring silver and black sea was lit by the most intense sheet lightning I had ever witnessed in Texas or the tropics. And silhouetted against the lightning (some would later describe them as intense black clouds of unusual shape) were the forms of angels.

These weren't the conventional Christian variety of angels, but the lords and ladies of the Higher Worlds, closing in pitched battle, Law against Chaos, while elsewhere Elric's struggle echoed theirs as he fought to herald in the Dawn. Lord Arioch, Duke of Chaos, and Lady Inald, haughty Countess of Law, leading their troops, faced each other across the boundary of the Middle March, fighting once again for control of the Balance.

I witnessed the chivalry of Law opposed, as ever, to the chivalry of Chaos, when they met on that Midsummer's Night in the worst summer storm England had ever known and which equaled, in the course of twenty-four hours, other huge storms across the world.

A rather florid anonymous account appeared in the *Craven Herald* and was quoted extensively in later literature. It described an assembly of winged horsemen, wielding fiery swords, who clashed in the heavens: one side representing howling Chaos and one side for stern, relentless Law.

As angels fought and fell, I tried to make out their true shapes: Lord Arkyn pointed his white sword Mireen. Lady Xiombarg, spitting black blood and blue fire, challenged him with her massive twin-bladed ax.

Jack's strongest memory, he says, is hearing the terrible smack of a winged body, the weight of an elephant, striking the limestone pavement above Chapel-le-Dale. It was Lady s'Rashdee falling down when half her left wing was severed. You can still see cracks in the rock. Large trees grow up through them now. Locals call it the Devil's Pavement.

In America, two doctor friends of my parents, living in Inverness, California, reported the extraordinary view over the moody marshland shallows of Tomales Bay. They were sitting on their deck that night, enjoying the clarity of the weather, when they heard distant thunder and then watched a slowly darkening sky until, against it, a series of grey clouds formed the shapes of twelve Amerindian warriors in great detail. These were without doubt tribesmen not of the West but of the Northeast, every one of them slightly different in costume and features as they ran out of the sunset sky and headed inland.

I also heard how the folk of Marazion, the little port across from Saint Michael's Mount, observed a gigantic figure in gold and ebony armor ride his warhorse over to the castle, a blazing brand in his right hand and a shard of flashing crystal in his left, make his horse rear, then bow in triumph and gratitude before galloping off across the water towards France.

I know most of it's true, because I heard the parts I didn't experience myself from Una Persson, as she calls herself now, that mysterious adventuress who spends so much of her time in Eastern Europe and never seems to age.

Sometimes I think of putting a book together of all the accounts, but this is probably all I'll write. To be honest, I've had enough of supernatural adventures in other worlds, and so has my husband. We have two young children now. We've resolved to live ordinary lives and let the fantastic past fade into an incredible dream, as we become plain old Mr. and Mrs. John Daker.

Mum and Dad live full-time in Ingleton, where they work at their computer business. Jack and I are thinking of moving up there to get the kids a decent education and some fresh air. London changes faster than I can take sometimes, and the price of houses is ridiculous.

When I get crabby and think the world is becoming too heavily populated, though, I let myself remember the vast population of the entire multiverse, in which nothing really ever dies, or can ever die, while the original universe still lives, where there is always some other version of you and me. Then everything falls into perspective, and I cheer up again.

I prefer not to consider that too much, though. I'd rather think of myself and all those living souls within my extended family who know that they can be pretty much whatever they want to be but who also know, better than anyone, that there really are no free lunches, that wherever you are in the multiverse, everything must be paid for, usually with hard work.

Lately, Jack's been having some bad nights. I think it's stress. I'm beginning to wonder if the stock market is represented by too few principled warriors like him. He gets sick of the lies and deceptions in the modern business world. We could do with a bit more courage and determination in public life, not all this Hollywood-style brand-name politics too many people fall for. People don't take enough responsibility for themselves or their actions.

We, too, have our ups and downs, of course. Jack says he

remembers his life on the bum rather than our interventions or adventures in the multiverse. He think it's for the best. Some of us can absorb that amount of information. Some can't. Personally, I understand his denial. I don't bring the past up very often.

I'm looking forward to moving. The first morning we get back to Tower House, we'll go for a walk in grass which the fresh summer rain has sweetened, and I'll show Jack Daker the real world his eye surgery has let him see again. It will be sparkling and beautiful in the golden sun, the evergreens dark against the pale blue sky. I'll pretend it's all as it was on that first day of my adventures, before I went looking for crayfish in the brook and met the most evil man in the multiverse. It now seems such a dream. As I often say to Jack, it takes a lot of courage and nerve just to face the terrors and anxieties of bringing up a couple of children in our modern world. Today's realities are violent and fantastic enough for us! He heartily agrees.

EPILOGUE

S HE FELL he knew that Law and Chaos both still pursued him and that somehow he was becoming an important piece in their perpetual battle. Struggle as he might to move against the Higher Worlds' plans for him, he was never entirely free of their influence. His enemies wanted lives which were absolutely free to expand and express themselves without any form of hindrance. He could not share that lust. He valued the power and compassion of the many over the individual power and greed of the few. This set him apart from his father and family but reconnected him with his forebears who had practiced his virtues and vices with more questioning of the moral uses of power.

He could not believe that it was enough to preserve Melniboné, and so he had come to think that only death could save his people. Every advance in his journey to this moment had been earned and had brought him some unwanted burden of knowledge, some dreadful doom. His fate had been to destroy an ancient nation and take on an ancient curse in the form of a blade which served itself by appearing to serve certain masters. Yet his very struggle contained both the elements which warred in the Higher Worlds, making him an unlikely Knight of the Balance, one of those few representative champions chosen to fight the fight of the many.

And still he fell until he felt a sharp salt wind in his face and warm iron in his fist, and knew he breathed with a new vitality. A vitality he had earned as he and his kind had earned it over and over again down the centuries, across all the worlds of the moonbeam roads. This understanding faded as he woke, screaming:

"Stormbringer!"

Hearing a curse from beneath him, Elric saw Jagreen Lern pointing up at him. "Gag the white-faced sorcerer, and if that doesn't put an end to his babbling, slay him!"

"Stormbringer!" called Elric again into that void, that terrible moment between life and death. "Stormbringer! Your master perishes!"

One of his guards reached up to tug at his bound foot. "Silence! You heard my master!"

But Elric had to take his remaining chance, his last knowing breath, to cry:

"Stormbringer!"

The guard put the sharp edge of his sword to Elric's naked feet. He made to slice off his toes. But Elric paid him no heed. There was still breath enough.

"Stormbringer!"

The guard had climbed the rigging and was almost face-to-face with Elric. His coarse features grinned in stupid triumph as he drew back his arm to stab at the albino's throat.

"Stormbringer!"

With an appalled gasp the warrior fell, his cutlass dropping from his fingers as he raised his hands to grapple with something invisible, which had him by the throat. Suddenly his fingers parted from his hands in little fountains of blood.

Flinging the lifeless corpse to the deck, the sword stood before its master for a moment. Then, in a series of rapid movements, it slashed at the bonds holding him to the mast, leaped into his hand and fed him the life-stuff they, in their dreadful union, sucked from their victims, making man and sword symbiotic predators.

Elric's story was moving towards its ultimate tragedy. Those who had fought to deny him his destiny were defeated. He could

fight his way to the ruins of his own past, betraying all who sought to help him, to find at least a kind of tranquility, one Champion among many in whom morality and bleak necessity continually made war.

And now the objects of power are in fresh configuration upon an Earth where Tanelorn may sometimes be found. Old friends go there to meet and rejoice, and enemies go to be reconciled. Another name for that city is the Old and the New Jerusalem. And it is all your soul desires.

I hope I will see you there.

An End and a Beginning

ABOUT THE AUTHOR

MICHAEL MOORCOCK is a vanguard author, editor, journalist, critic, and rock musician. As the editor of the controversial magazine *New Worlds*, he fostered authors who would go on to win accolades as prestigious as the Booker Prize. A member of the Science Fiction and Fantasy Hall of Fame, Moorcock has won the Guardian Fiction Prize, the Nebula Award, the World Fantasy Award, and the British Fantasy Award, among others. He received a platinum disc for *Warrior on the Edge of Time*, his band Hawkwind's bestselling Eternal Champion concept album. His song "Black Blade" is one of several produced with Blue Oyster Cult.

For further information about Michael Moorcock and his work, please send a stamped, self-addressed envelope to The Nomads of the Time Streams, P.O. Box 15910, Seattle, WA 98115-0910.